Mutilate

Nick Viljoen

A Malherbe Publishers Publication

Author: Nick Viljoen

Cover Design: Malherbe Publishers
Set in Franklin Gothic 10 pt.
All Rights reserved.
Copyright ©Nick Viljoen

ISBN 978-1-991455-88-8
First Edition 2025

Chapter 1
Hoedspruit. South Africa

Michael Morton, known as Mikey to his friends, sat astride the Kymco MXU300 quad bike. Earlier, he had stopped under the large Mopani tree to escape the sweltering heat of the Limpopo sun. The tree, hundreds of years old, provided shade for as many as twenty people. It was one of the few original trees still left on Wild Horizons. That day, it was just him and Red, the Rhodesian Ridgeback, taking shelter in the shade.

Most of the old Mopani trees had been illegally chopped down for firewood, and their bark had been stripped for use in *muti*, a traditional African medicine concocted by sangomas and witch doctors of the region. Removing the bark killed the tree, which eventually became firewood. Four years earlier, Mikey and his wife Cara had started planting young Mopani trees all over the farm and campsites. They grew relatively slowly and produced hardwood. Their leaves were edible and widely used in traditional medicines.

The temperature had reached forty-one degrees, and Mikey had decided earlier to quit working on the new chalet they were constructing. The temporary laborers and roof thatcher had returned to town and would resume work at sunrise. Alfred, a laborer Mikey had brought with him from Mozambique, had gone to his house on the southern border of the farm. Cara had granted Alfred a piece of land where he had built a one-bedroom dwelling.

Nearby, his neighbor Phiri, who had lived and worked on the farm since childhood, spent his retirement tending his vegetable garden. Phiri had lived on Wild Horizons his entire life. Cara had given him an acre of land years earlier, where he raised chickens and grew vegetables. Although retired, Phiri still saw it as his duty to patrol the bush regularly, keeping poachers and *muti* harvesters away. He knew every square centimeter of the farm and could move around stealthily, even on moonless nights, identifying any abnormalities. It was his home, and he fiercely protected the people who lived and worked there.

Wild Horizons was a holiday resort offering self-catering cottages and tree-covered campsites. Although game was occasionally spotted, it was not advertised as a game farm. Instead, it served as a retreat for camping, relaxation, and escaping city life. Unlike the upmarket game resorts catering to foreign tourists, Wild Horizons targeted South Africans, keeping prices reasonable. It offered trails for walking and cycling, as well as swimming in natural pools by the river. Mikey and Alfred handled daily maintenance, repairs, and care for the small menagerie of sheep, donkeys, geese, chickens, and an old mare named Margaret. The animals primarily entertained city kids and introduced them to a taste of farm life.

Mikey took his monocular from his backpack and scanned the area around him for anything unusual. Seeing nothing, he decided to ride around the perimeter of the 175-hectare farm to check the fences before heading home. He placed his wide-brimmed hat on his head, pushing it down firmly. His grey and sun-bleached yellow ponytail hung beneath it. He started the quad and slowly made his way down the hill. Red reluctantly got up and followed, moving from one patch of shade to the next to avoid the burning sand.

Mikey rode at a steady pace, inspecting the fence and poles for breaks or damage. He looked for signs of digging under the fences and tracked any spoor left by animals or humans in the soft, powdery sand.

Mikey, a man of the African bush, often referred to himself as a white bushman. Many years earlier, during the bush war in South West Africa (now Namibia), he had worked with a San tracker and hunter named Janna. Mikey had quickly learned Janna's skills and honed his tracking abilities over the years, achieving near perfection. He could read spoor and determine the identity, direction, speed, and size of the person or animal that left it. His tracking expertise and knowledge of the African bush and its people set him apart from his peers.

It wasn't long before he spotted some digging under the fence on the northern border. Before dismounting the quad, he scanned the area for spoor or signs of intrusion. Using his monocular, he checked the surrounding area for any movement.

Farm murders in South Africa had reached alarming levels, and vigilance was second nature to most farmers.

The flames of hatred were fanned by politicians manipulating the uneducated masses for their own gain, aiming to secure positions of power. Once in power, they gorged themselves, their families, and their cronies on tax money, neglecting infrastructure and leaving nothing for maintenance.

Seeing no sign of human activity, Mikey got off the quad. Red had taken advantage of a nearby bush and flopped down in its shade. Mikey approached the hole under the fence at an angle, cautiously observing for any indications of poachers or other criminals. After examining the scratch marks in the hard subsoil and the surrounding spoor, he quickly realized it was the work of a jackal. He planned to tell Alfred to set a trap that evening so they could catch and release the animal back into the nearby national park. Jackals and farm animals could not coexist.

Mikey climbed back onto the idling quad and resumed his inspection. Red, deciding his paws had endured enough punishment, jumped into the crate mounted on the back of the quad. The sun beat down through Mikey's bleached khaki shirt, and he unbuttoned it to allow air to circulate around his body. His muscular, tanned arms steered the quad up and down hills and through dried riverbeds.

Mikey had turned sixty recently but still possessed the strength and stamina of men half his age. His active lifestyle kept him lean and strong—qualities that had caught the eye of his much younger wife when they first met four years earlier at a seafood restaurant in Maputo.

Had she known then that he was a merciless vigilante, she might have avoided him altogether.

Chapter 2

Soweto

The agonizing screams of a small child ripped through the dark, cold Soweto night. Its bloodcurdling anguish could be heard kilometers away. The child screamed for his life and his mother. The cries pierced the night, silencing even the noisy township dogs, who ceased their barking to listen.

His mother was too far away to hear his desperate cries, and even if she had heard him, she would have been too afraid to look for him in the darkness. Everyone who heard the screams cowered in their homes, knowing that stepping outside meant almost certain death. Confronting the torturers of the little boy would have brought instant retribution—not only to the person who dared but also to their family. The gangs that ruled South African townships were ruthless.

Nobody answered the child's pleas. They chose instead to huddle under their blankets behind locked doors.

After fifteen minutes, the screams dwindled to a whimper and eventually fell silent. Gradually, the usual sounds and rhythms of the township returned. Neighbors heard one another coughing, and soft voices penetrated the stillness. Somewhere in the distance, a radio played the rhythmic beat of a kwaito song.

All was normal again. Soweto could sleep. At sunrise, the residents would go to see who had been crying for help in the dark of night in the dusty township, one of the largest on the African continent.

Under a bridge in Marshalltown, Johannesburg, the traders stirred as they began to wake.

It was summer, and the rain from the previous afternoon had created a flotsam of human debris that ran down the streets, eventually getting trapped by broken paving and blocked gutters. Among the papers, chip packets, and plastic bottles were human feces and used sanitary towels. The stench was unbearable, but the vendors paid it no mind.

They removed the black plastic sheets from their merchandise and began arranging their goods for the day's trading. Some sold cheap Chinese products, while others sold *muti*. Their trestle tables were covered with small boxes and Ziploc bags filled with pieces of bone, bark, sticks, hair, and dried animal skins. The skull of a baboon rested between the smaller skulls of monkeys. Sticks adorned with beads, sprouting horsehair plumes, and clay pots containing mysterious items were placed within easy reach of the vendors.

Multiple traders worked under the bridge, turning it into a bustling shopping hub for bargain hunters, witch doctors, and sangomas. The price of the *muti* varied based on its rarity—the more difficult it was to obtain, the more potent its supposed healing abilities. Some *muti* claimed to cure general ailments, while others were said to enlarge penises or shrink stretched vaginas. Certain *muti* even promised to reveal the winning numbers for the National Lottery or mysteriously fill a wallet with cash. Politicians were rumored to buy *muti* to boost their chances in elections. The sangomas' ability to bamboozle seemed limitless.

One particular *muti* was said to cure HIV/AIDS, but it wasn't visible on the vendors' tables. Trusted customers could inquire about it. If not in stock, it could be obtained on short notice. It was very expensive, requiring months of savings, as it was harvested from live humans—sometimes from small children.

Within minutes, the stalls were ready for trade. The black plastic sheets were folded and packed away in the shelters of the stall owners, ready to be used again at day's end. Nearby, food vendors lit their fires, the smell of burning rubber and plastic filling the air as they used these materials to start their fires. Even those educated enough to understand the environmental damage burning synthetics caused chose to ignore it for convenience.

Soon, meat was thrown onto the burning coals, sizzling and charring, filling the air with the mouthwatering aroma of roasted meat and spices. Plates of food, served with pap or bread, would be sold throughout the day in a cycle that would repeat for years to come.

The concrete pylons of the bridge served as a convenient toilet. The reinforced uprights were covered in dried urine, decades-old voting posters, and faded graffiti, some still bearing the face of Madiba, the father of the nation. Human feces lay at the base of the pylons, covered with pieces of toilet paper or scraps of newspaper.

The once-majestic bridge showed clear signs of neglect. Cracks ran through its concrete structure, and rust from exposed steel reinforcements streaked its surface with reddish stains. The decay of the city was unimaginable.

Money meant for maintenance and upkeep had long since been spent on expensive whiskey, exotic foods, and luxurious restaurant meals. Taxpayer money had been gorged upon, absorbed, and excreted in wealthy suburban toilets—converted into piles of waste by the chosen few of the ruling party.

Pieces of broken concrete that threatened to fall on the vendors below went unnoticed.

It was just another day in the City of Gold - Egoli.

****

The icy cold wind blew in from the frigid Atlantic Ocean, through the town of Saldanha, and across the dusty streets of the nearby township.

"Mammie, ek wil hier by jou bly, Mammie," pleaded the nine-year-old girl, her voice trembling with desperation.

Her heart-wrenching plea to stay with her mother was met with a vacant stare from the one person she believed would protect her. Her young mother had taken a hit of Tik just minutes before the two men arrived, sent to fetch the child. She shook her head and turned away from her daughter.

Her boyfriend, Jimbo, grabbed the child by her hand and hurriedly dragged her toward the two waiting men, anxious to complete the exchange before the mother changed her mind.

"Kom, die ooms gaan vir jou ice cream koop," he said, pushing her toward the men.

6

The girl tried again to turn back and run to her mother. The promise of ice cream wasn't enough to convince her that leaving with the two black foreigners was a good idea. As she turned, one of the men grabbed her by the collar. Losing patience, he yanked her back violently. The force tore the collar of her best dress—a white summer dress with flowers and a butterfly print.

The man seized her around the waist and carried her out of the yard toward a waiting black SUV. He shoved her into the back seat and climbed in with her. The other man reached into his jacket pocket, pulled out a rolled-up plastic shopping bag, and handed it to Jimbo.

"Twenty leopard," he said. "Spend it wisely. The cops will treat you two as suspects. If you flash money, they'll know you sold the child. If we ever see or hear from you again, it'll be when you come to die. Do you understand?"

Jimbo nodded quickly and peeked into the bag, which contained twenty R200 notes. His mind raced, calculating how much Tik the money could buy. He was too absorbed to notice that the girl was watching him from the car.

The man turned and walked to the waiting SUV. He climbed into the passenger seat next to the driver and motioned for him to leave.

"Stay on the West Coast Road and head straight to Gugulethu," he instructed. "The handover is near the beauty shop in NY101."

Turning to the sobbing child in the back seat, he said, "Mama Cebisile will give you ice cream. You look so pretty with your two little pigtails."

He glanced into the little girl's blue eyes, momentarily caught off guard by their unusual color. He thought she must have European blood somewhere in her ancestry. Jimbo was definitely not the father. His eyes were brown, and his skin was almost black. Perhaps Jossie, the mother, had a white boyfriend or a European customer who had fathered the child. It was rumored that the Dutch occasionally fancied a bit of chocolate.

He turned back to the driver. "Jamal, stick to the speed limits. There are manned speed cameras between here and Melkbos Strand. We can't afford to be pulled over."

Chapter 3

The white mansion with its red-tiled roof hung off the slopes of Tygerberg Hill. Its wide balconies overlooking the houses below in Plattekloof and Panorama. On clear days, the Atlantic Ocean and Robben Island were visible in the distance—the same island that had produced many millionaires who were once political convicts.

In the courtyard below, several cars were parked, indicating either a party or a meeting. The mix of Audis, Mercedes, and BMWs hinted at the wealth of the attendees. The last car to arrive was a white Ford Everest. Three people stepped out and were greeted by a white tattooed man dressed in black slacks and a tight-fitting black T-shirt. He led them to the entrance and up the stairs.

"The meeting is upstairs," he announced.

The three men made their way up the stairs and entered a large entertainment area, complete with a bar and two pool tables. Near the staircase, an expansive lounge area was furnished with grey leather couches and chairs. Six-meter-wide stacking doors opened onto the wide balcony. The owner of the house, Kallie Jansen, strode toward them with his hand outstretched.

"Tony, Milos, welcome to my home," he said, gesturing to the mirror on the edge of the bar where lines of cocaine were laid out. "Some candy for the nose?"

The eldest of the three men shook his head. "No, thank you. Maybe after we've concluded our business, ok? Could I get some refreshments for my driver? Non-alcoholic, please. He'll wait downstairs."

Without waiting for a reply, he walked over to greet someone he recognized, his Slavic-looking companion following close behind.

A few minutes later, their host returned after arranging refreshments for Milos' driver. He closed the double doors behind him and walked over to the lounge area.

"Ladies and gentlemen, please refresh your drinks and join me here so that we can begin the meeting. I also ask that all bodyguards and drivers leave the room. Drinks and food have been arranged for you downstairs. Speak to Zane if you need anything. Thank you."

He nodded at the barman, who acknowledged the signal to leave once everyone had a drink.

Eventually, the group settled, and Kallie got to his feet.

"Welcome, everyone. I'm sure most of you know each other, but some may not have been formally introduced. Starting on my left, we have my partner, John Robertson. Next to him is Chipo, the master of procurement and supply from Zim, who's traveled down from Joburg for this meeting. Then, we have Sharon, the only lady in our esteemed group, and as you all know, the mother of many daughters. Moving on, we have my old friends Milos and Tony, without whom we couldn't arm our soldiers. On my right are the brothers Rashaad and Shafique, our logistics and distribution team. Last but not least is Funani, our police liaison.

"These gentlemen and lady are the members of The Association. Let us discuss our current and future projects. Who would like to start?"

Shocked onlookers gathered near the stadium wall on an open field in Soweto.

It was early morning, and the sun had not yet risen above the horizon. The cold Highveld air bit into the crowd, who wrapped themselves in blankets and jackets. The women wailed and cried, while some older men, standing apart in quiet conversation, shook their heads in dismay.

The younger men had already gone to work, while the unemployed, with no reason to rise early, still lay in bed. The women clustered to one side, glaring at the men as if they held them responsible for the gruesome discovery. The men, feeling helpless and their masculinity under scrutiny, stood anxiously, waiting for the ambulance and police to arrive.

The corpse of a five-year-old boy lay on its side next to the wall. The rubbish that had been used to conceal it had been scattered by the icy wind. Those who had seen the body before the elders moved everyone away bore witness to the savage mutilation inflicted upon the child.

His ears, eyelids, eyes, nose, and lips had been cut from his face. His fingers and toes were severed. Worst of all, his genitals had been removed. The most significant blood loss appeared to have come from the mutilation of his testicles and penis, suggesting that he had still been alive when his organs were harvested. His little heart had pumped its last drops of blood before his short life ended.

The crowd turned as sirens approached. Two police vans skidded to a halt in a cloud of dust. Three policemen and a policewoman climbed out of the vehicles. The crowd pointed to the small corpse lying by the wall.

The policewoman was the first to approach the body. A police sergeant rushed over just in time to catch her as she fainted.

A young constable hurried to help, while the hefty warrant officer, struggling to extract himself from the van, finally reached the scene. One look at the corpse, and he turned away, vomiting a stream of yellow bile—the remains of the *kota* and energy drink he'd consumed moments before the call-out.

He stumbled back to the van, grabbed the radio, and frantically shouted, "Thumbela, uncedo nceda! Ngumntwana." (Send help, please. It's another child.)

Moments later, an ambulance arrived, its wailing siren piercing the somber silence. It, too, skidded to a stop near the police vans. The warrant officer stopped the medics from approaching.

"Stop there. It's a crime scene. We have to wait for the detectives and forensics."

The four SAPS members struggled to disperse the crowd but had little success. They set up crime tape from the stadium wall to the vans, trying to push people back. As the crowd grew, their initial shock and anguish gave way to anger—anger toward the gangs that tormented their communities and anger toward the corrupt police who enabled them.

The murmur of discontent rose quickly into shouting.

"Hamba! Voertsek! Hamba! Voertsek!"

The crowd advanced on the outnumbered police, fists raised. The officers, fear evident in their eyes, drew their weapons but knew they couldn't use them. Since the Marikana massacre, where untrained police killed 38 miners and seriously injured 76, officers knew opening fire on a crowd was no longer an option.

The frenzy escalated until someone shouted, "Nantso inyoka izisa! Here comes the snake!"

The crowd's attention shifted as a black BMW X5 approached.

"Kill the snake! Kill the ANC snake!" they chanted, their rage now directed at the vehicle.

The driver glanced nervously at the councilor in the passenger seat.

"Sir, I think they don't want you here," he said.

"Nonsense, man. They love me. Look how they're shouting," the councilor replied, folding his hands over his massive belly.

Unconvinced, the driver slowed and rolled down both windows. The chants became unmistakable:

"Kill the ANC! Kill the snake! Bulala inyoka!"

Without waiting for instructions, the driver made a U-turn, dust and gravel flying as he sped away.

Mama Cebisile tapped a message on her phone and sent it to a number saved in the directory.

'She is here'

The reply was almost instant, 'I will see you this evening.'

.She deleted both messages and put the phone in the folds of her traditional Sangoma dress. She looked over at the little girl with the blue eyes and, unable to return her stare, busied herself with the potions and paraphernalia on the shelf in front of her.

She was a traditional healer and a self-proclaimed sangoma. She treated many people every day. Sometimes, they came to her despite having received and used modern medicines. When some were cured, she took the credit for it. She knew that, a lot of times, her patients' ailments or social issues were imaginary, and most would disappear with time. When a patient was not cured and did not get a satisfactory outcome, the muti or the gods were blamed.

She was fully aware that having sex with a baby or a virgin could not cure Aids, but the financial rewards were too great to argue with her patients when they brought up that horrific 'cure'. She accommodated them as long as they had the money to pay. Afterwards she would sell the girl to the Nigerians and brothels. They would get her hooked on drugs and introduce her to prostitution.

She took the little girl by the hand and led her to a room at the back where she stripped her down and started washing her from head to toe. She would dress her in a white dress and present her to the patient. The blue eyes would definitely fetch a much higher price. Now, and later when she sold her on to Madam Sharon as a child prostitute.

A lot of money to be made off this one. For sure!

Chapter 4

Mikey parked the quad under the willow tree behind the house.

Entering the cool air conditioned sanctuary of his office, he sat down in front of his desk. He glanced at the clock hanging above the desk and saw he had about an hour before he had to go help Alfred start up the pump to irrigate the campsite. He stretched his arms above his head and closed his eyes. His mind went over the events of the past year.

It was a very hectic period. They had to prepare for the wedding. He asked Cara to marry him while they were holidaying in the Cape with his best friend Jaques du Toit. Jack, to everyone that knew him. They had to get the cottages repainted and spruced up and turn his workshop and garage into a reception venue. Flowers, catering, music and dresses were the main topic for weeks on end. Cara looked after every detail and made sure Mikey was up to speed and did all the tasks she had for him. At the same time they still had to run the resort.

The wedding was a huge success. All his friends from the Cape as well as two bikers from his hometown, Port Elizabeth, attended. Some old camper customers like Bob and Nancy came with their caravan to join in the festivities. Cara invited her school friend, Brigitta from Clermont. She flew from Paris to Oliver Tambo and Mikey fetched her with his Beechcraft Baron. She was a pretty divorcee with an amazing sense of humor and boundless energy. She had never met Mikey before, but hugged him like an old friend when he met her at the airport.

On the flight back she never stopped talking and Mikey learned things about his wife to-be that he never knew before. When they finally got to Wild Horizons she screamed with delight when she saw Cara. Mikey dumbly stood to one side while the two of them giggled and hugged.

When the excitement eventually subsided, Brigitta looked at Cara with mock seriousness and said, "Cara mia, you did not tell me Mikey is so handsome. I hope you don't mind, but I asked him if I could rub my tits against his muscular chest. You will forgive me, no?"

Cara put her hands on her hips and looked at Mikey with a smile on her lips, "You are so cheap and easy. The day I met you I could see you were easy. I hope you enjoy last flings. Next week you are married, you gigolo."

Mikey was blushing red under his bush tan and was at a loss for words. He grabbed Brigitta's two massive suitcases and headed for the spare room. Feeling the weight of the suitcases he should then have realized that she was here to stay for a long time.

On their return from the brief holiday in the Cape, Mikey purchased a small holding near town from an elderly man that had moved into a retirement home. It was very run down and needed a lot of renovation. With the help of local builders he managed to restore the building and convert it to the Eco and Nature Information Centre. Once a month Mikey invited 30 children from local schools and the community to attend videos and classes on nature and animals. It was normally followed by burgers and ice cream that Cara made for them.

During the building and renovations of the center Brigitta made herself handy by sorting out the garden and planting indigenous fauna and fruit trees on the one hectare property. She established a vegetable garden and somehow had convinced the builders to convert two of the rooms for her own use. It was converted into a bedroom with en-suite and a small kitchen. She had them put in an outside door leading onto a small deck under a veranda as well.

When Mikey brought this up with Cara she just shrugged and said, "What you want mon cherie, to let her stay with us in the house forever?"

"Forever? Do you mean to tell me she is not going back to France?"

Cara laughed, "Non. Not soon any way. You like her. Why not let her help at the Eco center? Is cheap labor, no?"

Mikey thought it over for exactly two seconds.

Within three months, Brigitta had turned the property into an inviting solace for nature lovers. She had added Arts and Crafts classes for the locals and regularly taught painting and home crafts to the local women. The kitchen had also been fully renovated, and the next step was for Cara and Brigitta to offer monthly French cooking classes.

Mikey just let them be and do what they wanted. He had millions stashed that he wanted to use for some good—money he had earned as a vigilante contractor over the last thirty years or more. He had more money than he knew what to do with.

He had not looked at the phone he always used for his contract work in months. His decision to retire was holding so far. For many years, he had been the avenging angel for others, doing a job that the police and justice system had been unable to do. His calm, calculated manner ensured that every job was completed professionally and on time. His clients were always more than happy to pay his fees, and references came regularly.

Pushing back the urge to put the battery and SIM card into the phone, he opened his eyes. Instead, he took his regular cell phone and called his friend Jack in Cape Town on WhatsApp video.

It was answered almost immediately.

"Hey, Mikey. How's married life, boet?" Jack greeted when he saw the smiling face of his friend.

"Brother, you do not want to know how busy she keeps me. I haven't been to a pub in months. How are you doing? Business okay?"

He wanted to speak to Jack about their other venture. Recently, during their previous adventure, they had managed to 'procure' several cell phones and recording devices from the crooks and politicians they had dealt with. It was a treasure trove of information, pointing to and proving corruption in big business and government. Instead of handing it over to the police, they had opted to create an offshore, secret website where they exposed everything. The site was called TRUTH. They had loaded all the proof onto the site and given limited access, with secret passwords, to select media outlets around the world.

15

It had proved devastating for a lot of people. Many had been arrested, lost their jobs, or were still being investigated. Politicians scrambled to keep their positions, shifting the blame from one to another. Instead of ridding itself of corrupt members, the ruling party had begun using state organs like the police and security services to try to find the whistleblowers and the source of the information.

The site had drawn interest from around the world, and tons of information concerning corruption, theft, and graft arrived every day. Only a very small percentage of submissions made it onto the site, as they had to be accompanied by verifiable, indisputable proof. TRUTH had one techie administering the site—Jeremy. They realized that very soon, they would have to get more help. Corporations, private donors, and concerned citizens from all over the world were contributing money to the site.

It was with the creation of this venture that Mikey agreed to hang up his guns and retire from contract killing.

He had not looked at the phone he always used for his contract work in months. His decision to retire was holding so far. For many years, he had been the avenging angel for others, doing a job that the police and justice system had been unable to do. His calm, calculated manner ensured that every job was completed professionally and on time. His clients were always more than happy to pay his fees, and references came regularly.

Pushing back the urge to put the battery and SIM card into the phone, he opened his eyes. Instead, he took his regular cell phone and called his friend Jack in Cape Town on WhatsApp video.

It was answered almost immediately.

"Hey, Mikey. How's married life, boet?" Jack greeted when he saw the smiling face of his friend.

"Brother, you do not want to know how busy she keeps me. I haven't been to a pub in months. How are you doing? Business okay?"

He wanted to speak to Jack about their other venture. Recently, during their previous adventure, they had managed to 'procure' several cell phones and recording devices from the crooks and politicians they had dealt with. It was a treasure trove of information, pointing to and proving corruption in big business and government. Instead of handing it over to the police, they had opted to create an offshore, secret website where they exposed everything. The site was called TRUTH. They had loaded all the proof onto the site and given limited access, with secret passwords, to select media outlets around the world.

It had proved devastating for a lot of people. Many had been arrested, lost their jobs, or were still being investigated. Politicians scrambled to keep their positions, shifting the blame from one to another. Instead of ridding itself of corrupt members, the ruling party had begun using state organs like the police and security services to try to find the whistleblowers and the source of the information.

The site had drawn interest from around the world, and tons of information concerning corruption, theft, and graft arrived every day. Only a very small percentage of submissions made it onto the site, as they had to be accompanied by verifiable, indisputable proof. TRUTH had one techie administering the site—Jeremy. They realized that very soon, they would have to get more help. Corporations, private donors, and concerned citizens from all over the world were contributing money to the site.

"If you can be a little patient you might be driving in my latest restoration. I am busy restoring an old Bedford postal van."

She frowned. "A van? Non, I prefer the MG."

Jack grinned and said, "It will have a double bed in the back."

Mikey put his finger in the air. "I vote for the Bedford. When will it be ready?"

"In a few more weeks. I am rushing it because Sweety is already looking at campsites."

Sweety, real name Brenda, was Jack's wife. She was a physiotherapist and had a practice on their smallholding near Klapmuts.

"How is your other business doing?" Mikey asked Jack.

"The Country Inn is virtually running itself. I have two very good partners. My civils consulting is slowing down. As time goes on, I am getting fewer calls, but I am grateful for that. I prefer tinkering in the shed at home."

Mikey and Cara excitedly told him about the new guest cottage they were building on Wild Horizons.

"It will be called Honeymoon Cottage," she said.

Mikey looked at Cara, who was sitting on his lap, with curiosity. "Honeymoon Cottage? When did you decide that?"

She nibbled his ear and, with a mischievous smile, said, "I decided on our honeymoon. It will be perfect for when we have wedding receptions at Wild Horizons."

Jack watched the two of them interacting. He knew that Mikey had yet to realize who was in charge in that relationship.

Mikey turned to look at her. "Where do you want to have the receptions? In the garage?"

She nuzzled his neck and winked at Jack. "No, silly. It will be in the hall you will build."

Jack laughed and said, "Looks like it will be a while before that Botswana trip happens. I will leave the two of you to your planning. Cara, be gentle with him. Remember, he is no spring chicken."

Before Mikey could protest, Jack ended the call. He sent him a WhatsApp message: 'Phone when the storm is over.' He attached a smiley emoji.

Chapter 5

The open-air market near Marshall Town was alive with shoppers and vendors.

Two men, dressed in *tsotsi* pants and running shoes, browsed through the merchandise on display. They knew exactly which stall they were heading to but did not want to make it too obvious. As they moved, they pointed at items and asked the vendors casual questions. Eventually, they reached the stall of the vendor they had come to see. The older of the two gave her a subtle signal, indicating they had something important to show her.

She got to her feet and gestured for him to follow her into the makeshift shelter. The younger man remained outside.

Inside, the older man pulled out a phone and showed her a video recording with the sound turned off. The footage showed the harvesting of genitals from a live young boy. A few seconds were enough to convince her it was real.

"Have you sold any yet?" she asked.

"I came to you first."

"Are the prices the same as last time?"

"I'm only the messenger. You have the number to call."

He turned to leave the stifling shelter, but she grabbed his arm, stopping him.

"Wait. I want to give you some *muti*. It will make you strong."

"Hai! I don't believe in that shit, old woman."

He yanked his arm free and walked outside, signaling to his friend to follow.

Neither of them noticed the teenager watching them from across the way. The boy trailed them for a while, snapping several photos with his cell phone. He continued his pursuit into a parking lot on the other side of the bridge but was forced to abandon it when they climbed into a white VW Golf and sped off. Quickly, he took a photo of the number plate.

****

It was just past eight p.m., and Gugulethu was relatively quiet, with most people having supper or staying indoors to escape the Cape South Easterly wind.

A red Audi A6 parked near the beauty shop, and the driver stepped out. He was skinny, with a sallow complexion. Anyone looking closely would have seen that he was not well. He walked slowly down the road.

A few houses further, he was met by a young man.

"Come. She is waiting for you. I'll stay and look after your car. It will be safe."

He was guided to a large house behind a shop. On the shop window, he noticed the name *Mama Cebisile* and a list of services and medicines she offered. The practice was closed for the night.

At the door of the house, she waited for him.

She led him into the kitchen and handed him a clay pot filled with a greenish liquid.

"For strength and to cleanse your mind. Drink it all," she instructed.

He sat down at the table and started drinking. The liquid had a strange grassy taste, but it wasn't unpleasant. She watched as he finished the mixture of herbs and Viagra. Soon, it would take effect, and his manhood would be strong. He didn't know what he had consumed, but he trusted her. She was an old friend of his grandmother.

Previous medicines she had given him had provided some relief, and at times, he had felt as if he was getting stronger. A friend had told him that the ultimate cure would be to have sex with a virgin. When he had discussed it with her, she had tried to put him off by telling him how expensive it would be.

He had a good job at an investment firm and earned a generous salary, but he had still been surprised when she told him it could cost up to one hundred thousand rand. When he realized he didn't have much time left, he instructed her to proceed with finding a virgin.

She handed him a slip of paper with banking details and an amount written on it.

He frowned. "Why is the price one twenty now?"

She smiled. "This is special *muti*. Very strong. Look—she has blue eyes. The spirits favor them. Very rare."

She showed him a photo of the girl on her phone. He stared at the image of an innocent, beautiful child. He was captivated by her blue eyes. He nodded and took out his phone, entering the banking details she had given him. Within moments, he had transferred R120,000. He showed her the confirmation.

She stood up.

"Wait here. I will call you."

She walked upstairs to check on the girl. The sedative she had given her earlier had taken full effect. The child lay on her back, staring at the ceiling. She was awake but unresponsive, dressed in a short white dress, her feet bare.

Satisfied, the *sangoma* returned downstairs.

The man looked up expectantly as she entered. She moved to stand beside him, placing a hand on his shoulder.

"Go upstairs. The room on the left. Close the door behind you. Do not kiss her—it will break the spell. She has no underwear on. When you are finished, leave the way you came. Speak to no one about this. In six months, you will be cured. Now go."

****

The members of *The Association* listened attentively to the speaker.

Milos the Serb was visibly upset. "I am being investigated by the police. My contacts say someone gave them information that I was selling guns stolen from police custody. I want to find that leak and plug it for good. I am not going to take the fall for this alone."

The menace in his voice was clear. Everyone knew that if he went down, they would all go down with him. He glared around the table, ensuring they all understood his message.

Most of them were already calculating ways to distance themselves from him.

Funani was the first to speak. "I have information regarding this."

All eyes turned to him, urging him to continue.

"Three months ago, two gangbangers from Macassar were interviewed by a Captain Teffo from the Durban Serious Crime Unit. This was regarding two 9mm pistols they had supplied to Branko Petrovic. One of them sang like a canary and told Teffo that they were instructed to give the guns to Petrovic. Instructed by Milos, the Serb."

Milos felt every gaze turn on him. He cringed.

He remembered it clearly. Petrovic had called him from the airport one day, looking for weapons for himself and his bodyguard. They couldn't risk bringing their own on the flight from Johannesburg. Petrovic had fought with him in the Balkan wars and was wanted for war crimes, just like him.

Petrovic had since disappeared off the face of the earth.

Milos had initially tried to find out what had happened to him but quickly realized that asking too many questions would implicate himself.

Now he knew.

The gangsters must have been in witness protection this entire time.

He looked around the table at the questioning eyes. He needed to say something, but words failed him.

Funani continued. "These two gangbangers are in witness protection, and no one can find them. My source believes the investigation has progressed and that arrests are imminent."

Milos turned to his friend Toni and shook his head in disbelief.

He decided to go on the offensive.

"What use is this Association and our highly paid police liaison if it cannot protect its members?" he shouted.

Sharon stood up, adjusting her skirt as she looked around the room.

At fifty-five, she was still a striking woman. A former prostitute, she understood the trade well. Tossing back her long black-dyed hair, she fixed her green eyes on the group and said, "I would like to pass a motion that Milos and Toni leave this meeting. They are clearly compromised, and until they are cleared, they should not be privy to what is discussed here today."

She sat down.

Everyone turned to Milos and Toni.

No one spoke.

After a long pause, the two men stood up and left without a word.

Kallie walked over to the balcony and watched them drive away.

He returned to the meeting, looking at each person in turn.

"Is everyone in agreement? Raise your hand if you are. We need a majority."

Every hand went up.

It was unanimous.

Milos and Toni would be eliminated.

Kallie acknowledged the vote.

"I will notify the Boer. What's next on our agenda? Would you like to keep the floor, Funani?"

Chapter 6

Captain Dan Mdlalose looked at the docket in front of him.

Before he opened the flap, he allowed himself a few seconds to look out of his first-floor window. Seeing the rubbish and papers blowing over the barren, dry plot that bordered Diepsloot SAPS, he felt even more depressed. He pulled the docket closer and opened it. He caught his breath when he looked down at the open file.

He struggled to look at the crime scene photos. The mutilated corpse of the little boy was shown from different angles. The face was unrecognizable. He shoved the photos under the pathology report and tried to concentrate on the contents. Soon, he realized that the report was just as gruesome.

He read the police reports. He had heard how difficult it was for the police at the scene to control the crowd. He was not surprised that the reports were incomplete and not very helpful. He put everything back into the folder. Then, he walked down the passage to the office of the Commanding Officer of Diepsloot SAPS, Brigadier Florence Rawlimi. He greeted her PA and knocked on the door.

"Come in," Rawlimi replied.

He entered the large office and greeted his OC.

"Good morning, Brigadier. Can I discuss a case with you?"

The Brigadier gestured for him to take a seat, and he sat down. He took a quick look around the office and, as always, was surprised by what he saw. It was adorned with pictures of the Brigadier posing with the President and a multitude of pictures of her with different Ministers and well-known businessmen. When he had been there the previous time, there had been a photo of her with Jacob Zuma, the former President. He was surprised to see it was no longer there. Everyone knew of her admiration for the now-deposed criminal. At the age of thirty-eight, she was by far the youngest Brigadier in the police force.

She looked at him over her reading glasses and asked, "Is it the case of the murdered child?"

He nodded and passed the docket to her. She slowly opened it and looked at the reports and the crime scene photos. She picked them up and scrutinized them one by one. Captain Mdlalose was astounded by her coolness. She put the photos down and read the report from the Pathologist. Then, she glanced at the reports from the officers at the scene. She closed the docket and shook her head.

"It is sad. What do you want from me?"

Captain Mdlalose got up and walked to the window. He took a few seconds to arrange his thoughts before turning back to her.

"Brigadier, this murder is the fifth one of its kind this year in Soweto. The people are getting fed up with us. My officers feared for their lives this morning. We have to find the person or people responsible for this. Soon. Very soon. The local councilor had to run for his life this morning. Not only are they blaming the police, but the ruling party as well."

She sat back in her chair, resting her elbows on the armrests. She tapped her manicured fake nails together, taking a moment to admire them.

She looked at him, shrugged, and momentarily showed her palms to him. "It is just another murder. What do you want me to do about it?"

He steadied his breathing and, keeping his cool, replied, "It was a five-year-old boy. He was alive when they harvested his genitals. This is a clear indication of a muti killing."

"We have no proof of that. How do you know it wasn't just a madman who takes souvenirs from his victims? We must be careful not to blame our Sangomas for this. They are very powerful."

"As I said, it is the fifth one this year. The other four were aged between four and six. The same parts were removed from their bodies. This is not a serial killer. This is killing for profit. It is savage and sadistic!"

He struggled to keep his emotions under control while looking at the emotionless woman sitting in front of him. She seemed bored and uninterested. She handed him back the docket and motioned for him to leave.

25

"Then you must find the killers. I have an important meeting to attend."

He snatched the docket from her outstretched hand and left her office. She sat down and took her cell phone from her bag. She dialed a number from her directory. It was answered immediately. She put it on speaker while she dug in her handbag for lipstick.

"My favorite policeman. Are you on your way yet?" the voice asked smoothly.

"I am on my way. Same address?"

"Same address. Make yourself at home. I will be there shortly. Have some champagne in the meantime. There is a bottle or two of Moët in the bar fridge. The key is with the janitor. I will let him know you are on your way."

She closed her phone and, using a mirror she took from her bag, touched up her lipstick. With a smile, she thought of the wonderful afternoon that lay ahead with the Italian. That morning, she had put on her most skimpy underwear and given extra attention to her makeup. Not only was it payday, but it also came with some carnal pleasure.

She was unaware of the small listening device under her desk.

****

Inspector Warrant Officer Maria Ruiters looked at her two fellow officers. "Can you believe the audacity of this woman?"

Captain Terrance 'Terror' Majoba and Sergeant Pieter Combrink both shook their heads. They were sitting in the ops room at the Hawks offices in Parktown.

"Do we know the address?" Lt. Ruiters asked.

Combrink nodded. "No, but I suspect it is the same place he used for the sex party he organized for the leader of the opposition and his 2IC a month ago."

Terror said to her, "The building is in Houghton Drive. You can be there before her. We need to find out what she has to do with him."

WO Ruiters grabbed her bag and headed out the door.

26

"Put your earpiece in. I will be nearby," Combrink shouted after her.

Chapter 7

The Boer looked out the window of his apartment on the second floor of Belsam Court in Parow.

He was checking for any suspicious vehicles or people on the street below. He was getting ready to go out to meet his contact at the pool and snooker hall on Voortrekker Road. The cryptic message had arrived just minutes ago. Seeing nothing out of place, he prepared to leave.

He had a Yamaha 700 Tenere as well as a mountain bike parked in his garage, but he decided it was too close to warrant using either.

Peering out to ensure no nosy neighbors were on the landing, he slipped out of his door. He headed toward the rear of the building and exited next to the garages. From there, he made his way down a side street to the main road. Walking at a steady pace, he glanced at shop windows, using the reflections to check for anyone following him.

He had grown up in this neighborhood. He knew every square inch of it.

As he neared the snooker hall, he zigzagged across the street, taking a detour past the entrance before doubling back. Stopping suddenly, he scanned his surroundings, ensuring he was not being tailed.

Satisfied, he made his way up the stairs and into the snooker hall.

He approached the bar counter.

"Cold one, Bennie. Anyone looking for me?"

"No. Just the regulars here today."

He slid Bennie a R200 note.

"Keep the change."

"Thanks, Dunc." Bennie pocketed the note and took R20 from his wallet to pay for the beer he had poured for Duncan Murray.

Duncan Murray was half-Scot, and on the insistence of his Afrikaans mother, he had attended a dual-medium school, learning in both Afrikaans and English. His mostly absent father had not objected too much—so long as no one asked him for money, he was indifferent to decisions about his son's future.

Duncan had finished high school and taken a job with a construction company as a general worker. The pay had not been great, but overtime had been plentiful. He had stuck with it for almost three years.

The work had been tough and physical, and soon, his lean frame had developed into a strong and agile one. But his temper was short, and he had always struggled with authority. He had held a special hatred for his foreman, and it had not taken long before he had finally snapped and clocked him.

The foreman had ended up in the hospital for three weeks with a cracked skull and broken ribs. Duncan had been fired from his job and given a stern warning from the magistrate for his part in the fight.

With a UK passport courtesy of his father's ancestry and his pension and leave paid out, he had kissed his mother goodbye and left for London. There, he had joined the British Army.

For two years, he had been a grunt, absorbing all kinds of abuse from his NCOs and officers. It had been tough, but it had taught him self-control.

A visiting captain from the SAS had taken notice of him. He had been scouting for new recruits, and Duncan's stamina, strength, and accuracy with a rifle had caught his attention.

Duncan had joined the SAS and begun specialist training.

During his time with 22 SAS, he had spent months in Afghanistan, hunting and eliminating Taliban fighters. Working with Delta Force from the USA, he had honed his skills to near perfection. In Libya, he had conducted reconnaissance missions and assisted in tracking down Gaddafi.

Throughout his time away, he had sent as much money as he could spare to his mother. Once, he had even visited her.

About a year ago, she had been diagnosed with lung cancer. He had resigned his commission from the British Army to be with her.

She had died soon after he had returned to South Africa. The funeral had been a small affair—some elderly residents from the flats and Duncan. He had no idea if his father was still alive, but he had not expected him to show up anyway.

Deciding to stay in South Africa, he had promised himself he was done fighting wars for little money.

He had drifted around for a while, living off his savings. He had grown his beard as he had vowed he would if he ever left the army.

To stay fit, he had taken to running up Tygerberg Hill in the early mornings. He trained with weights at home and maintained his army routine, waking at 5 a.m. every day. He ate well, keeping his diet balanced. He drank moderately and never smoked.

It had been during a pool competition at Nick's Pool Room that he had met Devlin.

He had been playing a friendly against a regular. It was mid-summer, and he had been wearing a blue T-shirt with the SAS logo—the dagger with wings—on the back.

Losing for the second time, he had grown frustrated and walked to the bar for a beer.

He had been bored.

Lounging around all day, playing pool, was starting to get to him. He had thought about returning to construction, but jobs were scarce. The economy was under pressure. The recent downgrade of South Africa's outlook by S&P and Fitch had worsened things. Corruption and graft had seeped into every new business venture, every project. The losses to taxpayers ran into the billions.

As he sipped his beer, he had noticed a stocky Coloured man standing next to him, glancing his way. The man had bulging biceps and a thin mustache. Duncan had turned to him, trying to figure out why he was watching him.

The man simply stared back, then nodded a greeting.

"Name's Devlin. I like your T-shirt. Where did you buy it?"

Duncan had sized him up, unsure if he was being baited.

"You can't buy it. You earn it."

Devlin had looked skeptical.

"A Boer in the SAS? I don't believe you."

Duncan had rolled up the right sleeve of his T-shirt. Devlin had leaned in to inspect the *Who Dares Wins* tattoo. Then, grinning, he had clinked his beer bottle against Duncan's.

"Respect, man. Respect."

They had become friends.

For weeks, they had hung out at Nick's. Once, they had gone for a steak at Barbeque Steakhouse nearby. Duncan had never invited Devlin to his place, and Devlin had never extended an invitation either.

After some time, Devlin had asked him about his plans for the future.

"I need to look for work soon," Duncan had admitted. "Doing nothing all day is getting to me. And I'm running low on funds."

"What kind of work are you qualified for?" Devlin had asked.

"I was in construction before the army. Mostly as a laborer. All I really have are the skills the army taught me."

Devlin had hesitated, then asked, "Would you use those skills if you were paid a lot of money?"

Duncan had gone quiet, thinking about it.

"I was offered work in the DRC," he had finally said. "But I can't work in that humidity and under those conditions. It was a security job at a mine. Not for me."

"What if someone offered you a ton of cash to sort someone out? Would you?"

Duncan had smirked and taken a slow sip of his beer.

"What do you consider a ton?"

Devlin had leaned in, whispering, "Five zeros, maybe even six."

Duncan had looked at him intently.

"Would this entail eliminating someone?"

"Sometimes. The fee is high for a reason. But don't worry—the targets are all bad people. Scum of the earth."

Duncan had felt something stir inside him.

Maybe—just maybe—this was what he had been subconsciously looking for.

"I have to think about it," he had finally said. "Taking someone's life isn't easy—unless you're a psychopath, of course.

Which I'm not. I wouldn't have been accepted into the SAS if I were."

Devlin had shrugged.

"Let me know if you get bored and change your mind, Boer."

He had started calling Duncan by that name from day one.

"You look like a Boer, and you have the accent of one," he had said when Duncan had asked why.

****

The vendor typed a message to the number given to her by the intermediaries of the supplier.

"I will take most of what you have. I will need a copy of the harvesting video. Price for the lower parts as well as the nose and the eyes."

She sent the message. Holding her breath, she kept the phone in her hand. This could mean a big payday!

She needed it badly. Too many vendors around her were selling the same things, and profits were low.

A moment later, her phone pinged. She glanced at the screen.

"Forty-five K."

She swore under her breath. She had expected better prices but knew bargaining was futile. There were too many buyers. She would have to pay the asking price and try to squeeze more from her own buyer.

She quickly typed a reply.

"Hold till morning. Need to secure funds."

"Ten a.m. No later."

She made a call to her buyer. It was past ten in the evening, but she knew he would be awake. The phone rang for a while before it was answered.

"Got it?" was all the voice asked.

"Yes. Price has gone up. Seventy thousand for all. With proof of harvest."

The voice on the other end went silent for a few seconds. She held her breath, praying the deal would go through. She desperately needed the money. The Induna running the stalls had been demanding his cut. If she didn't pay soon, she could lose her spot under the bridge.

"Okay. Will arrange delivery."

"Yes. How soon can you get the money to me?"

"It will be in your hands in an hour. Look for the Pizza Corner delivery bike. What's your favorite?"

"Meat lovers."

The call ended.

She immediately sent another message to the supplier.

"Funds ready. In one hour."

Her phone pinged again. She anxiously checked the message.

"Delivery in 90 minutes. Bring money to the taxi at the end of the bridge."

Chapter 8

WO Ruiters parked her car opposite the entrance to the upmarket apartment block.

While waiting, she checked her makeup in the rearview mirror. She was dressed in jeans and a linen shirt with a brown suede jacket. Always conscious of stares from most men, she deliberately tried to dress down to discourage them. Unfortunately for her, it was impossible to hide an almost perfect figure. She checked her hair, making sure the band holding the ponytail was not letting any strands escape.

Regularly glancing in her rearview mirrors and keeping an eye on the entrance to the building, she wondered what it was that made someone with a good career and salary become involved with people from the underworld. How did the crooks know who to target and who not to? Was it so blatantly simple to see if someone was corruptible? In her fifteen years of service, she had never been approached. Not once.

"Target arriving from the east. It's a black Mazda CX3," the voice of Combrink crackled in her earpiece.

"I see her! She's entering the underground parking. We need to get the address."

"I'm on foot. I'm near the entrance of the parking," Combrink replied.

"Follow her into the elevator if you can. I'm going to the foyer to check out the names of the occupants."

"Ok," his out-of-breath reply came over the earpiece.

Maria Ruiters exited her car and strode across the street to the main entrance of the apartment block. She entered and walked over to the desk, where the sole security guard, an elderly white man, was reading his newspaper.

"Good morning," she greeted him as he looked up from his paper.

He perked up at the sight of the attractive woman standing at his desk and politely greeted her. "Good morning, Miss. How can I help?"

Buoyed by his friendliness, she said, "I was sent here by my agency. I must meet with Mr. Manzoni, but I don't know which floor. Can you help me?"

His demeanor changed immediately. He had been under the impression she was a good girl. He was slightly disappointed to find out she was one of the escorts Manzoni regularly entertained upstairs. He really wished that man would disappear. The other tenants regularly complained about the parties and unsavory characters that frequented their building. Just the other day, that hated politician who always blamed whites for everything had been up there as well.

"It's on the seventh floor. 701. Right at the end," he replied gruffly and returned to his reading.

Maria smiled to herself. She had found a possible informer. The old guy clearly disliked Manzoni. She hurried to the elevator. Once inside, she called Combrink.

"Hang back. I got the address. Seventh floor. 701."

"Got it. She's talking to the janitor. Probably to get the key."

"We have to keep eyes on her and see if she returns the key to him. We need to get into that apartment later, and having the key will make it much easier."

The lift opened on the seventh floor, and Maria stepped into the passage. It was an L-shape, with one leg leading to apartments numbered 701 to 708 and the other from 709 to 716. She followed the passage to the end. Standing with her back to the lift, she pretended to talk on her phone.

It wasn't long before she heard the ping of the lift opening. When she heard the click of high heels on the tiles, she slowly turned around, just in time to see Brigadier Florence disappear around the corner. Quickly, she made her way to the intersection where the two passages met. She had her phone camera ready. She managed to take two photos before the Brigadier entered the apartment.

She called Combrink. "I got her on camera entering. Can you stay down in the parking garage? I'm sure Manzoni will be here soon. Get a pic of him before he gets to the lifts."

"Ok. Will do. Where will you be?"

"At the end of another passage, pretending to be on my phone. I want to get him entering the flat. Give me a heads-up, okay?"

"Maak so," he replied in Afrikaans.

The Boer spotted Devlin at the end of the room, sitting on one of the benches. Devlin showed him that he had a beer for him, and Boer walked toward him, greeting some of the regulars along the way. He sat down next to Devlin and took the cold beer from him.

"Cheers. Have you been waiting long?"

"No, I saw you coming down the road from that window and got the beers in advance."

The Boer was slightly annoyed by this but kept it to himself.

"What have you got?"

Devlin had his phone in his hands and forwarded a message to the Boer.

"All you need to know. Wipe it as soon as you've memorized it. This is a big one. Your first six zeros, man."

The Boer opened the message, carefully reading through all the pages, checking the photos and relevant information. He would study it in detail when he got home.

"Two guys?" he asked Devlin.

"They're buddies. Brothers in arms. They live and travel together. Always. If you get to one, the other will be right there."

"They look like Serbs."

"They are. Bad dudes. Killers of women and children. They're wanted for war crimes in the Balkans. Apparently, they were part of The Scorpions, a paramilitary group responsible for the killing of more than eight thousand Muslim boys and men. Two cruel old ballies."

"My favorite kind of target. Killers of the innocent. Time frame?"

"ASAP."

Maria was on the phone with Combrink.

"He was too quick. I couldn't get a photo."

"Don't worry, I got a couple before he entered the lift."

Maria heard the lift open and looked down the passage. She saw the elderly security guard walking toward her.

"I got to go. Wait outside and keep an eye on the parking exit," she told Combrink.

She put her phone in her jacket pocket and walked toward the guard. He looked very agitated.

"What are you doing up here? I've been watching you," he said, pointing to the camera above the lift.

She pulled her identification from inside her blouse and showed it to him. Taking him by the elbow, she steered him back into the open lift. He allowed himself to be guided. She pressed the button for the ground floor.

"I feel I can trust you. Is there a place we can talk?"

He looked at her, slightly embarrassed and partly relieved that he had mistakenly taken her for a hooker.

"Behind the desk is a tearoom. We can talk there."

The lift opened, and he walked ahead. He opened the door to a small room with a kitchen counter, desk, and chair. He offered her the chair while he stood in the open doorway, keeping an eye out for any tenants or visitors while also watching the security cameras below the counter.

"I'll close the door if someone comes. What do you need from me?"

She took out her phone and said, "Let me get my partner on a video call. He's watching the exit of the underground parking."

She called Combrink on WhatsApp video. He answered, and she could see he was sitting in his car.

"I'm talking to Oom Coenie Bothma. He's the security guy here. I think he could be a very valuable asset to us. Say hi to him."

She reversed the camera and held it toward the guard. She knew that calling him *oom* showed respect, and calling him a valuable asset would make him feel like part of their team.

Combrink greeted him, and Oom Coenie nodded in acknowledgment.

"Oom Coenie, we're staking out the apartment and the owner of 701. Do you have a problem talking to us?" she asked him.

****

Two weeks after the meeting with Brigadier Rawlimi, Captain Dan Mdlalose was still very frustrated and worried.

Despite encouraging the policemen and detectives under his command daily and offering every available resource to them, there had still been no breakthrough or suspects in the killing of the children. He was sitting with his head in his hands and his eyes closed when he heard a knock on his door. Looking up, he saw the desk sergeant standing in the doorway.

"I am sorry, sir, but you need to come speak to this woman. She says she is the mother of the slain boy. Her name is Busisiwe Ntuli."

"Call Detective Robson and bring the woman to my office."

He perked up. This was a break. If they knew who the boy was, it might help them follow new avenues of investigation.

Robson arrived almost at the same time as the young woman, who looked to be about twenty-five. She was neatly dressed and carried a handbag. She looked sad and very scared. Robson leaned against the wall while Dan offered her a chair.

"Please sit down, Miss Ntuli. I am Captain Dan Mdlalose. Can I get you some water?"

He tried to win her trust and make her feel at ease. She sat down, and tears started running down her cheeks. She clung to her handbag as if it were a last lifeline. She was too upset to talk. Dan gave her time to recover.

"Do you have a photo of your son, Miss?" he asked gently.

She sniffed and started digging in her bag for her purse. Removing two photos, she handed them to him. The first was of her kneeling next to her son with her arm around his shoulders. She looked happy and proud. The boy, about five years old, appeared well cared for and was smiling. The next photo showed the boy sitting on the top of a slide in a park, a look of absolute joy on his face.

Dan immediately noticed the T-shirt he was wearing. It was the bright yellow and green of the Mamelodi Sundown's soccer team.

The same T-shirt the slain boy had been wearing.

Dan felt a shroud of dread enveloping him. He showed the photo to Detective Robson before returning it to the woman. Robson, standing behind her, gave a subtle nod to Captain Dan, though she was unaware of it. She put the photo back in her purse and returned it to her handbag. Folding her hands on top of the bag, she looked expectantly at Dan.

He was sure that this was the mother of the little boy, but he decided to ask her some questions.

"What are your full names, Miss?"

"It is Busisiwe Ntuli. They call me Busi. Where is the body of my son?"

Dan shifted uncomfortably in his chair and remained silent for a few seconds before answering.

"We have to first confirm that the body we have in the morgue is your son, Busi. We will have to do a DNA test. It will take at least two weeks."

She looked at him angrily. "You looked at the photo. Can you not see if it is him?"

He looked at Robson for help. Robson saw that his boss was at a loss and sat down next to Busi. He took her right hand into his left and covered it with his right. Looking into her tear-filled eyes, he smiled gently.

"Miss Busi, I'm afraid his face is unrecognizable. We have to do a DNA test. We cannot show you the body. It might not be him. It could be someone else's child. If you can give us more information, it might make it easier and quicker for us to identify him. Will you assist us?"

Busi looked into the eyes of this middle-aged white man holding her hand, and for some unexplained reason, she suddenly felt safe and calm. She nodded and pulled her hand free.

"What do you need to know?" she asked them.

Chapter 9

Cara was in Hoedspruit to pick up supplies for Wild Horizons and the Eco Centre.

Mikey had just returned from the build site for breakfast. That day, they would be doing some tiling while the thatcher and his team carried on with the roof. He was very happy with the progress on **Honeymoon Cottage**. Plans for the wedding hall were being drawn up and should be submitted and approved by the time the cottage was completed.

Mikey took the old Nokia from the secret compartment in his desk drawer. He rolled it in his hand. Should he, or shouldn't he? The curiosity was too great. He inserted the battery into the phone without switching it on. Leaning forward, he peeled back a piece of upholstery from his chair. With his thumb and forefinger nail, he gripped the SIM card and pulled it out. Then, he placed his regular phone in the desk drawer.

Mikey walked to the garage and pulled the KTM out. He put on his helmet and climbed onto the bike. He pressed the start button, and the big V-twin fired up. He let the engine warm up a bit, then, keeping the engine at a low RPM, he left the farm. He rode through Hoedspruit and followed the R40 for about fifteen kilometers. Pulling off the road, he inserted the SIM card into the phone. He switched it on and waited for it to boot up.

Immediately, two SMS messages popped up. He looked at the older message first. It had been sent two months ago.

'All investigations ceased. No more enquiries. Thx again.'

He recognized the number. It was from Justin Fourie. Mikey had completed a contract for him a few months ago. He then checked the second message.

Contractor needed.'

He did not recognize the number. The message had been sent the day before.

He typed a reply: 'Reference?'

Mikey decided to wait a few minutes to see if there was a response. He got off the bike and removed his helmet. The phone pinged. He looked at the screen.

'Ron Brewer'.

Mikey remembered the case.

Ron Brewer owned a 4,300-hectare farm in Mpumalanga. He had done his homework before buying it three years earlier. He had made sure there were no land claims against the property and even had a soil test done to determine if the land was suitable for game farming. He had ensured that the water rights and all other documentation were in place before purchasing it.

Since then, he had invested millions in infrastructure and buildings. A few months into the development, he had been visited by a man who went by the name S'bu Mbali. He had arrived on the farm with two other men in a black Hyundai Sonata. The two men had stayed by the car while Mbali had walked over to introduce himself. The two big guys were there purely for intimidation. Mbali had taken Ron to one side and explained why he was there.

He had offered Ron 'protection' against land claims. The fee was one million Rand. Ron had laughed at him and told him there were no land claims against the property.

Mbali had smiled and said, "There will be if you do not accept my generous offer. And once the land claimers arrive, the price will become much, much higher."

Ron had declined the offer and asked him to leave.

A week later, small groups of people had started gathering outside the gates of the farm. Two weeks later, the group had grown to about sixty people with hand-painted placards reading: 'Give back our land' and 'One settler, one bullet'.

Mbali had arrived every second day, standing on the back of a pick-up, inciting the crowd into a frenzy with a loudhailer.

Ron had laid a charge of intimidation with the police. They had told him it was not their job to sort out land claims and that he must talk to the protesters. Ron had felt helpless. By then, the contractors had gotten scared and refused to come on-site. It turned out that unemployed members of their families were

41

part of the paid incited crowd. The project had ground to a halt, and Ron's investors had started getting nervous.

Eventually, one day, he had decided to give in and pay the extortion fee. He had approached Mbali outside the gate to talk to him. Mbali had kept him waiting in the sun for three hours before finally motioning for the crowd to quiet down.

He had waved Ron over to where he was sitting under a tree in a camping chair. He had been alone, and the camping chairs his two accomplices had been sitting on a minute earlier were folded and leaning against a tree. There had been no invitation for Ron to sit. Ignoring Mbali's rudeness, Ron stood in front of him, ready to talk.

"Did you bring the ten million?" Mbali had asked with a smirk.

Ron had looked at him for a few seconds, not saying a word, before turning and walking away.

Mbali laughed and shouted, "Tomorrow it is eleven million."

Ron drove to town and stopped at the Crow Bar. He needed a drink. Walking inside, he ordered a double whiskey. He didn't know what to do anymore. He had been clearly dealing with a psychopath. This guy would forever demand more and more. It would never end.

He had tried to involve the media in the beginning. Initially, they had shown some interest in the story, but with the release of the Zondo Commission Report, they had found bigger news to cover. Every journalist had been focused on the grand-scale corruption and theft involving the ANC and the government.

Ron was on his third drink when a smartly dressed black man had sat down at his table. Expecting more demands, he had sighed and said, "I suppose you also want a slice of the pie?"

The black man had just stared at him.

Ron became irritated and was about to move to another table when the stranger had spoken up.

"There is a solution, you know?"

Ron sat down again, intrigued.

The stranger put a piece of paper in front of him and said, "Leave an SMS message that says, 'contractor needed' at this number. Reference will be Bongi. The fee will be high, but I and some other businessmen will pay toward it to get rid of this irritating crook. He is interfering in our business as well."

"Who are you?" Ron had asked.

Without answering, the stranger had gotten up and walked out of the bar.

Ron sent the message to the contractor immediately. He had been desperate.

Five days later, the crowd had started to disperse. Mbali was nowhere to be seen. The contractor had come through. The workers had returned, and the project had resumed.

Almost a year later, Ron had received a call from a public phone. The caller had given him an address of a Home for the Infirm in a neighboring town not far from his farm.

"Ask for S'bu," the mysterious caller had instructed.

The next day, Ron had driven to the Home and asked for S'bu at reception.

He was shown to a lone figure sitting in the garden on a camping chair. The nurse had said, "He cannot hear or speak. He is impaired and has the mental ability of a four-year-old. He must have suffered severe trauma."

Ron approached the figure, only recognizing Mbali once he was standing in front of him.

Mbali stared up at him with an inquisitive look.

"I see you still have the camping chair," Ron had remarked.

Mbali had frowned, trying to comprehend. The moment his brain had made the connection, the look of incomprehension had been replaced by naked fear.

He had started screaming, trying to get up, but had fallen to the ground on his face. The front of his pants had darkened from spreading urine.

Ron turned around and walked toward the exit. As a nurse rushed past him, she had asked, "What happened?"

"I think he shat in his pants," Ron said with a smile.

****

The Boer sat in his kitchen with the file he had received from Devlin on his phone. It was late afternoon on Saturday, and he had to meet Devlin later.

The file was very comprehensive. It provided a brief summary of crimes allegedly committed by Milos and Toni during the Serbian war. Both were connected to gun smuggling in the Western Cape, and there were several photos of them dining and socializing with known gangsters and figures involved in protection rackets all over the Cape. The brief was to the point:

Eliminate. Indiscriminately. Fee: R1 million.

It would be his best payday yet.

He looked at the address provided in Camps Bay. He recognized some of the establishments where they had socialized. Some were in Camps Bay, and two were at the Waterfront. Bilboa in Camps Bay seemed to be their favorite.

The Boer examined the photos of their house. Images showing them dining with women confirmed they were not gay— just two old comrades sharing a home. The house was on a hill, and the aerial view showed a large dwelling with enclosed parking and a four-car garage. High walls surrounded the front, while a high electrified fence secured the back. The house backed into the mountain reserve behind it.

The Boer spotted a footpath running along the back of the houses. He traced it to where it started at a small parking area on Camps Bay Road. Reviewing the house plans that had been provided, he noted two upstairs bedrooms, both with en suite bathrooms, flanking the kitchen and lounge area on the left and right. Both rooms had an ocean view, making it logical that these belonged to Milos and Toni. Downstairs, there were three additional en suite rooms, along with a large reception room, a study, a library, and a laundry area. A single door and a few stairs connected this space to the garages.

He studied the information a while longer before closing the file and switching off the light.

He typed a message to Devlin: "All ok. Nick's. One hour."

****

Farouk Chukwu stared at the cellphone in his hand.

He read the message from the Vendor again, shaking his head in disgust. His driver and bodyguard, Nasir, stood nearby, waiting for Farouk to tell him what had upset him so much. Clearly frustrated, Farouk got up from the sofa and walked over to the lounge window. He punched his right fist into the palm of his left.

"Fuck! Fuck! These stupid fucking people always have to fuck things up."

Turning to Nasir, he threw his hands in the air in exasperation.

"You won't believe this, but that stupid woman got the body parts stolen from her. Someone grabbed the bag from her hand and ran off with it just after you gave it to her."

Nasir's face darkened with alarm as he stepped closer to his boss, unable to speak. The two men stared out over the driveway of their rented house, where the Black Toyota Fortuner was parked.

Farouk was the first to break the silence.

"We need to get rid of the other body parts in the deep freezer. She doesn't know who we are or where we live, but believe me—if whoever stole the bag takes it to the police, they'll use every cop available to try and find you."

"It's worth a lot of money. We can't just throw it away. We took risks getting it."

Farouk turned to Nasir. "We must find a safer place to store it."

"What about all the other stuff we have going on here? The guns, the SIM cards, the hackers, and the girls upstairs, for instance?"

Farouk looked out the window, searching for answers. He had made a fortune through the usual scams and smuggling, but trafficking the girls and getting them hooked on drugs was by far the most profitable. The demand and supply were never-ending.

Most of the girls were young Zimbabweans smuggled into South Africa via buses and passed on to Farouk and other traffickers. That evening, he was expecting three more girls, but he would have to let someone else take them. He needed to make a plan until things cooled off.

First, he had to get his money from the Vendor.

"The two downstairs are almost ready to go to Sharon in Cape Town. Let her know she can send for them. They have to be out of here by tomorrow. Box up the guns and the rest of the stuff. I'll take it to our storage unit. You stay here and wait for Sharon's guys—hand the girls over to them. Make sure they're both mildly doped up and give the guys enough H for the trip to Cape Town. Destroy their documents and anything else they had. Theirs and any other girls who have been here. Burn it all in the fireplace."

Farouk sent a WhatsApp message to Sharon:

"Two girls ready to go. Very young and pretty. R20,000. Pick up today. I am expecting a raid in two days."

He then went to check on the girls.

Walking downstairs to what had once been the maid's quarters, he unlocked the security gate. Inside, he saw they had eaten some of the food Nasir had given them the previous evening. Both were awake but very drowsy.

He helped the girl closest to the edge of the bed to the bathroom. Holding her upright, he pulled her dress over her head. She had no underwear on—he had removed it when she arrived two weeks earlier.

Farouk believed in "test riding" every girl when they arrived at the house. He had raped her in his own bed. She had been drugged when it happened, and, in his mind, she would probably not even remember it.

He turned on the water and, when the temperature was right, helped her into the shower. He passed her the shampoo and watched as she slowly started washing herself.

Turning away when he felt himself getting aroused, he said, "You must wash properly, girl. You're going on a long trip to your new home. There's some clean underwear and a pretty dress for you when you're done. Your friend over there is going with you. Leave her some shampoo."

Chapter 10

Milos and Toni were downstairs in the study.

Their driver had scanned the room for listening devices earlier that day. They knew they could talk freely. Each was nursing a Stoli on ice. It was not their first for the day and certainly would not be their last. Their housekeeper had cleared the plates away and would soon be on her way home.

"Toni, we need to discuss this situation we have. It's going to become a problem." Milos looked at his friend sitting on the opposite side of the desk. He seemed worried and deep in thought. Toni shifted in his seat and took a sip of his drink. The vodka burned its way down to his stomach—normally, it would have made him feel content, but since the disastrous meeting with the members of The Association three days earlier, his nerves had been on edge.

"There's only one solution to this problem. We have to find and take out the informer. What's his name?" He clicked his fingers, trying to remember.

"It's Sherman. He's in police protection. How are we going to find him?" Milos replied.

"Funani must help us. He's a Captain in the police. Surely, he can find out where they're keeping him."

Milos downed his drink and walked over to the cabinet to pour a fresh one. Toni got up from his chair and took his glass for a refill as well. Milos took the vodka from the small freezer and poured three fingers into each glass with some ice. The ice was made from distilled water so that it wouldn't influence the taste of the Stoli.

Milos and Toni took their drinking very seriously. They took their drinks and sat down.

Milos said to Toni, "Do you think we're still entitled to the benefits of The Association? I have a feeling we're not."

Toni nodded sagely. "You might be right. We could be kicked out permanently if we don't sort out this problem. What about your friend Branko? He has influence with some ministers in government. Has he surfaced yet?"

Milos shook his head slowly. "He's still missing. I regret giving him those guns. That's what started all this shit! The cops are still looking for him and his driver. They disappeared off the face of the planet."

"Do you think it might be a ruse? He might also be in police protection."

"No, Toni. I've known Branko almost as long as I've known you. I think he's dead, my friend. He was assassinated. I don't expect to ever hear from him again. We have to find someone else."

Toni sat up and looked at Milos excitedly. "What about that guy The Association used a while ago? Boerkie or Boere-something. He was good."

"The Boer. You're right. He was excellent. How do we contact him?"

Toni furiously paged through his phone directory until he found a name.

"Here. I got it. The contact is Dev. Must I phone him?"

Milos shook his head. "No. We'll call him in the morning. We've both had too much to drink. Would you like another? Your round." He held his glass out to Toni.

Toni took it, and with a spring in his step, he headed over to the drinks cabinet.

****

Devlin saw Duncan coming down the road.

He downed his beer and walked down the stairs to the sidewalk. Making sure Duncan had seen him, he turned and walked down the road. He rounded the corner and waited for Duncan.

"All okay?" he asked when Duncan arrived.

Duncan nodded. "No problems. Where are we going?"

Devlin walked over to a white Kia Sportage parked next to the road. He motioned for Duncan to get in. Duncan slipped into the comfortable leather seat of the Kia. Looking around appreciatively, he whistled.

"Who did you borrow this from?"

Devlin laughed. "It's mine. I use it sometimes when I feel like traveling in style. Do you like it?"

"Yes. Real nice. Very sophisticated. Somehow, I always pictured you with a dropped-suspension Beemer."

"Gangsta isn't my style, man." He put the car in gear and pulled away from the curb.

"Where are we going, Dev?"

"I want to introduce you to some good dudes. You're always complaining you don't ride your bike enough. These okes ride a lot. You'll like them."

"Can we talk about the contract?"

"Yes, on the way. We're going to a pub near Klapmuts. It'll give us time to talk. Is something bothering you?"

The Boer shifted in his seat to get comfortable and said to Devlin, "This is going to be difficult. From what I can see, it looks like a high-security area. Lots of cameras everywhere. I need time to plan it carefully, or I'll have to decline the contract. It won't be as easy as the other jobs. I need at least two weeks."

Devlin nodded and remained quiet for a while. He was heading up Mike Pienaar Boulevard toward the N1. Once on the highway, he turned to Duncan and said, "I understand. I'll contact the client later and explain. You'll know as soon as I hear from them."

"Who are they?"

Devlin shook his head. "I've never met them. I receive an SMS message on a cell phone I have that's registered to a gangster in The Plain. He's unaware that he even has a cell phone contract in his name. The messenger leaves a phone number. I send an SMS to that number with my handle and wait for a call with instructions. The fee is always paid in cash. I take ten percent for myself and give you yours. The money is picked up at different locations. I've never met any of the clients, nor do I know any names. They don't know who I am either. That's the truth. I'm a facilitator. I bring people together who have a common interest. Nobody will ever find you. You have to trust me."

"Talk to them. I'm not taking stupid risks for any amount of money."

Devlin concentrated on his driving and kept his thoughts to himself. He would need diplomacy to make sure this deal didn't fall flat. He felt slightly guilty for lying to Duncan. He was getting paid a flat fee of R100,000, as well as the ten percent he took from Duncan. If The Boer was successful with this one, he stood to make R200,000.

****

Mikey looked at the SMS he had received. It contained descriptions of mutilated children and raped little girls.

His blood ran cold. His blue eyes turned an icy shade of grey.

He typed the message. 'Where are you?'

'Parktown. Jhb.'

'Stand by.'

Mikey tried to think of a reason to give Cara for why he needed to go to Johannesburg—five hours from Hoedspruit. Slowly, an idea came to him, and he typed his message.

'Monday, 2 PM. Jo'burg Zoo. Café Fino. Wear a red beanie. I will find you.'

****

They were sitting in Devlin's car in the parking lot of The Country Inn. Devlin typed a message to his client.

'Need more time. 2-3 weeks. Very high security.'

He waited a while to see if there would be a reply. It wasn't long before his phone pinged.

'2 weeks max. Anywhere, anytime, anyway.'

He closed his phone and looked at The Boer.

"Can you do it in two weeks? That's the max they'll allow for the contract. If not, I have to let them know. They'll find another contractor. I suppose they're scared the Serbs will make a move."

Duncan thought it over and nodded his head. "Yeah, okay."

They got out of the car, and Devlin locked the doors with his fob.

"Let's go get some drinks and enjoy the evening, Boerkie."

****

Devlin had been up since 6 AM.

He was looking out the window of his apartment on the 12th floor of the Libertas building in Goodwood. He had several calls to make as well as a meeting with Rafique Meyer to secure a deal on some diamonds that had come into his possession. Rafique, or Fiekkie, as he was known by his gang members at The Jontieboyz, had inherited the leadership of the gang when the founding member, Jontyboy, was blown up by a parcel bomb. Fiekkie had been the 2IC at the time.

Devlin wondered where on earth Rafique had gotten the uncut diamonds from. As far as he knew, the gang had always been involved in drug dealing and gun smuggling—never diamonds. The meeting place was at the N1 City Mall, scheduled for 10 AM.

Devlin took out his phone to get hold of Ashwin, an ex-cop. He needed someone to watch his back at the mall. He noticed he had a message waiting and decided to check that first. He opened the SMS.

'Need the Boer for a job. T and M.'

Devlin almost burst out laughing. What the fuck? How easy is this going to be?

He replied to the SMS, 'Meet Monday?'

Almost immediately, the response came: 'Time and loc?'

He knew he had to discuss this new development with Duncan, but it would have to wait until the next morning. Duncan was out on that bike trip today, followed by the braai at Jack's place afterward.

He thought for a while before replying, 'Century City. 12 PM.'

'Good.'

Devlin couldn't believe their luck. This might make things easier to get to the two Serbs. He gathered his things and took the lift down to the parking area where his cars were parked. He exited the lift one floor below ground level and carefully looked around. He was always on alert, although he was quite certain that hardly anyone knew where he lived or what he drove. He changed addresses and vehicles regularly.

He approached the high-mileage Ford Fiesta from an angle and, standing behind a pillar, pushed the fob to remotely unlock the doors. Looking around, he saw no movement in the parking garage. Satisfied, he walked to the driver's side and got into the car.

He phoned Ashwin.

"Dev, how's things, bra?" Ashwin answered almost immediately.

"Hey, Ash. Are you busy?"

"Not right now. I'm heading off to the rugby club to watch the game later on. Why do you ask?"

"I need someone to watch my back. I'm meeting with a gangster at N1 City at ten o'clock. I'm heading that way now. The meet is at John Dory's in the food court."

"I'll hang around there and see if anyone is watching or following you. Who's the gangster?"

"Fiekkie."

"What business do you want with that idiot? He's trouble, man. Since Jontyboy got blown to bits, every cop and gang leader is watching him. They still think he was involved."

"He's laid his hands on some uncuts. He has to move them fast. Price is right."

"Okay. See you then. Normal fee?"

"Yes. R500 cash."

Chapter 11

Captain Dan called in all three detectives involved in the case of the mutilated children.

In his office sat Sergeant John Robson, the most senior, Sergeant Felicity Booysen, and Sergeant Lastborn Tobela. He looked from one to the other, making sure he had their undivided attention before speaking.

"We have the identity of the boy who was murdered at the soccer stadium. We are still waiting for the DNA results, but John and I interviewed a lady called Busi Ntuli a few days ago. From the pictures she showed us, it was clear that the child was hers. His name was Alfredo. She called him Alfie. His father is no longer alive. She had a fling with a journalist from Brazil six years ago and became pregnant with his child. That explains the lighter skin tone. The father died in Afghanistan before Alfie was born. Car bomb."

"We did not acknowledge the identification to her and told her we have to wait for the DNA results. As you all know, it could take months—if ever. In the meantime, we can go on the information she gave us and start investigating. It is not much, but at least it is a starting point. We have neighbors, family, and friends to interview, and as far as they and the media are concerned, we are treating it as a missing person enquiry."

He paused to make sure everybody understood the task.

"I cannot stress the importance of catching these monsters. I am convinced all the killings and kidnappings are the work of one group. We have to find them. I am splitting you up, and I am assigning a Constable to each of you to assist with your enquiries. These Constables are waiting outside as we speak. We will call them in later to assign and brief them. This way, I feel we can cover more ground. Please stay in contact with one another and let me know immediately if you find anything of importance. We will gather in this office every morning to discuss the investigation. I want to avoid any leaks to people who have nothing to do with the case. That way, we can limit rumors, false information, and hysteria. Is that clear?"

They all nodded and confirmed that they understood fully.

"Now, if you have any questions, ask them now before we bring the Constables in."

Sergeant Felicity Booysen raised her finger. "Sir, what is the Brigadier's involvement in this case? Do we discuss any of it with her?"

Captain Dan had expected the question and had his answer ready. He was aware that all of them had realized a long time ago that Brigadier Rawlimi was a political appointment and had absolutely no police skills or the will to do her job.

"I will brief her as soon as our meeting is over. Report to me directly. I will clear it with her."

He expected Rawlimi to be happy with the arrangement. It would give her more time to do more exciting things than the mundane tasks expected of an overpaid Police Brigadier.

After all, it took time and planning to spend a salary of R2 million a year.

They were gathered in the Parktown office of Captain Terrance Majoba.

They had decided to use his office instead of the Ops room next door. They realized that even the Hawks could be compromised. The investigation into illegal cigarette smuggling had been going on for more than a year. It was at a very delicate stage, and soon, the involvement of politicians and SAPS members might be exposed. They knew they had to be very careful about whom they trusted.

WO Maria Ruiters and Sergeant Pieter Combrink were looking at the footage they had taken at Manzoni's apartment and the recordings from Rawlimi's office.

They realized that the recordings could not be used, as the listening device did not prove any crime planned or committed. However, they did have proof—albeit useless for prosecution—that confirmed what they had been suspecting for a long time. The Brigadier was compromised.

The photos they had of Manzoni entering the building were also not worth much. They needed to get a camera inside his apartment. The problem was that they could not approach any authority for permission without running the risk of blowing their whole operation. They no longer knew whom to trust.

WO Ruiters looked at Sergeant Combrink, who said, "We need outside help. I'm sure Oom Coenie will get us access, but it cannot be one of us. Have you contacted your contractor?"

"We meet on Monday at 12 at the Jo'burg Zoo."

Captain Majoba was skeptical.

"How do you know about this guy? What will it cost us?"

"Sergeant Booysen at Diepsloot SAPS heard about him through her boyfriend. He used the contractor a few years ago when they had problems with S'bu Mbali. Remember him? He was in the news for trying to intimidate that guesthouse owner in Mpumalanga. He disappeared for two weeks and was found sitting next to a tree in a camping chair with blood coming out of his ears and his tongue cut out. He is living in a totally vegetative state at an institution somewhere."

Terror Majoba was uneasy about using someone like this. "Can we not find a common burglar for this?"

Ruiters shook her head. "We are not asking him to kill anybody, and it won't cost us a thing if we plan it well."

Terror looked at her, intrigued. "How do you plan to do that?"

She shifted in her chair and looked at her colleagues.

"Guys, what I am about to tell you is very confidential. If anybody finds out about this, we are all in deep, deep shit. Do you really want to know?"

Combrink nodded. "For sure. If it means we can catch these arseholes. Let's hear it."

Captain Majoba nodded and gestured for her to continue.

"Sergeant Booysen was approached by a youth from Jo'burg CBD with video footage of a muti transaction taking place in central Jo'burg. They suspect it might be the body parts of the little boy who was recently killed and mutilated next to the soccer stadium."

She held up her phone to them.

"This is Alfie, the little boy whose mutilated corpse was discovered at the stadium a few days ago. The youth is unidentified. He wants to remain anonymous. According to Felicity, his little brother was also killed for muti a year ago. This youth, about seventeen, approached her in the street. He showed her the footage. She asked him to accompany her to Diepsloot SAPS, but he refused. He does not trust anybody there. Least of all Rawlimi, the Commander at Diepsloot."

She continued, "They went to a coffee shop and talked. She says he is extremely determined to get anybody who had anything to do with the death of his brother and other children. The footage he showed her was of two men visiting a traditional medicine vendor. Her name is Nofolo Masondo. The two men are believed to be the middlemen in this transaction that took place that night. He has them on video getting into a VW Golf, registration and all."

She exhaled deeply.

"He has footage of her later that night receiving what looks like money and a pizza from the delivery guy on a motorbike. An hour later, he followed her and saw her getting into a taxi that went nowhere. The youth has the registration number of the taxi. She spent a good few minutes in there before heading back to her stall and shelter. She had the same shopping bag with her that she had taken into the taxi. This time, it looked heavier."

Captain Majoba sighed, looking at the photo of his six-year-old daughter on his desk.

"What happened to this country?" he thought.

"Do it," he said finally, looking at Combrink. "Set it up. Good luck. And remember, this meeting did not take place today."

Chapter 12

Devlin was sipping the orange juice he had ordered.

He was sitting alone at the back of the restaurant, waiting for Fiekie. His phone pinged, and he opened the message from Ashwin.

'On his way in. Alone. Will wait outside and follow when he leaves.'

Devlin sent him a thumbs-up emoji. He saw Fiekie enter the restaurant and held up his hand to guide him to the back. Fiekie was clearly out of sorts and visibly uncomfortable as he approached Devlin's table. He was not used to places like this. He was wearing a grey top with the hoodie up and jeans that were a few sizes too big for him. He slipped into a seat opposite Devlin and fist-bumped him. He had done business with Devlin before and trusted him. Devlin had a reputation for having the best contacts for whatever needed to be sold. He drew the line at narcotics and abalone smuggling.

"Hey, Fiekie. Howz it, bra?" Devlin greeted him, trying to make him feel at ease.

Fiekie nervously looked around and asked, "Is this a safe place?"

"Public places are the safest. No one knows about our meeting unless you told someone. Put down your hoodie—it looks suspect."

Fiekie reluctantly pulled down his hoodie and shook his head. "Not me. I told no one. Only you and I know. My crew doesn't even know about the merchandise. This is just you and me. And your buyer, bra."

Devlin sat back and asked if he would like something to eat. He held out the menu to him. Fiekie glanced at it and handed it back almost immediately.

"I don't know half the things on there! What are you having? Order that for me."

"Ok. Let me call the waitress over and place the order. Then we can talk in peace."

Devlin indicated to the waitress that they were ready to order, and she came over to the table. He ordered a juice for Fiekie and fried hake and salad for himself and his guest. She took the order and, with a perplexed glance at Fiekie, left to place it.

"So, are you going to tell me where the stones are from?" Devlin asked.

Fiekie glanced around nervously once again. He bent down and looked under the table.

Devlin laughed. "Bra, do you think I'd record you? Do you have any idea what that would do to my reputation? Relax now. Let's just talk. If I ask you something you're not happy to answer, just say so. Most of my questions are purely out of curiosity, man."

Fiekie sat back and looked at Devlin.

"Dev, if I get caught with these stones, my life is over. Do you understand? I can't tell you where they're from. I will sell them to you for much less than their true value just to move them quickly."

"Do you want to show me what you've got and how much you want?"

"I don't have them here on me. They're in my car."

Devlin considered this and said, "Ok. Let's talk about the neighborhood and people we know while we wait for our food. When we finish our meal, we can head over to your car and have a look."

Fiekie nodded and seemed to relax a bit.

"How is it being the leader of Jontyboyz? Is it what you thought it would be?"

Fiekie shook his head and sighed.

"It's terrible, bra. Everybody looks up to you to organize scores and deals. Things are tight in the Flats. Too many gangs and wannabes. Everybody is shooting at each other and poaching each other's gang members. We spend too much time fighting and too little time making money. It's chaos out there. A lot of the main manne are in jail. There's no one who can keep the peace among the gangs anymore. It's kill or be killed." He shook his head again and looked at Devlin.

59

"Dev, I don't know if I should tell you this, but I'm getting out after this score. It's not a life anymore. I feel like I'm going to die young if I stay in the Cape Flats."

Their food arrived, and the waitress placed the plates of fried hake and Fiekie's juice on the table. Once she was out of earshot, Devlin asked him, "Where would you go?"

Fiekie took a sip of his drink and smiled.

"Away. Far away from here."

Devlin nodded and dug into his food. Fiekie followed his lead, and soon, they were too busy eating to talk.

When they finished their meal, Devlin signaled to the waitress to bring his bill. He paid her in cash and included a tip. She thanked him and removed the plates. Devlin waited for her to leave and then asked Fiekie, "Where is your car parked?"

They got up to leave, and Fiekie indicated for him to follow. As they left the restaurant, Devlin spotted Ashwin loitering a few meters away. He knew Ashwin would follow them to keep an eye on proceedings. Fiekie motioned toward the western entrance, and Devlin followed him.

Fiekie suddenly turned and walked into the ablutions. Thinking he needed to piss, Devlin followed him. When they reached the urinal area, Fiekie whipped out a cloth bag from the front of his pants and opened it.

Devlin instinctively stepped back, thinking it was a knife or a gun. Fiekie held the bag open for him to have a look. Devlin leaned forward and saw the faint glimmer of polished diamonds at the bottom of the bag. He was surprised by this—he had been expecting uncut diamonds.

"How many are there?" Devlin asked suspiciously.

"Forty-seven stones. I must sell today, and I'll take R20,000. It's a fraction of what they're worth, bra."

Devlin tried to hide his excitement and said, "I'll give you the money today, but you have to understand that I need to have a close look at them. They could be cultured or lab diamonds. You hear what I'm saying, Fiekie? I'm your buyer, but I need to know what I'm buying. Let's go to my car and check them out."

He saw Fiekie hesitate and put his hand on his shoulder.

"You came to me because you trust me. Let me have a look, and we have a deal."

Fiekie nodded and motioned for Devlin to lead the way. Devlin walked ahead, now extra vigilant. This could be a trap, or worse—he could get caught in crossfire if another gangster was after Fiekie. These guys were on drugs most of the time and beyond reckless. They thought nothing of putting a hit on someone in a crowded shopping center.

He looked at Fiekie.

"Put your hoodie down and stop looking like a gangster. Chill, my broer."

Devlin saw Ashwin and indicated for him to follow. He scanned the area but saw nothing suspicious. As long as Fiekie had the diamonds on him, he was not too worried about cops. He walked casually toward the entrance and crossed the parking lot to his old Fiesta. Checking around one last time, he unlocked the doors with the remote fob. They got into the car.

He looked over at Fiekie and put the key in the ignition.

"I'm just going to drive slowly toward the car dealers on the other side to make sure we're not followed. Are you okay with that?"

Fiekie, who had calmed down a bit, nodded. Devlin started the car and pulled out of the parking area, heading toward Armstrong Ford.

He took his phone out and said to Fiekie, "I'm calling my bodyguard so he can also keep a lookout."

Ashwin answered almost immediately, and Devlin asked, "Are you near your ride? We're heading toward Armstrong Auto. I'll park on the side street. Park nearby and send me a message to let me know if everything is clear. We won't be long."

He slipped his phone back into his pocket and glanced at Fiekie, who was beginning to relax. Devlin circled the block twice, making sure they weren't being followed. Satisfied, he pulled onto a side street and parked.

Turning to Fiekie, he held out his hand. "Let me have a look."

Fiekie hesitated for a moment before reaching into his crotch area and pulling out the small bag. He handed it over to

Devlin, who carefully opened it and extracted one of the stones with tweezers from the console.

Holding it up to the light, Devlin examined it, then took a cigarette lighter from his pocket. He placed a small jar of water on the console between them, heating the diamond with the flame.

Fiekie's eyes widened, and Devlin gave him a reassuring smile.

After about thirty seconds, he dropped the diamond into the water. It sizzled and sank to the bottom of the jar. He repeated the same test with two more stones. Next, he took another two and rubbed them on a piece of sandpaper. Examining them closely, he found no damage at all. Finally, he retrieved the three stones from the water and inspected them for cracks. Finding none, he smiled and looked at Fiekie.

"They seem real, bra. I'm your buyer, but I need to know where they came from. I can't buy them if I can't cover my ass. I don't want to offer them to the wrong people. These are cut diamonds and can be traced. *Verstaan djy?* If I get caught, then you get caught. *Praat saam met my.*"

Fiekie shifted uncomfortably in his seat, his reluctance clear. Devlin waited. He knew he could sell these diamonds to Kallie Jansen for at least four times the price. But if Fiekie refused to reveal their origins, he would boot him out of the car right then and there. It wasn't worth the risk.

Fiekie eyed the bag in Devlin's hand, then looked up at him. Finally, he decided to trust him.

"The pawn shop in Voortrekker Road," he admitted. "I went there to pawn a watch, but the place was closed. I asked the *antie* next door where the pawnshop dude was, and she told me he was in the hospital. Had a stroke. They were waiting for his daughter to come from England to sort things out. They don't think he'll be able to work again, and they expect the business will be sold eventually.

"I decided to break in that night. I know the shop well—it was easy. Nobody set the alarm after they took him to the hospital. They just locked the door and gave him the key in the ambulance. I saw the blue alarm indicator by the front door wasn't on."

He glanced at Devlin, making sure he was following. Devlin motioned for him to continue.

"I broke in looking for rings and jewelry—stuff I could sell quickly. I took everything from the display cases and shoved it into my backpack. Before I left, I decided to check the office. The safe was locked, but the key was still in it. I opened it, and that's what I found."

He gestured toward the bag in Devlin's hand.

"What else was in the safe?"

"Some papers and money."

"How much money?"

Fiekie hesitated, shifting uncomfortably again. Devlin poked him in the ribs.

"How much?"

"Just over four thousand. I still have it—and the jewelry. I'm leaving the Cape as soon as you pay me. I'll never get another chance like this. In a few days, they'll realize the place was broken into, and since I'm a regular customer, I'll be a suspect. My crew doesn't know about this. My life will be in danger if they find out. Some of them still think I had something to do with Jontieboy's death, man!"

Devlin started the car and drove back toward the shopping center.

"Show me where you're parked."

They reached Fiekie's VW Golf, and Devlin pulled up near it. He spotted Ashwin slipping into a parking space close by.

Fiekie turned to him. "What now, bra? When are you getting my money?"

Devlin reached into his jacket pocket and pulled out a stack of R200 notes. He counted off one hundred bills.

"You think I'd come to a diamond buy without money?" he said with a smirk, handing over the cash.

Fiekie grabbed the notes and stuffed them into the front of his pants. He turned to get out of the car, but Devlin caught his arm.

"Fiekie, I hope you enjoy your new life. Now listen to me carefully. If you ever mention my name to anybody—ever—no matter the context, I'll put your crew onto you."

Devlin held up his phone and pressed play.

"The pawn shop in Voortr—"

He switched the phone off and met Fiekie's startled gaze.

"Verstaan djy, bra?" he said. "Mention my name, and it's the end of you. Now, go well and stay safe. Good doing business with you. One more bit of advice—get rid of the tattoo and start dressing like a normal person. Pretend you're not a gangster anymore. You might stand a chance that way."

He pointed to the *JTboyz* tattoo on Fiekie's cheek.

Devlin watched as Fiekie drove off before getting out of his car and walking over to Ashwin.

He handed him five R200 notes.

"An extra R500 for the overtime. I'll need you in a few days, okay?"

Ashwin pocketed the cash and fist-bumped him.

Chapter 13

Mikey was sitting on the veranda with Cara.

Red was lying by their feet. It was early evening, and the day's heat was slowly dissipating. A light breeze was blowing from the hill in the distance, making it much more bearable. They were sitting on the swing bench that Mikey had built for them, slowly swinging back and forth. Cara was sitting with her feet on the bench, facing Mikey. She was softly singing along to the song he was strumming on the Ibanez.

'Where do you go to, my lovely, when you're alone in your bed? Tell me the thoughts that surround you...'

She tickled him with her foot as she sang along. Her French accent added to the charm of the song's origin. He smiled at her attempt to disrupt him and moved away a few centimeters.

He still had not told her about his trip to Jo'burg the next day. He had decided to tell her later over dinner.

He finished the song and placed the guitar on the bench next to him.

"What's for dinner?" he asked her.

"Sabrina made chakalaka and pap. I just need to fry the Kudu sausage when we're ready to eat. Are you hungry yet?"

Mikey wanted to get an early start in the morning and get the meeting over with. He wanted to be back on the farm before dark. He rubbed his stomach and grinned.

"I wasn't until you mentioned the pap and chakalaka."

She got up and collected their beer glasses.

"We can eat in the kitchen, no?"

"Give me a shout when I should come. Can I have another beer with it?"

"I'll bring it before I make the sausage."

Red jumped up to follow Cara to the kitchen.

"Does he understand us?" Mikey asked.

Cara laughed. "Maybe, or it might be that he knows that when he smells the chakalaka, it normally comes with meat."

Mikey took out his phone and looked at the gruesome photos of the mutilated little boy's body again. A wave of fury threatened to overtake him. How could someone who did that to a child be expected to be treated like a human being and not a savage?

He closed his eyes and tried to control his anger. Losing his temper would not help. He had to keep calm and approach this methodically. He needed to get all the facts the next day.

He heard Cara coming onto the veranda and quickly closed the screen of his phone. She leaned over his shoulder and handed him the poured beer.

"Come sit in the kitchen while I finish the food."

He got up and followed her into the kitchen. Sitting down at the worn pine table, he took a sip from his beer. He watched Red salivating near the stove.

"I need to go to Jo'burg to pick up the new bulb for the overhead projector. It arrived from Taiwan on Friday. I think it would be best if I go tomorrow. I need it for the lecture on Tuesday. It might not arrive in time if they courier it."

Cara looked over her shoulder while flipping the sausage in the griddle pan.

"I can't go with you. I have two families arriving with caravans. If you're not here to welcome them, then I have to do it. You know they'll just park anywhere if no one shows them. Are you going to use my car?"

Mikey's old Nissan Patrol was in no shape for such a long trip. With more than four hundred thousand kilometers on the clock, much of it off-road, it was literally falling to pieces. The roof lining and door panels were long gone. So was the tailgate. When something fell off and Mikey felt it was not really needed, it stayed off. The reddish-brown paint was mostly covered with scratches and rust.

He would not get past the first traffic officer without being impounded in Jo'burg.

"I'll use my bike. It's better in the traffic and easier to overtake the coal trucks."

Corruption and cadre deployment had destroyed one of the best rail systems in Africa. Coal, logs, and manganese were now moved by private contractors and thousands of trucks. The roads were in bad condition. The KTM was the right choice for the trip. It would also make it very difficult for anyone to follow him after the meeting at Jo'burg Zoo.

Cara dished the pap and Kudu sausage with a generous helping of spicy chakalaka and placed the plate in front of him.

"When are you going to buy a new pick-up? That old skedonk is falling to pieces."

She took her food and sat down next to him.

He took a bite and savored the food before answering her.

"You have to remember, Chérie, I kissed the first love of my life over the driver's side door of that old skedonk."

She smiled at the memory of her kissing him for the first time. It had been outside a restaurant in Maputo, where they had met. It had already been dark, and he had been on his way back to where he worked, restoring a house for a friend. He had not expected her to kiss him, but she had—forcing her tongue between his lips for a proper French kiss.

He had not been expecting it. Neither had he expected her to arrive and stay at his worksite the following morning. She had gotten her friends to drop her there. Natalie had tried to talk her out of her foolishness, but Cara had already decided that Mikey was the man for her.

He had no choice in the matter either. She had stayed for two weeks, helping on the site. She had only allowed him into her bed on the last night there.

"If it wasn't for that door, I think I might have been impaled, no?" she said with a giggle.

"You are a very naughty girl," he said with his mouth full.

She giggled. "I have an idea! Why don't you take off the door and hang it in our bedroom, and every time you want a kiss, you lean over it?"

He smiled at her.

"And then you do naughty things with me?"

"Absolument." She gave him a mischievous grin.

He took another bite and a sip of beer before answering. He could not believe she could still make him blush.

"I'm taking that door off tomorrow as soon as I get back."

67

"Je suis déjà excitée."

"What does that mean?"

"You take off the door, and I will show you."

He had an idea of what she meant and smiled.

"What pick-up should I buy? Do you have any preferences?"

"Non. Pick-up buying is for guys, not ladies. You decide, but the air conditioner must work. Comprendre?"

"Okay. I will start looking for a bargain with an air conditioner," he said with a grin.

The sun was setting over the Cape Peninsula.

The dust-covered bikes and riders pulled into Jack's property, followed by an equally dusty Ford Ranger driven by Lofty. They parked the bikes in front of the shed and dismounted. Jack looked at the group of riders and could see that Duncan and Godfrey were taking some strain. They weren't yet used to the long rides. The older, more experienced riders like Dusty, Stoffel, and Tyre still looked fresh.

Martie, Dusty's girlfriend, climbed out of the passenger seat and headed off to the house to talk to Sweety.

"Come on, let's grab some beers and wash the Boesmanland from our throats," Jack said, leading the way into the shed toward the small bar area at the back.

He handed the first beer to Lofty.

"The rest of you can help yourselves. We'll have a couple here, then head to the back of the house for a braai. The women have already prepared *braaibroodjies* and meat for us. Cheers."

Lofty clinked his beer bottle against Jack's.

"This was one of the best days I've had in a long time, Jack. Thank you."

"You're most welcome. Would you like to become our permanent backup driver?"

Lofty's eyes misted over, and he looked away before replying, "I... I would like nothing better. I feel like I found a new family today. Are you sure?"

Jack nodded in the direction of Godfrey.

"Thank him. It was his idea."

****

It was close to midnight, and everyone had either left or gone to sleep.

Only Jack and Duncan remained, watching the dying embers of the *braai* fire glowing in the dark.

Sweety had convinced Duncan to sleep over in the guest cottage—riding back to Parow on a bike after dark, with a few beers in his system, was not a wise idea.

Jack had been watching Duncan all day. He had picked up on the awareness and alertness he showed. Jack was convinced Duncan had specialist training in the British Army and had experienced more than just the usual grunt work while fighting for Her Majesty. He could see it in the way Duncan moved—fluid, measured, always assessing the people around him. It reminded him a lot of a younger Mikey.

"Did you enjoy the ride today?" Jack asked.

"It's my first time riding with a group. It's something I've always wanted to do. I'm so glad I decided to come back to South Africa. We really have a beautiful country. I'd like to ride with you guys again if that's okay?"

Jack looked at him through the dim light.

"I like the way you ride. It's as if you've been riding with us for years."

"Thank you. Coming from someone like you, that's a compliment."

Jack stared at the glowing coals, choosing his next words carefully.

"Duncan, I need to ask you something. If you don't want to answer, that's okay. Whatever you tell me stays between us. That's how I roll."

Duncan felt a twinge of apprehension, wondering what Jack wanted to know.

"No problem. Shoot."

"Last night, you arrived with Devlin at the pub. I wondered what you two would have in common. You see, there's a retired policeman who drinks at the bar—an extremely astute observer. He recognized Devlin from a previous visit there.

69

"I know that Godfrey and Devlin grew up in the same neighborhood, so that's their connection. But Hennie 007, as we call him, says he knows Devlin as a sort of facilitator—he's sure he works with people on the wrong side of the law.

"So, how do *you* know him?"

Duncan looked over at Jack and said, "I met him at Nick's Pool Saloon one day, and we started talking."

"And?"

"What?"

"Does he know you're a specialist?" Jack asked quietly, pushing further.

Duncan didn't answer right away. Eventually, he decided he could trust Jack. He felt like the father he never had.

"I did a job for him. Only once."

"A job he facilitated?" Jack asked.

"Yes. It was to take care of a courier who stole from his bosses. Diamonds."

"Did you take him out?"

"Devlin thinks so. I took him to a warehouse in Stikland. Over four hours, I helped him realize the error of his ways—that anywhere beyond the Orange River would be better for his health. A career change wouldn't hurt either."

Jack nodded, somewhat relieved.

"Did you find the diamonds?"

"No. He said he sold them to a pawn shop. I gave him some money and dropped him off at the bus depot in Bellville the next morning. I gave him back his bank card, but I took his cell phone and destroyed it. He disappeared after that—left everything behind. A week later, Devlin gave me my money. He never asked me what happened."

"Why did you let him go?"

Duncan stared into the darkness and shrugged.

"I just knew he wasn't a bad person. He took a chance and got caught. I will only kill *very* bad people, Jack."

Chapter 14

Monday mornings were always the worst for Captain Dan Mdlalose.

After spending the weekend with his three children and his wife, Cynthia, it was almost impossible for him to face his job again. Just thinking about his dirty office, with its aged desk and chairs overlooking the rubbish-strewn open field next to Diepsloot SAPS, was enough to make him want to resign. Worse was the absolute drop in competence among the people he had to work with. Worst of all was his Station Commander, Brigadier Flo Rawlimi.

The only upside was that she was never there before ten in the morning and was usually gone by lunchtime. He just wished he had someone to lead him and give advice to his small group of detectives. He could see the futility in their eyes when he spoke to them. They felt the same as he did. They needed leadership and support from their commanders.

He looked at his wife and took her hands in his. She gazed at Dan, tracing the lines on his face, past his kind brown eyes, to the greying curls around his ears. He looked much older than a man of forty years.

"Cynthia, I hate my job. I feel so useless. If it weren't for weekends with you and the girls, I would go crazy."

Cynthia looked at Dan with tenderness and asked him what he would like to do if he had a choice.

He thought about it and said, "I want Langfaan Labuschagne to come back. God knows, we need his experience now."

"Why did he leave?"

"He was worked out to make space for cadres. If we could have had him for just a few more years, we could have learned so much from him. None of us know what we are doing. To most people in the force, it's all about promotion, ass-kissing, and graft. I can't give leadership to my detectives if I haven't been taught leadership."

She let go of his hands and got up to pack the lunches for the three girls before she had to go to work as well. She looked over her shoulder at Dan, who was staring into his cup. She had never seen him this bad.

They had planned so carefully for their future and children and had recently bought the house in Westdene. If Dan didn't work, they would have to move back to Soweto to live with her mother.

"Have you had any contact with him still?"

"I have his number, but after the way the department treated him, I'm too embarrassed to contact him." He got up from the table. "I'm going to work. Let me say goodbye to the girls."

He walked through the lounge toward the bedrooms.

Cynthia picked up his phone and, finding what she was looking for under LF Lab, forwarded the number to her phone. She checked her hair and made sure all her Nursing Sister badges were attached to her uniform. She called the girls to take them to school.

They were so happy at West Rand Primary since they had started there at the beginning of the year.

****

Devlin sent Boer a message.

'We need to meet. Urgent. 10 AM at Nick's?'

He could not wait to tell him about the two Serbs' request. He smiled at the thought. Once that was set up, he would have the afternoon to himself. His meeting with Kallie Jansen was only at 5 PM at La Prada in the Waterfront. They had happy hour from 5 to 7. Devlin had picked the place as he had been there before and really enjoyed the tapas.

Kallie did not know about the diamonds yet. Devlin had used his electronic diamond scale, and the stones had weighed almost sixty carats. He had looked at them with his loupe, and they had all seemed exceptionally clear to him.

He would offer them to Kallie for a third of their value. Eighty thousand sounded like a bargain. Devlin was sure he would be very excited to do the deal.

His phone pinged. '10 AM is good.'

Devlin smiled and fleetingly wondered how the bike trip had gone. He was sure Boer would have enjoyed it. He decided to treat himself to a McDonald's breakfast and headed that way.

****

Kallie Jansen put his phone in the inside pocket of his jacket.

It was a warm day in the Cape, and he had decided to dress in a white suit with a pale blue shirt. No tie.

He sipped his cappuccino while admiring the view from his mansion's balcony. He wondered why Devlin wanted to meet with him. He pulled his phone from his pocket and pressed a quick connect number in his directory.

John Robertson answered almost immediately.

"All okay?" It was their standard greeting—they never mentioned names over the phone.

"Okay. Are you at the office?"

"On my way. ETA ten minutes."

"I will see you there at ten. Something has come up."

Jansen cut the call and leaned over the balcony.

He called his driver upstairs and walked into the large lounge. He went behind the bar and made two more cappuccinos.

Zane entered the lounge, and Kallie motioned for him to take a seat.

Zane had been working for Kallie for almost two years now. He was dressed in his usual attire of black jeans, black Timberlands, and a tight-fitting black T-shirt. His left arm was covered in tattoos—the largest was a red heart with 'MOM' below.

Kallie would have preferred him to have no tats, but that was how he had arrived two years ago. He had learned to accept it. Zane was an excellent driver, and his size had come in handy a few times over the past years. Kallie had sternly warned him not to get any more tattoos.

"Zane, I need to get to the harbor by ten. I have a meeting with John at the office. We have to go via Milnerton to avoid any tails, okay?"

"No problem. Which car do you want to use?"

"The BMW. The blue one. It's less ostentatious. I want you to stay in the car and keep an eye out for anything suspicious."

Zane nodded and sipped his coffee.

"Okay. We leave in fifteen minutes."

****

Devlin saw Duncan coming down the road and ordered two beers. He carried them to the back of the pool saloon.

Duncan entered the establishment and, when his eyes adjusted to the gloom, walked over to where Devlin was sitting.

They fist-bumped a greeting, and Duncan sat down. He took a sip of his beer and looked over at Devlin.

"What's so urgent?"

Devlin smiled, and making sure no one was near them, he said to Boer,

"You are not going to believe this, Boer. The two Serbs that we have a contract to eliminate are looking for a hitman, and they asked for you."

The Boer leaned back and took his time to process the information. He was halfway through his beer before he answered.

"When do you have to give them an answer?"

"I'm meeting them in less than two hours at Century City."

"What do you think is the right way to approach this? Do you know who the target is?"

"No. Not yet. I think I must meet with them and hear what they want done. That way, we can plan our strategy. It could mean easy access to these old killers. I will contact you as soon as I'm done with them. Let's meet at Fish-Aways in Parow Centre for lunch at one. I will let you know if I am late."

74

Boer nodded. "I agree. We need to meet somewhere else for a change. I will see you there at one."

He got up and walked outside. Crossing the street, he made sure he was not followed as he made his way home.

He had a lot to think about.

Chapter 15

Mikey parked his bike and locked his helmet in the top box at a coffee shop in Birman Road, near Johannesburg Zoo.

With his backpack over his shoulder, he made his way to Café Fino, a couple of blocks away. He walked casually down the tree-covered street that ended at the restaurant. He was deliberately five minutes late. Stopping to observe, he scanned the area to see if anything seemed out of place. Satisfied that all seemed normal, he entered the restaurant and, without looking at anyone, picked the closest empty table. It was Monday, and the place was not busy. He picked up the menu and, while browsing it, spotted the black youth with the red beanie sitting alone at a table.

The boy was sipping on a milkshake and looked very nervous. Mikey took his time evaluating the people in the restaurant. He spotted the anomaly almost immediately. The guy with the short haircut, pretending to look at his phone, was clearly a cop.

The waiter came over to take Mikey's order. Mikey greeted him and asked for a cold Coca-Cola with ice.

He softly said to him, "Take it over to table number nine. I see my friend sitting over there."

Mikey waited for the waiter to bring his cold drink. He watched him walk to the table where the cop was sitting and followed him. As the waiter put the drink down, Mikey thanked him and sat down.

The cop, a man in his mid-thirties, looked up, bewildered. He opened his mouth to speak, but Mikey put a finger to his lips, signaling for him to remain silent.

"Why are you here? You have five seconds to tell me, or I walk out and disappear."

He could see the youth anxiously looking their way. The cop put down his phone and looked Mikey in the eye.

"I am here to speak to the Contractor. After that guy over there has told him everything."

He pointed to the youth sitting at the table not far away. Mikey grabbed the cop's phone off the table and got up.

"Stay here."

He walked over to where the youth was seated and sat down. He held out his hand toward him.

"Phone."

The youth handed over his phone to Mikey. Mikey could see he was scared.

"It is for mine and your security. Do not be afraid."

Mikey turned both phones off and placed them on the table. He could see the cop from where he was seated.

"Do you know that guy over there?"

The youth nodded his head.

"He is here to look after my interests. I was too scared to come alone."

"Do you know he is a cop?"

The youth nodded again.

"Yes."

"Tell me briefly why you are here."

"My name is—"

Mikey held up his hand.

"Stop. At this stage, I do not want to know your name."

The youth looked at this suntanned white man sitting in front of him and wondered if he was doing the right thing. Mikey saw him hesitate.

"I only need the facts and names that you have. I am only the middleman. Talk, or I leave."

The youth looked over to the cop and took a deep breath.

"My little brother was killed a year ago for muti. They cut off his ears, eyes, and toti. They cut his heart out while he was still alive. We found his body in a field. The cops at Diepsloot still have not found the killers. Then I heard of more small children disappearing. I have been watching the muti traders in the city for almost eight months now. A few days ago, I saw two tsotsis speaking to one of the women traders. Later that evening, money was delivered to her. She took that money and got into a taxi nearby her stall. The taxi did not move the entire time she was inside. She got out of the taxi with a heavy shopping bag. I followed her and grabbed the bag from her. Inside was a cell phone and body parts of a small child. I have video and photos of the number plate of the tsotsis' car and the taxi. Can I show you on my phone?"

Mikey pushed the phone over to him.

"I have seen it, but show me again."

The youth found the photos and handed the phone to Mikey.

"It is that boy who was killed at the stadium. I am sure."

Mikey looked at the phone and recognized the photos as the same ones he had seen a few days ago. He looked at the video and the other photos. He sent copies to his burner phone. He handed the phone back. The youth handed him another phone from his hoodie pocket.

"This is the phone that was in the bag with the body parts. It is locked."

"I need to take this with me. I have someone who can access it. Is it okay?"

"Yes. I know the name of the woman. It is Nofolo Masondo."

"Where is she now?"

"She still sells muti from her stall, but they will come for her soon. They will want their money or the muti."

"Why don't you give all this to the cops?"

He shook his head. Tears were forming in his eyes.

"I do not trust them. They are not good policemen. The one in charge, the Brigadier, told me it was my mother's fault that my brother was killed. She said my mother is a bad mother and that it was her own fault they took my brother from our house. My brother was playing in the yard when they jumped over the fence to take him. How is that my mother's fault?"

Mikey felt anger welling up inside him.

"Did anyone see them jump over the fence?"

"My mama saw them. She was looking out the window. It was two young tsotsis with balaclavas. She told this to the police. That Brigadier woman said she was lying. She said my mama sold my brother to them."

Mikey struggled to remain impassive.

"Where is your mother now?"

"She is in Transkei with my aunt. She cannot work. Her heart is broken."

Mikey was not sure what to do. There was still a lot of investigation to be done. He could not help the youth if he did not have the names of the kidnappers.

He motioned for the cop to come over. Combrink brought Mikey's cola with him and sat down opposite the youth. Mikey handed him his phone.

"What is your stake in this?"

Combrink shifted to get comfortable and leaned forward on the table.

"I was approached by a police detective working the case to accompany this boy. Her name is Sergeant Booysen. He does not want to tell her everything he knows. He wants to find and kill the men who killed his brother. So far, he has done and discovered a lot more than the entire police force has until now. I am with a different branch of policing and do not want to get involved in the details of it at all."

Combrink had realized earlier that Mikey would not be interested in planting devices for anyone. It was clearly beneath him.

Mikey had the youth's phone number. He decided to do some investigation of his own. He looked at Combrink.

"You can wait outside for him."

Combrink slowly got to his feet and walked outside.

Mikey looked at the youth sitting opposite him and said, "I will help you with the investigation to find these men. You must decide if you are strong enough to go ahead and kill them. Before you kill them, you have to realize you will probably have to torture them to find out what they know before you can move to the next suspect. It will become a way of life for you, and it will never stop. There are many like you—vigilantes. It could be a terrible, lonely life you choose. Are you willing to do this?"

The youth looked at him, fire blazing in his eyes.

"I will torture them before I kill them anyway. I will remove their body parts while they are alive, like they did to my little brother and all the other little kids! If you find one, I will find the rest of them."

Mikey felt a chill run down his spine and averted his gaze, looking out the window.

"I will contact you. Be ready at all times. Break all ties with the police. Leave now."

The youth got up and walked out of the restaurant to where the cop was waiting for him. They turned and headed toward the car park in front of the zoo.

Mikey placed a R100 note on the table and walked out in the opposite direction toward his bike.

He had the projector bulb he came for in his rucksack. He would be home in a few hours.

****

Devlin sat on a bench next to the old man, observing him.

They were on the first floor of Canal Walk shopping center near Cape Town. People bustled around them, lost in their shopping. Some, carrying branded shopping bags, rushed from store to store. Young people wandered past, eyes fixed on their phones, earphones in place. Men—mostly—strolled aimlessly, waiting for their wives and girlfriends to satisfy their need to spend money.

The old man looked like someone's grandfather. He did not fit the image of a war criminal and gun runner at all.

Devlin wondered if he had any regrets for what he had done—or what he was still doing.

His name was Toni. Milos must have been waiting in the car, Devlin figured. They were never far apart.

Toni spoke with a Slavic accent, rolling his r's. He handed Devlin an A4 envelope.

"It is a job we will pay R1 million for. He must find this man and silence him before he can testify. As soon as possible. His mother's address is in there. She will tell Boer where they are keeping her son."

Devlin had to fight the urge to laugh.

Are these old cunts for real?

80

Did they really think Boer would go hunting down a target for them? That he would torture women to extract information on a man they themselves had no idea how to locate?

These guys needed to lay off the vodka, man.

Keeping a straight face, he accepted the envelope and, in a conspiratorial tone, said, "He will contact you for a final meeting."

Toni nodded and got up, disappearing into the crowd.

Devlin was still sitting there, thinking it over, when he noticed Toni coming back toward him.

He did not look at Devlin as he passed by.

The old cunt is lost, Devlin realized, smiling to himself.

****

They were gathered once again in Terrence Majoba's office.

Ruiters and Majoba both faced Combrink, waiting for him to brief them.

"We have a problem," Combrink began. "This guy is not the right person to plant recording devices. First, he is way too professional—he is far above doing something as menial as that. And second, I could tell he will not do anything for anyone connected to the police. Our other problem is that the youth has disappeared. He jumped out of my car at a traffic light and ran off. I was stuck in traffic and couldn't chase him."

Ruiters looked dejected.

"What did he say after the meeting with the contractor?"

Combrink shook his head. "Absolutely fuck all. He refused to answer any of my questions. Wouldn't even speak to me. It's as if the Contractor hypnotized him."

Majoba rubbed his hands over his face and sighed, looking at them both.

"Honestly, I'm relieved. We made a mistake getting involved in this. Let Dan Mdlalose and his team worry about their case— we need to focus on ours. I want to bring that fucking cocky Italian to book. Him and that useless bitch from Diepsloot SAPS. She's an embarrassment to us all.

"Combrink, talk to Oom Coenie. Let's get access to the flat and plant our own devices.

"Ruiters, get the equipment we need.

"We meet here again early tomorrow morning."

Ruiters smiled at his reaction. It had been a long time since she had seen *Terror* so enthusiastic and forceful.

Chapter 16

Mikey made good time back to Hoedspruit and decided to have a beer at The Bush 'n Buck before heading home.

He had been thinking about the meeting he had with the youth and the cop. An idea had been forming while he rode. He parked the KTM in a side street next to the pub. He locked his helmet, gloves, and jacket in the top box and made his way around the corner to the bar. Seeing no one familiar, he walked to a table at the rear. He signaled the bar lady to bring him his usual.

Taking out the phone, he Googled the number for Diepsloot SAPS. He dialed the number from his burner phone and, after a long wait, was finally answered by a policewoman.

"Diepsloot. Sergeant Xoli speaking."

"Good afternoon, Sergeant. I would like to speak to Sergeant Booysen."

"Ehhh, she is not here."

The reply came just too quick to be believable. Mikey decided to try a different approach.

"Sergeant, I am Colonel Thiart from Special Crimes Unit. I need to speak to her urgently. Right now!"

"Sir, sorry, Sir. I can go look for her, but it is better if I give you her cell number. Is that okay, Sir?"

"That is fine. Give it. Next time, you answer the phone immediately when it rings. All calls to SAPS are serious. Do you understand me?"

Meekly, she answered, "Yes, Sir. I understand, Sir."

"Give me her number."

She read the number to him, and he stored it on the burner phone.

The bar lady placed the cold Black Label draught in front of him. He thanked her and took a long pull from it. The cold, bitter beer slid down his throat. Setting the glass back on the table, he waited for the yeasty burp to follow. It was one of the special pleasures in life.

He composed an SMS to Booysen with the registration numbers of the VW Golf and the taxi he had gotten from the youth. He provided the name of the vendor, along with brief information on what had taken place and what might happen next. He advised her to get someone to keep an eye on the vendor. The two tsotsis were bound to appear again. Lastly, he told her not to contact him again. When he had more information, he would reach out. She was never to mention the youth to anyone. Ever.

He sent the message to her and, after switching the phone off, removed the battery.

Mikey phoned Jack from his own phone.

"Howz it, Mike?" Jack answered in his usual way.

"Cool, Bru. Are you busy? I need some advice."

"I got time. Talk to me, Mikey."

Mikey knew Jack would be a bit disappointed when he heard that he was involved in contract work again, so he downplayed it as much as possible.

"I need Jeremy's expertise. I have a phone I need unlocked."

Jack was silent for a few seconds.

"What are you busy with, Mikey? I thought you were retired from that stuff."

Mikey told him what had transpired. He was brief and to the point. He urgently needed to get that phone unlocked.

Jack listened to the whole story and realized with dread that Mikey would not walk away from it. Not when there were small children involved.

"What will you do when you have the information?" he asked his friend.

"I'm not going to get involved physically, Jack. I will help this youth find these people and leave it to him. This guy is determined. He won't let it go, and without assistance, he will be in serious trouble. He lived in a cardboard box for months to get this info. I could see in his eyes—he won't let it go. I will advise him, and I want to support him financially. I have also sent all the info to a female police detective who has been working on these cases for a long time. If I can help her, then she can get her colleagues to assist in closing the case."

84

"What if they find the youth and lock him up? How will that help him?"

"Jack, this guy is super clever, and without his efforts, they would have nothing at this stage. Once I have the info off the phone, I will consult with you as well. This is urgent. How long before the next child is mutilated, Bru?"

Jack knew there was no turning back. They were already involved.

"Send the phone via Postnet to their Paarl branch. Use Jeremy's name and ID. If he can unlock it, I will forward the info from that phone to your burner."

"Jack, I know we are doing the right thing. This thing will keep me awake at night if I don't help this guy."

"I understand, Mikey. I am with you. Always. Let me know the waybill number as soon as you have it."

"Ok. Ciao, mon ami."

****

Maria Ruiters could not sleep.

She rolled onto her back and put her left arm under her head. Turning her head sideways, she looked at the sleeping form of her lover. He was snoring lightly, out for the count.

She smiled in the dark. Shame, she had ridden him to three orgasms tonight. It was as if the events of the past few weeks had unleashed the Amazon woman in her, with an insatiable urge that needed satisfying.

Her thoughts drifted to the youth.

Where was he now?

How would Felicity ever find him again?

She got up from the bed and silently walked downstairs. Entering the guest bedroom, she slipped into the shower. She might as well go home. Sleep was not coming to her now. It might be better if she was at home in her own bed.

She dried herself after the shower and wrapped the towel around herself. Quietly, she walked back upstairs. She put on her slacks and shirt and placed her underwear into her handbag.

Slipping on her shoes, she walked over to her sleeping lover and gently shook him.

He groaned and turned onto his back. She pecked him on the cheek.

"Hey, I will see you tomorrow, okay? I'm going home."

Half asleep, he mumbled, "Okay. Drive safe." He knew she wouldn't change her mind.

Combrink rolled back onto his side and was asleep almost immediately.

Chapter 17

Boer sat in his flat in Parow, at the kitchen table, nursing his first cup of black coffee for the day.

He had not slept well. After his meeting with Devlin, he had come straight home and looked at the notes he had received from the old Serb. It was absurd and ridiculous. There was no way he would ever contemplate taking on a job like that. The fact that they expected him to torture an old woman to get information about her son told him exactly what kind of people they were.

The only reason he had even studied their notes was to figure out how he and Devlin could go about getting the two together, alone. According to Devlin, their bodyguard was a vicious ex-hitman they had poached from a Cape Flats gang. His name was Jakes Jacobs, but he went by the name Lovey-boy. The two heart tattoos on his neck had earned him that name. He lived in a flat on the ground floor, next to the garages, and hardly ever left the premises.

Boer had to get the two Serbs away from the house—preferably without Lovey-boy.

He thought of his conversation with Jack two nights ago. He still could not understand what had made him confide in him. He had no doubt that Jack had also seen the evil side of humanity. He could sense the warrior in Jack. There was something about Special Forces guys that always showed—it was easily recognized by others.

But Jack had clearly learned to accept or deal with whatever had happened to him as a young man. He seemed happy and confident. It was clear that everyone on the bike trip had a very high opinion of Jack.

That's the person I want to become, he thought to himself.

He looked down at all his notes again. He had made up his mind to get this hit done as soon as possible. Slowly, he began formulating an idea in his head. It was still not ideal, but he was sure he could make it work. It would take some manipulation.

He opened his laptop and Googled Balkan War Crimes. He needed some names.

He found some names that had popped up in South Africa recently—ones he recognized.

He made a decision and wrote down the name Milan Beeka. It was fictional, but the two old Serbs wouldn't know that.

****

Devlin lay in bed, staring up at the bedroom ceiling.

He replayed the conversation he had had with Kallie the previous evening. Something wasn't right.

Kallie had seemed very eager when Devlin had mentioned the diamonds to him. He had seemed happy with the price as well. The quantity had not fazed him.

But it was after Devlin had shown him a photo of the stones on his phone that Kallie had become withdrawn and quiet.

Devlin took out his phone and looked at the photo of the diamonds.

It showed a small pile of diamonds—all brilliant white, except for two slightly yellow stones lying at the edge of the pile.

Kallie had kept asking about the origin of the diamonds, which Devlin obviously could not reveal.

After two drinks, Kallie had left, promising to contact him the next day.

Devlin had stayed on for a few more drinks till the end of Happy Hour. At the time, he hadn't thought much about Kallie's behavior, but this morning, as soon as he had woken up, it had immediately occurred to him that something had been off the previous evening.

He rolled out of bed and, on bare feet, walked to his Nespresso coffee machine.

He selected his favorite and popped it into the machine.

He walked to the shower and turned on the hot water. He stepped into the cubicle.

After the shower, he sat down at the kitchen counter and sipped his coffee. He sent a WhatsApp message to Boer.

'Where do we meet?'

It was not long before the message was answered.

'Still looking at the file. Is 3 PM okay?'

'Sure. Where?'

'Smugglers. Brackenfell.'

'I will be there.'

He briefly wondered why the Boer wanted to meet so far from their usual haunts.

Things seemed odd today.

He put the thought out of his mind.

****

The youth sat with his back against a wall, not far from where the vendor was trading.

He heard his phone ping and looked at the message.

He instinctively knew it was from the umlungu he had met at the zoo.

'You need to get a burner phone. Do you need money?'

Making sure no one was paying special attention to him, he typed his message.

'I need money. I am scared I will get caught shoplifting if I carry on doing it. I must complete my mission.'

'I will send via eWallet to this number. Get hold of a phone that is not registered in your name. SMS confirmation to me as soon as you have it.'

'Ok. I can get a phone.'

****

Sergeant Felicity Booysen looked at the message on her phone for the umpteenth time.

She was unsure what to do next. She had not told anyone in her office about the youth. He had been adamant that he would disappear if she did.

She had tried his phone a few minutes ago, but it went straight to voicemail.

She was at her cubicle at Diepsloot SAPS.

Most of the other detectives and officers had left—hopefully investigating crime and not shopping or lazing around somewhere.

Two cubicles away from her, deep in concentration, was Sergeant Robson, pecking at his keyboard with one finger.

Felicity sent an email to Gauteng Provincial Traffic, requesting information on the registration number of the Golf.

She accessed the SAPS database and started searching for cases of small children who had disappeared or been murdered in the past year.

She was shocked to find so many.

She narrowed her search to Gauteng Province only.

She found the names of five children, of whom three were boys.

The last reported case was Alfie.

She wrote down the names of the parents of the other two boys.

Joseph Diba, aged six, found in a cemetery near Duduza.

Father: Bongani Diba.

Mother: Patricia Diba.

They had three other children, aged between four and eleven.

Patrick Gola, aged six, found in the veld near Doornkop.

He was the son of a single mother, Buhle Gola.

She had one other child named Enoch Gola, aged seventeen.

Felicity felt her skin tingle.

This must be him!

Enoch Gola.

She accessed the file of the murder and read through it.

The mutilated body of the boy had been found by a group of young boys hunting with their dogs late one afternoon about ten months ago.

The body was already decomposing in the summer heat.

The autopsy revealed that the genitals, ears, eyes, and heart had been removed while the little boy was still alive.

It was a clear indication of muti harvesting.

90

The time of death was inconclusive due to the rapid deterioration of the corpse.

The case had been the first of this kind in many years and was handed to a young detective to investigate.

He had found the mother through a missing person report she had made at the police station five days before the body was found.

She read his short report.

Sergeant Petrus Tholo and his partner, Constable Mbabe, had visited the mother and notified her about her son's death.

They had interviewed her and collected DNA from her at her home in Dobsonville.

They could not let her view her child's body due to the gruesome mutilation.

They had interviewed the older son, Enoch, a day later, as he had been at school when they had visited.

Patrick had just turned six and was due to start school the following year.

He stayed with an elderly woman during the day while his mother was at work.

She lived three houses down the road from them, and he would walk home from her house to his own in the afternoon when Enoch returned from school.

The evening that Patrick was taken, Enoch was at a friend's house playing soccer in the street.

Buhle Gola had testified that she had been busy preparing dinner for her boys when she saw two men jump over the fence and grab Patrick.

The detectives had interviewed the neighbors who were willing to talk, but could not find anyone who had seen anything.

The interview with the son, Enoch, had not delivered any leads either, as he had not been home during the alleged kidnapping.

The detectives had noted in their report that the mother came to Diepsloot SAPS a week after the interview.

She had demanded to see her son's body, and when she was told that they had not completed the autopsy or received DNA results, she went ballistic.

She walked around the counter in the charge office and started shouting at the policemen and women working there.

She was taken to the office of Brigadier Rawlimi.

After a brief interview with the Brigadier, she was escorted outside the building and told to go home or she would be arrested.

The detectives had found no trace of the kidnappers as described by the mother, and the case went cold.

The last entry in the docket had been made seven months ago by Sergeant Tholo, stating that no further leads had been found and no witnesses had come forward, despite numerous calls in the media and social groups.

The DNA results were still unknown.

The mother had since given up her job and moved away.

Address unknown.

Felicity printed the docket and put it in her handbag.

She knew she would have to be very careful with whom she discussed it.

Brigadier Rawlimi was a very dangerous person to cross.

She typed a message to her friend Maria.

'I have his name. Waiting for trace on the VW Golf.'

She forwarded the same message to the Contractor.

She walked to Captain Dan's office and found him staring at the wall.

He indicated for her to close the door and motioned for her to sit down.

She looked at the kind man sitting across the desk from her and felt emotions of pity but also of anger.

She had to give him something to work with.

He turned toward her and looked at her expectantly.

"Do you have anything new?" he asked with trepidation.

"We have a lead. It was an anonymous call I got an hour ago."

She saw the hope in his eyes and felt guilty for not being able to take him into her confidence completely.

She could not risk losing the youth's help.

"What is it?"

"An unknown informer said he had information that a vendor in Jo'burg CBD might be trading with human parts. He gave me her name—Nofolo Masondo. He recommended we put surveillance on her. She is very cautious and will disappear as soon as she thinks we suspect her. The informer said she would not keep any human parts at her stall, so it would be futile to search it. He said the only chance we have is to watch her."

She hoped he would not think to try and trace the non-existent call.

She could not tell him about the registration number of the VW Golf she was trying to trace or the rest of the information she had without putting the youth in the spotlight.

He was doing the work and investigation that the police could not do.

She would wait until the time was right.

Her phone pinged.

She angled it away from Dan and looked at the message.

'Can we meet for lunch?'

'Busy till 2.'

'Late lunch. Culinary Table. Lanseria.'

'Do they still do oxtail?'

'Oh yeah.'

'See you there.'

Felicity closed her phone and looked over at Captain Dan, who was negotiating his way into the traffic toward the CBD.

"It was a friend I had to meet for lunch at two," she said.

"No problem. We should be back by then."

He had both hands on the steering wheel and constantly looked in his mirrors. She looked at him and said with a smile, "We will if I drive."

He took his eyes off the road for a moment and looked at her.

"Are you saying that I drive too slowly?"

"Captain, you drive like my father. If you let me drive, we will get there in half the time. I know these roads."

"I like driving, and I think I am a good driver," he protested.

"You are a good driver, but you drive very slowly."

He looked in his rearview mirror and pulled to the side of the road. He got out of the car without another word and walked to the other side. Felicity slid over to the driver's side and waited for him to buckle up.

"Make it tight. Ons gaan nou jaag," she said in Afrikaans with a giggle.

She pulled into the flow of traffic and saw him bracing his feet in the footwell. After a while, he started relaxing. She looked over at him.

"Are you feeling better?"

He nodded and grinned. "You are a very good driver. I think you must drive from now on. Felicity, there is something I have to discuss with you."

"I think I know what it is about, but tell me anyway."

He shifted in his seat and turned to face her. She could see he was very apprehensive and decided to give him time to tell her what was bothering him.

"I do not know how long I will still be in the police. Things at Diepsloot have become unbearable. I do not know what to do about the way our colleagues are going about things over there. Brigadier Rawlimi is not very helpful, and most of the older detectives know as little as I do. I sometimes feel like I have my finger in a hole in a dam that is leaking. Then another leak forms, and I stick another finger in there. I feel that I am running out of fingers. I feel helpless. The dockets are piling up in the passages, and almost no cases are solved. There is not enough experience and drive left in the department to fix things."

She nodded her head but kept quiet. She needed him to complete his story. She had noticed for a while now that he was not the same as when he had started there fifteen years ago.

"I do not know who to talk to. We need new leadership. Somebody that can take control, motivate, and get everybody doing what they are supposed to be doing again. The rot is from the top, I'm afraid. She has the Commissioner in the palm of her hand, and he has the backing of the ANC. Crime is getting worse every day."

She wished she could help him, but she felt exactly the same as he did. They had nowhere to turn. She looked at Dan sitting next to her. He had gone quiet.

"What will you do if you leave the police force?" she asked him.

He shook his head and stared out the window at the grime and graffiti that had taken over the City of Gold.

"I cannot leave. We bought the house in Westdene a while ago, and I need this job."

"Who else have you spoken to?"

"You, my wife, and Robson. They understand and know things are terrible, but they are as helpless as I am."

"We are close by. Do you want to park here and walk there?"

Dan looked around and tried to focus.

"Park right over there. I think it would be best if we split up. You go first, and I will follow and keep an eye on you. If you see anything suspicious, just put your left hand on your hip. I will do the same. Do you have your gun?"

"Yes, in my bag. Do we meet back here?"

"Yes."

She exited the car and waited for him to close his door before she locked the doors and set the immobilizer alarm. Luckily, it was a Ford Fiesta and not one of the high-risk models like Hilux or Golfs. Still, it was a risk leaving a vehicle unattended for too long in the CBD.

She walked casually toward the area where the vendors were. The sidewalks were crowded, and traditional medicines were sold next to knock-off branded clothing and running shoes. The air was thick with the smells of human waste and chargrilled meat. Wood smoke drifted between the stalls and the moving mass of shoppers and commuters.

Felicity had an idea of which vendor to look for and headed in that direction. She occasionally looked over her shoulder to see if Dan was still nearby. When she got nearer, she slowed down to browse. She was dressed like the people around her and blended in well with the crowd.

She neared the stall of Nofolo Masondo and saw she was talking to two women. Felicity looked closely at the items on offer

95

but saw nothing human-related. It was mostly animal horns, tree bark, and calabashes.

She saw the vendor hand over a brown paper bag to the two women, and they paid her for whatever they had bought. The vendor walked over to Felicity.

"What can I do for you, beautiful lady? Do you need help with a man, or do you have something troubling you?" she asked excitedly.

Felicity pretended to be deep in thought and plastered a troubled look on her face.

"Hallo, Mama. No, I do not see the medicine I need here," she replied sadly, pretending to walk on.

The vendor looked at the sad-looking, well-dressed young colored woman and saw an opportunity she could not allow to go to other traditional medicine vendors.

This one clearly had some money.

The buyer of the special muti had given her one week to return his money, or she would pay with her life.

She quickly moved around the tables, and taking Felicity by the arm, she led her to a stool in the shade. She sat her down and took a seat opposite her.

Dan saw this and was immediately alarmed, but held back. He slowly moved closer and was relieved to see Sergeant Booysen sitting down and talking to the vendor. The vendor was holding both her hands in hers.

"What is it that troubles you, ntokazi?"

"It is my heart, Mama," she said, looking at the vendor, hoping she had gotten this right.

"Your heart? Is it broken by a man?"

Felicity shook her head and cast her eyes downward.

"No, it is not broken for love. My heart is sick. It is going to die soon."

She gave a sniff and got up. The vendor tried to get her to sit down, but Felicity pretended to be too sad for further conversation.

She had planted the seed and knew she had to be patient.

She was sure the vendor would recognize her the next time she saw her.

She wiped her eyes with the palm of her hand and slowly disengaged from the reluctant vendor's grip.

She quickly walked away from the stall in the direction she had come.

She did not notice the youth standing nearby behind a row of soccer shirts hanging from rails.

Chapter 18

The youth had made friends with a young guy from Zimbabwe who sold soccer T-shirts and was now standing at his new friend's stall.

From where he stood, he could watch Nofolo Masondo, and he had been upset when he saw Sergeant Booysen approach the vendor and talk to her. He had initially felt tense, but after seeing the Sergeant pull off what was clearly an act, he had become more relaxed.

He had received a substantial amount of money from the Contractor the previous day. He had managed to get hold of a burner phone from a Pakistani vendor who sold and repaired cell phones. He had immediately sent a message to the Contractor. He had not yet received a reply, but the Contractor had told him it could sometimes take a while before he responded.

He had not seen anyone suspicious talking to the vendor. He was quite sure they would come for her after dark. Very soon. He had to follow them when they did.

He saw the policewoman leave in a hurry. He almost missed noticing Captain Mdlalose following her.

He was ready to follow when his burner phone suddenly rang. With trepidation, he answered.

"Hallo?"

"Can you talk?"

The youth started walking in the direction where he had seen the two detectives leave.

"Yes. I got the money. Thanks."

"I am going to give you the rules, and I want you to follow them one hundred percent. It is for your safety as well as mine. Do you understand?"

The youth could not understand why he trusted this guy, but he felt safe and relaxed while talking to him.

"I understand."

"If you need me, send an SMS to the number you used earlier. Use a small 'i' for info you have and an 'e' for emergency. Are you still watching the vendor?"

"Yes. Sergeant Booysen just made contact with her. I do not know what was said."

"Stay there. I will find out what they are up to."

"What if the buyers make contact with the vendor?"

"That, my young friend, I will leave for you to decide. Remember, you have to stay invisible."

The youth heard the call end and put the phone in his pocket. He looked around to see if he could spot the two detectives, but they were nowhere to be seen.

He went back to his friend's stall.

****

Felicity's phone rang just as she was getting into the car.

She saw no caller ID and suspected it might be the youth. She leaned in and said to Captain Dan, "My friend calling. I won't be long."

She walked to the rear of the car and answered the call.

"Hello."

"Can you talk?"

The voice was not familiar to her, but she instinctively knew it was the Contractor.

"Yes."

"What are you doing talking to the vendor? Do you want to fuck everything up?"

She looked around her, thinking she was being watched. She was shocked to hear that he knew her movements.

Who is this person?

She composed herself and fiercely replied, "Are you following me? I am a policewoman, and I will not be told by you how to do my job."

"Then you are not getting any more help from us. Goodbye."

Incredulously, she looked at her dead phone and immediately tried to reconnect the call.

'The number you have dialed does not exist.'

99

She was furious and worried at the same time.

Had she destroyed her chances to solve the child murders by being too aggressive?

She gathered her composure and got into the car.

"It was my friend confirming our lunch."

Captain Dan just nodded.

She moved the car into the traffic and headed in the direction of Diepsloot.

It was not long before he turned to her, a scowl on his face.

"What were you thinking? That woman now knows what you look like."

She had expected the question but was still trying to put her stupidity with the Contractor out of her mind.

"It was instinctive. I thought I would pretend to need special muti to see what her reaction would be."

"And?"

"I am hoping to build an acquaintance with her so that she might be ready to talk next time I see her. I am sorry, but I am desperate."

"We cannot do things that way. We are policemen, not vigilantes. We have to follow the law and what we have been taught. Do you understand?"

She could see he was very cross and decided to keep quiet for a while.

If he knew it all, he would probably have a fit.

Again, she felt guilty for not telling him everything she knew, but she now realized it had been the right decision. He was a stickler for the rules.

Dan stopped in the parking area in front of Diepsloot SAPS and waited for her to get out.

"I have to pick up my daughters from school today. My wife is attending a course at Johannesburg Gen today and tomorrow. I will see you later."

"Are you going to put surveillance on the woman?"

"As soon as I get back, I will talk to Robson about it. We still have the three Constables."

Slightly relieved, she got out and headed up to her cubicle.

She had a bit of time before she had to meet Maria.

Sitting down at her desk, she opened her emails.

She saw the mail from her contact at NaTIS and clicked on it.

****

Make: Volkswagen Golf GTI
Model: 2013
Vin No.: xxxxxxxxxxxxx
Engine No.: 0000000000
Owner: JX Thandise
ID No.: xxxxxxxxxxxxx
Address: Rockey Court, Flat No. 5,
Rockey Street, Yeoville

She accessed Google Maps and searched for the address, noting that the flats were above a supermarket.

It was an area she knew fairly well—well known for drugs and low-level crime.

She Googled the name JX Thandise, but got no hits.

Leaning back in her chair, she stared across the open-plan office.

She was unsure of what to do with the information she had.

Captain Dan had clearly shown he wanted to do everything by the book.

She could not blame him.

He had his family to think of.

She did not have that problem.

Her fiancé had lately been on her case to resign from the police.

He was a wealthy businessman and was worried about her safety.

He had corporate jobs lined up for her already.

The prospect of leaving the police was becoming more attractive to her lately.

She was getting fed up with her superiors and the lack of progress within the police force.

She shook the thoughts from her head and typed a message to the Contractor.

'VW owner is JX Thandise. Flat 5, Rockey Court. Rockey Street. 32 years old.'

She sent it before she could change her mind.

She grabbed her bag and headed out the door to her car for her lunch date with Maria Ruiters.

Chapter 19

Kallie sat on the sofa in John Roberson's office at the Cape Town docks.

John was pouring Jack Daniels into two glasses and added blocks of ice. He gave the drinks a shake and handed one to Kallie.

"What makes you think the diamonds are the same ones that were stolen from us?"

Kallie took his phone from his pocket, found the pictures he had taken of the diamonds, and showed them to John.

"See the two yellow stones on the edge of the pile? Look at the stone's quality and quantity, and you will see what I mean."

John examined the photos carefully. After enlarging and moving them on the screen a few times, he handed the phone back to Kallie.

"I'm afraid you're right. It's the same diamonds. What do you want to do? He's not asking much for them. They're worth ten times as much."

"You see, that's the problem we have. Should we kill him for the bit of money he's asking for, or do we write it off and keep his services?"

John took a sip of his bourbon and looked out the window across the harbor. He smiled and set his drink on the table.

"Does he know the previous contract and the one on the Serbs came from us?"

Kallie shook his head.

"No. If he knew, he would have realized that it could be the same diamonds that were stolen from us. He says he got them from a gangster who stole them from a pawnshop in Voortrekker Road in Goodwood. He wouldn't divulge the gangster's name. It sounds plausible."

"Okay. I trust your judgment on that. Let's wait until the contract on the Serbs is fulfilled. We could hold back what we pay him now for the diamonds and see what he says then. It'll give us time to check out the stones and decide if they are the same ones. Remember, every person we have a hold over is an asset. I feel young Dev is worth keeping."

Kallie nodded in agreement. "Good idea. You're right. How long until we get the Serbs out of the picture?"

"Not more than ten days. I'll be glad to get them out of our lives. How did we ever get involved with them?"

"It was during the time that police colonel was supplying guns to them. Now that he's in jail, the Serbs aren't of much use to us. Through their carelessness, they've become a liability to the organization. What about Sharon? She's seeking retribution against the Sangoma who sold her the girl with the blue eyes. She wasn't a virgin as she was told. One of her regulars from Russia confronted Sharon with proof that the girl had bruises on her genitals. She was used very roughly by someone a short while before. The Russian is livid. He flew all the way from Pretoria after his meeting with government officials to sample his virgin. Sharon had to refund him the twenty thousand she charged him and now expects him to badmouth her operation."

"How is that our problem?" John asked while refilling their drinks.

"She feels she has the right to call on The Association to assist her."

"What does she want?"

Kallie took his drink from John and sipped slowly. He knew he had to slow down if he still wanted to do the deal with Devlin later.

"She wants the Sangoma wiped out."

He looked at his partner, waiting for a reaction. John didn't like violence and would always try another way first. He took his time before he answered.

"I don't see any other way around it. If we warn her or hurt her, it won't mean much. These Sangomas believe they're above normal people, and she will probably think that throwing a couple of stones, burning some concoction, and mumbling some bullshit would keep her safe. She will have no regrets, and Sharon won't get a refund from her anyway."

Kallie held back before speaking. Personally, he would prefer if someone put a bullet in her.

John sat down next to Kallie and looked him in the eye.

"We have no choice. She must die."

****

Mikey saw via a link to his own phone that he had a message on the burner.

He pulled the KTM from the garage and put his helmet on.

Cara was at the bottom of the park and wouldn't even know he had left.

He started the bike and, at very low RPM, rode toward the farm gate. Once he was on the tar road, he opened the throttle.

He rode about twenty kilometers, then pulled off at the side of the road under the shade of a thorn tree.

He fitted the battery to his burner and switched it on.

He saw the message from Booysen.

He sent an SMS to the youth.

"Can you talk?"

It was not long before he heard the burner ring.

He answered without greeting.

"I have the name and address of the owner of the Golf."

The youth didn't respond immediately.

Mikey grew anxious and, for a moment, thought someone had stolen the youth's new phone.

He waited.

Finally, the youth spoke.

"Can I have it?"

"Yes. On condition that you scope out the place for now and wait until I give you instructions on what to do next. Remember, if you fuck up now, you will not complete your task. You have to follow my rules. If not, I disappear."

"I understand."

"I will forward the details now. I will contact you in two days to find out what you've got. Be careful."

Mikey ended the call and forwarded the information to the youth.

He fired up the KTM and turned around, heading back to Wild Horizons.

It was a glorious day in the Bushveld.

****

Felicity anxiously looked at her phone.

There was still no reply from the Contractor.

She decided to try something else and typed a new message.

'The youth is Enoch Gola.'

She sent it and put the phone in her bag.

She walked up to the restaurant and spotted Maria sitting outside on the stoep.

In front of her was an ice bucket with a bottle of Chardonnay.

After the customary hugs and air kisses, she sat down.

She did not normally drink alcohol on workdays, but she grabbed the bottle of wine from the cooler and poured a three-quarter glass full.

She added some ice and took a swig.

"Wow! You look thirsty today," Maria said with a smile.

"It's not thirst. It's fucking worries, girl."

"Boyfriend troubles?"

Felicity shook her head, unsure how much she could tell Maria.

She had to talk to someone. She couldn't bottle it up inside anymore.

"It's work. I don't know what to do anymore. I need advice."

She told Maria about her encounter with Captain Dan earlier.

"He is our leader in this investigation, but I get the feeling he is as lost as we are. This case is too complicated for anyone at Diepsloot SAPS. I'm worried that I might lose my job if things don't improve soon. I'm also sitting with info I can't share with anyone in the office. It's too delicate and might destroy our only chance to solve these killings."

Maria saw the waitress approach and motioned for her to give them a few more minutes.

She picked up her cell phone, making sure Felicity saw her switch it off.

She placed her phone on the table in front of her and waited.

Felicity removed her phone from her bag and did the same. Maria topped up their drinks.

"It is not because I didn't trust you. It was to put you at ease so that you would feel free to talk to me. I wanted you to trust me with everything. It was because of distrust between colleagues that the police were in shambles. It is going to take people like you and me to make a difference in the end. Tell me what you know, and let's see what the best way to move forward is. You are my friend, and I want you to always keep that in mind."

Felicity nodded her head slowly and started feeling relaxed. She picked up the menu.

"Let's order. It's a long story."

****

Duncan nursed a beer near the entrance of Smugglers, a bar in Brackenfell.

He watched the few patrons along the counter. Regulars, all, by the looks of it. Lonely souls looking for a bit of company, slowly sipping half-warm drinks, waiting for someone to buy the next round.

Devlin came in through the door and spotted Duncan. He sat down next to him and, without speaking, ordered a beer.

He needed to check out the people in the bar first—a habit he had acquired at a very young age.

He looked at the Boer while lifting his brows questioningly.

"Why here?"

Duncan grinned at him and took another sip of his beer before answering.

"My bike is at the bike shop down the road to have a new tyre fitted. After this beer, I'll treat you to lunch at Nando's."

Devlin smiled and bumped him on the shoulder with his fist.

Duncan looked over his shoulder at an old codger sitting at a table on his own. The man had been intently watching Duncan since he arrived.

He got up from his stool and walked over to him. He sat down at the table and greeted him.

"Hey, Uncle Rory. How are you?"

Rory looked at him intently and slowly recognized him.

"Thought ya looked familiar. Yer Alistair's son, ain't ya?"

"Yes, I am. That's if he's still alive, of course?"

Alistair and Rory, an ex-Brit, had been best mates. They had been Darts Doubles champs in the eighties.

They had also worked together at a company in Elsies River as boilermakers.

Rory slowly nodded his head and smiled.

"He is alive, all right."

Duncan looked to see if old Rory was pulling his leg.

Rory just grinned at him, showing off his nicotine-stained teeth.

"If you wait here long enough, you might see him. He normally comes in after six when his missus is off to work. She's a caregiver for some old gall in Durbanville."

Duncan shook his head and got up from the table.

"Maybe some other day, Uncle Rory. I have to go. Be seeing you."

He walked back to his seat, and while standing, he downed the rest of his beer.

He motioned the bartender over and paid for his and Devlin's drinks.

He left a R200 note on the counter.

"This is for Rory's drinks. I'll see him tomorrow and ask him what he got for R200."

He looked menacingly at the barman.

Devlin walked out with him, and they rounded the corner to where his car was parked.

Devlin unlocked the doors with the fob and got in on the driver's side.

He waited for Duncan to buckle up before he started the car.

"Who was that? What's the rush all of a sudden?"

"It's an old friend of my father's."

"That still doesn't explain why we had to leave in a hurry?"

The Boer looked out the passenger window of the moving vehicle, obviously deep in thought.

It was a while before he answered.

"He says my dad is still alive."

Devlin steered the car into a parking lot near Nando's and switched off the ignition.

They sat in silence for a while before he asked,

"Did you think he was dead?"

Duncan shrugged his shoulders.

"I haven't heard from or seen him since I was fourteen. He just left us. When I didn't see him at my mom's funeral, I assumed he was."

He went quiet.

"I'm not even sure I care."

Devlin decided to change the subject.

"Do you want to talk about the job here or in the restaurant?"

Duncan knew he had to be extra careful, and although he trusted Devlin, he could not risk ever being recorded by him.

"Let's get a table and talk."

"There is one more thing before we go."

Duncan was ready to open the door but turned back toward Devlin.

"I have a meeting this afternoon with a guy called Kallie Jansen. We've done some deals in the past, but today, I feel something is off. I'm going to send you a pin drop before I enter his house. If you don't hear from me by six o'clock, you'll know something is wrong. Is that okay?"

"Sure, Dev. I got your back."

They got out of the car and walked across the parking area to the eatery.

They placed their orders at the counter and found a table at the rear, where they could see everyone entering as well as keep an eye on the car.

Both placed their phones facing upward on the table.

Devlin told him about the meeting with Toni at Century City.

He handed him a piece of paper with the two Serbs' contact details.

"I don't need to know how, just when it's done."

Duncan nodded as he put the slip of paper in his pocket.

He looked at Devlin in earnest before he spoke.

"When this is done, I want it to be the last contract you and I are involved in. I consider you a friend, and I don't think we can continue like this. I will have enough money to lie low for a while. I think I might have a plan for the future. Is that okay with you?"

Devlin looked at the Boer with mixed emotions.

On one hand, he was proud and pleased to be considered a friend, but on the other hand, he stood to lose a lot of potential income.

He decided to play it cool. The Boer might change his mind when the money ran low.

"I'm proud to be your friend. What you say makes sense, and I agree. However, when the time comes and you feel you want to do another contract, you must let me know first. Okay?"

Duncan leaned forward and fist-bumped him.

The waiter was coming toward them with their Peri-Peri Chicken and rice.

"Let's eat. I'm going for a ride after this. I'll let you know when the contract is executed."

Devlin laughed.

"No need for proof. The media will provide it."

$$****$$

Felicity had finished her meal and was nursing a Cuppa Chino.

During the meal, she had told Maria everything she knew and had given her the information she had not yet divulged to Captain Dan.

She had deliberately not discussed her latest contact with the Contractor. It was just too incriminating, and she had a feeling it might come back to bite her.

Maria had listened to Felicity and taken in all the information she had provided. The biggest problem seemed to be inefficiency at Diepsloot SAPS, starting right at the top with Brigadier Flo.

She folded her napkin and looked across the table at her friend.

She understood her feelings of helplessness.

They had trust issues and corruption at The Hawks as well.

"Sister, I was going to tell you something that might make you feel a little better. I am also going to help you if you agree."

Felicity waited anxiously for Maria to continue. She gave a small nod in agreement.

"As you know, we were actively pursuing the illegal cigarette smuggling going on between South Africa and Zimbabwe. We were a very small group of agents working on this. All of them were people we could trust. Recently, we had followed your Brigadier to an apartment in the city that belonged to Manzoni, our main suspect. The two of them had spent some time there, and all indications were that she was romantically involved with him."

Felicity smiled and replied, "According to social media, so was the rest of the women in South Africa."

"They were not far off. He was a busy boy. We also suspected he might be funding the fascist left-wing party. Anyway, we got access to the love nest the day after they had met there, before the cleaners arrived. They were either very careless or very arrogant. On the coffee table in the lounge, we found a police docket. It seemed she had given it to Manzoni, and he had forgotten to take it with him. We were busy following up on its significance. We also found an empty bottle of Moët and two glasses, which we had sent for fingerprint and DNA tests."

Felicity shook her head in quiet amazement. Could somebody so stupid really be a Brigadier?

"That is nothing. We also found a used condom in the toilet that did not flush. We were waiting on DNA results."

"What will happen if Manzoni comes back for the docket?"

"He hasn't so far, and the apartment has been cleaned since. He will think it was dumped. Remember, he doesn't need the docket. All he needs is for the docket not to be where it should be. Pay a crooked cop to let out whoever is arrested, and it all goes away."

"I know too well. We have unsolved dockets lining our passages and office floors. There are thousands of dockets just lying on the floor."

"We have since planted a camera with sound in the apartment. We were monitoring it 24/7. We hoped to get more proof soon. Unfortunately, we could not reveal what we had on your Brigadier without exposing our case on Manzoni. Be patient, and I promise you it will be worth it."

"Is this not a job for IPID?"

Maria smiled ruefully and shook her head.

"They were also littered with cadres. I didn't see them pursuing a well-connected police Brigadier. Did you?"

Felicity smiled at Maria and nodded her head.

"I understand. Just knowing that the bitch was being watched by The Hawks was comfort enough. I just wished I could share it with Captain Dan. He needed a boost as much as, or even more than, our whole department."

Maria finished her coffee and removed lipstick from her purse. While applying a fresh layer, she looked over at Felicity.

"It was not all one-sided. I needed your help as well. We had a listening device in her office, but we needed more. We needed you to record her whenever she talked to you or your team. I needed someone there to let me know when she left the office and what her movements were. Her PA should have a diary. We needed it copied or photographed. It would give us a pattern."

Felicity looked very alarmed and started shaking her head.

"No way! I couldn't spy on her. I would lose my job in an instant, as well as my whole pension."

Maria put the lipstick holder back in her purse and snapped it shut.

"Did you want her gone or not? I wouldn't force you, girl, but we were desperate. We had to start fighting dirty. Always remember that if we stood back and did nothing, then one day, we would have to tell our children what we did—or didn't do."

She indicated to the waitress to bring the bill.

Felicity quietly looked at her friend. She knew she was about to walk on the wild side. More than she had done already.

"I will do it as long as it is just between the two of us. No one in your group can know that I supply you with info. Do you agree?"

Maria smiled and said, "It goes without saying. I will never let anyone know that you helped me."

Chapter 20

Captain Dan saw the white Isuzu pick-up parked in the street in front of his house, but assumed it belonged to someone visiting across the street.

He pulled into the driveway, stopping behind Cynthia's little Hyundai Atos. He sat for a while, alone in the darkness of the car, before grabbing his briefcase from the passenger seat.

He walked down the driveway to close the security gates. Satisfied, he headed up the stairs and unlocked the front door.

He heard voices in the kitchen and his two daughters squealing with laughter as he made his way down the passage of the old house.

Walking into the kitchen, he immediately smiled when he saw his old commander sitting at the kitchen table.

He kissed his wife and hugged his daughters before holding out his hand to greet LangFaan Labuschagne.

"Cappie, how are you? You look rested and fit. Are you enjoying retirement?"

LangFaan got up from the chair and hugged his old comrade.

"How are you, Dan? I thought I would come by and see if you're still looking after my girls."

Cynthia realized they had some things to discuss and shooed the two girls out of the kitchen.

"Come on, you two. You've heard enough funny stories for one day, and you still have to do your homework. I'm sure Uncle Faan will come say goodnight before he leaves."

Looking back over her shoulder, she told Dan, "I have a soapy to watch. I will join you in a while."

Dan sat down opposite LangFaan and folded his hands on the table in front of him.

"So, I assume Cynthia phoned you?"

LangFaan smiled and held his palms upward, questioningly.

"What can I do to help my friend? Your wife is concerned, and seeing you now after so long, frankly, so am I. You look haggard."

Dan was reluctant to share his feelings with his old Commander. He got up, took two glasses from the cupboard, and reached for a bottle at the back.

He poured each a double shot of whiskey and set one glass in front of LangFaan.

"A shot of courage. Not for you but for me."

LangFaan sat quietly, sipping his drink, while Dan talked about the problems at Diepsloot. He could not help but bring up Rawlimi and her shoddy way of running what had once been one of the best departments in the police force.

He told him about the aggression and distrust they experienced from the public. The slow results they got from pathology, fingerprints, and DNA departments.

"It's as if everyone has given up, Cappie! No one seems to have any direction or purpose. I have no one to talk to. No one to get advice from. I feel so... so useless."

"Who do you trust?"

Captain Dan stared out of the window and shook his head slowly.

He looked back at LangFaan and took a sip of whiskey before answering.

"I trust my detectives. Felicity Booysen, John Robson, and Lastborn Thobela—all Sergeants."

LangFaan shook his head in disbelief.

"Christ, Robson is almost fifty. He's been a Sergeant for nearly twenty years. I remember Booysen, but I don't know Thobela. Are they good detectives?"

Dan took a moment before answering.

"Booysen is very good, but impulsive and impatient. She needs strong leadership, something I feel I lack. Robson has experience and is reliable, but I feel he is also starting to lose patience. Thobela is keen and very astute. He was transferred from Bellville in the Cape. I think he will be excellent with the right guidance and training. We need someone like you there, Cappie!"

"I'm afraid that will not happen. I was asked to resign because I wasn't willing to take orders from ANC lackeys. Dan, I've started my own small investigative firm. I have three ex-detectives in my employ. All veteran cops. We do corporate investigations most of the time, but occasionally we're called by the public to investigate cases that the police refuse to or can't. As your friend, I'm willing to use the resources I have to assist you where I can and if financially possible. I'd like to suggest a bi-monthly meeting with your team to assist them with techniques and procedures. No one at SAPS has to know unless you feel you need to clear it with Rawlimi first."

Dan thought it over. The offer was irresistible, but he would be treading on thin ice.

Rawlimi would go ape-shit if she found out Dan was using a white man to train his detectives.

He made a decision.

"I accept your offer, but it will only be me and Robson. We will use what we learn and get from you to empower the other two. I feel it's safer if fewer people know about it. I cannot afford to lose my job, but right now, I am desperate."

LangFaan got up from the table, bringing the bottle of Three Ships with him.

He sat down, poured them each a healthy free-hand slug, and held his glass to Dan's.

They toasted.

"There is, of course, one condition."

Dan knew what was next and replied, "You need occasional help from SAPS systems. If it's not illegal, I don't mind. You fight crime, we fight crime."

"Cheers, Dan. Can we get together every second Monday in the evening?"

Dan nodded and grinned at his friend.

"So, our first meet will be in four days?"

"Yes, at my house. I still live in the same place. And Dan, just for the record, I need guys like you in my firm. If you ever leave SAPS, please talk to me."

Dan called Cynthia from the lounge.

She walked into the kitchen and was relieved to see Dan so relaxed.

The bottle of Three Ships on the table might have had something to do with it, of course.

"I have a chicken pie in the oven for supper. I just need to reheat it and put the rice in the microwave oven. Why don't you guys take your drinks to the lounge, and I will call you when I am ready? Leave the bottle here. I will open a bottle of white wine for us. I also need a drink."

They got up from the table and, with their drinks, moved to the lounge.

"How did she convince you to come here on such short notice?"

LangFaan grinned and slapped Dan on the shoulder.

"She promised to feed me."

****

The youth watched from a doorway as the two tsotsis exited the VW Golf and made their way up the back stairs to number 5.
While the driver was inserting the key into the door, the youth noticed the passenger fondling his friend's bum. *Interesting*, he thought, storing the information for later. He saw them enter and close the door behind them.

The youth slowly walked past the flat and took a few pictures of the door and locks with his camera. He then walked down the stairs to where their car was parked under a carport.

Looking around and seeing no one, he bent down and attached the magnetic tracking device to the inside of the rear fender.

He made his way out of the building and walked into the supermarket below.

Finding a quiet aisle, he accessed the app for the tracker and checked that it was working.

He had bought it from a stall holder who sold security gadgets near his friend's soccer shirt stall. He was surprised and relieved to see that it actually worked.

He closed the app, bought a bottle of juice, and walked out.

He had set an alert on the app and would know immediately when the VW moved.

Later, he would study the lock and other photos of the flat. With the money he had received from the Contractor, he had paid for a room near the market.

The couple he rented from both worked during the day. He had told them he worked at a restaurant in the City and might work late some nights. He used some of the money to buy jeans and shirts, along with a dark blue windbreaker.

He also treated himself to a pair of brown Timberland boots. He was getting used to the conservative clothes, and much to his surprise, he felt as if people treated him better than when he had been dressed in township gangsta kit. That night, he would dress in his old clothes before heading off to the market for surveillance.

Luckily for him, his friend slept at his stall and didn't mind company. Especially if the company brought food.

****

The Boer sent an SMS to the phone number he had gotten from Devlin to contact the Serbs.

'Ready to meet when you are. The Boer.'

He did not have to wait long before he got a reply.

'Tonight 9 PM. Pin to follow.'

He waited until he saw the pin drop register on his WhatsApp and was relieved to see it was at their house.

He sent a new message.

'9 PM.'

He switched off the phone. No more messages.

He had parked his bike in the garage and was enjoying the burger he had gotten from McDonald's on his way back from his ride.

The bike was fueled and ready. He had obscured the number plate with some mud.

He assembled the Glock 17, cocked it once to check the action, and waited a few minutes after finishing all his tasks.

Then, he took another burner phone from his rucksack and typed in the number for the Serbs and sent a message.

'Hi Milos, my name is Milan Beeka. I have information I got from my uncle Cyril's things. I have had it for a while. It has to do with things you did in the 1990s. A lot of pictures and detailed operations. Killing of Muslim men and boys. I need to leave the country in a hurry and I need money fast. I will hand it all over for 20K. Please do not see this as blackmail. This is a big favor I am doing for you. Can you imagine what someone else will charge you for this information? Send someone. Tonight. I will be at Quay4 from 8-10 PM. Red Serbia FC windbreaker. Cash only.'

He switched the phone off, removed the battery and packed his things into his rucksack and got ready to go to Camps Bay.

He needed to make sure the bodyguard left the premises for his plan to work.

****

Toni showed the message to Milos.

"I didn't know Cyril had a nephew. I wonder how long he's had this information. It must be since Cyril was assassinated. He must have found it in his uncle's belongings. Thank God he got it and not someone else. What do you want to do, Milos?"

Milos was sipping his second Stoli of the afternoon.

He sighed and looked at his lifelong friend.

"I am really getting fucking tired of this shit, Toni. I was hoping to have Jakes around when The Boer comes, but we'll have to send him to The Waterfront to collect the stuff from Beeka. Hopefully, all this shit will be behind us soon."

Toni nodded in agreement and took a sip of his vodka.

"Will we be safe alone with The Boer?"

Milos shrugged and said, "Sure. He works for us. We are going to pay him a million rand. Have you got all the other info we got from that guy in Macassar to give to him?"

"Yes, and the gun for the job. We can't have him use something that might be traced back to him. Remember, if he's safe, then we are safe."

Milos walked over to the drinks cabinet and poured them each another shot of Stoli with ice.

"Call Jakes. He has to leave by 7:30. Get twenty grand from the safe while you're at it. It's peanuts for what we get. Hopefully, it'll be the last of it."

"Ziveli. I drink to that."

Chapter 21

The Boer watched as the gates slid open, and he saw the nose of a silver ML350 appear.

He sat two houses away on his bike, pretending to look for directions on his phone. He glanced to his right when the car drove past and saw a well-built, younger guy driving. He looked at the number plate and memorized the last four numbers. It was all he needed. He allowed the car to build up a substantial lead before he turned to follow. He slowly rode to the Waterfront to give the driver time to park.

He parked his bike among some other bikes near Ferryman's entrance and locked his helmet in the top box. Slinging his rucksack over his shoulder, he went in search of the silver ML350. He walked through all the parking spots near the restaurant. He crossed the road to the underground parking arcade and soon spotted the back of the ML350 sticking out in the distance.

When he got closer, he noticed the driver still seated in the vehicle, seemingly occupied with his phone. The Boer double-checked the registration number as he walked past the rear of the car. He took up a position behind a pillar and, taking out his phone, he pretended to be in conversation. From where he stood, he had a clear view of the car. He looked at the time and saw it was close to 8 p.m.

Five minutes later, the door opened, and the driver stepped out. He locked the car and walked out of the parking arcade.

The Boer slipped a Special Forces fighting knife from the scabbard on his hip. Looking around to make sure no one was near, he walked between the ML350 and the VW Kombi parked next to it. He checked his surroundings once more. Seeing and hearing nothing, he bent down at the front tire and, with the sturdy short blade of the fighting knife, he punched a hole into the front tire. Checking again, he moved to the rear and did the same to that tire.

He quickly exited the arcade and casually walked to his bike. He checked to make sure no one was paying him undue attention, and when he was satisfied, he put on his helmet and started the Yamaha. Carefully, he rode out toward Green Point. He took a different route around Clifton to Camps Bay.

It was a warm evening, and he enjoyed the ride along the Atlantic coast. He reached Camps Bay Main Road and, while sitting on his bike, he took out his burner phone and sent a message to the Serbs.

'Nearby. ETA 9 p.m. How do I get in?'

It was not long before he received a reply.

'Hoot twice. Park and come upstairs.'

****

Milos looked at Toni and smiled.

"Our guy is on time. I like that. Let's have another drink before we talk business. Do you think he will be happy with half up front?"

"I can't see him not agreeing to it. Show him the bag with the money, and he will be happy. I'm sure that was how it was done the last time."

They were halfway through their drinks when they heard the hooting outside the gate. Milos pushed the remote while Toni peeped through the curtains.

"He is on a bike. You can close now."

Milos pressed the remote and placed it on the table next to him.

It was not long before they heard the steps on the stairs leading up to the lounge area. They had never met The Boer before and were surprised by how average he looked. The beard was the one distinctive feature he had. Toni walked up to him and held out his hand. The Boer completely ignored him.

He placed his rucksack on the floor next to him. He held an almost empty water bottle in his left hand and stood with his legs apart, facing Milos and Toni.

"What information do you have for me? I would like to get the job done by next week."

Milos indicated to Toni, who jumped forward with a few sheaves of A4. He held it out to The Boer. The Boer glanced through it, folded it in half, and stuck it in an inside pocket of his jacket.

"What are the terms?"

Again, Toni was the one to talk.

"We will pay half now and the balance when we receive proof of death. We do not care how you do it. We will be blamed in any case, but our lawyers will fight it."

The Boer looked from one to the other. He still could not believe these two old men were killers of women and children, but the proof was indisputable. Besides their crimes during the Balkan wars, their illegal guns were responsible for numerous deaths on the Cape Flats. A lot of children had been shot by incompetent, gun-wielding gangsters.

When he did not answer immediately, Milos nodded to Toni, who took a cloth bag with the money and held it out to The Boer.

"The gun you must use is inside. It is untraceable. It is loaded with nine rounds and nine more in the ziplock bag. Dump it in the ocean when you are done."

The Boer was dumbfounded and at a loss for words. Were these old fools really giving him R500,000 in cash and the gun to shoot them? He looked inside the bag and was astounded by how good half a million looked. He took the gun from the bag and placed the bag on the floor next to him.

"How do I get the rest?"

This time, Milos spoke.

"When we get confirmation, our driver will drop it anywhere of your choosing. On the same day. Is that acceptable?" he asked, a smirk playing on his lips, usually reserved for employees or people beneath him.

The Boer pulled back the slide on the pistol and saw there was a round up the spout. He recognized it as an old 9mm Star, the same model the cops used years ago.

"How do I know this thing can still fire?" He was making sure he asked the right questions to keep them at ease.

"It will fire. It is a good gun. Now we have a drink together. Maybe we become partners, and you do more work for us. You drink Stoli?"

"Yes. Thank you. It is my favorite." He had no idea what it tasted like.

Milos indicated to Toni to pour the drinks. As he got up to help him, The Boer emptied the water bottle and put the gun barrel into the opening.

He shot Milos through the bottom of the skull, and before his body hit the floor, he put two rounds into Toni's head as he was turning. The shots were muffled by the imitation silencer and would be barely audible outside the house.

The two old men lay dead on the parquet floor, blood pooling beneath their heads. They lay a meter apart—brothers-in-crime— justice delivered for a lifetime of atrocities.

The Boer grabbed the security cam recorder, took their phones, and placed the bag of money in his rucksack. He walked down the stairs, wiped the gun clean, and dropped it into a flower bed.

He pressed the remote to open the gate, rode out slowly, and closed it behind him.

Justice had been served.

****

Devlin looked across the bar counter at Kallie, who was mixing three rum and Cokes. He placed two of the drinks in front of Devlin and John Robertson.

"There you go, enjoy. How do you want the money, Dev?"

Earlier, John had checked the diamonds and found them to be real. It was all for show because as soon as he poured the diamonds out on the cloth, he recognized them immediately. He had valued and thoroughly checked them less than two months before.

Devlin took a sip of the rum, and although it was not something he normally drank, he enjoyed the sweet molasses taste of it. He looked at the two buyers. He had dealt with them before, but today something just felt off. It was as if they had invited him over to size him up. He found it difficult to shake the feeling of doom.

Why did they ask how he wanted the money? It was always cash, every time.

"There is only one way for me. I do not kop Bitcoin, and other methods will leave a trace. Cash is best." He looked from one to the other.

Robertson was the first to speak.

"We have it ready. I will give it to you when you leave. Tell me again how you got the stones."

Devlin shifted position on his bar chair and took another sip of the rum. He really liked it. He glanced at the label on the optic-mounted bottle that Kallie Jansen had poured it from—Captain Morgan. He made a mental note to get some for his pad on the way home.

He wanted to finish his drink and be on his way.

"I was approached by a gang member that I have done deals with before. He told me that he broke into a pawn shop in Goodwood and burgled the place. He found the diamonds in an open safe. The burglary has not yet been discovered, as the owner had a stroke and is still in a coma in N1 Hospital. Unfortunately, I cannot give you the name of the gangster, as you will undoubtedly understand."

He downed his drink and stood up.

"I have to go now. My bodyguard is waiting at N1 City for me. I gave him a time when I will meet him."

Kallie Jansen scowled and said to Devlin, "Do you feel threatened by us that you have to put security in place?"

Devlin expected the question.

"That is why I'm still in business after all these years. I learned a long time ago that trust is something that can get you killed."

John Robertson got up and took Devlin by the elbow, desperate to get him away from Kallie's uncontrollable temper.

"Come, let me pay you, then you can be on your way. Let us know if you have any more deals like this for us, ok?"

They walked down the stairs, with Robertson leading the way. He opened the safety gate to let Devlin out. He pulled a thick envelope from his inside pocket and handed it to Devlin.

"It's a pleasure doing business with you. Buy yourself a new car. That old Ford looks beat."

Devlin took the money from him and walked to his car. He waved the envelope in his left hand and turned toward Robertson.

"This is not enough for a new car. Maybe I should have sold it on the open market."

He got into his car and waited for Robertson to open the gate. As he drove out, he caught sight of Kallie Jansen standing on the veranda in his rearview mirror, watching him. A shiver ran down his spine, and he tried to shake the feeling of suspicion.

He sent a text message to The Boer.

'All ok. Will call you tmrw.'

Chapter 22

Mikey was in town to pick up pipe fittings for the farm. He inserted the battery into his burner phone and sent the youth a message.

'Can you talk?'

He sat in the pick-up and waited for the reply. It wasn't long before the phone rang. He answered it.

"Is everything okay?" he asked.

"Yes. I planted the tracking device on the car. This morning, I got into their flat. I put a camera in the kitchen. It is open plan to the lounge."

"Good. Did anyone see you?"

"No, it was quiet there during the day. I will send you the link to the tracker and the camera."

"Did you look around? Any sign of human remains or evidence of their involvement?"

"The flat is spotlessly clean. These guys are gay. There is only one bedroom. There was a laptop on the counter, but it was password protected."

Mikey analyzed the information the youth was giving him before he asked, "What do you want to do next?"

"I want to kill them!"

"These guys are not the main ones. We need to get the ones doing the killing. If you kill them, you will never find the killers."

"What must I do then?"

"Observe them. Wait until they make contact with the vendor and keep an eye on them. If you don't spook them, they won't go anywhere. Wait for me to contact you again. Send the link for the tracker and camera."

Mikey disconnected the call. He rubbed his hands over his face. He felt helpless being so far away, and he wasn't sure what skills the youth had besides sleuthing. Mikey decided to phone Jack.

"Yo, Mikey. How are you, boet?"

Mikey smiled when he heard how upbeat his best friend was.

"I'm cool, Jack. Man, I need some advice again."

He proceeded to tell Jack everything he had so far, knowing very well that Jack would not approve of his involvement in such things again.

"Jack, I have to help this guy, but I don't know how without going with him. He does not have the skills to get information from these guys to move to the next target. That is the only way to get to the killers."

Jack would do anything to prevent Mikey from going anywhere near these people. He also realized that Mikey would not rest until the killers were found and dealt with. He had an idea, but would need time to make it work.

"Mikey, I want you to promise me you will not go there. I have an idea and will discuss it with you in a few days, okay? Let the youth just observe for the time being. Is it possible to get a tracking device on the vendor? I have a feeling she will split soon."

"I will work on something."

Mikey knew he could trust Jack to come up with a plan. He felt guilty for dragging him into this mess, but every night he closed his eyes, he saw the video of the mutilated little bodies.

"How is Jeremy getting on with that phone we took from the vendor?"

"He is struggling with it. It is PIN and fingerprint protected. He is sure he will eventually get it open. I will ask him this evening when I get to the bar."

"Okay. Phone me as soon as you've got something for me."

"Will do. Ciao."

****

Captain Dan drove toward the market where the vendor operated. In the car with him was Sergeant John Robson. He had been briefing him on the way there. He looked at John to try and gauge his reaction to the suggestion of working with LangFaan

Labuschagne. John was tapping his finger on the door panel, obviously deep in thought. It was a while before he answered.

"LangFaan contacted me last night. He has a job for me, and I am seriously considering it. I will not get a promotion where I am now. I have given more than thirty years to this job, and because of my skin color, I am overlooked for promotion year after year. Fuck, Captain, did you know that Captain Mkize used to be the garden boy here at Diepsloot when I started? I doubt if he even made it to grade seven at school. And I must salute him every day! Do you have any idea how that feels?"

Dan felt helpless. There was nothing he could do to change Robson's mind if he decided to go. He had been working with John for more than fifteen years and yes, he too had been passed over for promotion.

"John, I understand how you feel. Affirmative Action is hurting whites and is not good for the force or the country, but remember, it was the same during Apartheid. You are now experiencing what blacks experienced for a very long time. I need you, and if you leave the police now before we catch these killers, I will not be able to do it on my own. Please give LangFaan a chance to help us. The minute I told him you are still a Sergeant, I knew he would offer you a job. Thanks for confiding in me."

"I hear you, and I have been telling myself every day that Affirmative Action is trying to correct imbalances, but you have to admit that the whites who benefited during Apartheid did their jobs. Not like now."

Dan sighed audibly.

"I hear you. The rot is coming from the top. The very top. Are you going with me to the meeting this evening?"

John nodded his head.

"Yes, I told LangFaan already that I will be there. Can you keep quiet about the job offer for a while? At least till I make up my mind."

"I will do that. What did he offer you, if I may ask?"

John smiled and looked at Dan.

"More than you earn."

****

129

The team was gathered in Captain Terror Majoba's office.

They had a new member, recruited from Durban Serious Crimes Unit—a young Indian guy called Rikki Patel. He was a Captain, the same rank as Majoba. He was a temporary addition to the unit, sent there to work with Majoba's group to gain experience in fighting illegal cross-border imports. Durban had become the export hub for the rest of Southern Africa's illegal diamonds, gold, and now cigarettes. Many shipments from Durban had recently been intercepted in Australia and New Zealand. Their governments were demanding action from South African authorities.

They were all gathered around Majoba's desk, watching his computer screen. A while ago, the motion-sensitive camera in Manzoni's love nest had been activated. It had been dead since Combrink installed it more than a week ago. Everybody was excited that they finally had action.

On the screen, they observed three very beautiful women. They were dressed in short, tight-fitting knit dresses and skimpy tops. All were young and very well-endowed. The two black girls were a little more voluptuous than the blonde with them, though she was no scarecrow either. They were unpacking groceries and assembling plates of snacks on the bar counter. There were two crates of Moët, ready to be packed into the bar fridge. On the counter, they could see bottles of Hennessy brandy and at least six bottles of Johnnie Walker Black.

The girls seemed to be acquainted but not particularly close friends. They were giggling excitedly while preparing what looked like a party.

Chapter 23

Sergeant Felicity Booysen was working late, waiting for everyone to leave so she could get into Brigadier Rawlimi's office.

She sat in her cubicle, going over interviews the constables and Sergeant Tobela had conducted with the neighbors of Buhle Gola. They were investigating all the previous abductions. She did not pick up on any new evidence from the interviews. Most of the neighbors had not seen anything. Two of them had heard a car speeding away but had not seen anything.

Felicity was ready to close the docket when her eye caught something she had overlooked. She read the paragraph again and felt a tingle run down her spine. The six-year-old son of a neighbor, three houses down the road, had seen a white VW Golf 7 GTI drive past his house earlier that morning. The constable who had conducted the interview with the boy's father had been interrupted by the kid and had not paid him much attention. However, he had asked how the boy knew which model it was. According to the father, his older son, who worked in Secunda, owned a Golf 3 GTI. The younger son adored his older brother and could identify every VW Golf model ever produced.

Felicity pulled up the Natis report she had received earlier on her screen. She looked at the information but felt disappointed when it did not specify which model the car was. She sighed, leaned back in her chair, and started chewing on the back of her pen. She Googled VW Golf GTI 7 and found plenty of pictures of the car. She scrolled until she found a white one. She opened the photo gallery on her phone to locate the photo the youth had taken of the Golf belonging to the two tsotsis. Once again, she felt disappointed—it only showed the number plate and a small part of the boot.

She looked up to reply to a greeting from the last detective leaving the office.

"Good night, Petrus. I will lock up and leave the key with Captain Andile."

The open-plan offices of the detectives were a no-go area for anyone except the detectives who worked there. It was a directive from Captain Dan to prevent dockets from disappearing.

She watched the disappearing back of Petrus Kama, one of the few dedicated ones left in vice. She decided to wait a while before making her move. Looking back at her screen, her eye fell on the VIN number.

She opened Google and typed in the VIN number. She could not help but grin when all the information for the Golf popped up on her screen. It was a Golf 7!

She sent a message to the Contractor.

'Urgent. Contact me any time.'

She waited for a while but received no answer. She bent down, picked up her handbag from the floor, and pulled out the small spy cam she had gotten from Maria. She slipped it into her pocket and made her way to the Brigadier's office. She moved around the PA's desk and opened the top drawer. A few weeks ago, she had to wait for a meeting with the Brigadier and had seen her PA take the key from the top drawer and hand it to Rawlimi when she arrived.

She took out the key and unlocked the door. Slowly, she pushed it open and peered inside. It was relatively dark as the blinds were drawn. Felicity closed and locked the door behind her, then pulled out the key. She moved to the window and slowly opened the blinds until enough light from the spotlights around the police station illuminated the room. She looked around for a good spot to hide the tiny camera.

She noticed an imitation plant on the bookshelf behind the desk, took it down, and placed it on the desk. It was covered with a thin layer of dust. The little camera had a wire attached, and she used it to tie the device to the stem of the plastic plant. She returned the plant to the top shelf. Moving to the door, she tried to see if the camera was visible, but it was too far away to spot. She listened at the door to make sure she was alone, then took out her phone from her jeans pocket.

Suddenly, she heard knocking on the outer door of the detective's pod. Her blood ran cold. She pressed her ear to the door. She heard the door open and someone enter. Was it the night Commander, Captain Andile, or someone else coming to snoop? She pressed her eye to the keyhole and saw a male hip move past her view. Her heart pounded in her chest. She wiped the perspiration forming on her brow. She heard the person moving in her direction.

A hand went out and tried the handle of the Brigadier's door. Felicity was relieved that she had locked it. She held her breath and heard the person move away. Through the keyhole, she caught a glimpse of a large male in uniform. She listened as he walked out of the office and pulled the door closed behind him. She took a deep breath and decided to continue.

She sent a WhatsApp message to Maria.

'Check.'

She knew Maria was waiting for her message, ready to link the camera to the app on her phone. She heard her phone ping and looked at the screen.

'Move it a little more to your left. I can see you.'

Felicity walked to the pot and adjusted it a few millimeters. She waited. Almost immediately, her phone pinged again.

'Perfect. I could hear your phone ping, so sound is good. Get out of there.'

Felicity closed the blinds and locked the door behind her. She walked around the PA's desk and returned the key to the drawer. She picked up the PA's diary from the desk and went to her cubicle. It took her a while to photograph each page, but she was unhindered. No one entered the office while she was busy with her task. When she was done, she returned the diary to the desk exactly as she had found it.

She shut down her computer and left the office. She handed the key to Captain Andile and asked him if he had been looking for her earlier.

He shook his head. "No, I was just checking all the doors to the offices. I went into the detectives' pod and thought it had accidentally been left unlocked. Then I saw your laptop was still on and realized you must have gone to the toilet."

Felicity felt very relieved and smiled at him. "I heard a knock from the washrooms. I thought it was someone looking for me. Good night, Captain."

She walked past the charge office counter to the back where her car was parked. As she got into her car, she saw a new SMS from the Contractor.

'What did you find?'

She called the number, and he answered crossly.

"Yes?"

She was slightly taken aback by his rudeness but was careful not to antagonize him. She desperately needed him and the youth.

"You need to ask Enoch if he can send the photo of the two tsotsis to his mother. We tracked the car that was spotted near her house earlier that day. It might be the same guys that took his little brother Patrick."

He did not answer for a while, and she looked at her phone to see if the call had been disconnected. He eventually spoke.

"Are you willing to work with us?"

She did not hesitate and answered, "Yes. I am sorry about my outburst."

"I will ask him to do that and let you know. Do you have any leads on the latest killing?"

"Not yet, but we have surveillance on the vendor."

"I know. Tell your guys to dress down a bit. They stand out and will be spotted. We have a tracker on the Golf and a spy cam in their flat. Nothing to report yet."

He ended the call.

She was a little pissed off because he had spotted their surveillance and also because of his rudeness, but she felt very excited to be working with them again. The fact that they had eyes on the tsotsis was a big bonus. She felt the stress of the past hour drain from her. Suddenly, she was in good spirits and called her boyfriend, Bongi. He answered with a question.

"Are you working late, or do I have to worry about another man?"

"Lover, I am just leaving the office now, and I had a wonderful day. I need you to cook pasta for me, feed me a lot of wine, and shag the shit out of me. Do you think you can do that?"

Bongi laughed and said, "I think you have the right number. I think I can accommodate you and your desires, madam. Come right over and meet the naked chef."

"Get naked. I will be there in fifteen minutes."

****

Maria was very pleased with the work Felicity had done and showed the phone to Majoba. He took his eyes off the screen he had been watching and looked at it. The rest of the group had gone home, leaving just the two of them in the office.

"Amazing the definition we get from such a small cam. Look at this feed from the apartment," he said.

She looked over his shoulder at the screen. It was still only the women there. They were nibbling on the snacks and slowly sipping champagne. Clearly, they were waiting for company. Majoba had turned the sound down, evidently bored with their conversation. Maria put her phone away.

"Are you going to be here all night? You do know we are recording this?"

He looked over his shoulder and said, "I want to know who they are expecting. It will keep me awake all night if I do not know."

"You are right. I'm going to get some coffee. Can I make you a cup?"

"That would be nice, thank you... Whoa, come look at this."

Maria turned and rushed over to his desk. On the screen, she saw three men entering the apartment. One of them was Manzoni. The other two she recognized immediately. She pointed to the screen.

"Is that who I think it is?"

"It is the leader of a political party and his sidekick. We suspected they had partied there before. Now we have proof. Let's hear what they are saying."

The men accepted drinks from the women and seemed very enamored by the attention they were getting. Majoba turned the volume back up. Everybody was talking at the same time, greeting each other. The two guys with Manzoni were already groping the bums of two of the girls. The leader of the political party, Mamello, was clearly very much into the blonde. His sidekick, Sehloho, was keeping the girl in the leopard-print skirt busy. Manzoni, however, seemed preoccupied, frantically opening and closing drawers while talking to the other girl.

Maria pointed at him on the screen.

"He's looking for the docket."

Majoba smiled and looked at Maria.

"Let him sweat. He'll forever wonder what happened to it."

The conversations gradually became more modulated as the excitement wore off. Mamello downed half the drink the girl had put in his hand and shouted at Manzoni, "Chief, what are you looking for? Come here. We must dance."

Maria could hear he was already half-drunk. They must have partied somewhere else before coming to the apartment. Manzoni ignored him and went into the bedroom. They had no camera there, but they suspected he was searching for the missing docket. It wasn't long before he returned. By now, Sehloho had his tongue buried deep in Leopard Print's ear. She squirmed to get away, but he had her around the waist. Eventually, they collapsed on the sofa, and he slid his hand up her dress. She desperately tried to pull her dress down while he groped her.

"My god, he is an animal. Who are these girls? How can they take such abuse?"

"High-class prostitutes. They're paid to take it," Terror replied.

Manzoni tapped Sehloho on the shoulder, trying to get his attention. He had to shake him before he was successful.

"Hey, Sehlo, take it easy, man. That's what we have a room for. Relax and have a drink first, enjoy their company."

Sehlo looked at Mamello, who clapped his hands, laughing.

"The night is young, brother. Here, have a Johnnie Black."

He offered him his glass. Sehlo took it and sheepishly sipped while Leopard Print rearranged her dress. Manzoni's girl switched the TV on and selected a dance music channel. Soon, everyone was dancing to the rhythm of the hip-hop music. Manzoni still had a slightly worried look on his face.

"Terror, do you think we can use that docket as leverage or bait?"

"Here you go again. Is it not bad enough that we have unauthorized surveillance in the apartment? Now you want to use a stolen police docket—one that we have illegally obtained—to scare the poor sod?" He grinned widely. "Fuck, yes, of course, we are going to use it to make his life miserable."

She tapped him playfully on the shoulder and turned to the percolator to pour the coffee. After half an hour of watching the drinking and dancing, Majoba got up from his desk.

"I'm going home. I know where this is going to end up. It's recording, so I'll watch it tomorrow. I'm sure these guys conducted their business before they got to the apartment. They won't discuss anything of importance in front of the whores anyway."

Maria pulled on her jacket and picked up her bag from her chair.

"I agree. It would be like watching a bad X-rated movie. You're right. They're done with business for the night. I'll see you tomorrow."

"Ok. I'll lock up. Do you have your key?"

Majoba had installed new high-security locks six months ago when he suspected someone had been snooping around his office. Only the two of them and Combrink had keys to the new locks.

Before she opened the door to leave, Maria turned back to him.

"I meant to ask—what do you think of the new guy?"

"Patel? I haven't really given him much thought. Why?"

She shook her head and flipped her hand.

"Do you think he might be a plant? You know everyone on this floor always asks what we're doing."

Majoba pulled on his jacket and walked toward her, waiting at the door.

"He comes highly recommended, but I think you might be onto something. Let's play our cards close until we get to know him better."

"He knows we have surveillance on Manzoni's place."

Majoba nodded. "Yes, but he thinks it's authorized. You better tell Combrink to be careful around Rikki as well."

"Wouldn't it be easier and quicker to set a little trap for him?"

Majoba shook his head and smiled.

"You know, Maria, I think you joined the wrong force. You should have been with State Security. You're a real spy. What do you have in mind?"

She smiled.

"I'll think about it and tell you tomorrow. I'll see you then. Bye, Terror, send regards to Patricia."

He nodded. "I will. Let me know if you see anything worthwhile on Rawlimi cam. I want to nail that bitch."

She hurried down the steps and pulled her phone from her bag once she was safely in her car. She called Combrink.

"Hey there. Are you still at the office?"

"I'm just leaving. Pieter, I had a conversation with Terror, and we both feel we need to be careful what we say in front of Patel. At least until we know he's not a plant."

"Serious? I quite like the guy, but if you think so, I'm fine with it. Are you coming over?"

"No, not tonight. I'm giving you a few more days to get your strength back," she said with a giggle.

"I'll let you know when I'm at full strength again. I like the Amazon Maria. Anything more from the surveillance?"

"I'll tell you tomorrow at the office. Even better, I'll show you. We got tired of watching people drink and dance to crappy music."

"Ok, I'll wait till tomorrow."

She put the car in gear and drove to her flat in Edenvale.

Chapter 24

Rikki Patel sat back in his chair and looked at the Section Commander of Parktown Hawks, Colonel Bongani Diba. Diba was fiddling with his phone, trying to store the conversation he had recorded of Patel's information. He finally put the phone down on the table and looked at Patel.

"I will check tomorrow if they have authority for the camera. You must try to stick to them and learn as much as you can. I am sure these guys are not operating according to protocol. They are very secretive about the progress they have made. They report directly to the Area Commander, and I am not happy with that."

"They do seem like a very tight group and are obviously very dedicated. What does it matter, as long as they get the results?" Patel asked.

Diba scowled at him.

"We cannot let units in DPCI go rogue. I want to know what they are up to."

Patel put his hands in the air. "Ok, Colonel. I will let you know if they do anything out of line."

Diba got up from the table and greeted Patel before leaving. Patel sat a while longer, contemplating the position he found himself in. He still could not understand how Diba had found out about his drug dealing in college. He felt like a traitor spying on what was obviously one of the best units he had ever worked with.

He finished his tea and called the waitress over to pay for it.

****

Duncan had stashed the bag with the money he got from the Serbs behind the old geyser in the bathroom of the flat in Parow.

He saw the message from Devlin and replied with a short SMS.

'Contract executed.'

He put the phone on the table and went to the fridge to get a beer. He opened the Black Label and downed half of it. He felt the beer relaxing him and drained the rest. His phone buzzed on the table, and he looked at the message from Devlin.

'Tmrw.'

He got up from the table and grabbed a second beer from the fridge. While sipping it, he thought about what to do with the money. It was a problem. He couldn't put it all in a bank. He couldn't declare it as income. He had an idea.

He would ask Oom Jack.

****

It was early in the morning, and Kallie was sitting in bed, having the coffee and toast his housekeeper had brought in earlier. He was scrolling through his News24 app, reading the news headlines as he usually did every morning. The second headline caught his eye.

'Serbians killed. Bodies found by driver.'

He immediately switched his TV on and went to the News24 channel on DSTV. He read the article. Other than the fact that the driver came home after a night out at The Waterfront and found the bodies of his employers, Milos and Toni, there wasn't much else. He took a screenshot of the TV and forwarded it to John Robertson.

He suddenly realized that today would be a busy day. He hopped out of bed and walked into the huge designer shower, turning on all the faucets and spouts it had.

He looked forward to his first line of coke for the day. He planned to have a quick snort when he opened the safe to get the money to pay The Boer later.

He was sure Devlin would ask for it very soon.

****

The youth saw a message from the Contractor.

'Phone me.'

He told his friend he had to go for a pee and walked to the end of the market area. Taking up position next to a fence, he made sure no one was watching before dialing the Contractor. The call was answered immediately.

"I have information that the two tsotsis you photographed may be the same guys who took your little brother. You told me your mother saw them when they jumped over the fence. Show the photo to her and see if she can identify them."

"She is in Transkei with my aunt. I will send it to my aunt to show her. When must I do it?"

"Do it right now. I will wait right here for your call."

Mikey ended the call and prepared to wait. He was parked next to the road about fifteen kilometers from Hoedspruit. He had to visit the Eco Centre to discuss the wildlife show he was preparing for a class of Grade 7 school kids on Friday. Brigitta had agreed to do the burgers and ice cream for them after the lesson, as Cara had gotten herself involved in decorating the new Honeymoon Chalet. He was not far from there.

It wasn't long before his phone rang. He saw it was the youth and answered.

"What did she say?"

The youth spoke fast and excitedly. "She says she is sure of one of them. The driver. I want to kill him! I am going to do it now."

Mikey quietly said to him, "Enoch, if you cannot learn to control your emotions, I will not help you."

"How... how do you know my name?"

"I know everything. If you are willing to be patient and listen to me, we will find everyone involved in the killing of your little brother. When we do, I will equip you with the skills and tools to avenge all you like. If not, I leave now, and you are on your own. This is the absolute last time I will ask if you understand our deal."

It was a while before he answered. "I'm sorry. I understand. I need you. What do you want me to do?"

"Surveillance. We have to get these guys to lead us to the kingpins. When you see their car move, you have to follow."

"But I am watching the vendor! How must I follow them? I cannot drive."

"I gave you a lot of money. Use an Uber driver if you have to. You have a tracking device on their car. It should not be too difficult to find and follow them."

"You are right. The traffic is so dense here, they cannot move very fast."

"Good. Enoch, I would not mind if you feel the need to give your mother some of the money I gave you. It is not a loan. It is yours to use as you please."

Mikey ended the call and started up the old Nissan. He had still not found another pick-up to buy.

****

Duncan parked his bike outside the pub in Klapmuts and walked inside.

He sat down at the bar and ordered a beer from Junior, the barman. Apart from an old dude with a grey beard sitting on the opposite side of the U-shaped counter, he was the only other customer. It was still early, and although he had hoped to run into Jack, he still enjoyed the ride. The old guy watched him closely as he drank his beer, and he started feeling a bit uneasy. Junior had gone to the back somewhere and was out of sight. Duncan tried to avoid the stare of the old guy by turning around and looking at all the photos plastered on a notice board behind him.

Junior, in the wash-up area behind the bar, pulled out his phone and typed a WhatsApp message to Jack.

'He is here.'

He walked back into the bar and asked Duncan if he was waiting for someone.

"I was hoping to find Oom Jack here."

Junior smiled. "He will be here shortly to pick up the orders from the bar and the kitchen."

He turned to the old guy sitting opposite Duncan. "Another drink, Hennie?"

Hennie nodded but continued to stare at Duncan. He accepted his drink from Junior and then spoke.

"You are mates with Dev, aren't you?"

Surprised, Duncan looked at him and suddenly remembered the conversation he had with Jack the evening after their trip. He tipped his glass toward Hennie and said, "I do know him, yes. Where do you know him from, Hennie?"

If Hennie was surprised that Duncan knew his name, he didn't show it. He smiled and took a sip of his brandy and Coke.

"So, if you know my name, then you probably know that I am a retired policeman. And you will then know that I know your friend Dev is not always playing on the right side of the law."

Duncan looked at Hennie over his drink and realized that he had to be very careful around him.

"I have no idea what Dev does or does not do for a living. I met him at a pool club a while ago, and he brought me to this bar because I told him I was looking for some off-road bikers to ride with on trips. Are you trying to warn me about something? If so, then I will appreciate it, because I play on the right side of the law."

He looked at Hennie challengingly while sipping his beer, considering coming back some other time to talk to Jack.

"I'm not in the police anymore, so I cannot tell you anything about his movements now. I just recognized him from way back. I saw you talking to Jack the other night, and knowing Jack, he will accept you readily. Until you make a mistake, of course. If you were in my position, you would also feel uneasy when someone like Dev enters your domain. This is like my second home, and the people that come here are all known to me."

Duncan finished his beer and called Junior over.

"I would like another. Please pour one for Hennie as well. I will go sit over there by him."

He moved to the other side of the bar and sat next to Hennie. He put out his hand and, in Afrikaans, said, "My naam is Duncan. Aangename kennis."

Hennie took his hand and, also in Afrikaans, said, "Bly te kenne, Duncan."

Duncan smiled and tapped his beer glass against Hennie's glass.

"So, tell me, Hennie, what did you do in the police?"

****

Hennie was still rambling on about his time as a policeman by the time Jack arrived. He greeted Hennie first and then Duncan.

"Junior, just an Appeltizer for me. I still have to cook the books."

He sat down next to Hennie and asked what they had been talking about.

"I was just about to tell Dunc about the time we did that raid with Sanap in Woodstock when we found all those bales of marijuana hidden in the storeroom of the curry shop. They were selling it in small containers as dried Dania with the Roti's and Bunny Chows. These guys were doing a roaring trade. Every couple of months, one of the brothers would travel to Durban to pick up the hot Durban curry spices and at the same time get a bale or two of Durban Poison. It worked well until an undercover cop from Sanap stopped there late one night for a Roti. There was a kid serving, and he misunderstood when the cop asked for some salad with the Roti. The kid gave him a tub of A-grade dagga with his Roti. The next evening, we raided the place and arrested everyone that worked there, as well as two customers."

Hennie's eyes glittered as he finished telling the story. They all had a good laugh. Hennie pushed his drink away and got up from his chair.

"I need to go point old Percy at the porcelain. When I come back, I will tell you about the swingers' club we raided in Clifton."

Duncan waited until Hennie was out of earshot before he turned to Jack and said, "Oom Jack, I need some advice, but I can't talk here."

"I need to discuss something with you as well, so meet me at my place in an hour. I just need to get the grocery and booze orders from Junior and Amanda. Watch what you say in front of Hennie. He is very astute. I'm going to finish this drink and leave. You can stay and listen to his stories. I've heard them all."

144

"Ok, I'll have one more, then come over to your place."

Chapter 25

Devlin sent a copy of the News24 report on the Serbs as confirmation to the customer who had contracted them.

He exited the site and closed his laptop. He knew it might take a day or so until they notified him where to pick up the payment. He was not worried. He had dealt with these people before, and they had always paid within a few days. He wondered where the pick-up would take place this time. The previous time, they had left the money in an unoccupied flat in Oakdale. He had picked up the key from the café around the corner near the flat.

Devlin took his laptop and set it up in the lounge, where he planned to spend most of his day. He had recorded the Formula 1 race and intended to spend the day watching it.

He felt good about the big payday coming up.

****

Sergeant Felicity sat in her cubicle, once more going over the interviews the constables had conducted with neighbors and families over the past four days.

If she had found a lead there once, it could very well happen again. Captain Dan had called for a meeting in his office at ten. She heard her cell phone ping and saw that there was a message from the Contractor. Making sure no one was near her desk, she opened it.

"Look at the driver of the Golf as one of the abductors of Patrick Gola. His mother has recognized him as one of the two who jumped over the fence and took her son. Do not contact her under any circumstances. Go back to Alfie's abduction and see if anybody recognizes the driver and the other guy. They are a gay couple, so I would assume they work together. Show a photo of a white Golf GTI 7 around. Do NOT arrest them. They will lead us to the main guys. Give us time."

Felicity drew a deep breath and deleted the message, as she had done with all the previous ones. She felt a rush of excitement and could not wait for Captain Dan's briefing to be over so she could head out to Soweto and see if she could find anyone who recognized the two tsotsis or their car.

When she saw Sergeant Robson get up from his chair and head toward Captain Dan's office, she followed him. She indicated to Sergeant Tobela to come along.

They were all seated in front of Captain Dan's desk. He looked surprisingly upbeat, smiling at everyone. He seemed comfortable and at ease when he started his briefing.

"Good morning, all. How is the best detective unit in SAPS doing today?"

They were all taken aback, and only Robson replied, "Excellent, Captain. We are ready to roll."

Felicity glanced at John Robson, wondering what the hell was going on. What had happened since yesterday? Had the Contractor given Dan the same information? She noticed that Lastborn Tobela was also at a loss for words as Dan continued.

"From today, we are going to approach this investigation in a completely different way."

He began laying out the new approach for them. They listened intently, surprised by how logical it all sounded.

Captain Dan had his team's full attention.

****

WO Maria Ruiters saw the door to Captain Majoba's office was open and walked in without knocking. She took a seat next to him. He passed her a memory stick. "It's all on here. Watch it from a secure place on your laptop. I came in early to copy it. I've erased all the footage from my computer. If anybody asks anything about surveillance cameras, let me know immediately. Have you figured out a way to test our new guy?"

"I haven't. I take it we're not telling him about the camera in Rawlimi's office?"

"Absolutely not. Just you, Combrink, and I know about that. Have you got anything from it yet?"

Maria laughed. "Don't hold your breath, Captain. That chick is hardly ever there. I'll let you know as soon as I see something worthwhile. I'm going to get a coffee at the place across the road and scroll through last night's party footage. I'll be back to pick up Patel and show him a few warehouses we suspect are being used for storing illegal cigarettes. It'll give me time to check him out."

Maria took her bag and left the office. She saw Patel sitting at his desk and walked over. "Good morning, Rikki. I'm just going to grab a coffee across the road and catch up on some reports. I'll fetch you when I'm done. We're going to check out some warehouses."

"Hi. That would be great. I should be done with my emails by then."

Maria walked across the road and found a table at the back of the coffee shop. She placed her order with the waitress and waited for her latte to arrive before opening her laptop. She inserted the memory stick, and with one earpiece in, she started viewing the footage recorded in Manzoni's apartment the previous evening. She was hoping to find proof of him engaging in sex with one of the prostitutes. It would be dynamite to rattle his suave confidence a bit. His wife was not aware of his philandering.

Very soon, she became bored with the dancing, drinking, and constant giggling of the prostitutes and fast-forwarded the video. She couldn't hear much of the conversations with the music so loud anyway. Suddenly, she saw something and rewound back to the scene where Sehloho was seen dragging the woman with the leopard print into the bedroom. She watched the faces of Manzoni and Mamello and was surprised to see them ignoring it. Clearly, it was the way it had been done before. Maria watched a while longer before she fast-forwarded again.

It wasn't long before she saw the bedroom door open. Only the woman emerged from the room. There was no sign of Sehloho. Probably passed out, she decided disappointedly. No one could use the room now. She fast-forwarded again, and looking at the time counter on the video, she realized that the evening was fast coming to an end. She slowed it down and watched in real-time. It wasn't long before the music was switched off, and everyone sat down to finish their last drinks.

She saw Manzoni eventually get up and shoo the girls from the apartment. They grabbed their handbags, putting the Moët he had given each of them into their bags. She could hear him say to them that an Uber was waiting for them downstairs. They had obviously been paid earlier or were being paid by an agency because Maria didn't see any money change hands. Manzoni closed the door behind him and turned to Mamello.

"Nice girls. Pity your sidekick annexed the room. Do you want to go see if he's awake yet?"

Mamello walked into the room, and after about a minute, he came back. He sat down again and accepted a drink from Manzoni. Maria noticed that Manzoni poured himself a glass of Coke with ice. She made a note to watch the whole video again to see if this was his modus operandi the whole evening—pretending to drink.

Mamello was clearly very drunk, and she could hear his speech slurring when he asked Manzoni, "When you pay the donation over, I'd appreciate some of it in cash. One bar. Can you manage that?"

Manzoni smiled at him as if he had expected the request the whole evening.

"No problemo, Chief. I'll leave it in our post box for you. You can pick it up in two days. Do we tell him?" He indicated with his thumb toward the room.

Mamello grinned. "No. I think he's had his fair share tonight."

Manzoni put his drink down, indicating that the party was over. He laughed at Mamello's comment. "I wonder if he'll remember it."

Mamello got up when he saw Sehloho stumble from the room. He grabbed his friend around the waist and walked him to the door.

Maria watched as they said their goodbyes and left. Immediately after he closed the door, she saw Manzoni start searching the room again. He opened drawers and moved furniture away. He walked to every room in the apartment and searched for the missing police docket. Eventually, he gave up, and with one last look around the apartment, he closed the door behind him. A few seconds later, the camera switched off.

She closed her laptop and walked across the road to go get Patel.

Chapter 26

Jack saw Duncan sitting on his bike in front of the closed gates to his smallholding. He opened the automated gate and indicated for Duncan to follow him. He parked in front of the shed and got out of the car. He watched as Duncan removed his helmet and jacket.

"Come inside, buddy. I've got cold beers in the fridge."

Jack led him to the back of the shed and got two beers from the fridge. He handed Duncan one and indicated for him to sit down. Jack took a long pull of his beer and waited for Duncan to speak. He saw he was grappling with indecision and decided to give him time. Duncan looked around the workshop.

"We're alone here; you can talk freely. I've told you before that everything you tell me stays with me. You have my word on that."

Duncan took a sip of beer, searching for the right way to approach Jack. He felt he could trust the man in front of him and began.

"I have money—cash money—I don't know what to do with."

Jack smiled and said, "Now that is a problem most people wish they had. How much money are we talking about?"

"I'll have almost R2.6 million that I can't declare. The money I saved from my time in the army is in a Money Manager account, but I can't put this 2.6 in that account without questions being asked."

Jack finished his beer and put the bottle on the workbench. He looked Duncan in the eye and saw a hint of steely determination.

"Is this money from a recent contract?"

Duncan nodded slowly. "Some of it is from the previous contract. I don't have it all yet, but I should have it within a couple of days."

"Do you have any new contracts lined up?"

"No. I've already told Dev that I'm going to lie low for a while. I have to take stock of my life and decide what I want to do in the future. I realize that I can't be associated with Dev anymore. I wasn't aware that he was on the police radar until you and Hennie told me. I can't take that risk. I need to disappear for a while—lock up the flat and go somewhere—but I can't travel with a bag of money."

Jack looked at the young man in front of him and saw an opportunity. He took a while to formulate his plan and got up to get more beer from the fridge. He handed one to Duncan and sat down.

"How would you like to help a friend of mine find some child killers? No pay, but your expenses will be covered. You'll have to travel to Jo'burg and stay there for a few weeks."

Duncan's eyes lit up. "Child killers I'll wipe out for free. Tell me more."

"I must first make some calls. Keep yourself busy for now. Bring your bike inside and do a light service on it. All the tools you need are over there by the bike bench. I won't be long."

Jack left the shed and walked over to his house. He had to talk to Mikey.

****

Enoch sat in the passenger seat of the Chevy Spark, indicating to the Uber driver where to go.

He had the Tracker app open on his phone and was watching the dot move along the map of Joburg. The tsotsis were on the move, and he was following them. He saw their car on Baard Road in Centurion. They were less than a kilometer from where he was in the Uber car. He watched the screen and saw them turn into a parking area and stop in front of The Burger Box roadhouse. He urged the Uber driver to speed up.

The Uber driver entered the parking area, and Enoch told him to stop. He passed the Uber driver a R200 note.

"Wait here. I'll give you another R200 off the books on top of your fee. I need you to take me back to where you picked me up. I won't be long."

Before the driver could argue, he exited the car and started walking around the building. He entered the restaurant from the rear entrance and made his way through the kitchen to the front. He ignored the stares he got from the grillers and waitress. He took a seat at a bench in front of the restaurant. He ordered a milkshake from the same waitress who had followed him from inside. She still seemed slightly puzzled.

He looked across and saw the white VW Golf parked next to a black SUV. The passenger of the Golf was in conversation with the driver of the SUV. Enoch watched them for a while. The waitress placed the milkshake in front of him. He looked up at her and smiled.

"Bring me another one for takeaway, please."

She smiled back at him and asked, "Are you going to eat something?"

Enoch looked at the young waitress and, for the first time, noticed how beautiful she was. She looked about eighteen. He gave her his best smile and shook his head.

"No, not now. I might come back later for something. You can bring the bill with the takeaway, please."

He almost missed seeing the brown paper bag being passed from the SUV to the passenger of the Golf. They were discussing something, but Enoch was too far away to hear anything. He looked over to where the Uber driver was still waiting patiently for him. He finished his milkshake and walked into the restaurant. The waitress stood ready with his takeaway milkshake.

He paid with a R200 note and told her to keep the change. She smiled and told him to make sure to find her when he came in later for a meal. Enoch took the milkshake from her with a grin.

"I won't let anyone else serve me. You're very good, and if I may say so, you're beautiful. Your boyfriend must be very much in love with you."

She blushed and gave him a shy smile. He gave her a last look and made his way out the front. While keeping to the right of the car park, he made his way back to his Uber driver. He passed the milkshake to the driver, and taking another R200 from his pocket, he handed it to him.

"Here. Enjoy your milkshake. I need you to follow that black car over there when it leaves. Can you do it? It can be off the books. I'll pay you R20 per kilometer. Cash."

The driver took a sip of the milkshake and smacked his lips. "R20 a kilometer till I drop you? I can do that. How long do we have to wait?"

Enoch looked over to where the black SUV was parked. It was a Toyota Fortuner. He took his phone, and zooming in with the camera, he took several photos of the two vehicles as well as their registration plates. He saw the cars start up and indicated to the Uber driver to be ready.

They were a few car lengths behind the Fortuner, and he had to constantly remind the Uber driver to keep his distance. He knew how important it was to find out who these guys were. He had not yet been able to see them clearly. They were driving within the speed limits and were heading toward Eldoraigne. They turned into Shirley Road, and midway up the road, the Fortuner turned and waited for a gate to open. The Uber driver had by now caught on and waited for the Fortuner to enter the premises.

"Drive slowly past the property and look straight ahead. Do not try to look at them."

Enoch had his phone ready and started snapping as they neared the entrance. The high gate was still closing when they passed. He was happy that he had photos of the address as well as photos of two large black men exiting the Fortuner before the gate was completely closed. He put his phone in his pocket and told the Uber driver to take him back to where he had picked him up earlier.

"Why are you following these guys?" the driver asked.

"My mother wants to know where he lives. He made my sister pregnant. Now he's hiding. I don't blame him. She's not very pretty. I think they want to sue him to marry her. It's her only chance to get a husband."

The driver looked at him incredulously and shook his head. "Wow! And I thought we were following some bad okes, man."

Enoch laughed with him and, shielding his phone from the driver, forwarded the photos to the Contractor.

****

Jack walked back into the workshop where Duncan was busy adjusting the drive chain on his Yamaha.

Jack walked to the rear and sat down near the fridge. Duncan locked the rear wheel in place and, taking a rag, started wiping the tools before putting them back. Jack noticed this and smiled to himself. Duncan sat down and looked at Jack expectantly.

Jack started telling him about the situation Mikey had got himself into. He called him Mackie. Duncan listened intently without interrupting. Jack could see Duncan was both intrigued and shocked by the story.

"If you're interested, he'll come fetch you with his plane. He'll take you and the youth to a smallholding near Lanseria. There's a comfortably furnished house on the property, and there will be a vehicle for you to use. You'll have to train the youth in weapon skills as well as hand-to-hand combat. I'm pretty sure Mackie will teach him some other things as well. He'll contact you in a day or so to finalize everything. He'll also be able to help you with your cash problem. There are different options."

"I can't leave before I've received my payment."

"That's okay. He's aware of it. Are you ready to do this?"

Duncan looked at Jack and grinned. "Oh yeah. This is the break I need. I'm so glad I came to talk to you today."

"You can't tell anyone where you're going, and when you come back, you can't tell anyone where you've been or what you did. What you decide to do afterward is up to you."

"I got it. How old is this youth? Can you tell me a bit more about him?"

Jack looked at Duncan and told him what he knew.

"He's Xhosa. His mother is living near Idutywa in the Eastern Cape. He's seventeen, turning eighteen in five days. He passed Grade 11 and left during Grade 12 when his little brother was killed. He's very inventive and has a high IQ. He's determined and thinks on his feet. He's set on avenging his brother's death as well as that of all the other children who were killed and mutilated for their body parts. In fact, we think he might be the perfect soldier. He needs training, and even more importantly, he needs guidance. He tends to get a bit emotional at times. He'll be introduced to you by another name. You can decide what name you want him to call you. The rest, Mackie will tell you."

"I can't wait to train this soldier. I'll get my things in order. Can I leave my bike with you when I go upcountry?"

"Anytime. I'll run it and make sure the battery stays charged. Would you like another beer?"

"Thanks, but I think it might put me over the limit. I have to keep my wits about me for the next few days. I'll leave now and let you know when I'm ready."

"Okay, ride safe, and leave your phone at home. Mackie will issue you with a burner."

Chapter 27

Mikey looked through the photos the youth had sent him. He picked the one that clearly showed the registration number of the Fortuner and forwarded it to Sergeant Booysen with the message: 'Need a name and anything else you can get.'

Mikey sent the message and then phoned a number from his personal phone. It rang a few times before it was answered.

"Mikey! Are you in England, boet?" The jovial voice of his old friend greeted him.

"No, I'm at home. How are you keeping, Butch? When are you coming for a visit again?"

"I'm due to fly to Australia to attend the christening of my granddaughter. I was planning to stay there for a few months and then come to SA for a month or so in time for the Lions rugby tour. I can get you a ticket for one of the games if you want."

"I wish I had the time, man. I have a lot going on lately. It would be nice if you could come visit us here at Lost Horizons. A lot has changed since I saw you last."

"Married life changes a lot of things, my friend. Get used to it."

"Butch, the reason I'm calling is to ask if I can use your place near Lanseria for a few weeks. We want to train two game wardens, and they're both from that area. It'll just make things easier for us. I'm willing to pay rent."

Butch Prinsloo didn't answer for a while, and Mikey feared he had expected too much from his friend.

"Are they house-trained?"

"Absolutely. One of them used to be in the British Army."

"I'm just joking. Mikey, you are welcome to the place. I prefer it if it's occupied anyway. You don't owe me anything for it. I can never repay you for what you did for me. It's yours to use. The key is with the neighbor."

Mikey had helped Butch get even with the person who had killed his wife during a burglary a few years ago. Veronica had come home one afternoon and walked in on an ex-employee of theirs who was burglarizing the house. He had attacked and killed her before making off with her car and the electronics he had looted. Despite footage showing him on the premises, the police had refused to lock him up. According to them, he was within his rights to help himself to their belongings because, as he claimed, he had been dismissed unlawfully without pay, and he accused Butch of calling him a kaffir.

The killing of Veronica, he claimed, was because she had also called him the same name and had tried to stab him with a knife. The police had decided it was self-defense and never even bothered opening a case against him. They had threatened Butch with a case of racism if he pursued his claims. Heartbroken and disillusioned, Butch had emigrated a year later.

One rainy afternoon, while walking to a shop in Watford in the UK, he had received a photo of his wife's murderer hanging from a tree near the police station that had refused to arrest him. He was still wearing the jacket he had stolen from Butch's cupboard. It was covered in blood that had poured from his throat where the wire had cut into it. Butch had then received a phone call from a detective investigating the death of his wife's assailant, asking him where he had been at the time. Learning that Butch had been in the UK, the detective had seemed happy to eliminate him as a suspect.

Mikey remembered that the house had a tandem garage, and he asked Butch, "Is it okay if we soundproof the garage for pistol practice?"

"No problem. Do whatever you like there, Mikey."

Mikey thanked him, and with promises to see him in three months, he ended the call.

****

Devlin stared at the email he had received from the client. It had been sent from an anonymous, encrypted email account.

'Funds ready. Area: Stikland. Proton Street. Street number same as target minus 21. Door at rear of building. In and out. One hour.'

He remembered the Serbs' street number and subtracted 21 from it. Opening Google Maps, he found the location. He grabbed his jacket and the keys to the Fiesta and made his way down to the car.

He slowly drove past the industrial building and tried to see around the back. The building had a To Let sign on the fence and seemed empty. He looked around to see if there were any CCTV cameras on the building. Except for two workers having their lunch on the grass in front of the building next door, there was no one around. Devlin noticed that he had a few minutes to spare and drove around to Brito's for a takeaway sandwich.

He parked the Fiesta a hundred meters down the road and got out. Casually, he walked to the industrial building and made his way to the rear. He saw a red steel door and pulled on the handle. The door squeaked open, and he looked inside. It wasn't necessary for him to enter, as he immediately spotted a sports bag on the floor right at the entrance. He picked it up and hefted it over his shoulder.

As he closed the door, he looked around to see if he could spot the watcher, knowing for certain that someone had been posted to keep an eye on the bag. He saw no one and made his way to his car, eager to get away. Devlin placed the bag on the passenger seat and started driving. At the first traffic light, he pulled the zip open and saw the tightly tied bundles of R200 notes. He whistled as he drove on, heading back to his flat.

On his way there, he changed his mind and drove in the direction of Smugglers in Brackenfell. He parked nearby and, making sure no one was watching, he started counting the money in the bundle. He counted R50,000 and a total of forty-two bundles.

Total: R2.1 million.

He removed six of the bundles and shoved them under the passenger seat. Zipping the bag closed, he placed it on the floor behind the passenger seat. He took out his phone and sent a WhatsApp message to The Boer.

'At the same bar we met last time. I have the moola.'

*****

159

Mikey lay in bed.

Cara sat with her back against the headboard, a laptop on her knees. She had stopped typing, her hands hovering over the keys as she listened to Mikey telling her his plans.

"I need to fly to Cape Town tomorrow to pick up someone. He's a specialist, and he's needed in Joburg to train and teach combat skills to a young black guy. I agreed to help them with the logistics, so I might need to go help them once a week—to deliver supplies and oversee the training."

She turned her head to look at her husband lying next to her.

"Aren't you supposed to be retired from all that shit, Mikey?"

It was a while before he answered. She watched him and waited patiently.

"Cara, it may not make sense right now, but this is the process I have to put in place to be able to retire permanently. Hopefully, when this is all over, these two guys will take over what I've been doing. They're young and hate injustice. I have to assist them with what's needed now. Small children are being killed and kidnapped all over South Africa. Their body parts are cut from them while they're still alive. Young girls are raped and sold into prostitution. Can you imagine what their parents must be going through?"

Cara saw the anguish on his face as he spoke, and she knew there was nothing she could do or say that would deter Mikey. All she could hope for was that he stayed safe.

"And your role is only logistics and training? You'll be safe?"

Mikey sat up and turned to look at his wife. He took her hand in his and kissed her on the cheek.

"Cara, I promise you, that's all I'll do. I'm doing this exactly for that reason. I'll be content knowing someone is delivering justice where our country's systems fail. I need to be there once a week to make sure these guys are ready and have the know-how to keep themselves safe."

"I understand, mon amour. What time do you leave?"

"I need to be in the air by sunrise. I want to be there before dark. I'll stay with Jack and Sweety tonight and fly back tomorrow."

Cara put the laptop down and got up from the bed.

"Where are you going now?" he asked, alarmed.

She looked over her shoulder as she walked out of the room.

"I'm going to make food for the road for mon amour. I'll make beef sandwiches with Dijon. No?"

****

The Boer sat at the kitchen table, looking at the things he needed to pack for the trip. Meticulously, he went over every item and started placing them in a blue duffel bag. When he had finished packing, he sat down at the table and thought about the conversation he had with Devlin earlier.

He had told Devlin that he would be out of town for a while and would be leaving his cell phone behind. Devlin had immediately become inquisitive and wanted to know if it was another contract.

"Why not take your phone with you?" he asked Duncan suspiciously.

Duncan laughed at his friend's concern.

"I have a job training some guys from an Anti-Poaching Unit in the Eastern Cape. There's no cell phone reception there anyway, and because this training camp is in a secret location, I've been asked not to bring it with me. The team will be supplied with two-way radios while we're in training, and no outside calls will be allowed for the first two months."

"How did you hear about this job?"

"I was contacted by the guy in charge of wildlife protection in the Eastern Cape. He got my name from an old army colleague. The job pays very well, and it could open doors for me."

Devlin, clearly not happy about losing his friend for such a long time. said so.

Duncan looked at the sports bag sitting on the chair next to him. He had put all the cash he had hidden around the flat, plus the money he had received from Devlin earlier, into the bag. It could barely close. Yesterday, he had left his bike with Jack, and the Ford Ranger he had loaned him was parked in the garage behind the flat. He was set to meet the Contractor tomorrow evening at Jack's house.

Duncan and the Contractor would share the guest cottage there before flying out early the next morning. Duncan had no doubt that he would still have to pass the Contractor's approval before being allowed to board the plane. He shook off the nervousness and went over his itinerary.

He had arranged with the elderly Mrs. Brand from next door to keep an eye on the flat. He had given her a key in case anything went wrong. Earlier, he had pre-paid his municipal accounts for three months and loaded enough electricity on the prepaid meter to last twice as long. His personal belongings had been stored in the garage until he returned.

He got up to check on his microwave lasagna.

Chapter 28

Sergeant Felicity Booysen briefed the two constables using her Bluetooth, while driving as fast as she could toward the market.

"Constable, keep an eye on those two. Record as much as you can, but make sure nobody sees you do it. Move closer and try to hear what they're talking about. If they become aggressive or try to get her into the shack, move in and inquire about muti for stomach cramps. I'm on my way."

The long days of surveillance looked like they were about to pay off. The tsotsis had been hanging around the market for over an hour and were now talking to the vendor. She parked the car near the entrance and made her way toward the vendor's stall. She took up position nearby, pretending to look at purses and handbags on display at a vendor two stalls away. She saw her constable loitering near the muti vendor's stall, inspecting the items for sale on the table. She sent him a WhatsApp message.

'I'm here. Stay close. It looks like they're arguing.'

She saw him read the message. Her phone rang, and she saw the call was from him. She pressed the answer button and listened. She could clearly hear the vendor talking to the two standing next to her behind the display tables.

"Next Friday, I swear! I will have the money for you. I got customers looking for special muti. I will pay from that money. I swear to you. Please, Buti, ask him for just one more week."

"No, mama. He told me today he wants his money. Plus 30 percent interest. Right now."

Felicity saw the one guy, whom she now identified as JX Thandise, the owner of the Golf, pull up his shirt—probably to flash a weapon at the vendor, who immediately took a step back toward the safety of her shack. She saw the constable looking around, trying to find her. She stayed where she was, careful not to intervene and give the whole game away. She had her phone to her ear when she became aware of someone close behind her. As she was about to turn, she heard the youth's voice.

"Do not interfere. They are just threatening. They will not do anything to her. She owes a lot of money."

She watched as the tsotsis pushed closer to the vendor, crowding her space. She was slowly being pushed inside her shack.

"Do you want to die, mama? These guys do not play. We have been sent to collect or kill you today," JX said to her in a very threatening voice.

Felicity turned to talk to the youth, but he had vanished. She saw the constable starting to panic as he lifted the phone to his ear.

"Move closer and ask her about the muti. Now!"

She watched as the constable put his phone in his shirt pocket and motioned to the vendor. She could hear him asking her for some assistance. Felicity saw the relief on the vendor's face.

JX pulled his shirt down and menacingly said, "Next Friday."

He motioned to his sidekick, who had been quiet the whole time, that it was time to leave. Felicity listened to the constable talking to the vendor and was very impressed by the way he handled the situation. She made a mental note to recommend him to Captain Dan later. It was a pity that his cover was now blown. She watched him leave the stand and take his phone out of his pocket to talk to her.

"Well done, Constable. Hang around out of sight till we get someone to replace you. You did well, but unfortunately, we will have to use you somewhere else from now on. She will recognize you."

Slowly, she moved amongst the different vendors, looking to see if she could spot the youth. She dearly wanted to talk to him.

The youth was already on the move, following the two tsotsis to their car. He watched them get in and saw the driver making a call. The call did not last very long, and the car started up and drove away. He watched on his tracker app and saw them heading in the direction of Rockey Road. Soon, he would get a ping from the spy cam when they entered the flat. He knew the

Contractor would get the same warning. He hailed an Uber to take him home.

He had given the couple notice, and his belongings were packed, ready to go to the farm near Lanseria Airport tomorrow. He was looking forward to the training.

He wiped a tear from his eye as, for a split second, the emotion overwhelmed him.

****

Captain Rikki Patel looked across at WO Maria Ruiters.

She was driving with one hand on the steering wheel past the factories, pointing out to him the one they suspected was storing illegal cigarettes.

"If you know it's there, then why don't you raid it?" he asked.

She shook her head and smiled. "This is a very slippery customer, Captain. We won't be able to connect him with these cigarettes. We have to catch him right there with the product or with proof that he owns it. We've been watching him for almost a year now, but we don't have any definite proof yet. We suspect he might be funding one of the opposition parties, hoping that they can help him keep the corridors that were created with the ban on cigarettes and booze during Covid-19 open. We know that SARS is also investigating him and hope they find something to pin him down—him, as well as anyone assisting or benefiting from this cigarette smuggling."

She stopped the car next to an empty warehouse and turned to him.

"We know that the cigarettes come through the border at Beitbridge from their factories in Zimbabwe. We've given the information to SAPS, but they haven't done anything to stop the imports yet. We know some of the cops, as well as some of the Home Affairs officials, are on the take. Sometimes it feels as if we are all on our own and that everyone in government is part of the corruption. Captain, our little unit is watched all the time by our superiors, and we feel that we could be shut down at any time. There are forces at work here that want to see us fail."

Rikki Patel nodded his head and looked out the window so that she wouldn't see the guilt and emotions dueling inside him. He felt guilty for spying on this dedicated group of investigators. Maria could see something was bothering him and watched him as he stared out of the passenger window. She started the car and pulled away. He turned toward her and put his hand on her arm.

"Stop, Maria! Please stop. I have to tell you something."

Maria stopped the car and switched off the engine. She suspected she knew what he wanted to tell her and asked, "What is it, Captain?"

Rikki took a deep breath and slowly exhaled.

"I did something very stupid when I was in Police College. I was caught selling dope. Because of my parents' influence, I was let off. I thought it was all forgotten until Colonel Diba dug it up somewhere. He's using it as leverage to get me to spy on you guys. I am so fucking sorry, Maria. I just don't know what to do!"

Maria was relieved that her suspicions were correct, but she was still shocked to hear it. She wiped her hands over her face and looked at him.

"What have you told him so far?"

"I told him about the camera you have in Manzoni's apartment. He said he would find out today if it was authorized. The rest of what I told him was just everyday investigating stuff. I was told to get any notes lying around and to record your conversations. So far, I've given him nothing else. I can't stand that fucking asshole, Maria. I only do it because he has me by the balls. I love being a detective and don't want to lose my job. I've never worked with a team as dedicated as you guys before, and I told him that, but he seems determined to destroy your team. I have a feeling he's taking orders from higher up."

Maria could see he was very upset, and she realized it had taken a lot for him to admit his deceit. She had to make a decision but decided to speak to Captain Majoba first. She snapped open her seatbelt buckle and opened the door.

She looked over her shoulder at Patel. "Rikki, I need to speak to Majoba. I won't be long."

She walked to the back of the vehicle and phoned Captain Majoba. She explained what had happened and that she needed advice.

"Will he be willing to work for us?" he asked.

She hadn't thought about it and was unsure.

"I don't know. Should I ask him?"

"Yes. Report back to me as soon as you've spoken to him. In the meantime, I'll try to arrange authorization for the camera. I hope it's not too late."

She got back into the car, and looking at Patel's anxious face, she started the engine.

"Let's go for a coffee, Rikki. We can talk there."

****

Spotting a spotted a scarf in blue and white hanging from the rail, Sergeant Felicity Booysen asked the vendor, who had been eyeing her suspiciously, for the price.

She haggled with the vendor over the price, as was customary at the market. They eventually settled on R120, which she paid. She selected the record app on her phone and switched it on. Taking the scarf, she folded it over the phone and, holding it in her hand, slowly made her way to the muti vendor. She put a sad look on her face as she began browsing through the items on display, keeping an eye on the vendor, who still had a very worried expression. When the vendor recognized her, she came around the display, took Felicity by the hand, and led her to a chair.

"I see you are back, ntokazi. What is it that ails you? I can help you."

Felicity sniffed and pretended to wipe a tear. She looked down and fiddled with the tissue in her hand.

"Mama, I need special muti. My sangoma told me it is all that will heal me, but she cannot find the special muti for me. She says I must find it myself. It is my heart. It is sick, and if I do not find this muti, I will die soon."

The vendor struggled not to grin as she held onto Felicity's hand. How much money does she have? she wondered. She looked very well-dressed. Speaking in a soft voice, she tried to convey compassion and trust.

"Ntokazi, you need the essence from the heart of a young child. It is hard to come by and very expensive. One hundred thousand. Do you have that money?"

Felicity nodded her head and wiped another tear from the corner of her eye. She sniffed and looked at the vendor.

"I have a lot of money. My parents are rich. Can you get me my medicine?"

The vendor was normally very careful, but her predicament was causing her to be reckless.

"I can get the medicine for you in one day. If you come back tomorrow evening at about six o'clock, I will have it for you, and you can take it to your sangoma. I will send a letter with it so that she will know it is real and how to administer it. Will you have the money ready?"

Felicity nodded, and balancing the scarf on her knees, she took the vendor's hands and kissed them.

"Thank you. Thank you. I am so happy now. I will be here at six tomorrow evening. With the money."

She picked up her scarf and stood, knowing she had to be careful not to overdo it. The vendor guided her around the table and bid her goodbye.

Felicity walked to the car and only took the phone from the scarf once she was seated inside, with the doors locked. She rewound the recording and listened to it. She could clearly hear herself and the vendor talking. Felicity sent the recording to the Contractor with a message attached.

'Urgent. Contact me.'

She started the car and headed to Soweto to meet up with Sergeant Tobela. He was busy re-interviewing some of the witnesses in Soweto.

****

Maria took the coffees from the barista and carried them over to where Patel was sitting near the window.

She placed his cup on the table in front of him and took the seat opposite. She took a sip of the hot coffee and looked at him. He looked very apprehensive, as she still had not told him the details of her conversation with Majoba. She made it obvious that she had shut her cell phone off and placed it on the table in front of them. He quickly caught on and did the same.

"So, Rikki, it comes down to this. Are you willing to work for our side?"

He shifted in his seat and nodded. He had been hoping she would ask him to do that.

"What do you want me to do?" he asked nervously.

Maria smiled and blew over her cup.

"Not much, really. We want you to clear any info you feed him with us first, but we also want you to record every meeting you have with him. Do not try to catch him out or lead him—just feed him the info. Whenever you meet with him, make sure you are alone with him in a public place. We will take your recordings and keep them safe in case we need them to defend ourselves in the future. Hopefully, he will get fed up with all the useless info and leave us alone. We just want to carry on with our work. We do not have time to pursue him."

Rikki Patel smiled at her and sipped his coffee.

"I can do that. I want to be an asset to your investigation and help you smash this smuggling bastard. Thank you for the chance."

Maria clicked her cup against his.

"You are welcome. Do not discuss this with anyone but Majoba, Combrink, and me, and you will be okay. Let's drink up and go find out if Combrink managed to locate their secret post box. Manzoni is going to leave one million rand there for Mamello. We need to find out where this post box is. Combrink has been keeping tabs on Manzoni. I think it is safe to tell you that we have a tracking device on his car. Unfortunately for us, he has more than one car he uses."

They finished their coffee and headed to Maria's car.

Chapter 29

Mikey had landed the Beechcraft at Cape Winelands Airport a few minutes ago.

He loved the plane and the freedom of movement it offered him. He had owned it for a good few years and still marveled at how he had come to acquire it.

He had taken the plane from a target he had eliminated in Luanda a few years ago. He had needed to get out of Angola in a hurry and, through weeks of surveillance, had known that Quitera, the target, owned a plane. Mikey had taken the plane from his hangar and flown it out of Angola the same day he had eliminated Quitera. He had found all the documents related to the Beechcraft inside the plane, as well as company registration papers to which the plane had been registered. Back in SA, he had greased some palms and had the documents of the company that owned the plane altered. He had sprayed it a different color and put new numbers on it.

He taxied the airplane next to some other light aircraft parked on the apron. He had already refueled and paid his landing fees. Exiting the plane, he folded the ramp back and locked it. He saw Jack sitting in his Pajero nearby and, waving to him, walked over. He got into the passenger seat and grabbed his friend's hand.

"Jacko, it's great to see you again, man."

"Good to see you too, Mikey. Was the flight okay?"

Mikey laughed. "A bit bumpy at times, but I made good time. You know how these small kites bump and jump when you hit turbulence. Are we heading straight home?"

"Yes, I want to introduce you to your protégé. I'm sure you'll like him. Do you want to give him your real name, or do you want to use Mackie?"

"I'd prefer to keep my distance until I know him a bit better. He can know me as Mackie for the time being in case you or Sweety makes a slip-up. It'll be easier to explain away."

"Erm... Sweety isn't here at the moment. I asked her to stay with Vera and Martie for a few days."

Mikey looked at his friend and nodded.

"I think you did the right thing keeping her away. We don't know where this thing will end up. How did you manage it?"

"John is repainting the inside of the house over the next few days, and she gladly accepted Vera's offer to stay over until it's done. I'm also sleeping there tonight."

"What can you tell me about this guy? What do I call him?"

"He also asked me to keep his name secret until he gets to know you," Jack said with a wicked grin.

"Cheeky fucking bugger. I already like him," Mikey replied, clapping his hands together.

Jack told Mikey what he knew about Duncan, highlighting his training and time in the SAS. He explained how they had met, become friends, and started trusting each other.

"You can call him Boer. He's got a Scots father and an Afrikaans mother. He speaks Afrikaans as well as English. He's a very pleasant, slightly shy person. He reminds me a bit of the young Mikey I met more than thirty years ago."

Mikey grinned and sat back, enjoying the drive to Jack's place. He suddenly remembered to check his burner phone. He saw there was a message and a recording from Sergeant Booysen. It had been sent a few hours earlier. He read the message first.

"Jack, would you mind pulling over? I need to make an urgent phone call."

"Is it Cara?" Jack asked worriedly.

"No. It's someone helping me with the case. I won't be long."

Mikey opened the door and got out of the car as soon as it came to a standstill.

He walked a few meters away and opened the recording Felicity had sent him. He could hear the two women speaking and immediately recognized Felicity's voice. When he finished listening to the recording, he dialed Felicity's number.

"Did you listen to the recording? It's me talking to the vendor that the child's body parts were taken from," she immediately asked him.

"I did listen. What made you do that? It can fuck up everything."

"JX Thandise and his sidekick were there to threaten her. He showed her a gun and told her if she doesn't come up with the money she lost, she'll be dead in a week. I want to have her arrested when she hands over the muti to me. We can't let her get killed. She's a very important link in this. They'll be able to get to her while she's in custody."

Mikey thought about it for a while before answering.

"I know they were there. I also have video footage and recordings of the two discussing the whole saga in their flat after they got back from her. They seem confident that they've scared the shit out of her."

"What else do you have?"

"They phoned someone from the flat, and although the conversation we heard was one-sided, it sounded like they were talking to the big boss."

"Do you know who it is?"

"Not yet. I want to send you a registration number to see if you can get a lead on it, but you must give me your word that you won't follow up on it. Do I have your word?"

Felicity felt a ripple of excitement run down her spine. They were getting closer!

"I give you my word, but I have to give my team something to work on."

"Give them the vendor and the muti. Nothing else."

He ended the call and sent the registration of the Fortuner to her.

****

Combrink watched Manzoni get out of his car, with a wrapped package in his hand, at Sunninghill Post Office.

He took a few quick photos of him walking into the post office. Getting out, he followed him inside. Keeping his distance, he watched as Manzoni opened a post box and put the package inside. Combrink counted three rows from the top and four boxes from the end. He took a quick photo of Manzoni locking the box.

172

He turned his back and picked up a form from the counter when he saw Manzoni coming his way and waited for him to walk outside.

He watched him drive off and moved toward the post boxes. There was no one around in the post box area. Combrink put on latex gloves and took the lock pick from his little folder. With his back to the door, he started working on the lock. It was relatively simple, and within seconds, he had it open. He removed the package and, using the picks, locked the box again. Carrying the parcel in his left hand, he made his way to his car and phoned Maria.

"Hi. Where are you?"

"I just witnessed and photographed the Italian stallion at Sunninghill Post Office."

"Sergeant Combrink, that is fantastic news," she replied.

He quickly realized she wasn't alone and said he would meet her at the office in an hour. He started the car and headed toward Parktown. He hadn't gone more than two blocks before his phone rang. Seeing Maria's name on the screen, he answered.

"Can you talk?"

"Yes. I could hear there's something else you want to tell me. What is it?"

"I removed the parcel from the post box, and it feels like a million bucks."

"Oh my god, can you imagine how pissed off Mamello is going to be when he gets there and finds Manzoni has shortchanged him?" Maria couldn't help but laugh out loud.

"I wish I knew when Mamello planned to pick up the parcel. I want to video him opening the post box."

"We can't spare you to stake out the post box. Sorry. I can, however, see a big break in that bromance very soon. I'll wait for you at the office. We need to record the money and see if we can lift some prints off the parcel. Majoba and Patel are also here. They're having a serious meeting. I can't wait to tell you what happened today."

"Okay, I'm on my way."

****

Mikey sat on the workbench in Jack's shed. They were waiting for the Boer to arrive.

"After you guys get to know each other, we can meet at the pub. You can get supper there. Just remember, you are still an author of South African pubs and guesthouses, just like when you visited here last year. Hennie and Junior will surely recognize you. I'll wait there for you after I've introduced you to Boer. You can use the Ford. There's a remote for the gate on the key holder. Boer will be here with it soon."

"Has Jeremy managed to get anything off that phone yet?"

Jack shook his head. "I haven't heard from him yet, but I'll ask him when I see him later today."

"It's important."

"Yeah, I know, Mikey, but the poor guy is so busy with TRUTH work that I feel guilty putting pressure on him to unlock that phone. We'll have to get him some help soon. The site is inundated with cases of corruption from all over the world. I still change the password whenever I'm out on the country roads. I must tell you, it's quite a job deciding which publications to give the new passwords to."

"Jack, starting that site was pure genius. Look how many of these crooks have already been fired, investigated, or are being prosecuted. I often recognize information from TRUTH being used by the media worldwide to expose these cunts."

"It's become huge. I'll have to get him some help, but who do you trust?"

"I don't know, bud. I don't know anyone who's both computer literate and trustworthy enough. It's your problem for now. I've got a vigilante to train."

Jack heard the exhaust note of the big diesel at the front gate and walked to the shed's door to welcome Duncan. They walked into the shed where Mikey was still sitting on the workbench.

"Mackie, this is Boer. Boer, Mackie."

They shook hands, and Jack excused himself.

174

"There's beer in the fridge over there. Close the shed doors when you leave. I'll wait for you at the Inn."

He walked out of the shed and got into his old Pajero. He planned to make a turn at Vera's before heading to the Inn. He was sure Mikey and Duncan had a lot to talk about.

He just hoped it was all worth the effort.

Chapter 30

Mikey and Duncan were at the airfield, storing their kit in the cargo compartment of the plane.

Jack had dropped them off a few minutes earlier before heading back home. The two of them waited for a bit more daylight before taking off. Mikey pulled out his phone and sent a message to the youth.

"Get an Uber and go to the following location. Be there at six p.m. and wait for us."

He attached the pin location he had stored and checked to make sure the youth had received it. Then he turned to Boer, who was sitting next to him, rolling his shoulders and getting comfortable for the flight.

"We'll fly direct to Lanseria, get the pickup, and meet the youth at the gate of the smallholding. I'll spend two days with you guys before heading home for a week. I've put together a basic training schedule—fitness, weapons, explosives, hand-to-hand combat. Most of that will be on you. I'll use my two days to teach you guys undercover surveillance, abduction methods, and a few of my personal favorite weapons."

Boer nodded, a glint of anticipation in his eyes. He bumped fists with Mikey, already sensing that the coming weeks would be intense. There was a lot to learn.

"Do you think the kid will cope?" he asked.

Mikey considered the question for a moment before answering. "Yeah. He's determined and smart. He'll go through anything to get to the people who killed his little brother. He's rough around the edges, but sharp. You'll find him to be a quick learner."

Satisfied, Mikey fired up the Baron's engines, the deep rumble vibrating through the aircraft as he began taxiing to the runway. He stopped at the top of the strip, running his pre-flight checks with practiced efficiency. Everything was in order. With a push of the throttle, the engines roared, and as he lifted his foot off the brake, the Baron surged forward. The wheels raced over the tarmac, gaining speed. Three-quarters of the way down, Mikey pulled back on the yoke, and the plane lifted smoothly into the sky.

He glanced over at Boer. "If you're keen, I'll show you how to fly this kite. Who knows, you might want one of your own someday. You can take the controls once we clear the mountains."

Boer grinned, his excitement evident, and gave Mikey a thumbs-up. As the Cape Winelands stretched out below them, he turned back to the window, watching the world fall away beneath their wings.

$$****$$

Felicity replayed the events of the night before in her mind, going over every detail of the takedown.

Masondo, the vendor, had been waiting for her, eager and anxious. She had already packed up her wares, folding the trestle tables away. Sitting on her lap had been a small beer cooler bag, her fingers drumming against the lid. When Felicity arrived, Masondo had carefully lifted the cover, revealing a jam jar inside, half-filled with an amber liquid. Suspended within it was a pink chunk of flesh, floating in the liquid like some grotesque relic. The jar rested on a bed of ice.

Felicity had given her a quick flash of the wad of R200 notes peeking from her handbag.

"We can't do this here," she had murmured, lowering her voice. "I feel like we're being watched, Mama. Is there somewhere safer?"

Masondo had darted a quick look around, her beady eyes scanning for threats. Then, after a moment's hesitation, she had nodded.

"There is a place around the corner where I eat. It's safe and not far. Follow me."

She had risen with an ambling gait, leading Felicity toward the restaurant. Felicity had taken her arm, allowing herself to be guided, knowing Maria was following close behind. A subtle nod had been all it took to confirm Maria's presence.

The moment they had sat down, Sergeants Lastborn and John Robson had appeared, taking seats directly opposite them. Robson had reached into his pocket and flashed his police ID.

"Nofolo Masondo, you're under arrest. I won't cuff you if you come peacefully."

Masondo had stared at him, her breath hitching. Slowly, with a resigned sigh, she had stood, allowing the officers to lead her out of the restaurant without resistance.

****

Felicity walked over to Captain Dan's office, leaning against the doorway.

"Any word yet?" she asked.

They had sent the jar's contents to the lab, where DNA samples from the mothers of the last two mutilated boys were on file. An urgent test had been requested, and they expected results soon. The pathologist, a mother of two young boys herself, had promised to give it top priority.

Captain Dan looked up from his desk. "You'll know the minute I do. Want to sit in on the interview?"

Felicity shook her head. "No, I'll watch from the observation room next door. Take Robson—she's afraid of him."

Dan nodded, leaning back in his chair. "Any leads on the two guys who gave her the jar?"

Felicity hesitated. She knew where they lived, but she couldn't reveal that. Not yet. To catch the real killers, she had to be patient. She had to play by the Contractor's rules.

"We'll find them, Captain. One of the constables is keeping an eye on her stall. He's under instructions to tell anyone looking for her that she's tending to a sick aunt and will be back soon. It's important they think everything is normal. Hopefully, they'll come for the money soon."

Dan nodded, his fingers tapping against his desk as he returned to typing his report. Felicity could tell he was pleased with the progress. There was new energy in him—an urgency that hadn't been there before.

She returned to her desk and typed a quick message to the Contractor, explaining why they had to arrest Masondo and warning that the two tsotsis might also be taken down soon, possibly within the next few days. She hoped he would understand that some things were out of her hands.

Her thoughts drifted to her earlier conversation with Maria. On their way to the market, Maria had told her about their unit's goal—building stronger relationships with other teams that weren't compromised. It made sense, but Felicity knew she could never admit to Captain Dan that she had planted a camera in Rawlimi's office.

Dan was too rigid, too by-the-book. His respect for the law wouldn't allow it. If he found out, he might even arrest her. It was safer to keep it quiet—or remove the camera altogether.

Maria had agreed to keep it between them. What Felicity didn't know, however, was that the rest of Maria's unit already knew she had planted the device. Maria had even shared some of the more damning findings from the surveillance.

Rawlimi, it seemed, did little—if any—actual police work. She spent less than three hours a day in her office, most of that time on the phone with friends or adjusting her makeup in the mirror. Once she left for lunch, she didn't return until the next morning.

Felicity stole another glance toward Dan's office. The wait was starting to eat at her. She couldn't sit still.

She wanted to be in that observation room. She needed to hear what Masondo had to say.

Chapter 31

Mme Cebisile settled herself on the grass mat and springbok skin covering the floor of her practice.

A new client was coming for a consultation, and first impressions mattered. She adjusted her beaded headdress, ensuring it sat straight, and smoothed down her leopard-print skirt to properly cover her legs. Reaching for the leather pouch that held her bones, she emptied its contents onto the springbok skin. She liked to reacquaint herself with the different objects before each session, refreshing her connection to their meanings. Her eyes traced over the scattered pieces of bone, small pebbles, seashells, and the two chipped dominoes. Satisfied, she gathered them up and returned them to the pouch.

The front door chime rang. She looked up, parting the beads hanging in the doorway to the reception area. A well-dressed young Coloured man stood waiting. She smiled. It was rare for members of other races to seek her services, and when they did, they often expected to pay more for the privilege.

She called out, "Come, young man. Sit here by me."

He hesitated before stepping into the room, scanning his surroundings with wary eyes. When he looked down at her seated position on the floor, she gestured to the cushion she had placed opposite her. He lowered himself carefully, crossing his legs as he settled in.

"What ails you, unyana? What can Mama Cebisile do for you?"

The young man glanced around the sparsely furnished room, listening as though making sure they were alone. Then, shifting as if to get more comfortable, he pulled the cushion out from under him—along with a small .32 pistol tucked into his waistband.

In one fluid motion, he pressed the barrel against the cushion to muffle the shot and pulled the trigger twice.

The first bullet tore through her left eye. The second shattered her gaping mouth.

Mme Cebisile fell backward, lifeless. Blood pooled beneath her head, soaking into the springbok skin. The air filled with the acrid stench of gunpowder.

He sat still, listening. No voices, no rushing footsteps. The shots had been contained.

Leaning forward, he checked for a pulse. None. Her beaded headdress was already dark with blood, her unseeing eye a red ruin. Taking out his phone, he snapped a photo of the body. Certain his work was done, he slipped the gun back into his waistband, rose to his feet, and walked out the way he had come.

He pulled up his hoodie, keeping his head down as he strolled casually toward his car, parked a few houses away. A handful of kids played in the street, but they paid him no attention. He got in, started the engine, and pulled away at a steady pace.

By the time he was back on the N2, heading toward Delft, he sent a WhatsApp message along with the photo.

'Done. Leave money with Manny at Dooley's Take Away.'

****

Kallie Jansen leaned back in his chair, pleased. The hit had gone off without a hitch.

He had dispatched Zane to Dooley's with the payment—a mere twenty grand for such a clean job. A bargain. He'd be using that hitman again. Possibly sooner than expected, depending on how his upcoming meeting with John Robertson went.

Today, he had to drive himself to the office, but he didn't mind. It gave him a reason to take the Z4 he had bought a few weeks earlier.

He pulled out his phone and sent a quick message to Sharon.

'Mama C no more. 😊 '

Tossing his keys in his palm, he headed down to the garage, where his four luxury vehicles gleamed under the lights.

****

Mackie and Boer cruised down the gravel road in the recently purchased Isuzu D-Max, heading toward the house they would use for training the youth.

Their flight had gone smoothly, the tailwind over the Free State making up for lost time. It had given them a chance to land early, settle in, and recon the property before nightfall.

As they neared the entrance, Mackie spotted the youth waiting by the gate, his posture stiff with anticipation. Pulling up to the locked entrance, both he and Boer climbed out.

Mackie approached first, nodding at the young man before turning to Boer.

"This is your instructor," he said. "You'll know him simply as Boer. And to you and me, I'll be Mackie. Remember, I asked you what name you wanted to go by? So, introduce yourself."

Boer stepped forward, extending a firm hand. He had been assessing the young man from the moment they arrived, noting his broad shoulders and solid frame. He was nearing six feet tall, with a presence that hinted at the man he would become.

The youth clasped Boer's hand, his grip steady and filled with quiet determination.

"Good to meet you," Boer said. "What do I call you?"

The youth studied the well-built man before him, his gaze flicking to Mackie and back.

"You can call me Piet."

Boer grinned at the choice—a solid, unmistakably Afrikaner name.

"Good to know you, Piet."

Mackie took the youth's hand next, squeezing it firmly. "Good to see you, son. Just call me Mackie, okay? I'm nobody's uncle."

Then, turning to Boer, he added, "I'm going to unlock the gate and check out the house. How about you give Piet his first driving lesson? Looks like we've got a few tracks over there to practice on. Piet, toss your stuff in the back."

Mackie pushed open the gate and made his way up to the house, unlocking the front door with practiced ease. He had visited Butch a few times before and was familiar with the layout. Heading straight to the kitchen, he switched on the electricity mains, listening as the appliances hummed to life. A quick check of the taps confirmed the water pressure was good.

Stepping through the side door, he entered the long garage and unlatched it from the inside.

Outside, the Isuzu was moving in starts and stops. Mackie smirked to himself. The lesson wasn't going well.

Minutes later, the Isuzu lurched into the garage, this time with Boer behind the wheel. Mackie pulled the garage door shut behind them as Boer and Piet climbed out. The youth hoisted his kit from the back of the pickup, his expression unreadable.

Mackie grinned. "How'd it go?"

Boer shrugged, tossing a glance over the cab at Piet. A knowing smile played on his lips.

"Not too bad for a first time." Then he turned back, his face serious. "Do we have something strong to drink?"

Mackie burst into laughter. "That bad, huh?"

Boer exhaled heavily. "Let's just say, I can't wait to see how the bike-riding lesson goes tomorrow."

Chapter 32

Felicity's phone rang.

She glanced at the screen—Maria. Turning slightly in her chair, she scanned the office, making sure no one was close enough to overhear, before answering.

"Hi, Maria. How are you?"

"I'm fine, but I need some help."

Maria launched straight into an explanation about the docket Rawlimi had handed to Manzoni and how they had managed to retrieve it. She hadn't planned to tell Felicity, but now, she had no choice.

"I just overheard a call between Rawlimi and Manzoni. You won't believe how stupid this bitch is. She had him on speaker while filing her nails. We caught the whole conversation. The Italian Stallion is panicking about the missing docket and trying to find out if it has surfaced anywhere in SAPS channels. If a cleaner found it in his apartment and turned it in at a station, it would automatically be sent back to the investigating office. We watched her fumble around on her computer, but honestly, I don't think she even knows how to search for it. She told him she'd send an email to the person she got it from. Which she did—right after they hung up. Fee, we need that email."

Felicity knew Rawlimi was in her office, but getting to her computer with both her and her PA present was impossible.

"You're asking for a lot. How the hell am I supposed to get to her computer while she's still here? She always switches it off when she leaves for lunch. It's not possible."

"Yes, it is. We have her password—it's Gucci. We've got a perfect view of her screen from the camera you planted in her office. Does her PA leave for lunch too?"

"She does. A full hour. Sometimes longer. She knows Rawlimi hardly ever comes back after lunch. But that doesn't mean I can just walk in there. Someone could come looking for her and catch me. What do I do then?"

Maria paused for a moment before responding. "Wait fifteen minutes after they leave. Everyone at Diepsloot knows she doesn't come back in the afternoons, so no one should be looking for her. Take a memory stick and download all her emails if you can."

"What? Are you fucking crazy?"

Maria went silent for a few seconds before speaking again. "Do you want her gone or not?"

Felicity exhaled sharply, glancing around the half-empty office. Guilt twisted in her gut.

"Okay. I'll try. You better have a job lined up for me at the Hawks if Captain Dan catches me. I'll call you when I have something."

****

In Cape Town, Kallie Jansen brought the Z4 to a stop in front of their factory near K-Berth at the Cape Town harbor. Climbing out of the car, he couldn't resist turning back to admire it for a second. What a ride.

Stepping through the door to Robertson's office, he gave John a casual wave before dropping onto the sofa. John was still on a call—something to do with freight clearances. That was his side of the business, the logistics and paperwork. Kallie didn't care much about that. As long as the shipments reached their destinations and the money kept flowing, he was happy.

When John finally ended the call, he turned his attention to Kallie.

"How's that other thing going? Sharon's problem."

Kallie smirked, lacing his fingers behind his head as he leaned back.

"It's done. Twenty grand. Zane is delivering the money as we speak."

John frowned. "Are you sure we can trust this guy? I don't want this thing coming back to bite us in the ass. Why so cheap?"

"John, stop worrying. It's someone Zane knows. We can use him again—very soon."

Robertson narrowed his eyes. "What do you mean?"

Kallie told him about his conversation with Funani and what he had found out about Mostert.

"We paid half a mil to have him wiped out! What happened?"

"That, we don't know yet. But I'll find out. You got any ideas?"

John rubbed his face, letting out a slow breath. "My god, Kallie. Does Mostert know it was us who tried to have him killed?"

Kallie grinned. "Relax, John. If he knew, why would he be trying to contact Funani? He's in the dark. Neither Boer nor Devlin know it was us, either. We're safe."

Robertson sat back behind his desk, rubbing his temples. Through his fingers, he muttered, "What do you want to do now? You can't get to Boer."

Kallie's smirk deepened. "I can—if I get hold of Devlin."

John shook his head. "I think we should let it go. Wait and see if Mostert contacts us again. We can take it from there."

"You're serious? You're willing to let that fucking contractor and his contact cheat us out of half a mil?"

Robertson studied his partner. He was getting tired of this business—of Kallie's obsession with control. What Kallie didn't know was that he was planning to get out soon. He had enough money stashed away to disappear somewhere far from South Africa.

SAPS had a new commissioner, and this one seemed to know what he was doing. Things were changing. It was getting harder for an honest criminal to make a decent living. Time to cash out.

"Kallie, leave it. Revenge isn't worth it. Just don't use them again. Your new guy can handle Mostert."

"What's his name, anyway?"

"Zane calls him Boetie. I don't know his surname. Probably some Cape Flats lowlife."

Robertson sighed. "Fuck me. Boer and now Boetie. Can't we hire an Englishman?"

Kallie laughed. "Must be Affirmative Action. No other work for Afrikaans-speaking men."

Robertson met his gaze from across the desk. "Are we agreed? We're backing off from Devlin and his contractor?"

Kallie shrugged. "Fine, John. You always know best. I'll let you know if Mostert resurfaces."

He stood, leaving the office without another word.

Sliding into the bucket seat of the Z4, he pulled a silver pen from his pocket. Unscrewing the end, he tapped out a thin line of cocaine onto his palm and inhaled sharply. Checking the mirror, he wiped away any lingering residue from his upper lip. The rush hit fast, sharpening his senses, making everything feel clearer, more precise.

He put the Z4 in gear and floored the accelerator. The rear wheels spun on the loose gravel, fishtailing briefly before gripping the road.

He felt invincible.

Fuck John Robertson. Devlin and his buddy had to pay.

****

Felicity sat at her desk, waiting for Rawlimi and her PA to leave for lunch when an unread email caught her eye.

It was from her contact at Vehicle Registrations. She opened it and scanned the details.

Black Toyota Fortuner. Farouk Chukwu. Shirley Road, Eldoraigne.

Quickly, she copied the information to her phone and sent it to the Contractor. She didn't know why he needed it, but she was certain she would find out soon.

Out of the corner of her eye, she spotted Rawlimi walking toward the lift. A minute later, her PA followed.

Felicity glanced around. The office was quiet—most of her colleagues were either on lunch or still out on assignments. Captain Dan's office door was closed.

Now or never.

She rose from her chair, walking casually down the aisle, heart hammering. Reaching the reception area of the Brigadier's office, she paused.

One last check over her shoulder.

No one in sight.

Sliding open the PA's desk drawer, she retrieved the key to Rawlimi's office.

Chapter 33

Jack was walking from the house to his workshop when he saw Jeremy stop at the gate.

He pressed the fob to open it and continued toward the workshop, pausing outside to wait for Jeremy to step out of his car.

"Morning, Jeremy. What brings you here so early?"

Jeremy held a cellphone in the air. "Hi, Oom Jack. I managed to get this phone working. I made a backup of all the numbers, photos, and videos. It's all on this memory stick. I know you warned me about the content, but I couldn't resist having a peek. This is gruesome stuff. What country did this happen in?"

Jack frowned. "What, Jeremy? I have no idea what's on it."

Jeremy scrolled through the phone's gallery, stopping when he found what he was looking for. Holding up the screen so Jack could see, he played a video.

Jack barely lasted a few seconds. A little boy, still alive, screaming for his mother as his ears and nose were sliced from his face.

Jack turned away, raising a hand to signal Jeremy to shut it off. He wiped his palms over his face, his gut twisting at the horror of what he had just witnessed. God, what had become of this country? How had they reached this level of depravity?

He glanced at young Jeremy, regret pooling in his chest for allowing him to see such a thing.

"I'm sorry you had to watch that," Jack muttered. "We suspected it might be bad, but this... this is worse than anything I imagined. I'm sorry, son."

Jeremy swallowed hard, his voice uncertain. "Is this happening in South Africa, Oom Jack?"

Jack hesitated before nodding grimly.

"Yes, I'm afraid so. And it's not the first time either. It's harvesting—body parts for muti." He exhaled heavily, steadying himself. "I need to get this to Mikey as soon as possible. This is why what you do is so important, son. Can you help me?"

189

"Yes, but we should send it directly from the memory stick via email."

Jack led him into the workshop, settling down at the workbench in front of his PC. He turned the screen toward Jeremy and pushed the keyboard closer.

"Just type 'Mikey,' and his email will pop up."

While Jeremy got to work, Jack methodically dismantled the phone. With a clean rag, he wiped every component free of fingerprints, then slipped on a pair of mechanics' gloves before carefully reassembling it. He wrapped the device in a sheet of clean A4 paper and wrote down the new PIN code Jeremy had given him. Setting the package aside, he turned his attention back to Jeremy, who showed him a thumbs-up, indicating the email had been sent.

Jack pulled his own phone from his pocket and dialed Mikey's number. It rang for a while before he answered.

"Hi, buddy. What's up?"

Jack glanced at Jeremy. "Mikey, Jeremy managed to crack that phone you got from the youth. It's fucking horrific, man. Be prepared to be shocked. He emailed you everything. I've cleaned and wrapped the phone. What should I do with it?"

Mikey sighed. "Jack, I'll check the email later. We're in the middle of weapons training right now. Can you send the phone via PostNet? I'll collect it at the Lyttelton branch. And tell Jeremy I'm impressed. I owe him a beer. I'm sorry for exposing you guys to whatever it was you saw. I need time to go through everything. I'm working closely with a police detective and will probably bring her in on this. I'll contact you later."

"Okay. Bye."

Jack ended the call and reached for the memory stick. Slipping it into his toolbox, he pushed back his chair.

"Come on, Jeremy. Let's head to the kitchen and rustle up some breakfast. I've got fresh chorizo and will make you my Tex-Mex Huevos Rancheros. You like chili?"

"Love it." Jeremy grinned, following him inside. "Oom Jack, when am I going to get help with TRUTH?"

They walked into the kitchen before Jack answered.

"To be honest, Jeremy, we don't know who to get. Who can we trust?"

Jeremy sat at the kitchen counter, drumming his fingers on the laminated surface. An idea had been forming in his mind, but he wasn't sure if Jack and Mikey would go for it.

"There's a guy who's contributed to the site a few times. He's from Sweden. Seems just as passionate as we are about exposing corruption."

Jack paused his chopping. "What if he's a spy trying to infiltrate us? We can't risk being exposed."

Jeremy scratched his head, nodding. "I thought of that. But there's a way. We could have him set up his own network under a different service provider—call it TRUTH Europe or something. That way, he handles everything from Europe and the U.S., and we never have to reveal our own location. Eventually, we could expand to Asia and South America, making it a global operation. It would also allow me to focus solely on South African and African corruption."

Jack considered it for a moment, then smiled. "That's a good idea. Let me run it by the others. How do you like your eggs?"

****

Mackie stood in the lounge area, where they had set up the kitchen table as a makeshift lecture space.

His gaze swept over the two men sitting in front of him. Earlier, he had spoken to them about the psychological aspect of their work, trying to gauge their mental strength. He sensed their absolute hatred for injustice, their frustration with government incompetence.

In Boer, he saw a kindred spirit—someone who reminded him of himself years ago. Piet, however, was still untested. His commitment to revenge was clear, but whether he had the resolve to follow through remained to be seen.

"I want to briefly discuss alternative methods of eliminating a target," Mackie began. "You won't always have a gun. And even if you do, it might not be the best option. Over the next two days, we'll cover explosives, knives, and weapons of opportunity. Piet, once I leave tomorrow, Boer will handle your training in hand-to-hand combat and firearms. We've already worked out a schedule."

He placed several items on the table—pieces of wire, rope, and a rolled-up length of nylon.

"This morning, we're focusing on one of my favorite weapons—the garrote. There are several types, but I prefer three. The first is piano wire. It can be carried rolled up in your pocket or disguised inside a guitar string packet. Looks completely innocent. For handles, you can break two small branches or use wooden dowels. Personally, I prefer two 8x120mm coach screws. I loop the wire ends permanently and screw them in when needed."

He saw Boer smirk while Piet frowned, his forehead creased.

"The wire garrote is deadly," Mackie continued. "With enough strength, it can decapitate a man. If the target manages to get fingers under the wire, it won't matter—it will still cut through."

He picked up a massive zip tie, handing it to Piet.

"This is a construction-grade cable tie. Unbreakable. It's a modern garrote—allows you to watch the target die or extract information from him before he goes. I'll demonstrate later."

Piet passed it to Boer while Mackie picked up the rope.

"This one is simpler, but effective. Less messy, though it requires more time and control. Let me show you."

Handing Boer a leather strap with buckles, Mackie gestured for him to put it on. Then he lifted the rope garrote.

"Put this on—it'll protect you. I'll demonstrate for Piet first, then he'll try, and then it'll be your turn. When I leave, I want you two to keep practicing. You only get one chance in a real situation."

Piet's eyes gleamed with excitement. He had already decided—this was how his brother's killers would die.

****

192

Mikey sat alone, staring at the video playing on his phone.

The boy's arms and legs were bound, his elbows and knees pressed together. A man methodically cut away pieces of him, using a panga and a knife. The boy screamed.

Mikey shut the email.

He dropped his head onto his forearms, his chest tightening with grief. Then, slowly, it morphed into something else.

Fury.

He exhaled through his nose, clenching his fists. No government, no law, no justice. Only men like him.

He walked to the gate, looking at the blackened field across the road. Scorched, waiting for rain.

Maybe it was time to see what Piet was made of.

Chapter 34

Felicity had just replaced the key to Rawlimi's office when she heard Captain Dan's office door open. Her heart kicked up a beat as she hurriedly took a few steps down the aisle, away from the door, composing herself. When she saw him emerge, she called out.

"Hi, Captain. Have you seen the Brigadier's PA? There's something I need to ask her."

Captain Dan shook his head and glanced at his watch. "You'll have to wait until after lunch. I'm about to interview the vendor. Do you want to watch?"

"Ooh, I can't wait. Let's go."

He motioned for Sergeant Robson to join them. The three of them walked down to the holding cells. As they entered the interrogation room, Felicity stepped into the adjacent observation room, where she could watch through the one-way glass. Inside, Dan Mdalose and John Robson took seats on one side of the table at the center of the room, leaning back as they waited for the arrival of Nofolo Masondo.

Felicity was unaware that, while she had been inside Rawlimi's office downloading emails, Captain Dan had been on a long call with LangFaan. He had needed pointers on how to conduct the interview without giving Masondo an opening to demand a lawyer.

She watched as a constable escorted the vendor into the room and seated her across from the two detectives. Dan pretended to flip through a file while Robson stared at her, unblinking. The vendor's eyes darted between the two men, her face tight with worry. After a moment, Captain Dan closed the file and gave her a slight smile.

"My name is Captain Dan Mdalose, and this is Sergeant John Robson. This interview is being recorded. Can we get you anything? A cold drink, maybe some water?"

LangFaan had told him to ease her into it—make her feel like they had her best interests in mind, but not too comfortable.

Masondo shook her head and sniffled into a handkerchief.

"Can I call you Nofolo?" Dan asked.

She nodded hesitantly. "Yes."

"What about your business? Your medicines?"

Nofolo's expression twisted in distress. "What will happen to them?"

Dan leaned forward slightly. "Nofolo, you're in serious trouble. But if you assist us with our investigation, we can help you. The main reason we arrested you today—rather than waiting—is because we heard some people are planning to kill you." He paused, letting that sink in. "Don't worry about your stall. Someone is keeping an eye on it while you're here. Do you understand?"

She gasped, a loud cry escaping her lips. Her shoulders shook as she broke into sobs. Dan knew he had to keep her mind engaged, keep her from thinking too much—keep her from asking for a lawyer.

"Nofolo, we've been watching you for a long time. We know you're not the mastermind here. You're just trying to make a living. Yes, what you've done is a crime, but if you help us catch the people actually killing these children, we'll be lenient."

He had no authority to make that promise, but at this moment, it was just a suggestion.

Nofolo's face contorted with fear. "He—he will kill me! I'm scared! You don't know him."

She was sobbing uncontrollably now, tears streaming down her cheeks. She clutched her hands around her ears, rocking slightly, teetering on the verge of a full-blown panic attack.

Dan caught Robson's eye and gave a small nod. Without a word, Robson stood and left the room. Nofolo's attention flicked to him, tracking his movements. By the time the door closed behind him, her wails had softened.

She turned to Dan again, searching his face. He gave her a reassuring smile.

"Nofolo, we will protect you. You can stay in the holding cells until we arrest all of them. We're stronger than they are, and we have numbers on our side. Help us, and you'll be safe. They'll never see daylight again. Trust me."

She sniffled and turned to look at the camera mounted on the wall. Her tears were drying, her hands still trembling slightly. Dan leaned back, waiting.

Finally, she sighed and looked at him. "What do you want to know?" She hesitated, then added, "You must catch all of them. If they see me in the streets, they will hurt me."

Dan hid his smirk. *Does she really think we'll let her go?* He pulled the file closer, readying his pen. LangFaan had told him that taking notes made people feel more connected to you.

"Okay, let's start at the beginning. Who were the two guys threatening you at your stall?"

"They work for Chukwu," she said, lowering her voice. "The one is called Jax. The other is his intombi." She made a crude gesture of copulation. "His name is Lollo."

"Do you know their surnames?"

She shook her head. Dan jotted the names down and looked back at her.

"Who has the muti?"

"It's gone. A ulutsha grabbed it from—"

Too late, she realized she had slipped. She tried to cover it up. "Sorry, I thought you meant the herbs they stole from me."

Dan feigned indifference, waiting for her to continue.

"The muti comes from Mister Chukwu. He's Nigerian. Very rich. Very cruel. Very big. I am afraid of him."

On the other side of the glass, Felicity was taking her own notes. *That's why the Contractor wanted me to trace the Fortuner's owner.* She shook her head in disbelief. *How does he do it?*

"Where do I find Mister Chukwu?" Dan asked. "Is that his name or his surname?"

"I—I don't know. I think it's his name. I contact him on WhatsApp. His number is in my phone."

Dan pulled the cellphone they had confiscated from her earlier and placed it on the table.

"Unlock it."

She hesitated before tracing her security pattern on the screen and handing it back.

"It's under 'Mr C.'"

Dan found the number. There were only two numbers saved in her contacts.

"Why only two numbers?"

She shifted in her seat, licking her lips before answering. "My other phone is lost. This is my new one. I had these two numbers written down. I need to rebuild my contacts."

Dan fought the urge to laugh. Where you're going, you won't need contacts.

"Who's the other number?"

"A customer," she said quickly.

Dan dialed it and put the phone on speaker. She stiffened. Her fingers twitched on the table.

The line clicked. A voice answered in rapid Xhosa.

"Where is my fucking money? You lied to me! I paid you for the muti, and if you don't deliver, I want my money back or I will kill you!"

Dan ended the call.

The phone rang again immediately. He let it go to voicemail. The ringing stopped, then started again.

Dan locked eyes with Nofolo.

On the other side of the glass, Felicity cringed. Any moment now, Dan is going to find out about the stolen bag. The phone. The boy's body parts. She could see the vendor was terrified, on the edge of confessing.

"How do you pay for the muti? And how is it delivered?"

Nofolo hesitated. She wiped her nose, sniffed, then spoke.

"If it's a big buy, I borrow the money from the buyer. Then I message Chukwu. He sends the muti with a taxi. I pay the driver. That's all."

Dan sent a text from her phone to the last caller.

'I will get your money. Two days.'

He stood and motioned for her to follow him. Outside, he handed her over to two constables.

Back in the observation room, Dan turned to Felicity.

"We have two names, a supplier, and a pissed-off buyer. He thinks he'll get his money in two days. Let's make sure he doesn't."

He handed her his notes.

197

Chapter 35

Manzoni stared at the WhatsApp message on his phone, reading it for the second time.

'Are you now playing games with me, wena? There is no money in the post box.'

He hesitated before replying, uncertain of Mamello's intent. Was he trying to con him for more money, or was he laying the groundwork to break free from their agreement? Manzoni's jaw clenched as he pulled his Mercedes SUV into the driveway, the weight of the situation pressing down on him.

Stepping out, he tossed the key fob to his butler.

"Ask Reggie to wash it before he parks it, please, Cyril. I'll use the Cayenne if I need to go out again."

Without waiting for a reply, he climbed the grand stairs leading to the front entrance of his mansion in Blair Atholl Golf Estate. The 850-square-meter house was an architectural masterpiece—designed in an H-shape, featuring a 20-seat cinema, a private library, a fully equipped gym, an indoor heated pool, a putt-putt course, and five opulent bedrooms, each with an en-suite bathroom. His exotic car collection rested in an eight-car garage, equipped with humidity control and a state-of-the-art workshop.

At the center of the entrance hall, standing atop a pedestal, was a large Venetian vase, filled with blood-red roses. Twice a week, as per Donatella's strict instructions, a florist from the city delivered and arranged fresh flowers.

Manzoni glanced at the security screen in the kitchen. The Alfa Romeo Stelvio was missing from the garage. That meant Donatella had not yet returned from whatever function or luncheon she was attending.

With a heavy sigh, he dropped his keys onto the huge marble island in the kitchen, his thoughts circling back to the message. He strode to his study, closed the door behind him, and sank into the black Telluride executive chair behind his desk.

He read the message again.

Undecided, he rested his right elbow on the armrest, pressing his fingertips to his temple. His pulse pounded in his ears. Mamello had accused him of deception, and while the accusation enraged him, he couldn't ignore the nagging doubt clawing at his mind.

He knew Mamello would see the blue ticks—the message read receipt—and would be waiting impatiently for a response. Avoiding it was not an option.

He made the call.

The line rang twice before Mamello answered.

"What's the story? Talk to me, wena. I'm busy." His tone was curt, dismissive.

A prickle of irritation ran up Manzoni's spine, but he forced himself to stay calm. His voice remained measured.

"I put the cash in the parcel and wrapped it myself. I went to the post box alone, personally placed the package inside, and as always, I made sure it was locked. Is there anyone in your crew who knows about the post box? Someone who might have access to it that you're unaware of?"

"Hey, wena, don't talk shit to me." Mamello's voice sharpened with hostility. "You go put the money there again. Today. Sharp, sharp. Don't waste my time. My guys aren't crooks."

Manzoni clenched his jaw, swallowing down the burning fury rising in his chest. He needed Mamello's cooperation to move his trucks across the Zimbabwean border. Mamello had the contacts, and right now, that was more important than his pride.

"I'll drop it at the post box in an hour. I'll send you a photo of the parcel."

Mamello's voice turned silky. "See, Marco? It's not difficult. You and me, we are brothers. We cannot have these misunderstandings between us." A low chuckle followed, his amusement grating on Manzoni's nerves.

Manzoni ended the call without replying.

Rising from his chair, he walked over to the safe, concealed behind a hidden panel in one of the ornate pillars. Glancing over his shoulder to ensure no one was watching, he opened it.

Inside, stacks of currency sat in neat piles—South African Rands, American, Canadian, and Australian Dollars, Euros. Below them lay sheaves of bond and share certificates worth millions.

But what caught his eye, as it always did, was the note taped to the inside of the door. A note Donatella's father had handed him on their wedding day.

He read it again, as he did every time he opened the safe.

'Tienila al sicuro o vedrai il tuo sangue prima di esalare l'ultimo respiro.'

'Keep her safe, or the blood you see will be your own before your last breath.'

He could still picture Don Attorio's smile, those ice-blue eyes piercing through him as he pressed the note into his palm, whispering, "Welcome to the familia."

Shaking off the memory, Manzoni quickly pulled stacks of R50 notes from the shelf and shoved them into a large brown courier envelope. With a final glance at the note, he closed the safe and replaced the panel.

He walked to the kitchen and checked the security screens, searching for Reggie, his driver. Spotting him in the garage, he pressed the intercom button.

"Reggie, bring the Cayenne around. I need a lift to the post office."

As he waited for Reggie to retrieve the Porsche, his mind churned.

What had happened to the original cash he left in the post box? Was Mamello scamming him? Or had someone seen him make the drop?

A post office worker, maybe?

The uncertainty gnawed at him. Nothing about this sat right.

The distant roar of the Cayenne's engine reached his ears. Shaking his head, he grabbed the envelope and stepped out the front door.

****

Mikey read Felicity's message.

Flipping his phone shut, he walked back to the house. Inside, Boer had a stripped-down 9mm Vektor Z88 pistol laid out on the table. It was one of two guns Mikey had given him—weapons taken off previous targets.

The other was a Unique .22 Automatic pistol—small, compact, with minimal recoil. While it lacked stopping power, fifteen rounds of high-velocity bullets made it deadly.

Boer was pointing to different parts of the Z88, giving instructions to Piet, who was meticulously reassembling the firearm under the pressure of a stopwatch. Mikey leaned against the doorway, watching.

When Piet finally set the reassembled gun on the table, Boer showed Mikey the time on the stopwatch.

"Not bad, Piet," Mikey said, nodding. "My first time was slower than that. Now, I can strip and reassemble in under fifteen seconds. Learning this is important—it's how you understand your weapon. Handle it often enough, and it becomes an extension of you. Could mean the difference between life and death."

He turned to Boer. "Piet will be busy with this all day. Strip, reassemble, repeat. Drill it into muscle memory."

Piet grinned, getting to work again. Mikey motioned for Boer to join him outside.

They stepped onto the stoep, the late afternoon air thick with the scent of dry earth.

"We have a problem," Mikey said, his voice low. "Two of our targets are about to be arrested. If that happens, we won't get what we need from them. We've got less than 48 hours."

Boer's expression remained unreadable. "Where?"

"They're in a flat in Yeoville. Now that SAPS has identified them, they'll be under surveillance."

Boer folded his arms. "Do you have a plan?"

Mikey exhaled. "Not yet. I have an idea—but it means Piet has to be proficient with the .22 by tonight."

Boer cracked his knuckles. "Then I'd better start. He'll be deadly accurate by six p.m."

Mikey nodded.

Mikey remained seated for a while, turning an idea over in his mind. He pulled out his phone and checked the app to see if the two men were at their flat. The screen showed no movement inside.

Switching to the tracking app, he scanned for their vehicle. The VW Golf was parked near Simunye Beer Parlor—a known hotspot for beer and inyama braai. If they were drinking, they would likely stay put for a while.

Good. That gave him some time.

Rising from his chair, he stretched briefly before heading inside to prepare lunch.

As he stepped into the house, he noticed a shift in training, Boer had set the Z88 aside and was now focused entirely on the Unique .22, guiding Piet through its handling.

That was exactly what Mikey wanted. Tonight, the kid would need to be ready.

Chapter 36

Captain Terrence Majoba and WO Maria Ruiters took their seats at the conference table, two floors above Majoba's office.

Across from them sat Colonel Zero Mbalula from IPID and Colonel Regina Ngoro from Hawks Commercial Crimes. They had already exchanged introductions earlier over coffee in the conference room, setting a formal yet cautious tone for the meeting.

Majoba had decided to let WO Ruiters lead their presentation. His team had discussed their progress earlier and unanimously agreed—they needed help to take the case further. Arranging this meeting with the two department heads had been Majoba's call, a necessary step in pushing their investigation forward.

Maria took the lead, turning her attention to Colonel Mbalula first. She slid a thick file across the table toward him.

"Colonel, I don't expect you to go through this now. It's extensive—recorded phone calls, video footage, surveillance photographs, emails, and diary entries. My report is also in there. It contains evidence exposing the incompetence of Brigadier Florence Rawlimi, the head of Diepsloot detectives.

"You'll read about her disregard for investigations into the child killings, her failure to lead, and her general lack of commitment to her duties. The report also names a police sergeant from whom she obtained a stolen police docket—a docket she then handed over to Marco Manzoni. We are currently investigating Manzoni in connection with cigarette smuggling. We know they have a sexual relationship.

"We came across this evidence by accident, during our own investigation. It was sent to me anonymously—delivered to my home in three separate drops over the past three weeks. To this day, I don't know the source."

Mbalula tapped the top of the file with his fingernail, his expression tightening.

"Why are you presenting this at this meeting?"

Maria had anticipated the question.

"Because some of the players in that report also feature in the case we are about to present to Colonel Ngoro."

Mbalula's eyes swept across the faces around the table. He sighed, pulling the file closer, clearly uneasy.

"These are serious allegations against a high-ranking officer. I'll have to tread carefully." He paused before adding, "Do I need to be here for the rest of this meeting?"

Maria knew exactly what was happening. They had handed him the report in front of witnesses, ensuring it wouldn't conveniently disappear. His hesitation made it clear—he was uncomfortable. She also knew why. Mbalula had political ambitions and had been careful not to step on the wrong toes.

She kept her voice neutral.

"No, sir, not at all. We are not investigating Brigadier Rawlimi ourselves. When this evidence was sent to me, it became a matter for your department. You will decide whether to prosecute or not—it's out of our hands. If we receive any further evidence, we will send it directly to you."

Mbalula gave a curt nod and removed the file from the table. He hesitated for a moment, scanning the room, then stood and exited the conference room without another word.

Maria exhaled, relief flooding her chest. She didn't know what would happen next, but at least they had proof that Mbalula had received the report.

Trust was a rare thing these days. You never knew who would stab you in the back.

Her gaze shifted to Colonel Regina Ngoro—one of the few people she did trust.

Ngoro was already smiling faintly. Maria pushed the second file—the one on the illegal cigarette smuggling case—toward her.

"Colonel, this is what we have so far. This file contains photos, video footage, and surveillance reports. The video footage, like the other case, was sent to us anonymously.

"It seems like a lot of whistleblowers are coming out of the woodwork lately. Maybe people are finally getting fed up with corruption and crime. Unfortunately, it also suggests they don't trust our witness protection program.

"Our small team has done everything we can, but now we need your department's help to take this further. We're also hoping you'll involve SARS. This case is far-reaching, and we can't handle it alone.

"It's a comprehensive report—too much to go through today. I suggest you review it first, and then we can set up another meeting to discuss our next steps."

Colonel Ngoro turned to Captain Majoba, her eyes narrowing slightly.

"How are you coping, Terror?" she asked, using his old nickname. "I hear there's a lot of backstabbing on your floor. Rumor has it you keep all your office doors locked, and your team holds briefings behind closed doors."

Majoba smirked. "Colonel, we do what we have to. These are difficult times. It seems like everyone is just out for themselves.

"It will take people like you—and the people in my team—to clean out the rot that crept into the Hawks during the state capture years."

Ngoro picked up the file, her expression thoughtful as she rose from her chair. She turned to Maria with an approving nod.

"I hear good things about you," she said. "Let me know if you ever want to transfer to my department."

Maria shook her head politely.

"Thanks for the offer, Colonel, but I don't think I'd be much use sitting in an office, staring at reports and figures all day. I belong in the field."

Majoba chuckled, rising from his seat. He winked at Maria.

"Let's get out of here before the Colonel makes you an offer you can't refuse."

He turned back to Ngoro, extending his hand.

"Thank you for your time, Colonel."

Ngoro shook his hand, her grip firm. "I'll review this report and get back to you soon."

As Maria and Majoba left the conference room, Maria allowed herself a small, satisfied smile.

For once, it felt like they were a step ahead.

Mikey navigated the thick knot of afternoon peak-hour traffic in Yeoville, his hands steady on the wheel as he edged through the congested streets. He turned down Rockey Road and pulled into a parking spot half a block from Jax and Lollo's flat.

From his vantage point, he had a clear view of the entrance to the narrow stairwell leading up to the first-floor apartments. He unlocked his phone, the surveillance app already open on the screen. The live feed from the hidden camera inside the flat flickered in real-time.

He turned to Piet, showing him the screen.

"There's one camera in the flat. According to the tracking app, their car is still at the beer hall. That means they're still inside. Remember, the gun is only to subdue them. Fire only if things go wrong—and if you do, make sure you kill both.

"Once they're down, tie up Jax first while keeping an eye on Lollo. Then tie up Lollo. Sit them back to back and tape their mouths shut.

"After that, put the cable ties around their necks—tighten them until they struggle to breathe. Use another one to bind their heads together. Don't rush the interrogation. Let them feel it. Let them believe they're about to suffocate. That's when they'll start talking.

"When you question them, focus on Chukwu and his business. Remove the tape only if one of them has something useful to say. Do you understand?"

Piet nodded without hesitation. His jaw was set, his eyes hard. Mikey could tell—he was already in the zone, ready.

"I'll be watching from here," Mikey continued. "I'll also have an eye on the feed from the camera. If I see anything off, I'll call you.

"When you're done, bring me their phones and get their passwords. Once you have everything you need from them—eliminate them. Tighten the cable ties until there's no coming back. It's quiet, and it should take less than two minutes. Make sure they are dead.

"Before you leave, remove the cameras we installed. Take all their cash—keep it. Consider it part payment for what they did to your family. Lock the door behind you, and on your way out, try to retrieve the tracker from their car."

Piet nodded again, methodically checking the pistol and silencer tucked safely inside his jacket pocket. He pulled his cap low over his forehead and yanked the hoodie up, shadowing his face.

Mikey tapped his shoulder just as he was about to exit the Isuzu and handed him a folded cardboard sign, a piece of string threaded through the top.

It read:

'ubungqingili'

"Here." Mikey pressed it into his hand. "Hang this around Lollo's neck. It'll keep the cops chasing a different angle, looking for homophobic killers.

"Good luck. Stay calm. Keep your gloves and balaclava on—it'll scare them more.

"I'll be here."

Piet took the sign, tucking it under his arm as he stepped out onto the dirty pavement.

Chapter 37

In Cape Town, Devlin was getting ready to go out for the evening.

He had planned on playing a couple of games of pool at Nick's before heading to Barbecue Steakhouse for a well-earned supper. Pulling on his leather jacket, he grabbed the keys to the Kia from the wall next to the front door. Then, sticking to his usual safety ritual, he made his way cautiously to his car.

Once inside the Sportage, he started the engine and slowly rolled out of the underground parking, scanning his surroundings with habitual vigilance.

Tonight, he felt good.

He had spent the afternoon sleeping, and now, with a fresh stash of money, he was on top of the world. The only thing dampening his mood was Duncan's absence. Hell, he missed his friend. He hadn't heard from him in days, and the silence was unsettling. He couldn't wait for him to get back.

Turning left into Voortrekker Road, he headed toward Parow.

He parked the Kia around the corner from Nick's and strolled toward the snooker saloon, taking in the familiar atmosphere. As he climbed the narrow staircase, he exchanged quick greetings with a few regulars before heading straight for the bar. He ordered a beer, slipping into his usual rhythm.

But then, something shifted.

A strange feeling crept up his spine—the unmistakable sensation of being watched.

Keeping his expression neutral, he turned his gaze to the mirror behind the bar, using it to scan the room without being obvious. His eyes moved carefully from face to face, analyzing the crowd. It didn't take long before he spotted a familiar face.

Boetie Solomons.

The name alone made his stomach tighten.

Boetie was the brother of one of the gang leaders from Philippi. What the hell was he doing here? And more importantly—why was he watching him?

A cold prickle ran down Devlin's neck.

Pretending not to notice, he casually picked up his beer and walked toward the back of the room, where he and Duncan usually hung out. A couple of guys he knew were already there, engrossed in a game, while a third player stood waiting for his turn.

Devlin placed his money next to the stacked coins on the table, securing his place in line. He greeted the group, but his mind remained on Boetie. As the game progressed, he made a habit of moving around the table, using the angles as an excuse to steal glances across the room.

Boetie was still watching him.

Devlin kept his expression neutral.

He had to be sure.

Taking out his phone, he pretended to search for signal.

The moment Boetie turned to speak to the guy next to him, Devlin acted fast. He zoomed in and snapped a photo of Boetie's profile, the dim lighting casting just enough shadow to make him look more ominous.

Sliding his phone back into his pocket, he waited for his turn to play, his mind racing.

Something wasn't right.

Boetie looked out of place here.

While taking his shots, Devlin stole quick glances in Boetie's direction, watching his movements. It felt like a setup. But for what?

Opening his phone discreetly, he found the picture he had taken and immediately forwarded it to Duncan, along with a message:

'Keep an eye out for this dude when you get back. He's been watching me for a while now. Boetie Solomons.'

By the time nine o'clock rolled around, Boetie was gone.

Devlin exhaled a quiet sigh of relief.

He said his goodbyes to the guys at the snooker tables and made his way back to his car, the evening still unfolding exactly as he had planned.

His celebratory mood remained intact. He had had a few beers and was planning on a few more at Barbecue Steakhouse.

More than anything, he was looking forward to a rare, flame-grilled rump steak with that tangy house sauce.

What he didn't notice was the dark blue VW Golf with tinted windows, parked discreetly nearby.

Inside the car, a figure slouched low in the driver's seat, watching him closely as he walked past, completely unaware.

****

Sergeant Felicity Booysen sat at her desk, reading through the internal report she had pulled from the SAPS network. It contained an article quoted directly from *The Cape Times*.

'*Sangoma found murdered in Gugulethu, Cape Town.*

A well-known sangoma, Mme Cebisile, was found murdered in her consulting room in Gugulethu, Cape Town. She had been shot twice in the face.

Unconfirmed sources suggested that further searches of her premises had uncovered clothing that could possibly belong to Belinda-May April, the kidnapped girl from Saldanha Bay. Belinda-May had been taken from her home two months ago, and authorities had since found no leads.

Investigations had not turned up any suspects in Mme Cebisile's murder.

Police had also failed to prove suspicions that the girl had been sold by her mother and her mother's boyfriend. Both had been questioned several times by local and City Police, but no concrete evidence had been found to implicate them. They stuck to their story.

The sangoma's home and consulting rooms had been cordoned off, and forensic teams were conducting a thorough search. Several boxes of traditional medicines and witchcraft-related items had been removed from the premises.

Police had declined to comment.'

Felicity printed the article, grabbed the sheet, and walked straight to Captain Dan's office.

He looked up when she entered.

"Good afternoon, Felicity. How's our investigation into the two guys from Yeoville going?"

She sat down, placing the printed article on his desk.

"We're still watching their flat and keeping an eye out for their car. Nothing from the surveillance feed yet. The constables watching the premises are going off duty in ten minutes, and we don't have anyone to take over."

Dan nodded. "Nothing we can do about that until we get more people. It should be fine until then. Just make sure we have someone back there first thing in the morning."

Felicity pushed the article closer to him.

"Read this. Maybe contact the investigating officer in Cape Town. It could be linked to our cases—abducted child, sangoma involvement—it's worth looking into."

She knew it was just a hunch, but any lead was valuable at this stage.

Dan read through the article slowly, then looked up at her, skeptical.

"It's on the other side of the country, Felicity."

She shrugged, meeting his gaze, willing him to see the connection.

Dan sighed, read it again, then nodded.

"Okay. I'll find out tomorrow who the investigating officer is and get in touch."

She stood to leave but hesitated. She sensed there was something else on his mind.

She folded her hands in her lap and waited.

Dan fiddled with the cell phone they had taken from the vendor. Finally, he looked up.

"I sent Masondo's buyer a message from this phone—told him he'd get his money back in two days. I want to set a trap for him. Any suggestions?"

He would ask LangFaan the same question when they met later, but he wanted her opinion too.

Felicity raised an eyebrow.

"Is this something the Brigadier has to sign off on?"

Dan smirked and shook his head.

"Probably. But she's too busy with other things. I'll make the call on this one."

Felicity studied him for a moment, a flicker of approval crossing her features.

He had finally grown a pair of balls.

She had to hide her smile as she answered.

"Good. It'll help speed things up. I'll come up with a plan for the trap. Can we talk tomorrow?"

Dan stood and grabbed his jacket from the back of his chair. He had to meet LangFaan in half an hour.

"Sure. Come see me when you're on duty."

Felicity nodded, watching as he walked out.

For the first time in a while, she felt hopeful.

****

Mikey watched the camera footage on his phone while keeping an eye on the front entrance to the flats.

Darkness had settled over the streets. Through the grainy camera feed, he could see Piet leaning against the kitchen counter, his posture still, his breathing steady. It looked like he was meditating, mentally preparing himself. Earlier, Mikey had watched him unscrew the bulbs from the lounge area, plunging it into shadow.

A ping from his phone broke the silence.

Switching to the tracking app, he saw the VW Golf leaving the beer hall parking lot. He tracked it for a few seconds—it was heading in his direction. Without hesitation, he sent Piet a message.

He scanned his surroundings, making sure no one was paying too much attention to him.

The streets were still alive—commuters returning home, shopkeepers lingering outside, exchanging idle conversation while waiting for the last stragglers.

Mikey knew that later, when the city quieted, he would stand out more.

For now, his baseball cap and jacket collar tucked around his hair gave him some cover. The cloned plates on the Isuzu would keep him untraceable, but his biggest concern wasn't law enforcement—it was civilians with smartphones.

People took pictures of anything that looked out of place.

He glanced back at the tracker app. The Golf was nearing Rockey Street.

He waited. Then he saw it—turning into the flat's parking area through the security gate.

Mikey sent Piet another message.

Switching back to the camera feed, he saw Piet move toward the front door. The moment was close now.

Not long after, the tension in Piet's posture shifted.

The building's entrance door opened.

Through the harsh passage light, Mikey saw them—Jax and Lollo, clearly illuminated.

One of them reached for the lounge light, flicking the switch. Nothing happened.

After a moment's hesitation, they gripped onto each other, carefully navigating their way toward the kitchen, their movements sluggish.

Drunk.

Completely wasted.

Mikey shifted his focus to Piet.

The silenced pistol was steady in both hands, his steps silent and controlled as he advanced on them.

The moment they reached the kitchen, Lollo flicked on the light switch.

Jax, blinking against the brightness, was the first to spot the gunman.

The sight of a black silk balaclava sent a jolt of terror through him.

He tapped Lollo on the shoulder.

Lollo turned.

His bloodshot eyes went wide as he let out a shrieking gasp.

Both men froze.

Slowly—very slowly—they raised their hands.

Chapter 38

Maria lay with her back against Combrink's chest, still breathless from their lovemaking. His arm draped over her, his hand cupping her breast. She held his hand, her fingers resting lightly over his. He kissed the soft skin behind her ear and whispered,

"I want you to stay tonight."

His other hand wandered downward, tracing over the flat plane of her belly, fingertips teasing toward her mound.

She laughed softly, swatting his hand away.

"Not tonight, lover. I don't want to become a fixture in your apartment. This is a friendship with benefits, and it's best if it stays that way. I'm not the type of woman who wants to be tied down."

"So, you're keeping your options open until something better comes along?"

She didn't answer, but instead wrapped her fingers around his half-erect length, stroking him lazily. It didn't take long before he was ready again.

She mounted him, pressing her palms to his chest, her lips curling into a wicked smile.

"No," she murmured. "It means I need to keep you hungry."

$$****$$

Piet stared at the two men, their hands raised in surrender.

The arrogant drunken swagger they had displayed earlier was gone, replaced by raw fear. Sweat poured down Lollo's round cheeks, his entire body trembling.

Piet motioned with the barrel of his gun, gesturing for Lollo to move to the counter.

His hands tightened around the grip. Every muscle in his body screamed at him to pull the trigger—to end them right there. These men had taken his little brother. They were responsible for Patrick's cruel death.

His chest heaved as he forced himself to stay calm.

214

Not yet.

"Turn around, both of you," he ordered, keeping his voice low and even, just as Mackie had taught him. "Put your hands behind your backs and keep quiet. I just want information. I'll let you go when you tell me what I want to know."

Keeping his eyes on Lollo, Piet slipped an industrial cable tie around Jax's wrists and yanked it tight, ignoring his cry of pain. He shoved Jax's head against the wall, kicked his feet backward to throw him off balance, and swiftly moved to secure Lollo.

Lollo had already started whimpering. Piet grabbed his collar, jerking him onto one of the high kitchen chairs.

"Sit down and don't move. Or I will shoot your friend."

He kept his gun trained on Jax, watching for any sign of resistance. The moment Jax twisted slightly, Piet brought the butt of the gun down hard against his skull.

Jax's knees buckled, and he slumped forward, groaning. Piet grabbed his hoodie, dragging him toward the chair he had already positioned back-to-back with Lollo's.

He shoved Jax down, then took a double-linked cable tie, slipping it over both their heads and pulling it tight. The two men gasped, their chests heaving, struggling against the tightened plastic digging into their throats.

To make sure they were completely restrained, Piet added another two cable ties around their necks separately, making it nearly impossible to move.

They were half-choking, squirming, their backs pressed against each other in a desperate attempt to find relief.

Piet didn't care.

Not yet.

He wrapped another tie around their upper arms, pulling it so tight that Lollo let out a muffled cry. Then, he bound their legs to the chair, securing them completely.

Jax tried to look at him, his eyes pleading.

Piet slammed another blow into the side of his head.

Jax groaned, his body jerking against the restraints.

"What... do you want from u—?"

215

Piet cut him off by slapping a strip of duct tape over his mouth.

Lollo let out a muffled sob, and Piet did the same to him.

Then, he stepped back and stared at them, his breath steady, his heart pounding.

****

Piet paced slowly around them, stopping in front of Jax.

"Who do you give the children to?" he asked, his voice calm, controlled.

Jax's eyes widened, and panic flooded his face. His head shook violently from side to side, his body trembling.

Piet's jaw clenched. He knew Jax would deny everything, try to waste time.

Without a word, he walked around to Lollo.

Taking another piece of duct tape, he pressed it tightly over Lollo's nose.

The effect was immediate.

Lollo began to thrash, his body convulsing, fighting for air. His nostrils flared, collapsing as he desperately tried to breathe through the tape.

Jax could hear him heaving, feel his struggles against his back.

Piet returned to Jax's chair, sitting directly in front of him, watching.

"I know about Farouk Chukwu. I know where he lives. It's not worth letting Lollo die for the rest of the information."

The terror on Jax's face deepened. His nose ran, mixing with the sweat beading on his cheeks.

Finally, he nodded.

Piet yanked the tape from Lollo's nose.

Lollo gasped, his chest heaving, his nostrils flaring in desperation.

Piet turned back to Jax, holding the gun to his forehead as he peeled back part of the tape.

Jax blurted out, "Are you crazy? You'll kill him—"

Piet pressed the tape back down, sealing his lips shut again.

"If I tape his nose shut again, it stays that way until he suffocates." Piet's voice was cold, steady. "I don't have time to waste.

"You get one more chance to talk."

Jax's body shook violently, his eyes darting to Lollo, seeing the desperate, terrified state he was in.

"I'll tell you everything I know," he whimpered. "Please... don't hurt us."

Piet leaned forward, keeping the gun trained on Jax's belly.

"Tell me about the operation in Shirley Street. Names. Numbers. How many children have you given them? And I want to know who was in the harvesting video.

"Don't lie to me. I already know enough to catch you. If you lie, I'll know."

Mikey was recording everything.

Jax swallowed hard. "Chukwu's second-in-command is Nasir Aku. He's the one who did the cutting. Both are from Nigeria. They're the only ones we ever met."

Piet's hands tightened around the gun.

"How many children?"

Jax hesitated, glancing at Lollo, then whispered, "Three boys... one girl."

Piet's vision blurred with rage.

The boy from the yard.

The boy who fought back.

Patrick.

His little brother.

Piet took a step back, his breath shaky, then looked up at the camera.

His phone pinged.

He checked the screen.

One word.

'Eliminate.'

Piet wiped his tears away, then turned back to the men who had destroyed his family.

The last thing they ever saw was the pure hatred in his eyes.

He tossed the sign Mackie gave him on their bodies that were still tied to the stools. The stools had toppled over in their struggles to get air into their lungs after Piet yanked the cable ties tight. They had made the wrong choices in life and had to pay for it in a gruesome way. Piet gathered the camera and stashed it into his rucksack with the bundles of money he found in the refrigerator.

Making sure no one was around he made his way out onto the landing and softly pulled the door closed behind him. He made his way down the stairs to the parking area to remove the tracker from the Golf.

Chapter 39

Sharon Moore prepared a cocktail for herself, a ritual she had grown to cherish.

She added the bubbly to her shaker, carefully pouring the Mimosa into a wide-brimmed cocktail glass. Experimenting with different cocktails had become a daily indulgence, a way to unwind in her uptown apartment before heading out to the clubs later in the evening.

Life hadn't always been this good for her. A decade ago, she had been just another R100 streetwalker, hustling to survive.

It was Kallie Jansen, an old client of hers, who had given her a break and set her up with this operation. He had pulled her off the streets, renting out two ground-floor flats in Panorama, turning them into the foundation of what had since become a thriving business.

The setup was simple but effective—clients met the women in the lounge, drinks flowed, negotiations were made, and deals were struck. Each flat had three bedrooms, each equipped with a small en-suite bathroom, allowing the girls to refresh between clients.

Over the years, the business had expanded. They now had four flats, operating with nearly thirty women, all highly paid and exceptionally beautiful.

There were strict rules.

No drunkenness. No drug addicts. Sharon demanded that her girls stay in peak condition—trim, healthy, and fit.

When they grew older or found themselves less in demand, she moved them to her other brothel in Goodwood, where the clientele was less particular and the rates were lower. If they wanted to retire, they were free to leave at any time. But most stayed.

The security, the care, and the money Sharon provided made them loyal.

But her most exclusive service catered to the filthy rich and the deeply perverted—the supply of virgins for those willing to pay six-figure fees.

Her last transaction would probably be her last.

Not only had it become nearly impossible to find virgins, but it had also become too dangerous. The last girl had been barely ten years old, and already spoiled when that sangoma bitch sold her to Sharon.

She had been lucky to offload her to Chukwu in Gauteng, but even after paying back the Russian, the two new prostitutes she had received in exchange would take months to break in before they turned a profit.

The girls from Chukwu were always hooked on heroin, and most needed rehab before they became worth anything. Some never kicked the addiction, and Sharon sold those off to a pimp in Parow—destined to walk the streets.

Sharon's own flat sat on the top floor, five levels above the business below. From there, she had a clear view of Table Mountain and, more importantly, absolute privacy.

Not once had she brought anyone into her home.

She still enjoyed the occasional fling, but always on her terms. Always at his place. Always driving herself.

Her pride and joy was her postbox-red Audi A1.

She never slept over, and she never hooked up with the same man twice.

Sharon took a small sip from her glass and walked to her office, where a split-screen monitor displayed live surveillance feeds from the lounges downstairs.

Kallie had once suggested they use footage of their more famous clients for blackmail.

Sharon had shut that idea down immediately.

She refused to put herself or her girls in danger.

Kallie often came up with crazy ideas, but she knew better than to take them too seriously—especially when he was riding a cocaine high.

She sipped her cocktail, clicking through the different camera feeds, watching the flow of clients and girls.

Each flat had its own bouncer—their job was to collect the "job card" from the girl before she took the client to a room.

Only card payments were accepted.

The bouncers also kept time, ensured clients left when their time was up, and handled security.

They oversaw cleaning staff between 9 a.m. and 11 a.m. each morning, made sure laundry was picked up and returned, and restocked the fridges with snacks and liquor.

Eight bouncers worked in shifts.

The business shut down every Sunday at midnight, reopening on Tuesday at noon. Everyone took a break then.

Sharon's mind drifted to the message she had received from Kallie earlier that day.

It was about Mme Cebisile.

She smirked.

You don't fuck with The Association.

A warm tingle spread through her loins, and she sighed in satisfaction.

Tonight, she would find herself something tall and muscular.

The bouncers at the clubs were always eager.

She got up, poured the rest of the cocktail mix into her glass, and settled back in front of the monitor.

She enjoyed watching the clients arrive, the negotiations, the playful flirtations.

Sometimes, she wished she were young again.

Some of their clients were absolutely delicious.

****

Mackey and Piet arrived back at the house, the tension from the night's events still hanging in the air.

Mackey knew better than to press Piet with questions. Some things a man had to work through on his own. He watched as Boer placed a firm hand on Piet's shoulder, guiding him inside.

Alone for a moment, Mackey walked to the front gate, pulling out his burner phone from his pocket. His personal phone had been left at home days ago—a precaution he had learned to take long ago.

He dialed the landline at Lost Horizons and listened as the ringing echoed in his ear. The office was attached to the house, and he knew Cara would be expecting his call.

After just a few rings, she answered.

"Lost Horizons, how may I help you?"

"You can tell me how much you miss me," he murmured.

"Mon ami! Where are you? I miss you so much," she responded, her voice lighting up with excitement.

"I'll be home tomorrow morning—should be flying out at ten o'clock. I can't wait to be back."

"I will make a special lunch for you," she purred. "And we can try out our new bed in the honeymoon suite, no?"

Mackey groaned. "Cara, don't do that to me. How am I supposed to sleep tonight?"

She giggled softly. "You sleep and dream of me, and tomorrow you fly fast. Go sleep now, and time will go quickly."

"You're right," he admitted. "I'll see you tomorrow. Ciao, mon amour."

Ending the call, he slipped the phone back into his pocket and turned toward the house.

Inside, Boer and Piet were sitting at the table, having a late supper. Mackey sat down, reaching for a lamb chop from the braaibak at the center of the table. Boer had lit a fire and grilled chops and boerewors while they had been in Yeoville. The first bite of succulent lamb hit his tongue, and he realized just how hungry he was.

He gave Boer a nod of approval, acknowledging his skill at the fire.

He glanced at Piet, who was devouring a thick piece of boerewors, his appetite clearly uninhibited.

Boer grinned and playfully punched Piet's shoulder. Then, he looked at Mackey, smirking.

"He's okay. I was just as hungry after my first time."

Mackey watched as the two men worked through four kilograms of grilled meat. A bond had already formed between them. It was a natural thing for men of their background—when you had the same kind of history, you understood each other without words.

Despite everything, Piet looked calm, as if the night's events had centered him.

When the meal was over, Mackey got up, went to the fridge, and grabbed three cold beers. He opened them and set one down in front of each man.

"Okay, boys," he said, leaning back in his chair. "Let's go over this week's training. I'm leaving tomorrow and will return on Sunday. While I'm gone, I want you to focus on fitness, strength, and weapons skills.

"Piet, you did exceptionally well today. You have the temperament for this life—of that, I have no doubt. Boer and I will give you the tools and skills to complete what you set out to do.

"But always remember—emotions will get you killed. Never go ahead with an operation unless you are sure you have a good chance of getting out unscathed and undetected."

He turned to Boer.

"You understand the psychology of this work, and it's important that Piet does too. I've put together a list of training exercises that need to be completed this week. If you need to reach me, leave a message on my burner—I'll check it once a day.

"Keep that phone off unless you're expecting a message from me. No unnecessary risks. Any questions?"

Both men shook their heads.

Mackey drained the last of his beer and stood up.

"Alright, I'm heading outside to make some calls and then I'm going to crash. It's been an eventful day. Boer, can I talk to you for a second?"

Boer nodded, following him outside into the night.

Mackey stopped a few meters from the house and turned to him.

"I've been thinking about the cash still lying in the Beechcraft. The only real option is to put it in a safety deposit box at a bank. Keep some stash handy for unexpected expenses—you never know when you'll need it.

"Cash is a problem in our line of work. I suggest setting up an offshore account for future payments.

"If, of course, you plan on continuing with what you're doing."

Boer shifted his feet, his expression thoughtful.

"That's a lot of money—about two-point-five bar."

Mackey grinned and clapped a hand on his shoulder.

"You'd be surprised how quickly you can burn through it."

He let the words sink in, then added, "Invest in assets. Industrial or commercial property—especially in the Western Cape—will always appreciate in value.

"If you have the space and interest, classic cars are also a good investment. There's a high demand in Europe for them. Exporting them is easier than ever these days."

Boer nodded, looking more relaxed now that he had some options.

"I need you to take me to the airport tomorrow," Mackey continued. "Then you can take the money and open a safety deposit box for now.

"Here." He handed Boer a bank card. "There's money on this for expenses this week."

Boer took the card, slipping it into his pocket.

Mackey's tone lowered slightly, turning serious.

"Boer, get to know Piet better before you trust him too much. Okay?"

Boer hesitated, then nodded. "I think he's okay, but I hear what you're saying. I'll focus on training like you suggested.

"What if he wants to go somewhere?"

Mackey thought for a moment.

"Take him if he needs a break, but stick with him. I gave him some money a while back, and with what he took from Jax, he should be flush for now.

"But stay out of the townships and the city center. He must not visit any of his old stomping grounds.

"If he wanders off, it'll be a problem.

"You and I will need to ditch him if that happens."

Boer nodded slowly, his face serious.

Mackey's voice dropped lower.

"He can do whatever he wants after this job is done—after the killers are dead. Until then, he's *in training.*

"We cannot let him compromise us by doing something stupid. I'll talk to him before I leave tomorrow."

"I understand," Boer said, turning to head back inside.

Mackey watched him go, then walked toward the gate, pulling out his burner phone.

It was time to make a call to Jack in Cape Town.

Chapter 40

Devlin placed his knife and fork down on the empty plate, his stomach full and satisfied.

He wiped his lips with the white serviette, then picked up his glass, draining the last drops of rich red wine. His gaze dropped to the stripped T-bone on his plate, still amazed that he had managed to finish the entire 500g steak.

It had been grilled to perfection, and the hand-cut chips that came with it had been crispy, golden, and delicious.

He wiped his lips once more, then pushed back his chair, rising from his table at the rear of the restaurant.

Walking toward the counter to pay, he spotted Gawie, the head griller, chatting with Basil, the owner. Devlin pulled out his wallet, laying R500 on the counter.

"Thanks, guys," he said, nodding in appreciation. "That was, once again, the best of the best. You really know your stuff, Gawie."

Gawie fist-bumped him, grinning. "Thanks, Dev, but I think we need to give the farmer and the butcher some credit. Without quality meat, I wouldn't be able to give you a good steak."

Devlin smirked, turning to Basil. "I suppose you won't give me the butcher's name, will you?"

Basil shook his head slowly, a knowing smile playing on his lips.

"No chance, Dev. The recipes I got from the old guy who sold me this place will die with me, son."

"So they should."

Devlin tapped the cash on the counter. "Give the change to my waitress. It was great coming by again."

Basil crossed his arms, tilting his head. "What happened to your buddy, the Boer? I need him to come eat here more often. The man has an appetite."

Devlin chuckled. "He should be back in a few weeks. He's with a group of guys in the Transkei. Anti-poaching training or something along those lines."

"Great. Come for a steak when he gets back."

"I'll probably see you before then."

Devlin twirled his car keys around his finger, heading for the door.

As he stepped outside, his eyes swept up and down the street, checking for anyone watching him.

Nothing seemed off.

The streets were still active, filled with people heading home and shopkeepers finishing up for the night. But later—when the city quieted—he knew he would stand out more easily.

He crossed the main road, walking toward Parow Centre's basement parking. Inside the shopping center, he moved past the food courts, his senses always on alert. He took the lift down to the parking lot and strode toward his car.

He had a few drinks earlier, but he still felt okay to drive.

Reaching for the remote, he pressed the button to unlock the car.

His brows furrowed.

The door was already unlocked.

He glanced down at the remote in his hand, wondering if he had forgotten to lock it earlier.

Walking around the Kia, he spotted something else.

The boot lid wasn't fully closed.

"Idiot." He exhaled, shaking his head. "It won't lock if that's open."

He pushed the boot shut and tried the remote again. The locks engaged and disengaged smoothly, as they should.

Satisfied, he slid into the driver's seat and started the engine.

Just as he leaned back to fasten his seatbelt, he felt the cold edge of a knife press against his throat.

****

Mikey sat back, phone pressed to his ear, as he updated Jack about his plans.

"I'm flying out to Wild Horizons tomorrow morning."

Jack's voice came through clear.

227

"How's it going with the new recruit? Is Boer helping?"

Mikey nodded, even though Jack couldn't see him.

"He's great. The two of them get along well. Piet's a quick learner—does everything without asking questions. He would have made a great soldier."

He took a breath before continuing. "I left a list of things Boer needs to work on with him. I plan to be back by Sunday."

Jack chuckled. "I bet Cara can't wait to have you home."

"I miss her," Mikey admitted, "but I know there'll be a list of jobs waiting for me. Between her and Brigitta, I have no peace anymore."

Jack laughed. "You're happy, man. That's better than chasing crooks and murderers across the world. It's time to let someone else handle that. Enjoy retirement, Mikey.

"Sweety and I will see you soon. The bus is almost ready, and we're heading in your direction. I'll help you with that wedding hall you're supposed to build."

Mikey grinned. "Hey, Jack, that'd be great! Then you can see what we've done with the Eco Centre."

But he hadn't called just to chat.

"The real reason I'm calling is to check in on Jeremy. You said he's struggling with the load."

Jack exhaled. "Yeah. Had a meeting with him. He thinks it might be smart to franchise TRUTH—get sites set up in Europe, America, and the East. That way, he can focus on corruption in South Africa and the rest of Africa."

Jack sighed. "God knows, there's enough of it."

Mikey stayed silent for a moment, considering the idea.

Jack knew better than to interrupt his thinking.

After a pause, Mikey finally spoke.

"I think it's a great idea. I was worried TRUTH would grow too big for us to handle. I've got an idea, but I'll discuss it with you later. Let me first see how things play out with Boer and Piet."

Jack chuckled. "Who gave him the name Piet?"

Mikey laughed. "He picked it himself. It suits him."

Jack snorted. "Sounds about right."

Mikey glanced at his watch. "Jack, I'll talk to you tomorrow when I'm back home. I've already been on this phone too long. Ciao."

"Take care, my friend."

Mikey ended the call.

Just as he was about to shut off the burner phone, it pinged.

A message from Sergeant Booysen.

'A trap is being set for the buyer. Name unknown. 48 hours.'

Mikey quickly typed a reply.

'The buyer is yours. Leave Chukwu to us.'

He sent the message and switched off the phone, sitting back in his chair.

Things were finally moving.

$$****$$

Maria felt her frustration rise as she looked at Pieter.

He could be such a fucking prude sometimes.

She blamed his strict Afrikaner upbringing.

Glancing around the restaurant, she saw that no one was paying them any attention. She leaned forward slightly, her fingers slipping open two buttons of her blouse. Her toffee-colored breasts swelled against the fabric, threatening to escape.

She licked her lips and batted her eyelashes at him.

"I will pay."

Pieter smirked, clearly struggling not to look at her cleavage.

"Let me see if I understand this correctly," he said, his voice measured. "You want to bribe me with sex to do your dirty work?"

His eyes flicked up to hers, amusement dancing in them.

"Why don't you drop the memory card off at Mega Media's offices yourself? I'm not even sure I agree with your plan. What happens if it's traced back to us?"

Maria sighed, realizing he wasn't falling for her tactics.

She leaned forward, resting her elbows on the table, her voice dropping to a whisper.

"Nobody can prove it's us. I told the Colonel we got it from an unknown source. Anybody could have given it to the media."

Pieter didn't look convinced.

"Yes, and what about Terror? He'll know it's one of us."

Maria shrugged. "Who says he doesn't know what we're planning?"

She buttoned up her blouse, sighing in annoyance as she sat back. Her eyes locked onto Combrink, willing him to agree to her plan—leaking the party video to the media.

Pieter took a bite from his cheeseburger, chewing thoughtfully.

A grin tugged at his lips as he shook his head slowly, seeing how irritated she was getting. He wiped his mouth and finally spoke.

"There's a better way to get it to the media."

Maria's eyes lit up. She leaned forward eagerly.

"How? Tell me."

Pieter smirked, his gaze dropping to her partially buttoned blouse.

"Is the offer still on the table?"

Maria shifted on the bench, studying him before answering.

Was she falling for this tall, ropy Afrikaner?

She couldn't deny the attraction—his sharp blue eyes, straw-blond hair, and strong, muscular frame.

But love?

No.

She had made a rule—never get emotionally involved.

Her last relationship had been a disaster. She had moved in with him, thinking it was love, but within months, the verbal abuse had started. Two years of mental torment had followed before she finally walked away.

Now, her job was everything.

She had seen marriage up close—her mother had taken many beatings from her alcoholic father, and Maria had sworn she would never allow herself to be in that position.

Love?

Love was the first step toward losing control.

And Pieter?

She knew he was crazy about her, but their work made any kind of real relationship impossible.

Their weekly romp was as far as it could go.

She tilted her head, her voice teasing. "That, White boy, depends on the quality of your suggestion. What do you have?"

Pieter smirked, enjoying her restlessness.

He had been in love with her since the day they met.

It had taken him three years to gather the courage to ask her out for a drink, and even then, it had been Maria who set the pace. For over a year now, he had been waiting, hoping she'd let him in a little more.

He wanted more than just sex.

He wanted all of her.

But he also knew he had to be patient.

"I was thinking," he said, drawing out the moment, "it would be quite devastating if Florence Rawlimi herself accidentally leaked it to the media."

Maria's eyes darkened with interest.

Pieter leaned in.

"We have photos of her and Manzoni at their love nest. We have recorded phone conversations between them. If we add a short story explaining the stolen docket, with both their fingerprints on it, plus the champagne glasses they used that night?"

He let the thought sink in.

Maria's breath hitched, her lips parting slightly.

He had her.

"You could ask your friend to send it from Rawlimi's computer."

Maria blinked, then let out a low chuckle.

"You're a very clever boy, Combrink. But it's going to be a major job convincing her to do it. She'll shit a brick when I ask her."

Pieter shrugged.

"Like you said—how badly does she want Rawlimi gone?"

Maria took a slow sip of her wine, her fingers twirling the glass as she stared out the window.

Pieter watched, waiting as she savored the thought of nailing both Rawlimi and Manzoni in one move.

She turned back to him, her elbows resting on the table, and whispered,

"All this excitement is making me horny."

Pieter laughed, shaking his head at her bluntness.

But he felt the stirring in his khaki chinos.

"Your place or mine?"

Maria downed the rest of her wine, grabbed her bag, and stood up.

"My place. It's closer. Tonight, you can sleep over—but no coffee or breakfast in bed. By seven o'clock, you hamba. You hear?"

Pieter raised an eyebrow, surprised.

Maria had never let him stay the night before.

This was new.

It was a start.

And he would take it.

Grinning, he followed her out of the restaurant, his eyes locked on the sway of her hips.

Chapter 41

Devlin smelled the sour stench of his attacker's breath, hot and foul against his skin.

He instinctively knew it was Solomons.

The razor-sharp blade pressed against his throat, and he forced himself to stay calm, raising his hands slowly.

"What is it you want with me, Boetie?" he asked carefully.

"I hear you recently got paid. Where is it?"

Devlin's mind raced.

Only Kallie Jansen and his partner knew about the diamond payment. That meant Boetie must have been sent by them.

But why did they want him dead?

Had something gone wrong with the diamonds?

His instincts screamed that taking Boetie to his flat would be a death sentence. If that was the case, he might as well die right here.

"I don't know what money you're talking about," he lied smoothly. "I've got about two grand on me and some savings in the bank."

"Don't talk shit to me!" Boetie hissed, pressing the knife harder. "I know you! You'd never put that kind of money in a bank. Start the car and drive. We're going to your place. I know it's there. Move it."

Devlin swallowed hard and started the engine, shifting into drive.

A trickle of warm blood ran down his neck where the blade had nicked him.

As he pulled out of the parking garage, he noted the booms were up—no need to stop.

He cracked his window slightly, hoping for fresh air, but Boetie's sour, dagga-laced breath still filled the car.

His mind raced, desperately searching for a way out.

With the knife at his throat, it was hard to focus. He needed to distract Boetie, keep him talking.

"Does your uncle know you're a hitman for Kallie?" he asked casually.

Boetie didn't respond—just pressed the knife harder.

Devlin had to tread carefully. If Boetie was even half as dangerous as his uncle, he was in serious trouble.

"Boetie, your uncle and I grew up in the same neighborhood. We did jobs together. He wouldn't be happy if he knew you'd killed me."

"Fuck my uncle," Boetie spat, screaming into Devlin's ear. "He's in jail, man!"

Bingo.

Devlin knew he had hit a nerve.

He kept driving, heading in the general direction of his flat, though he still didn't know if Boetie actually knew where he lived. He doubted it. But he couldn't risk it.

He needed to keep him off balance.

"I have to ask myself," Devlin continued, his voice thoughtful, "why Kallie paid me and then sent you to take the money back. Was there something wrong with the diamonds I sold him? Or are you planning to keep it for yourself, Boetie?"

He glanced at the rearview mirror.

The streetlights illuminated Boetie's face just enough for Devlin to see it—hesitation.

He was getting to him.

Boetie's scowl deepened. "What fucking diamonds, man?" he snapped. "Zane only told me about the hit on Mostert you got paid for. Mostert was spotted in Joburg a week ago. Alive and well. Kallie is pissed off, man! He wants you dead. Tonight."

Devlin's blood ran cold.

Mostert was alive?

Impossible.

Boer had eliminated him. Devlin had seen the proof—the photos, the blood, the corpse.

This had to be a mistake.

Unless...

Unless Kallie had been the anonymous contractor all along.

Devlin's thoughts spun wildly. If Kallie had been behind the job, why was he using his driver, Zane, to contract Boetie? Did he not realize how reckless and unreliable Boetie was?

Nothing added up.

"That's got to be a mistake," Devlin said, keeping his tone even. "I saw photos of Mostert's body. Someone's setting you up, Boetie. The cops are probably onto Kallie and Zane, and they're looking to shift the blame. How much is Kallie paying you?"

He slowed for a red light, watching Boetie in the rearview mirror.

Boetie's eyes darted uncertainly.

The pressure of the knife eased slightly.

Devlin pushed his advantage.

"You know your uncle hates Kallie. I think he'd be very pleased if you and I worked together to get rid of him."

Boetie's face twisted in confusion. "What do you mean? You expect me to kill KJ?"

He laughed, but Devlin could hear the edge of fear in it.

"You must be fucking mad, man! Do you know how strong The Association is? Those people are everywhere! They'll come for me!"

Devlin saw the fear in his eyes and knew he had him.

He calmed his tone.

"Boetie, I don't expect you to do anything except let me live. My guy will handle the rest. I'll tell your uncle you came to me with information and helped us eliminate Kallie and his gang. He'll be proud of you. Now tell me—who else do you know in The Association?"

Boetie hesitated.

"And what about the money Kallie promised me?"

"How much?"

Boetie grinned, showing the gaps where he was missing several teeth.

"Twenty thousand."

Devlin almost laughed.

Now he understood why Kallie had chosen Boetie for the job—he was cheap.

"Did Zane tell you who's in The Association? Any names? Give me names, and I'll pay you twenty thousand plus five thousand for each one."

Boetie's eyes narrowed. He was thinking hard.

Devlin felt the knife ease away a little more.

He had him.

Boetie was doing the math, and Devlin drove slowly, letting him figure it out.

Finally, Boetie nodded.

"Go get the money. No tricks, or you're dead. Move it!"

Devlin flicked his indicator and turned toward his building's underground parking.

As he pulled into his usual spot, Boetie's eyes darted around.

"Where are we? Why did you stop here?"

"This is my place. I'll get your money."

Boetie didn't trust him.

"Hold your hands above your head. Thumbs together."

Devlin hesitated, but complied.

He felt something tight snap around his thumbs—thumb cuffs.

Shit.

Boetie chuckled. "Got them off eBay."

He jabbed the knife into Devlin's back.

"Okay, put your hands in front of you and get out. And remember—I have the knife. Don't force me to kill you, Dev."

Devlin slid out of the car, taking the keys with him.

He had no choice now—he had to take Boetie upstairs.

As he walked toward the lift, he plotted. He had two grand in his pocket and fifty grand in the freezer. The big money was in a safety deposit box.

He would have to give Boetie the fifty and hope it bought him enough time.

As the lift doors closed, Devlin glanced at his captor's twisted grin, the glint of the knife in the dim light.

He had one chance to turn this around.

And if he failed—he was dead.

Devlin had seen the knife briefly when Boetie climbed out of the car after him.

It was an evil-looking thing—long, sharp, and well-used.

His mind raced. Could it be true? Was Mostert really alive, or was it just bullshit Kallie had fed Zane?

The worst part?

The Association knew who he was.

They had probably always known.

The lift doors slid open, and Devlin walked slowly to his door, his mind working through possibilities and escape routes.

He turned toward Boetie and said, "The alarm pad is on the right. The code is 44411."

Boetie pushed him forward, his free hand punching in the code.

The beeping stopped immediately.

Boetie grabbed the collar of Devlin's jacket and shoved the knife harder into his back.

"Okay, partner—where's the money?"

Devlin could feel his hesitation. He knew Boetie was undecided and that now was the time to take the lead.

"How many names do you have?" he asked. "Remember our deal."

Boetie hesitated.

Devlin nodded toward the bathroom.

"You can lock me in there after you give me the names. I'll tell you where the money is then. That way, you can count it without worrying about me. You can leave whenever you want, and I won't even know when you're gone."

Boetie's eyes darted around the apartment, taking in the furniture, the electronics, and whatever else he could steal.

His lips curled in excitement. He nodded.

"If you fuck me over, I'll kill you, Devlin. Uncle or no uncle."

Devlin kept his voice steady and neutral.

"I don't plan to do anything, man. I'm grateful to know about Kallie's betrayal. I'm happy to pay you what I promised. Give me the names, and you can go about your business. I'll disappear tonight."

Boetie watched him for a long moment before rattling off the names.

"Kallie, John Roberts, Milos, Toni, Sharon Moore, and Captain Funani. That's six. You owe me fifty grand."

Devlin turned his head slightly, meeting Boetie's eyes.

"Kallie and John—who is actually Robertson, not Roberts—I already know about. Milos and Toni are dead. I'm not really getting a good deal here, but I'll keep my end of the bargain. The money's in the deep freeze."

Boetie shoved him into the bathroom and locked the door.

Devlin heard him walking to the kitchen, the sound of the freezer door opening filling the silence.

This was his chance.

He wrestled his phone from his shirt pocket, struggling with his thumbs cuffed together. Using his forefinger, he managed to snag it and drag it out.

The screen was still dimmed, the volume muted.

He typed fast.

To Ashwin: 'Help. Boetie Solomons has me locked up in my flat. Edward Court. Eighth floor. No. 812. Urgent! Careful.'

He pressed send and then listened at the door.

Boetie was ripping through the layers of cling film, pulling out the bundles of cash.

Devlin quickly typed another message, this time to Boer.

'Solomons has me locked up. He says Mostert is still alive?? The Association has a contract on me—and maybe you too. Members: Kallie Jansen—Jim Fouché Avenue, white house with red portico. Partner: John Robertson. Sharon Moore—Goodwood brothel owner. Captain Funani—Bellville SAPS.'

Send.

Devlin stuffed the phone under some clothes in the laundry basket.

Boetie couldn't find it now.

He sat down on the toilet, trying to wriggle his thumbs free. The cuffs bit into his skin, sharp edges cutting into his flesh.

He listened carefully.

Boetie was moving around the flat, probably looking for something to put the money in.

238

There was nothing Devlin could do now but wait.

After a few minutes of opening and slamming drawers, Boetie's footsteps approached the bathroom.

The key turned in the lock.

The door creaked open slightly, and Boetie peered inside.

"Hey, Dev..."

Devlin stared back, his pulse steady, his expression neutral.

Boetie's smile was twisted, almost nostalgic.

"Do you remember the day you came to pick up the booze at my uncle's smokkelhuis in Kensington?"

Devlin nodded slowly.

"I was in high school, visiting him," Boetie continued, stepping further inside. "I was standing in the kitchen while you guys were making a dop in the dining room. Do you remember?"

Devlin remembered it vaguely.

Boetie's expression darkened.

"Do you remember what you said about my mother?"

Devlin's stomach dropped.

Fuck.

"You said the reason I'm so stupid is because my alky tikkop mother drank and did drugs while she was pregnant with me."

His voice was calm, but the rage beneath it was unmistakable.

Devlin remembered the remark now.

His uncle had been complaining about Boetie's school progress, and Devlin had made a flippant comment, trying to explain rather than insult.

But to a teenage boy craving validation, it had been a knife to the heart.

Boetie's eyes burned with years of resentment.

"I looked up to you, Dev."

His grip tightened around the knife.

"Until that day. Since then, I've hated you. I've hated you for a very long time, man."

Devlin felt a deep, terrible dread settle in his chest.

He had been played.

Boetie had never intended to leave him alive.

239

The bastard had been waiting for this moment for years.

Devlin shook his head, regret flickering in his eyes.

But it was too late.

Boetie's other hand appeared from behind the door—clutching a large automatic pistol.

Devlin's stomach twisted.

It was his own 9mm Glock.

Boetie must have found it under the mattress.

The hammer fell.

A flash erupted from the muzzle.

The impact hit Devlin's chest like a sledgehammer, slamming him back against the cistern.

His breath hitched, eyes dropping to his chest, watching blood gush from the wound as his heart still pumped.

Through the blur, he saw Boetie step forward, unlocking the thumb cuffs.

He felt him yank the fake Rolex from his wrist, slipping it into his pants pocket.

Then—

Devlin saw no more.

Chapter 42

Mikey had been back at Lost Horizons for two days, working furiously to catch up.

Though Alfred and the rest of the staff had managed to keep things running smoothly and assist Cara in his absence, the building work had fallen behind.

Cara had done a remarkable job getting the function hall plans approved, and she expected it to be completed in three months. In the last two days, the builders had dug and set the foundations.

Now, the building inspector was due in an hour.

Mikey took the free time to hop onto his KTM Adventurer and ride into town.

He needed to communicate with Boer.

Booysen's message had made one thing clear—they needed to speed up the training if they wanted to reach Chukwu and his accomplice before the police got to them.

Once those men were in custody, it would be impossible to take them out.

Mikey pulled out his burner phone, typed a quick message, and sent it.

'Need to talk. Buzz me.'

He slipped the phone into his shirt pocket, started up the KTM, and headed to the hardware store.

Lighting was on his list.

Cara and Brigitta would likely have designs of their own, but it wouldn't hurt to see what was available off the shelf.

He parked the bike near the entrance and walked inside, making his way down the lighting aisle.

Halfway through, his phone buzzed.

Mikey turned around, walked outside, and rode to the shopping center parking lot for privacy.

He dismounted, pulled out his burner phone, and dialed the one he had left with Boer and Piet.

Boer answered immediately.

"All okay?" Mikey asked.

"Sort of. Can you talk?"

"I'm alone, standing at your spot by the gate. What's wrong?"

Mikey exhaled, choosing his words carefully.

"Got a message from my contact at SAPS. They're setting a trap for the buyer today. They think they'll catch him. He's not our concern. They also know the name of the killer, but they don't know where he is yet. I do."

There was a slight pause before Boer responded.

"Shit."

"If the cops track him down first, we'll never get to him. You need to go to a pawn shop and get a second-hand, late-model cellphone. Tell them you want it for spares. Pay cash."

"That's easy enough. What do I do with it?"

Mikey knew this was risky, but there was no other choice.

"Keep it with you until I get back. In a few days, someone will arrive at the smallholding and give three hoots. A woman will hand over a small parcel. Take it and keep it in a safe, cool place. Do not open it. Do not speak to the courier. She doesn't know what's inside."

"Got it." Boer's tone was sharp, business-like. "Anything else?"

"Yes. I'll be there by Saturday. We'll likely need the silenced .22 again. Let Piet be accurate and comfortable with it by then. How's his strength training?"

Boer chuckled. "This guy is focused, man. He takes to training like a born soldier. He's still young, but he's already strong. We wrestled this morning, and I'll tell you—if he keeps going through protein the way he does, he'll have the better of me soon."

Mikey smirked. "Good. I'll call from Lanseria after I land."

He ended the call and shut off the phone.

He then rode to the Post Office, relieved to see that the public phone was still operational. He dialed a number from memory.

A female voice answered, "Timber Down Tree Felling."

"Hi Grace. Is Gustaf around?"

"Mikey! How are you? I hear you got married."

He grinned. "Yeah, I finally gave in. How have you been?"

"To tell you the truth, I'm pissed off that you got married. I was still hoping I had a chance, you know." She giggled playfully.

"I'm putting you through to Grumpy Gustaf."

Mikey waited patiently, listening as Gustaf shouted at someone over a shortwave radio before finally answering.

"Gustaf. What can I do for you?"

Mikey smirked. "Is this Mister Grumpy?"

Gustaf's tone immediately changed.

"Mikey, you old dog! How's life? I hear you got married."

"News travels. I wanted to invite you, but heard you were in Australia."

"Yeah, I was visiting my daughter. I'm a grandfather now. Can you believe it?"

"Oupa Gus! That's got a nice ring to it. Congrats, man. We have to get together soon. Listen, Gus, I need some stuff."

Gustaf's tone shifted. Serious now.

"Some grey putty?"

"Correct. About 125 grams and a small det. The smallest you have. Can you help?"

"Need it to fell something?"

"Yeah. An ugly tree from Nigeria."

There was a short pause, then a low chuckle.

"Well, seeing as it's for a good cause, I can accommodate you. Where do you want it?"

"Delivered to a smallholding near Lanseria in two days. Possible?"

"Yeah, man. Is it for Butchy?"

"No, he's in the UK. I'm borrowing his place. We're training some anti-poaching wardens."

"Yea right. Anti-poaching? What will you think of next?" Gustaf laughed. "I'll send her ladyship with the parcel tomorrow morning. I need stuff from the city anyway."

****

243

Boer walked to the back of the tandem garage, where the target sheet hung.

He unhooked it, inspecting the bullet spread before turning back to Piet, who was reloading magazines at the table.

"Not bad, Piet. Thirty shots, and you hit the black circle twenty-seven times. But the problem is those three that went wide. What went wrong?"

Piet examined the sheet, then shrugged. "I think it was the first three shots. I have to get used to the recoil. I expect it, and when it doesn't come, I overcorrect. I'll do better this time."

He slammed a fresh magazine into the pistol and cocked it. Boer watched as he emptied fifteen rounds into the target.

Before he could reload, Boer stopped him.

"Put the gun down. Run the perimeter of the property. Two minutes, thirty seconds. Go!"

Piet hesitated but obeyed, sprinting out of the garage.

Boer emptied the spare magazine, setting the loose rounds on the table. He waited.

A minute later, Piet burst through the side door, breathless, and grabbed the gun.

He slammed the magazine into place, cocked it, and pulled the trigger.

Nothing.

Boer raised an eyebrow. "You're dead, bru."

Piet's face flushed, realizing his mistake. Boer tossed the bullets onto the table.

"Load and fire."

Sweating, Piet reloaded and fired fifteen more rounds.

Boer shook his head. "Again. Three times. Run between each round."

For the next hour, Piet fired, ran, reloaded, and fired again. Boer changed the targets after every two rounds, watching closely.

By the end, Piet was drenched in sweat.

Boer examined the sheets. "One hundred percent accuracy on the first round. Second, you missed five. Third, only one miss. Not bad."

Piet nodded, exhausted.

Boer smirked. "We'll do combat knife drills after lunch."

Piet groaned.

"Make the sandwiches," Boer said. "I don't want to stab you on an empty stomach."

Chapter 43

Captain Dan sat near the entrance of the eatery at the market, a plate in front of him.

He had ordered a spicy grilled pork bun and a cola, but he barely touched them.

His eyes drifted to the back of the restaurant, where Felicity sat, her back toward him.

She was dressed to blend in—a colorful dress and headscarf adorned with African-style patterns, mimicking the vendor's usual attire. From behind, she looked just like her.

At a nearby table, two Constables in plain clothes sat, eating, their eyes casually scanning the entrance.

Outside, two more Constables, dressed in township clothes, loitered near the Lotto kiosk, pretending to fill out betting slips.

On the table in front of Felicity, a brown paper bag rested—stuffed with scrap paper.

She sipped her cola slowly, her gaze fixed straight ahead.

Earlier, Dan had used the vendor's confiscated phone to send a message to the mystery buyer—telling him the funds were ready and where to meet.

The buyer had responded immediately, demanding that she bring some of her more expensive medicines as a show of goodwill.

Dan had sent a thumbs-up emoji in response.

Now, all they had to do was wait.

Felicity stiffened slightly when a man in a waiter's uniform slid into the seat opposite her.

He studied her face, his expression hesitant.

He had only seen the vendor once before, and that had been in a dimly lit taxi.

His eyes flicked to the brown paper bag, and without a word, he grabbed it from her hands.

Opening it, he peered inside.

His face twisted in confusion.

The vendor had been darker, her features different.

This woman had the complexion of a Coloured—not the vendor he had dealt with before.

The moment he saw the bundles of scrap paper, realization dawned on him.

He jumped up from his chair.

But before he could make a run for it, the two plainclothes Constables were on him, forcing him to the ground.

He struggled violently, but they were younger, stronger—his fight was short-lived.

Captain Dan walked over, pulling a pair of handcuffs from his belt.

He tossed them to Felicity.

"Here," he said with a smirk. "You can have the honor."

As she snapped the cuffs onto their suspect's wrists, Dan turned to the other four officers.

"Good work, men. Now don't lose him, you hear?"

****

Chukwu motioned to Nasir to slow down.

"Pull over a few houses before ours," he instructed.

Nasir didn't ask why.

It wasn't unusual for Chukwu to be cautious.

For the past two days, Chukwu had felt something was off—as if they were being watched.

After the initial scare a while back, things had returned to normal—but something in his gut told him otherwise.

He sat quietly, his sharp eyes scanning the street ahead.

Nasir knew better than to question him.

Chukwu took out his phone, his thumb scrolling through his gallery.

He turned the screen toward Nasir.

"Check this out."

Nasir glanced at the photo—a young girl, nine years old, with striking green eyes.

"She's the one Sharon is sending us."

Chukwu grinned, his voice oozing satisfaction.

247

"Can you imagine what someone will pay for those eyes?"

Nasir barely looked.

He grunted noncommittally.

He didn't like killing girls.

Boys were different—they were expendable.

But little girls?

They grew up. They could be useful in other ways.

Chukwu closed the gallery, slipping the phone back into his pocket.

"We need to start looking for another location soon," he mused.

"The neighbors are going to start asking questions about the six guys who arrive for work every morning."

"The women aren't as much of a problem," he continued. "We're two good-looking men. It makes sense that we'd have girlfriends. But six men coming and going? That's going to raise eyebrows."

He exhaled.

"Besides, the internet business is taking off. We could use six more guys on the laptops."

Nasir frowned.

"Where are we going to find them?"

Chukwu laughed.

"Are you serious? There are hundreds of wannabe IT guys looking for work."

Nasir hesitated, then asked, "How safe are we, Chukwu? What if one of them talks?"

Chukwu snorted.

"Why would they? We pay them well. And we have them recorded committing crimes. They won't talk. If they do..."

He dragged a finger across his throat and grinned.

Nasir still wasn't convinced.

"What about the stuff in the deep freeze? I thought you said we'd move it."

"Don't worry about it. I'll move it when I have a new place."

He scanned the street one last time.

Nothing looked out of the ordinary.

"Start the car. I think we're clear."

Nasir obeyed, slowly pulling into their property.

The automated gate slid shut behind them.

"Park over there and check on the guys in the office," Chukwu instructed. "I have something to do. A new girl came in from Zim last night. I need to grade her."

He grinned, swaggering up the stairs, humming the Rocky theme song under his breath.

Combrink sat at his desk, updating their investigation timeline, when Maria dragged a chair next to him.

He ignored her, pretending to be absorbed in his screen.

She tapped his shoulder.

"Hey, Casanova, I have something to show you."

He stopped typing and turned toward her.

"I've seen them."

His eyes dropped to her chest with a grin.

Maria punched his arm.

"You one-track-minded beast! I didn't mean that."

She handed him a small note with a web address.

"I tried to convince Fee to send our stuff from Rawlimi's PC, but she absolutely refused. Instead, she gave me this link."

Combrink glanced at the note.

"What is it?"

"A site called TRUTH. They collect evidence of corruption, crime, fraud—you name it. They analyze everything, and if the evidence holds up, they post it."

She leaned in.

"They give passwords to trustworthy media outlets, relevant authorities, even opposition parties. According to Fee, most of the big corruption scandals we've read about recently started here."

Combrink raised an eyebrow.

"If it's secret, how do we know it's legit?"

Maria smirked. "Fee's boyfriend posted evidence there. A few days later, it was all over the news."

Combrink entered the web address into his phone browser. He scanned the page, then showed it to Maria.

"It has step-by-step instructions for logging evidence. This could be huge."

Maria nodded slowly, her excitement growing.

"We should post something. See what happens. If it works, we post the rest."

Combrink grinned.

"We need a handle. Something catchy."

Maria smirked.

"What about: Gotcha?"

Combrink laughed, fist-bumping her.

It was time to take down the untouchables.

Chapter 44

It was late evening, and the streetlights of the N1 stretched into the city, disappearing among the hundreds of thousands of others that illuminated the Mother City.

Kallie leaned over his balcony, admiring the view.

In his hand, he swirled four fingers of Tullamore Dew in a crystal glass. His system buzzed from the two lines of coke he had just sniffed off the tile on the bar counter.

The rush of power and euphoria made him feel invincible—sharp, untouchable.

From his vantage point, he noticed the gate open as Zane's black Ford Focus ST rolled through.

Zane parked in his designated spot and stepped out. He looked up, spotting Kallie on the balcony. Kallie waved him up.

Stepping back inside, Kallie hid the tile with the remaining two lines of coke under the counter.

That was his personal indulgence—something he didn't share with his staff.

The door swung open, and Zane entered the vast lounge.

Kallie greeted him with a grin.

"Zane, good to see you back. How did it go?"

Earlier, he had sent him to meet and pay Boetie.

Zane pulled out his phone and showed Kallie the photo Boetie had sent—the very dead Devlin.

Kallie smirked and took a moment to soak in the image.

He would have Zane send him a copy later.

He liked to savor these moments.

Devlin had always been too arrogant, too cocky—a prick who thought he was untouchable.

Kallie grabbed a beer from the fridge and handed it to Zane.

"It went okay, Boss. Boetie seemed a bit... off. I think it's because he knew Devlin pretty well. I gave him the money, told him we'd be in touch if we need him again."

Kallie scoffed, swirling his whiskey.

"Fuck Boetie's emotions. He gets paid to have none. Cheers to dead Dev!"

He clinked his glass against Zane's beer bottle, oblivious to the fact that Zane wasn't as excited as he was.

Kallie knocked back his whiskey, slamming the glass on the counter before walking around the bar.

He grabbed an envelope, stuffed with cash, and slapped Zane's shoulder.

"Here's a little bonus. Take the night off, enjoy yourself. I won't need you until tomorrow afternoon. And Zane?"

Zane paused, pocketing the envelope.

"Not a word to John. Okay?"

Zane nodded, beer still in hand, before heading downstairs to his quarters.

Kallie poured another stiff drink, slid the tile back onto the counter, and grabbed a rolled-up R100 bill.

It was party time.

****

Zane sat on his bed, his shoulders slumped, staring at the floor.

The beer in his hand had gone warm, but he hadn't even noticed.

Since his meeting with Boetie, his doubts about this job had only grown worse.

He had originally signed on as a driver, but now Kallie expected him to do a lot more.

He shook his head, placing the beer on the bedside table.

Reaching for the envelope, he counted the cash.

Five thousand rand.

He tucked it back into the envelope and stood up, heading to the mirror.

Slipping on his favorite black leather jacket over his T-shirt, he ran a hand through his hair.

A thought crept in—one he had been pushing aside for weeks.

Where was Kallie's money coming from?

The bastard never went to the bank, yet he always had stacks of cash.

How much was stashed in the house? And where?

Zane shook off the thought.

This wasn't his business.

Grabbing his keys and envelope, he walked out to his car.

Before starting the engine, he glanced up at the balcony.

No sign of Kallie.

But he could hear Neil Diamond's *Cracklin' Rosie* blasting from inside.

Hot August Night.

Kallie's favorite album.

Zane sighed, closed his door, and dialed a number from his contacts.

"Hi Mammie. Is Mammie nog wakker? Ek is op pad en ek bring vir ons van Golden Plate se roti's."

****

Captain Dan leaned against the balcony railing outside LangFaan's office, looking over the park below.

"We have the buyer and the vendor in the cells at Diepsloot. He says his name is Bongani Mzobe. I need to get Chukwu's whereabouts from them."

LangFaan listened quietly, his hands resting on the railing.

Dan continued.

"I don't have much time before I have to report it to Rawlimi. I have to get Chukwu before she hears about the arrests. She'll use it to her advantage and go public. Chukwu will be out of the country before you can blink."

LangFaan sighed, staring at the people moving through the park below.

He missed being out in the field, working with his old team, dealing with the scum of the city.

Finally, he spoke.

"Use surprise and fear first, then promise leniency to the first one who talks. Let them see each other as you take her to the interrogation room. Have the officer escorting her tell her she'll likely spend thirty years in jail."

Dan nodded, absorbing the strategy.

"Once she's in front of you, ask only one question. Give her time to think. Ask her if she wants to give up Chukwu's location for leniency, or if you should offer that deal to Bongani. Then say nothing else."

Dan rubbed his chin, considering it.

Then he shifted topics.

"Is John Robson coming to work for you?"

LangFaan didn't answer right away.

He watched the people in the park, some rushing to their destinations, others wandering aimlessly.

It was a beautiful autumn day in the City of Gold—as long as you ignored the thick brown pollution hovering over the distant skyline.

"He said he'd think about it," LangFaan finally replied. "But I think it'll be a hard decision. He's a career policeman. Affirmative action is killing good white cops, Dan. How do you work for years, knowing you'll never get promoted because of your skin color? How do you take orders from someone who doesn't even know what they're doing?"

Dan sighed heavily, rubbing his temples.

"I can't afford to lose him too, Cappie. He's been with us so long. He's one of the best."

LangFaan shook his head. "Well, Dan, you'll have an even bigger problem when Lastborn or Felicity gets promoted before him. He's been here fifteen years longer than either of them. You might have time—but not much."

He held out his hand.

Dan shook it.

"Good luck, Dan."

****

Felicity pinched her nose, the stench of decomposition overwhelming as she entered the flat.

Captain Dan followed closely behind, both of them struggling not to gag.

The two corpses inside were bloated, their skin yellow and green, leaking fluids from their eyes and mouths.

Felicity quickly surveyed the room.

The fridge doors stood open, the prepaid electricity meter dead.

No power. No refrigeration.

She turned to Dan.

"Close the door. Call it in. Have forensics and the meat wagon sent over."

Dan nodded, pale.

Felicity stepped outside, pulling out her phone.

She quickly typed a message to the Contractor.

'Found the rotting JX and friend. Power ran out. Gruesome. Time is running out on Chukwu.'

Chapter 45

Jeremy leaned over Jack's desk, his expression serious as he brought up the information they had received during the night.

Normally, he wouldn't bother Jack with every bit of intel that came in, but this—this was dynamite.

On the screen, photos, videos, and voice recordings flickered between a female Brigadier and a well-known smuggler.

They listened intently to the recorded phone conversations, their eyes scanning the photos of the two figures entering a high-end apartment complex.

The next file played a video—a party, filled with booze, music, and women.

At the center of it all?

An opposition leader and his sidekick, cavorting with scantily clad women.

Among them, Marco Manzoni, his hands all over a half-naked woman, his face flushed with alcohol.

Then came a series of stills—Manzoni slipping a parcel into a post office box.

The final piece?

A recording of Mamello, blatantly demanding a bribe.

Followed by a concise report that tied all the pieces together.

Jack exhaled sharply, his fingers tapping the edge of the desk as he took it all in.

"Jeremy, this is good stuff, my boy. Make sure every worthwhile media outlet gets this—ASAP."

His voice was laced with satisfaction.

"This bastard has done enough damage to our economy. I can't wait to see how this plays out."

Jeremy nodded, already moving to execute the order.

Jack rose from his chair, running a hand through his hair as he left the room, his mind racing.

****

Jack walked down the passage to the bar, finding it still closed.

Inside, Junior was busy cleaning and restocking the fridges.

Jack greeted him.

"Good morning, son. Everything okay?"

Junior glanced up from where he was packing bottles, flashing a grin.

"Morning, Oom Jack. All good on my side. We had a busy night. Just before closing, a group of very thirsty guys showed up—straight from a bachelor's party. They stayed till midnight."

Jack chuckled.

"Did you book your overtime?"

"Not yet. I haven't seen Tannie Amanda yet, but I will."

Jack nodded, then leaned against the counter, lowering his voice slightly.

"Tell me, Junior, have you seen that guy who came here once with Godfrey? Devlin?"

Junior paused, his brow furrowing.

"No. I saw him that one time only. But now that you ask... Hennie 007 has been asking about him."

Jack's stomach tightened.

Hennie? Asking about Devlin?

Why?

"What exactly did he ask?"

Junior wiped his hands on a bar towel, thinking.

"I heard him asking Duncan how he knew Devlin. That was a while back, though."

Jack frowned.

"When did you last see Duncan?"

Junior shook his head.

"Haven't seen him in a long time."

Jack sighed, rubbing his jaw.

"He's in Transkei, training game park rangers. He'll be back soon."

But his mind was elsewhere.

Why the hell would Hennie be asking about Devlin?

Hennie was retired from SAPS, but he still had his ear to the ground. The man knew things.

Jack's instincts prickled.

Hennie knew something.

And if he was poking around, it meant Devlin was either dead...

Or in serious trouble.

Jack exhaled slowly.

They needed to be very careful around Hennie.

****

Mikey scowled at the message Felicity had sent.

Shit.

They weren't ready to move on Chukwu yet.

He typed quickly, sending a message to Boer.

'Schedule is changing. I will see you at 10 a.m. tomorrow.'

Then, he sent another to Felicity.

'Hold off as long as possible. We are almost ready.'

Satisfied, he switched off his phone, stuffing it into the pocket of his enduro jacket.

He started the KTM, twisting the throttle as he headed back to Lost Horizons.

There was packing to do.

And Cara was going to be pissed.

****

It was Saturday morning, and a cold breeze swept through Cape Town.

Zane lay awake in his flat beneath the main house, staring at the ceiling.

Above him, he could hear movement.

Footsteps crossed the lounge floor, doors opened and slammed shut.

He remained still, listening.

Kallie had told him he wouldn't be needed until noon, and Zane knew better than to make himself visible too early.

He let his eyes drift closed again, slipping into light sleep.

****

The next time he woke, it was to banging on his door.

"Zane! Wake up! Open the door!"

Kallie's voice rang out, impatient and agitated.

Zane rolled out of bed, still half-asleep, dressed only in his pajama shorts.

He shuffled to the door, rubbing sleep from his eyes, and swung it open.

Kallie stood there, already high, his body jittery, his eyes darting around restlessly.

Zane sighed inwardly.

He had seen Kallie like this before.

It was going to be one of those days.

"Good morning, Boss. Do you need me?"

Kallie barely acknowledged the question.

"I'm off to a meeting with Funani. Can you clean up the mess in the lounge and kitchen? Miriam has the day off—she's visiting her daughter. I'm expecting company later, so I need the place spotless."

Zane, still fighting off the cold from the morning breeze, took the keys Kallie held out to him.

"Sure, Boss. You want me to drive you?"

He could see it clearly—Kallie was in no state to be behind the wheel.

But Kallie waved him off, irritated.

"No, I'm driving myself today. You clean the house. I'll take the M5—clear the cobwebs from it."

Zane winced inwardly.

That meant Kallie was off to party.

With Funani and the Petersen brothers—Rashaad and Shafique.

Which meant drugs, alcohol, and God knows what else.

Not his problem, Zane reminded himself.

Kallie handed over the house keys before walking toward the garage.

Zane watched him go, still half in a daze.

The BMW M5—Kallie's latest purchase—was a beast of a car.

More than 450 kilowatts under the hood.

Zero to a hundred in about three seconds.

Not exactly a car you wanted to be driving high.

From inside his flat, Zane heard the engine roar to life.

The sound rumbled deep, vibrating through the walls.

Then, the M5 shot forward, tires squealing as Kallie gunned the motor, tearing off down the street.

Zane glanced outside—Kallie had left the gate open.

With a sigh, he grabbed his fob and closed it.

Then, he climbed back into bed, pulling the covers over himself, trying to get warm again.

He'd clean the house later.

For now, his mind drifted back to last night—a quiet evening spent with his mother.

They had shared a meal, watching reruns of The Golden Girls—his mom's favorite show.

A rare moment of peace.

Within minutes, Zane dozed off again.

✳✳✳✳

In Hoedspruit, the early morning air was crisp, but the sun peeking over the hills hinted that the day would soon turn warm under a cloudless sky.

Mikey secured his rucksack to the back of the KTM, tightening the straps.

He glanced at Cara and saw the worry in her eyes.

"I'll be back in two days. And I have a surprise for you."

He hadn't told her about the new pick-up yet.

She would love it.

Right now, she had to rely on the old Patrol whenever she needed to cart things around, and with over four hundred thousand kilometers on the clock, it was literally falling apart.

Cara's eyes lit up with curiosity.

"A present for moi?" she asked in her French-accented English.

"More like a surprise," he said, trying to change the subject.

He knew how easily she could pry information out of him, and he wanted to keep this a secret.

"Are you helping Brigitta at the center today?"

Cara narrowed her eyes, but let it go.

"We're doing a cooking demo for the ladies from the Bushbuck Ridge Community Forum. We're making cassoulet—but with game meat, smoked chicken, and samp along with the usual beans. We made our own Toulouse sausage a few days ago."

Mikey zipped up his jacket, then grabbed his helmet from the handlebars.

He pulled her close, pressing a kiss to her lips.

"Enjoy it. And don't worry about me. I'm only there in an advisory capacity—nothing dangerous."

Cara arched an eyebrow, unconvinced.

"You say that, but I know you. If things go wrong, you won't just stand by."

Mikey grinned and pulled his helmet over his head, flipping up the visor.

"Then I'll make sure nothing goes wrong. I'll call when I'm on my way back. I love you."

He started the bike, the engine roaring to life.

Cara gave him a small wave as he pulled away, kicking through the gears.

He was looking forward to the trip.

It had been almost a year since he had taken a worthwhile ride—the last time being on a borrowed 1200 Tenere, riding like a madman to rescue Cara from her abductor.

As he turned onto the road to Lanseria, the KTM's speed climbed to 140 km/h, the engine humming beneath him.

A dark thought flickered in the back of his mind.

Had Cara's abductor's corpse ever been found?

That remote farm near Van Wyksdorp, where Mikey had hung him from the rafters in the garage, had been isolated enough that it could still be a rotting secret.

＊＊＊＊

Dan stood by the bedroom window of his house on the hill in Westdene, staring out into the cold morning.

Through the thick, polluted air, he could see that the day would be clear and cloudless—likely warming up within an hour.

Still, he shivered involuntarily, stepping away from the window to glance at the bed.

Cynthia was curled up beneath the blankets, still asleep, but he knew that once the girls woke up, their peaceful morning would be over.

They always ended up in bed with them on Saturdays.

Dan sighed, his mind shifting to work.

They were finally making progress with LangFaan's help.

But they still didn't know where Chukwu was hiding.

If they could find him, it would mean everything—for him, for his team, for the families of the murdered children.

Dan knew he already had enough evidence against Chukwu.

But if they could catch him in his hideout, there would be more—probably enough to bury him forever.

He climbed back into bed, wrapping an arm around Cynthia's waist.

Still half-asleep, she held onto his arm, her body warm against his.

Last night, for the first time in months, they had made love.

She had cooked his favorite meal, and after the girls were in bed, they had shared a few glasses of wine, sitting in comfortable silence, watching the fire burn in the hearth.

Then, she had started stroking his thigh.

He had been more relaxed than usual, and she had sensed it.

Maybe it was because of the deaths of Jax and Lollo.

After their bodies were removed and the flat ventilated, Dan, John, and Felicity had gone through the place for clues.

They had been shocked by how careless the two had been.

There were pieces of children's clothing, notes with directions to where kids had been abducted.

But the biggest discovery?

Lollo's diary.

It had given them another name—Nasir Aku.

And Chukwu's first name—Farouk.

Dan would need to talk to Robson and Booysen.

They had to find a way to trace Chukwu through the number they pulled from the vendor's phone.

The usual methods had failed—the phone was unlisted.

Dan's other problem?

Keeping the media off their backs.

So far, they believed it was just a robbery gone wrong.

He couldn't let them know this was connected to the child killings—not yet.

And now, looking back, he was certain—

The sign they had found on the bodies had been a plant.

A diversion.

Someone was deliberately trying to mislead them.

Chapter 46

Mikey slowed his KTM as he reached the gate, preparing to dismount and open it when he spotted Boer walking toward him.

Boer unlatched the gate, allowing Mikey to ride through toward the back of the house, where Piet was waiting.

As Mikey killed the engine, he was surprised when Piet clapped him on the shoulder and reached for his helmet.

Mikey greeted him with a fist bump, declining when Piet offered to take his rucksack.

His tools of the trade were in there—along with a special surprise he had been secretly working on for Piet.

"Howzit, Piet? You're looking fit, buddy."

"Uncle Mackie, I'm glad you're back! Boer got us some meat for a braai, and I promised to teach him how to make pap."

Mikey could see the change in Piet—he was in good spirits, a vast improvement from the last time he had seen him.

"Well, let's head inside, and you guys can fill me in on the training."

Stepping inside, Mikey found Boer standing in the doorway and gripped his hand, slapping him on the shoulder.

"How's it going, Boer? Our student looks fit and happy."

Boer grinned, nodding toward Piet.

"This guy is tough, man. I've never met anyone who learns this fast. Can you see how much bigger he's gotten?"

Piet rolled up his sleeve, flexing his bicep with pride.

Boer and Mikey burst into laughter.

Mikey walked into the garage, now fully transformed into an army-style training space.

He set his rucksack on the table, picking up the stack of target sheets.

Flipping through them, he studied the scores before looking up and smiling.

"Are these all yours, Piet?"

Piet puffed out his chest, his pride evident.

"All mine, Uncle Mackie. Can you see how much better I got as the days went by? I hardly miss the bullseye now. I'm equally good with both calibers."

Mikey nodded approvingly, then turned to Boer.

"How's his hand-to-hand combat? And the other weapons?"

Boer leaned against the workbench, arms crossed.

"Very good. You should see him handle the Isuzu. Drives like a pro. When this is all over, he can apply for his license. Unfortunately, I have to admit—bikes aren't his thing. He struggles with the clutch and pulling away. We gave up on that—it was wasting too much time."

Piet glanced at the two Hondas parked nearby, shaking his head with a half-embarrassed grin.

"I'll try harder. Maybe I just need a better instructor—one with more patience."

Boer shrugged, smirking.

Then he pointed to the broom closet.

"That parcel that arrived is in there."

Mikey nodded.

"Great. We'll check it later. First, I've got a present for Piet."

Mikey opened his rucksack, pulling out a parcel wrapped in newspaper.

He set it on the table in front of them.

"Guys, we need to speed things up. The cops are closing in on Chukwu, and we still have training to finish—not to mention figuring out how to get to those two cunts. We'll need to start surveillance over the next few days, studying their movements. I have some tools to help with that, but first—Piet, I have something for you."

Boer and Piet leaned in as Mikey spoke.

"We have to eliminate these killers—but it's just as important that we send a message. We need to discourage others from doing the same to innocent children."

His eyes moved between them, ensuring they understood the gravity of what they were about to do.

Then, he unwrapped the parcel.

Inside, a calfskin holster lay neatly tied with leather thongs.

Mikey untied the straps, revealing a scaled-down machete—polished steel, gleaming under the light.

The blade was razor-sharp, smaller than a traditional machete or panga, but just as lethal.

The handle was wrapped in kudu hide, with an attached leather wrist strap.

Piet picked it up, testing its weight, his movements fluid as he swung it in chopping arcs.

His eyes darkened, his jaw tightening.

He was completely transfixed.

He swung again—and again—as if already picturing his target.

Then, his grip tightened around the handle.

His thumb traced the edge, his lips curling into a smile.

"This is how they will die."

His voice was low, almost a whisper.

His expression hardened, his face twisting with hatred.

"I will chop them up like they did my brother."

Boer and Mikey exchanged glances.

Piet's eyes had turned black with rage.

A dark, feral energy radiated from him.

He looked at the weapon in his hands, then closed his eyes, his smile deepening.

Mikey knew he had to break the spell.

"Uhm... well, I'm glad you like it."

He cleared his throat, shifting the focus back to strategy.

"Let's work on how to get to these two assholes."

He spread a map across the table, freshly printed from the internet, displaying the suburb where their targets lived.

****

Zane unlocked the door to the house and headed up the stairs toward the lounge area.

He had decided to start cleaning there first.

The counter held an empty whiskey bottle and a glass—Kallie's leftovers from the night before.

Beside them, he noticed a black tile dusted with traces of white powder.

Zane left it untouched.

He had no interest in getting his prints on it—or having any residue on himself.

Aside from that, the lounge looked fine. Not much needed to be done.

He gathered the glass and bottle, then walked down the passage to the kitchen.

Once inside, he sighed.

It was a mess.

Flour covered the counters, spread across almost every surface.

Zane opened the oven door and found half-risen bread—burned to a crisp.

On the stove, a pan held a half-eaten roll of fried sausage, also charred but still partially consumed.

Zane smirked, shaking his head.

Kallie must have gotten the munchies last night.

Too stoned to drive and get food, he had tried to make something himself—with disastrous results.

Zane picked up the pan, about to start cleaning, when he suddenly froze.

Something was off.

He replayed his walk through the house, realizing that when he had passed Kallie's bedroom, something hadn't felt right.

Slowly, he set the pan down and turned back toward the passage.

****

Combrink nodded at Oom Coenie as he approached the reception counter of the upmarket apartments.

He gestured upstairs, waiting for Oom Coenie to hand over the key.

Captain Terror had decided it was best to retrieve the camera before it was discovered.

Taking the key, Combrink entered the lift, pressing the button for a floor above Manzoni's.

Exiting the lift, he descended one flight of stairs to Manzoni's floor.

He pulled on latex gloves, then dialed Maria.

She was monitoring the camera feed from her office.

"All clear?" he asked.

"All clear," she confirmed.

Combrink glanced around, making sure no other tenants were nearby, before unlocking the apartment and stepping inside.

He quickly located the camera, removed it, then scanned the apartment for anything incriminating.

Nothing.

Satisfied, he locked the door behind him, then returned the key to Oom Coenie before heading out.

****

Captain Rikki Patel dialed Maria's cell phone.

"There are a lot of trucks arriving at the warehouse. More than usual. I think something's happening—you need to get out here."

For days, Patel had staked out the warehouse Maria had pointed out.

It had been quiet—only the occasional delivery van or kombi entering and leaving.

But in the last hour, four large enclosed trucks had arrived, disappearing inside.

The rolling doors shut behind them, blocking any view of what was happening inside.

Maria's voice sharpened.

"I think you're right. They're either moving in a massive shipment or clearing out. I have a search warrant pending. I'll get it and meet you there within an hour. Do you have the registration numbers of the trucks?"

"Yes, I do. What if they leave before you get here?"

268

"I'm sending a reaction team now. Captain Terror has people on standby."

Maria hurried into Terror's office, dropping into the chair across from him.

"Captain, Patel just reported heavy truck activity at Manzoni's warehouse. It could be a major shipment arriving—or they could be clearing out. We need to move now."

Terror nodded once, already reaching for his phone.

"Get your guys over there. No trucks leave. We're bringing a search warrant. Captain Patel is on-site—I'm forwarding you his number now."

He glanced at Maria, who was already dialing Combrink.

"Pieter, go get that search warrant from the magistrate. Manzoni's warehouse is active. Meet us there. The reaction squad is already on their way. No truck leaves. You know what to do."

Terror rose from his chair, strapping on his service pistol before grabbing his jacket.

"You drive."

****

Combrink checked his phone, considering Maria's last instruction.

He was still parked in front of the apartment building, not far from the industrial area where Manzoni's warehouse was located.

He made a decision.

Flipping through his contacts, he found the number he needed and dialed.

A female voice answered.

"Metro Media, Janke speaking."

Combrink took a breath and spoke carefully.

"Raid on Manzoni warehouse. Jetpark."

Chapter 47

Mackie, Boer, and Piet were in the Isuzu, slowly driving down Shirley Road. Boer sat across in the space behind the front seats of the super cab pick-up. He had the Nikon ready as they slowly passed the front of their target's house. He started taking photos as they approached, and seeing that the huge gates were closed, he concentrated on the upper floors of the double-story house.

Piet and Mackie looked straight ahead in case someone was watching for suspicious cars driving past. Two blocks further, Mackie parked next to the road, and Piet got out, starting to walk back in the direction of the house. Mackie and Boer viewed the photos on the camera's screen.

"Zoom in on that one. Is that a person standing at the top left window?"

Boer nodded. "Yes, it's a male. Quite young, I'd say. Drive around to the house that backs up to that one. Let's check it out. We might be able to see something from there."

Mackie put the Isuzu in gear and drove around the block. He stopped across the road from the house that backed up to the target's house. It was a single-story house, and they could see the top floor of Chukwu's house.

"Use the camera. The zoom will give you a better view. See if you can spot something."

Boer held the camera pointed at the house, and it wasn't long before Mackie heard the shutter noise of the camera.

"Okay, I got some pics to look at. We can go get Piet."

Mackie pulled away from the curb and drove around the block to pick up Piet, who was waiting on the corner. Piet got into the passenger seat, and Mackie drove off. He seemed very focused and hadn't been very talkative since they left the house an hour ago. Mackie had to prompt him.

"Did you see anything?"

Piet shook his head but didn't reply. Mackie glanced in the rearview mirror at Boer. He gave a small shake of his head.

"Piet, you can't zone out now, son. It'll take time to get the info we need. The more information you have, the better you can plan. You have to be patient, do you understand?"

Piet turned his head and looked at Mackie. "What if the cops get him first?"

"There's a risk of that happening, but I have a contact in SAPS who will give us the heads-up if they plan to move on Chukwu. Why don't you look at the photos on the camera in the meantime?"

Piet nodded and took the camera from Boer.

Mackie drove to an open field next to the old Joburg Road. He followed a dirt road until he was far enough from the houses. He turned the Isuzu around to face the way he had come. Taking a small pouch from his rucksack, he opened it and started assembling the drone he had removed from the pouch. He looked at the other two watching him and smiled.

"It's on loan from Oom Jack. Luckily, I've practiced a bit with it."

He got out of the pick-up and placed the drone on the bonnet. He opened the app on his phone, and it wasn't long before the drone started up and took off. He watched the live camera feed as he flew it to Chukwu's house about 100 meters away. Piet and Boer leaned over his shoulder to see.

"It's recording, so we can analyze the results later."

Mackie took the drone high enough to avoid attention. Hovering on the eastern side of the house, he adjusted the camera. He then flew directly over the house until they had a clear view of the yard in front of the garages. They saw several vehicles parked in the yard. He moved the drone to the other side of the house and got a view of an oval-shaped swimming pool.

Next to the pool were some beach chairs, and on one sat a figure bent forward with a cell phone to his ear. They could see it was a large African man. They could only see his head and his back. Mackie was tempted to fly closer, but the risk was too high of being detected. The last thing he wanted to do was alarm these killers. He moved the drone to the side of the house where they had seen the person earlier. Carefully, he edged from the end of the house around to where the windows were. Soon, they saw a lot of people sitting in front of computer screens. A few men and two women. They were intent on the screens in front of them and didn't notice the drone hovering outside.

Mackie maneuvered the drone until he was satisfied that he had recorded almost everyone there. He took the drone down to the front of the house to have a look and record the registration numbers of the cars there. He flew the drone to almost ground level and could see the number plates clearly. He noticed that the cars were mostly economy-class models. They probably belonged to the workers in the computer room.

He slowly took the drone around the side of the house and was shocked to see a young girl staring out of one of the windows. Her hands clutched the burglar bars, and she had a vacant look in her eyes. She didn't seem alarmed by the drone hovering in front of her. She had straw-colored hair, creamy brown skin, and blue-green eyes. She looked about ten years old, and she was crying. She gave a shy wave, and Mackie found it difficult to move away from her.

Mackie slowly took the drone higher and started returning it back to its landing spot on the bonnet. No one spoke while he folded up the drone and returned it to its pouch. They got into the pick-up, and slowly, Mackie drove back to their base.

Shocked at what they had seen, they didn't talk for the whole drive back to the smallholding.

****

When Maria and Captain Terror arrived at the warehouse, they saw it was surrounded by Tactical cops and some of their own guys. She stopped the car nearby and got out. Walking over to the leader of the Tactical squad, she handed him the search warrant.

"We will wait for you to breach the door and keep watch. We have to arrest everybody, even if you have to shoot anyone trying to escape—through the leg."

As far as she could tell, no one inside was aware of their presence outside, so the element of surprise was theirs. She moved to where Combrink, Patel, and Terror were gathering. Terror looked at her when she got near.

"Are they ready to go?"

"Yes, sir. We will watch the door while they go inside to block anyone from getting away. They will let us know when we can come in. I told them that Captain Rikki spotted four drivers with four co-drivers entering."

"Good. There will probably be a few more who work here. Pieter, can you stay on this corner and see if the guys at the back need any help?"

Combrink nodded and smiled excitedly. At last, they were taking action. It had been almost a year of watching, searching, and guessing. He walked over to the corner to take up his position—just in time, because the TAC guys were busy jacking up the steel door. The metal squealed and protested, but the two 4x4 jacks were very strong. It wasn't long before they had enough space to roll under, and within a few seconds, more than twelve of them had entered the warehouse.

Maria leaned down to see under the half-opened door. She spotted a loading platform stacked with hundreds of carton boxes and four trucks parked with their rears against it. Most of the people inside had their hands up, but one guy suddenly sprinted toward the door. He looked to be about forty years old and dove, rolling under the door when he got close. Maria reached for him, but Terror already had him around the neck, dragging him to the wall. Patel raced forward and slapped cuffs on him. Terror dragged him over to a streetlight pole and cuffed him to it.

The man looked at Terror and grinned. "The boss will have me out before the day is over."

Maria turned around and walked up to him.

"Are you talking about Manzoni? I've got news for you, asshole—he only cares about himself and his product. You'll find out how little you mean to him over the next few days. If I were you, I'd start thinking about cooperating with us. Remember, we can offer a deal, but there's only one, and it's on a first-come, first-serve basis. And at your age, you should really avoid going to jail. Can you serve ten years? Ask yourself that."

She turned her back on him and walked back to the half-opened door, squatting down next to Terror and Patel. They watched as, one by one, the people inside the warehouse were arrested. None of them put up much of a fight. They were just employees. And as expected, Manzoni was nowhere to be seen.

He never got his hands dirty.

Chapter 48

Brigitta held her face to the sun, enjoying the warm rays of the Bushveld on her skin. Cara sat in the shade on a rustic bench nearby, watching her friend soak up the African sun. They were taking a break before the next group arrived for pottery lessons. Cara looked around her and was once again astounded by how much they had accomplished since Mikey bought the rundown smallholding from old George Travis more than a year ago. It had become a very popular spot for tourists, and the locals had embraced it, with almost everyone promoting it as the new tourist attraction in the area.

In the short time they had it, they had started offering cooking classes, pottery classes, and wildlife education. The old house had been converted to include a real farm-style kitchen and dining area, as well as a large room with overhead projectors for educational lectures. Local plants had been planted all over the property, and recently, a small livestock farm enclosure had been built to teach visiting school kids about farm animals, allowing them to touch and pet them.

Two goats, two sheep, and a donkey were all they had so far, not counting Brigitta's chickens. They regularly rotated the animals with the ones they had at Lost Horizons. Brigitta had her own quarters at the back of the building, where she comfortably resided. She had yet to decide when to head back to France—if ever.

"Brigitta, I have an idea," Cara interrupted her tanning.

Brigitta opened her left eye and peered at Cara. When Cara did not expand on her idea, Brigitta turned toward her, her eyes questioningly exploring Cara's face.

"I want to invite the old guy for lunch."

"Cara mia, what old guy?"

"George Travis. The old guy that used to own this place. I'm sure he would be delighted to see what we've done with it. What do you think?"

Brigitta had never met him but had heard about the old man who used to own the smallholding.

"I wonder what kind of food he likes."

"I can find out from the old age home where he stays. They'll be able to recommend something. He can invite two or three friends as well. What do you think?"

"I think it's a wonderful idea. Will you wait till Mikey is back?"

Cara knew that eventually, Brigitta would bring the conversation around to Mikey's absences. She took a deep breath and slowly exhaled before answering.

"He'll be back soon, Brigitta. It's a job he has to do."

"He's gone a lot lately. Aren't you worried?"

Cara turned to her friend. "Why would I worry? He's training game rangers and will come home when the job is done. It'll be soon—you'll see."

Brigitta, herself recently divorced from a philanderer and distrustful of men, asked Cara, "You think he is with another woman, no?"

Cara laughed loudly and shook her head.

"No, I definitely know he's not. Mikey is in love with me, with life, and with this country. He has no place in his heart for another woman, silly. Let's get ready for the pottery class. I need to get back to Lost Horizons."

They got up to prepare to welcome the group of ladies eager to learn how to play with clay.

****

Mackie opened the can of Coke that Piet placed in front of him.

They had uploaded all the photos and recordings from the morning onto a laptop and had reviewed them over and over. Each had made his own mental notes and was ready to discuss what they had learned so far.

Boer went first. "I think the people upstairs in front of the computers are internet scammers. The cars we saw parked in the yard indicate that they don't live there. I'm certain the pretty girl we saw downstairs is there against her will. The guy we saw next to the pool could be Chukwu."

He looked at Piet, who had been very quiet since they returned. Piet looked up from the screen. "I agree with everything you said. If they can murder small boys, what stops them from kidnapping young girls? Do you think it's the white girl that disappeared from Dunottar—the one Jax confessed to?"

Mackie shook his head. "No, this girl isn't her. They wouldn't keep her this long—it's too risky. That was a white girl, and this one is of mixed race. But whoever she is, we need to get her out of there. She's clearly not happy to be there. We need a plan, and we need to act soon."

The group went quiet, each lost in his own thoughts. Boer cleaned his nails with a commando knife, waiting for one of the others to speak. Eventually, he returned the knife to its scabbard and looked across the table at Mackie. He decided to go first.

"We need to capture one of the guys who work there. We need information on who is there during the day and who stays after everyone else leaves. I think we should go watch the house now and see if we can nab one of them. If we can get someone with a car, it could help us get into the premises later."

Mackie thought it over and couldn't think of a better plan.

"Okay, let's formulate it as we drive. We'll need cable ties and duct tape. Boer, can you take the Z88? It's untraceable. Anything you want to add, Piet?"

Piet was already on his feet, his rucksack with his tools of the trade in hand, ready to go. He shook his head and smiled.

Mackie was glad to see him so focused and ready.

****

Felicity, John, and Lastborn gathered around Captain Dan's desk.

Dan had the phone they had confiscated from the vendor on his desk. He looked at his team seated in front of him.

"We've done very well with this investigation so far, but we need to arrest Chukwu and Aku before they find out we know about them and leave the country. We have a contact number

277

for the buyer that we've tried to trace, but the process is cumbersome, and we're going to lose them if we don't do something ourselves. Do you have any suggestions?"

They had all been aware of that fact, but no one had come up with a workable plan yet. They looked at each other and shook their heads. Felicity had an idea, but she wanted to give the Contractor as much time as possible.

"Captain, we have to be very careful not to alert these guys. We need to keep it to ourselves as long as possible if we don't want it leaked to the media. We could try sending a WhatsApp message to them, pretending to want to make a purchase, but if we don't get the wording right or ask for the wrong product, it might scare them, and they'll take flight."

"What do we do in the meantime?"

"We have to be patient and keep investigating. It's still possible that one of them might contact the vendor, and then we can take it from there."

She heard her phone ping and looked at the screen. It was a message from Maria. She read it and showed it to Dan.

'Raided Manzoni's warehouse in Jetpark. Arrested 16 and confiscated four trucks, computers, as well as millions of cigarettes. We're getting closer.'

It was followed by a laughing emoji.

Chapter 49

Zane entered Kallie's sleeping quarters.

It was a large room with huge bay windows. The king-size bed was unmade, and glasses along with a plate of leftover food sat on the table in the small sitting area. Above the bed, mounted on the ceiling, was a fifty-inch flat-screen TV. Leading off to the left was a massive walk-in closet that extended into an en-suite bathroom, complete with gold taps, heated rails, and a tub with water jets.

What had caught his attention from the passage earlier was the huge painting of a nude woman. Zane had seen photos of Kallie's ex-wife around the house and immediately recognized her as the woman in the painting.

The painting hung askew against a large column that supported the beam crossing the roof of the room. Zane moved the painting to the side and, behind it, saw a solid safe door. He carefully lifted the painting off the wall and placed it on the floor. Turning the handle on the safe, he was surprised to feel the heavy door slowly opening. He peered inside, and his mouth involuntarily dropped open. The safe was at least 500mm deep and a meter high.

Stacked from back to front on the top three shelves were massive bundles of R200 notes. Zane had never seen so much cash in one place. The bottom two shelves were filled with Rolexes, Breitling, and Patek Philippe watches of all shapes, as well as multiple packs of white powder. He shook his head, finding it difficult to comprehend what he was seeing.

He stared at it for a moment longer and decided to leave everything as it was. As he started closing the heavy door, shifting his weight to apply more strength, he noticed a strip of paper taped to the inside of the door. He paused, leaned in to look at it, and immediately realized what it was.

Taking out his phone, he snapped a photo of it. He carefully examined the inside of the safe and the door for any sign of alarm detectors or wiring. Satisfied, he closed the door and turned the handle back to its original position. He rehung the painting, stepping back to admire it for a few seconds. She truly was beautiful.

Before leaving the room, he took a final photo of the painting.

****

At 4:45 p.m., they were parked at the top of Shirley Road.

Mackie had the Google Maps app open and was studying the property and the surrounding houses. It would be very difficult to scale the walls or gate of the property without ladders or grapple hooks. The close proximity of the houses and the relatively busy street made it nearly impossible to get inside unnoticed. Most of the houses in the fairly upmarket suburb had palisade fencing in front, including the house across the road from the target house.

Mackie had changed position twice already and had once driven past the house. He had noticed a sign on the wall next to the pedestrian entrance gate.

It read: Mzoli Inc. Accountants.

No email, no phone number, and strangely, no bell either. Mackie realized this was just a cover, which he confirmed when he googled the company. It was clearly meant to fool the neighbors. The more affluent the suburb, the more the residents ignored each other, and Chukwu obviously knew this. As long as he paid his rent on time, the owners wouldn't bother him either.

Boer was using his monocular to watch for any movement in or out of the property. They expected the workers to start leaving soon. They had parked on the western end of Shirley Road, hoping this would be the route most of the workers would take to go home.

Piet kept a lookout for anyone paying too much attention to them while they sat parked in the empty street. There was hardly any traffic. He also had to help identify their target.

At precisely 5:01 p.m., Boer warned Mackie that the gate was opening. Mackie closed the app on his phone and started the Isuzu. He reversed into the driveway of the house where they were parked. Two people—a man and a woman—walked out of the gate first, heading in their direction. Soon, a VW Jetta nosed out of the gate, but there were two occupants, which would make it too tricky for them. It turned in the other direction anyway. Another car, a Toyota Tazz, approached but also had more than one occupant.

The next car to exit the gate was a Ford Fiesta with slightly tinted windows. It was only when it turned in their direction that they saw it had only the driver inside. As the car came closer, they saw the driver was an African man in his mid-thirties. Piet tapped Mackie on the shoulder.

"That's the one."

Mackie waited for the car to pass before turning out of the driveway to follow him, keeping a healthy distance. They could hear the booming hip-hop music coming from the car. They needed to hijack him soon, before he reached the highway. As they turned down the next road, Mackie saw a stop sign coming up ahead.

"Get ready. This is it."

He pulled past the Fiesta and cut in front of it, forcing the driver onto the pavement. Boer jumped from the passenger seat, allowing Piet to follow. The driver slammed on his brakes and got out, ready to confront the stupid white guy who had nearly crashed into his pride and joy. But he realized too late what was happening. As Boer approached, the driver panicked and tried to get back into his car, suddenly too afraid to take on the muscular man with the Z88.

Boer allowed him to slide into the seat but followed him in, nudging him over to the passenger side. Piet jumped in the back, behind the owner. Mackie was already on the move, confident that no one had witnessed the abduction—and those who had wouldn't have time to react. He couldn't believe their luck in gaining such easy access. They had planned to smash the driver's side window if necessary, but the car remained completely intact and undamaged.

Boer smacked the driver on the side of his face with his left hand, the Z88 still in his grip.

"Shut up and behave. We're from State Security. We just need information."

Mackie had taught them that it was better to calm the target, making him believe it wasn't all bad.

The man took the blow to the side of his face and leaned back against his seat. Too late, he felt the cable tie slip over his head, securing him to the headrest. He panicked and tried to pull free.

"Sit still! You'll suffocate yourself. We won't harm you if you behave. We're taking you somewhere quiet to question you, and then we'll release you."

The man calmed slightly and tried to glance behind him, but Piet rewarded the effort with a sharp slap to the ear. Boer looked in the rearview mirror and saw Piet grinning. He maneuvered the Fiesta onto the road and followed Mackie. Then, handing the Z88 to Piet, he glanced at their captive, who stared straight ahead, his bottom lip quivering slightly.

As they neared Lanseria, Boer turned to him.

"We're close now, but unfortunately, we have to cover your eyes. Our base is top secret. Do you understand?"

The man nodded, though he still jumped when Piet applied a double strip of duct tape over his eyes. Boer smiled, knowing the poor sod would lose some eyebrows when they ripped it off.

They followed Mackie through a gate and drove to the back of the building. Piet got out first, and while pressing the barrel of the Z88 against the captive's neck, he cut the cable tie. Boer came around, roughly grabbed his hands, and tied them behind his back with a fresh set of ties. They shoved him through the back door and forced him onto a chair in the garage. Piet tied his upper arms and legs to the chair.

Mackie walked in and stood behind their captive. Boer pulled up a chair and sat in front of him.

"What's your name?"

When the man refused to answer, Piet pulled his wallet from his back pocket.

"Petrus Sibongile Thoko. Thirty-seven years old. What do you do for Chukwu?"

The surprise on Petrus' face was evident. He lowered his chin to his chest, slowly shaking his head. Piet grabbed his hair, jerking his head up. Boer smirked at the tactic and glanced at Mackie.

Mackie took the Z88 from Piet and fired a shot next to the captive's head.

Petrus screamed like a slaughtered pig, writhing in his seat. He was berserk with fear for a few seconds before realizing he was still alive. His left ear had gone completely deaf.

He sobbed. "I can't, I can't. He'll kill me. That guy is an animal."

They let him calm down, knowing he was close to breaking. Finally, Boer leaned in.

"Well, Petrus... do you want to help us, or do you want to die today?"

Chapter 50

Jack saw his last WhatsApp message had gone through to Mikey.

He had been trying to get him to call back. Lofty and Godfrey had been asking about Duncan, and there had been unbelievable requests for the latest info they had posted on TRUTH. The media outlets they had given the passwords to were gobbling up the info.

Jack was curious to know how Duncan was doing and wanted to share the news of TRUTH with Mikey, but the main reason he was dying to talk to his friend was to tell him about his and Sweety's planned trip with the revamped school bus. They had named it Dorothy, and she came equipped with the latest technology. Jack had installed a hot water geyser, solar panels, and lithium batteries, as well as an induction cooker and fridge. The 3.0 TDI Ford Ranger engine and gearbox pulled like a train, and the difflock from the same crashed Ranger would get them through most bad roads. He had fitted brawny all-terrain tyres on old-style steel epoxy mags. In front were comfortable leather heated seats he had taken from a Pajero at the same scrapyard. The old Bedford bus had gotten a white, blue, and red spray job and looked very stylish with the map of Africa painted on the back.

Realizing he had to be patient, he still couldn't help worrying about his friend and Duncan. He zipped up his Cordura jacket and pushed his helmet onto his head. He looked back at Lofty, who was sitting in the driver's seat of the pickup, and gave him a thumbs-up. The other guys on their bikes were all ready to go. Dusty took the lead, and the group drove out of the Inn's parking area. They had a long trip ahead to Middelpos, where they would sleep over at the hotel there before heading down the Gannaka Pass the next morning through the Tankwa Karoo's rugged beauty on their way home.

They made their way toward Ceres, where the group of twenty-two would stop for breakfast.

Maria was finishing the report of the bust while Combrink, Patel, and Terror were interviewing the drivers and workers they had arrested the previous afternoon.

She walked over to where the holding cells and interrogation rooms were. She watched through the one-way glass of the first room and saw Terror and Patel interrogating one of the younger African drivers. She noticed Combrink exiting one of the other rooms and called him over. Seeing no one was around, she gave him a peck on the cheek.

"Has the older driver been interrogated yet? I'm talking about the one we caught trying to make a run for it."

"Alfons Da Mata. He's from Mozambique. I'm off to get him from the cells now. Terror wants to talk to him next."

"I want to be there. I will wait in that room. Bring him in and leave as soon as you have him shackled. I won't start without Terror." She pointed to the room he had just come from.

Maria went to the kitchen first and made three cups of coffee. She carried them to the interrogation room and put them on the table. She sat back and, while browsing through the docket, sipped her coffee. It wasn't long before Combrink brought Da Mata in and shackled him to the ring on the steel table. Maria passed him a cup of coffee and proceeded to read the docket, totally ignoring him. She noticed that he wasn't drinking the coffee immediately, but she knew the aroma would soon make him change his mind. He hadn't been fed since he was arrested.

She slowly paged through the docket. She knew he was a Mozambique citizen and was working in South Africa on some dodgy work permit. She had sent his details to a contact at Home Affairs the previous afternoon but hadn't yet received a reply. She noticed him dragging the cup closer and sniffing the coffee. It wasn't long before he took a sip. She pretended not to notice.

He had almost finished the coffee when Terror walked in and sat next to Maria. He looked over at her and winked. He passed her a slip of paper.

"We got a lot from the first guy, but I'm still holding out for more info. Shall we start?"

Maria closed the docket and looked at their captive.

"So, Alfons, I hope you enjoyed your last night's sleep in a bed with a mattress and your asshole still intact. You have probably been wondering if your boss has come to find out about you. I'm sorry to tell you he hasn't, and I will bet my month's pay that you will never hear from him again. He is probably already looking around for new drivers. Did you know that the trucks you lot were driving were leased from another company? He already has other trucks and drivers, meu amigo. The cigarettes he will write off, and he will just carry on as if nothing happened. To him, you are nothing."

She sat back and looked at him coolly, giving him time to think it through. She could see he was getting more and more agitated. Terror, not speaking at all, was just watching Da Mata intently.

Maria opened the docket folder and paged through it. She pretended to find what she was looking for and looked up at him.

"The work visa your boss got for you is also fake. Not only are you now illegally in South Africa, but you are an illegal criminal sitting cuffed and tied to a steel table in a cell being interviewed by the Hawks. Not the best place to be, is it?"

She saw she had hit a nerve. He couldn't meet her eye and looked toward the opposite wall. He was developing a twitch under his right eye, and sweat was starting to form on his forehead. Maria looked at the slip Terror had passed her earlier and now knew that this guy was more than just a driver for Manzoni. She continued talking, bending the truth a little.

"This is Terror Majoba, and he is head of the Hawks. The reason he is here is because he has the authority to offer you leniency. Who knows, you might be home in Maputo in a few days, amigo? We are giving you this one chance to become a state witness. The alternative, my friend, is a very long jail sentence. And it will be very far from here, I promise. Your bambinos and esposa will have to come visit you in Pollsmoor. I'm sure you've heard of that place where you share a four-man cell with ten of the worst gangsters the Cape Flats has ever seen.

You might survive one or two nights, but soon your rectum will look like jelly, and we don't care. It's cheaper for the taxpayers if you die soon after getting there. You and your boss have stolen enough from the taxpayers of this country with your illegal imports."

She drained her coffee and started gathering her items off the table. As she and Terror started to get up, Alfons cracked.

"I will tell you everything you want to know. I'm not going to jail for him."

Maria looked down at him and asked, "Are you talking about Marco Manzoni?"

"Yes, yes, him."

"Are you willing to testify in court?"

"If I live that long, yes, I will."

"We will put you in witness protection if we are happy with your testimony."

He looked down at the cuffs holding him prisoner and whispered, "I know a lot."

****

Petrus finished telling them about the internet scam and how it worked.

He knew the names of two guys who worked with him. He did not know their surnames or where they lived. They had been instructed by Farouk to address each other by an allocated number only. They started at ten a.m. and worked until five p.m. without a break. No one was allowed to roam. Their permitted area was the room with the computers, an adjoining kitchen with a coffee machine, and a bathroom. They arrived for work, parked in a designated parking spot, walked straight up the stairs at the back to the office, and started hustling. No one complained because the pay and commission were very good. Everything was paid in cash.

Boer was still the only one talking to him and asking questions.

"Have you seen any women or children around?"

Petrus shook his head. He was still blindfolded.

"I've heard screams on two occasions, but when I looked at the others, they just pretended not to have heard anything. I am the newest guy there and did not want to stir. The screams I heard were definitely female, but they were very faint."

"Do you know the layout of the building?" Boer asked. He noticed Mackie indicating to him that he already had that covered. Petrus answered hesitantly.

"I can draw you the areas that we are allowed in, but the rest of the house I do not know. The windows we pass to the stairs are always covered."

"What about Chukwu?"

Petrus looked perplexed.

"Chukwu? Who is that?"

"Your boss. The big Nigerian. The other one is Nasir."

Petrus looked genuinely surprised.

"We know him as Faro and the other guy as Nazzy. Faro comes into the office regularly, especially if someone makes a big score. He never talks, only walks over and watches the screens. We suspect he monitors our progress from another room. He always knows everything. That is why everybody is always on their best behaviour. I was interviewed by Nazzy and have never personally spoken to Faro, ever."

Mackie showed Boer it was time out, and he and Piet got up and walked to the kitchen. Boer got up and checked Petrus' binds.

"We will be back. In the meantime, think of anything that might help us and your case as well. Just chill. Ok?"

As he turned to follow Mackie and Piet, Petrus said, "The two of them leave at about one every day for an hour or so. We can hear when the V6 Toyota starts up. We think they go for lunch."

"Good. That might help us. You will be okay, Petrus. Just be patient. I will bring you something to drink and eat later. Do not try to escape. You will be shot."

"What about my money? It is payday tomorrow."

Boer ignored him and closed the soundproofed door behind him. He joined Mackie and Piet at the table. He saw Mackie had the parcel that was delivered by the woman on the table in front of him. Mackie looked at him questioningly when he took his seat.

"Did he say anything else?"

"Farouk and Nasir go out for lunch at about one every day, and tomorrow is payday. They get paid in cash."

"That is useful to know. I was hoping he could give us more info. Anyway, we will have to make do with what we have. I want to show you guys how to load and prime a cell phone with explosives."

Piet looked at Mackie and asked him, "Does this mean I am not going to use my panga to kill the murderer of my little brother?"

Mackie nodded.

"I'm sorry, Piet, but it is possible that you might not get the chance to kill him with the panga, but let me assure you, they will both die a horrible death, and you will still be the executioner. We have to prepare you for whatever chance you might get. If we are going to concentrate on one weapon only, we might miss other opportunities."

Piet seemed satisfied by this. Mackie started stripping down a fairly late-model cell phone, removing everything inside the covers. He detached the screen and fitted it back to the face with a few drops of superglue. He showed them how to pack the Semtex into the cavities and fitted a small battery that he soldered to the on/off switch. They watched him quietly, amazed by his dexterity with the fine wires and the small detonator. He clipped the cover back on and carefully placed the phone on the table in front of him.

"It is now live and will go off as soon as someone tries to switch it on. There is enough explosive to kill anyone within a meter of the phone."

Boer smiled and was delighted with what he saw. He slapped Piet on the shoulder.

"What do you say about that, Piet? It is foolproof, buddy. No one that I know of, finding a cell phone lying around, will resist trying to switch it on. Kaboom!"

Piet rubbed his face with both hands, and when he looked up at Mackie, he asked, "How much damage will it do?"

"I've never gone to look myself, but reports afterward indicate that most of the head gets blown away."

Piet liked what he heard and grinned from ear to ear.

Chapter 51

Dan read the email from the forensic lab.

He called Felicity on her cell phone. He could see her working at her cubicle through his office window. She answered and turned to look at him.

"The DNA from the jar is in. Are any of the others around?"

She looked over the partition that divided their workspaces and shook her head, looking back at him in his office.

"Just me. Lastborn is in Soweto with two constables to interview the neighbors again, and John is on his way to Rocky Road to interview the shopkeepers and other tenants."

"Come here. It's bad news."

She put her phone in her jacket pocket and got up from her chair. She walked the short distance to his office, and he indicated for her to close the door. She took a seat in front of his desk.

"The DNA from the jar is a match with the DNA we took from Busi Ntuli, Alfie's mother."

Tears formed in the corner of Felicity's eyes and started running down her cheeks. She looked at Dan and shook her head.

"These fucking monsters! They do not deserve to live."

Dan sighed and looked at her, waiting for her to get her emotions under control.

"We will have to tell her."

Felicity wiped her tears and blew her nose in a tissue that Dan offered her.

"I will do it. Can I ask Lastborn to come with me?"

Dan felt relieved and nodded his head.

"It would be best to tell her at home, where she has friends and hopefully family around her."

They became aware of a sudden commotion outside the door, and Dan got up to investigate. He was astonished to see people walking around amongst the cubicles where some of the detectives were working at their desks.

"Who are you?" he asked the person walking toward him.

The man flashed an ID at Dan and said, "I am Major Mzobe. We are from IPID. Where is Brigadier Rawlimi?"

"She is not here in the afternoons. Her office is over there, but it is locked. Her PA is also still on lunch."

Dan pointed down the passage to the offices and suite of Rawlimi and her PA.

"It is three o'clock. Why is she still on lunch?" he barked.

Dan looked at Felicity, who had joined the conversation. He was at a loss for words, not knowing how to answer the question. Felicity answered on his behalf.

"Sir, the Brigadier leaves at around one every day, and soon after, her PA follows and most days only returns after three. She hardly ever returns on time. She does not answer to anyone but the Brigadier. You will have to ask the Brigadier that question, and that will be tricky because she will only be back tomorrow at about nine a.m." She folded her arms and looked at him.

He turned to Dan and scowled.

"I have a warrant for her arrest and to search her office. Get hold of her."

He turned and indicated to two of his men to follow him as he headed down the passage. It wasn't long before Dan and Felicity heard the crunch of a door being kicked open. She turned to him and, with a mischievous grin, asked, "Captain Dan, may I have the honor of phoning our esteemed leader?"

He stepped into his office and handed her the Brigadier's cell phone number.

"Be my guest, Sergeant. It has turned out to be not such a bad day after all, you know?"

Maria dialed the number from the phone on Dan's desk. It rang for quite a while before Rawlimi answered it rudely.

"Yes, Captain. What do you want?"

Felicity said in a sweet tone, "Brigadier, it's Sergeant Booysen. There are some people busy going through your things in your office. I think you must come here right now."

"My office? Who gave them the right to go into my office? Who are they?"

"I've never seen them before, ma'am. Shall I tell them you are not happy?"

Dan was biting on his knuckle to keep himself from laughing. He walked to his office window and opened the blinds to watch the commotion outside in the passage. He saw agents arriving with empty cardboard boxes, walking toward Rawlimi's office. He could hear Rawlimi shouting over the phone from where he stood.

"Where is Julie? Tell her to chase them out of there!"

"She is still on lunch, ma'am."

"On lunch? It is three o' fucking clock. I will fire her, the useless white bitch!"

"Must I tell her when she gets back from lunch, ma'am?" She looked at Dan, who was holding his stomach. He was doubled over, still biting his knuckle, struggling to keep himself from screaming with laughter.

"I am on my way. I will fire everybody that I find in my office. Do you hear me? Go tell them!" she screamed before ending the call.

Felicity burst out laughing and looked at Dan. He was clearly having the time of his life.

"I suppose I better go tell the Major she is on her way and that she is going to fire him."

Dan started another fit of laughter, and through the tears, he motioned for her to go. She walked down the passage, making way for agents emerging from Rawlimi's office with filled boxes. She stepped into the office and gave a quick glance to where the camera was hidden, relieved to see it had not been discovered. The Major was seated behind Rawlimi's desk, opening drawers and piling the contents on the desk. Felicity's eyes widened when she saw some of the items on the desk and almost forgot what she was there for. The desk was scattered with all types of extremely expensive makeup, skimpy underwear, and right on top of the heap was a huge pink dildo and a purple vibrator.

"Major, I got hold of the Brigadier. She is on her way. She says no one is allowed in her office. She will personally fire anyone who is."

Major Mzobe sat back in the comfortable recliner and put his hands behind his head.

"What a pity. You should have told me earlier," he said with a huge grin. Another agent was under the desk, busy disconnecting the Brigadier's PC.

Felicity turned and walked out of the office back to where Dan was waiting for her. He looked up at her when she sat down.

"Should we let the others know?" he asked, his fist in front of his mouth, clearly battling to stop laughing.

"I will contact Lastborn and John and invite them for a drink after work. Where would you like to brief them, Sir?"

She let out a soft giggle.

****

Maria looked at the message she had received from Felicity. She quickly opened the app and watched the footage from Rawlimi's office. She immediately regretted her doubts about Colonel Mabulula. It looked like he was doing his job and not wasting any time in doing it. She sent Felicity a smiling emoji with a message.

'Can you get the camera out of there?'

'Yes, I'm waiting for them to finish up. They have arrested her and taken her away.'

Maria stayed in her car in the underground parking of her apartment building. She put her head against the window and closed her eyes. It had been a tough day for all of them. The information they had gotten from Alfons was dynamite. He had given them details of routes, procedures, and contacts. He had named the officials at Beitbridge on both sides of the Zim border, as well as the cops there and along the way, whom they could call or depend upon to look the other way. He had told them where and from whom he collected the documents needed to pass unchecked.

The cherry on the cake was when he told them that he had kept every load slip, permit, and document for every load he had brought over the border. He had given them other locations where he had dropped loads. He had even recorded some conversations he had with Manzoni regarding shipments and the contacts he had provided.

It was more than they could ever have hoped for. They had to put it all into context, draw up an arrest warrant, and see if the higher-ups approved it. With the state of corruption in South Africa, nothing was a given. Some people were just too well-connected politically to be prosecuted. She hoped that this would be enough to stop the import and sale of illegal cigarettes and put the culprits behind bars. If not, there was always TRUTH. She had to get all this information to them.

With a spring in her step, she walked up to her flat.

****

After cleaning up the kitchen and the lounge area, Zane went back to his room.

The wind had still not stopped blowing, and it had brought along more rain. He wished he had the day off to visit some friends. He contemplated sneaking off, but Kallie would probably need him later on. He picked up the book he had started reading the day before. The writer was Lee Child, and it was about an ex-army guy who became a drifter. Zane imagined himself hitchhiking through South Africa and the rest of the continent, experiencing one adventure after another. Helping people out of trouble and getting girls to fall in love with him wherever he went.

He couldn't help it, but his mind kept wandering back to the money in the safe. What could he do with that money? It must be millions! He shook the thought from his head and concentrated on the adventures of Reacher, the character in the book. Kallie would know if he took the money, and his life would be over. It wasn't long before he drowsed off under the warm duvet with the book on his chest.

Chapter 52

Mackie was on the Honda Africa Twin, parked down the road from Farouk's house, pretending to be looking at his GPS.

He had his helmet on and was keeping a close eye on the gate to Farouk's compound in his rearview mirror. Boer was parked at the bottom of the road on the other side of the entrance in Petrus' Ford Fiesta. It was close to lunchtime, and they were hoping these two killers stuck to the schedule that Petrus had sworn to.

Piet was sitting in the passenger seat with Boer. He was impatient and anxious. Mackie saw an elderly guy walking from the front. He had a very old Jack Russell on a leash and was slowly ambling along, allowing the dog to sniff and squeeze a few drops as they came along. When they got close to Mackie, the old guy lifted his hand in greeting.

"Good day. That's a fine-looking motorcycle you have there."

Mackie acknowledged his greeting and replied, "It sure is. I am still getting used to it. I got it yesterday."

The old guy looked the bike over, shaking his head in wonderment at the technology he was witnessing. The dog strained at the leash to get to the rear wheel of the bike, hoping to find more unfamiliar scents.

"Don't be daft, Chappie. Yer cain't piss on it. Did yer not hear he said it is still new?" The *new* coming out as *noo*.

Mackie smiled and, while keeping an eye on the mirror, looked the old guy over. He had to be from Scotland, he decided.

"Don't worry, it's what dogs do. Mine are constantly pissing on everything to mark their territory. I'm waiting for a mate of mine who's riding with me. We got separated, and I can't reach him on his phone. He probably doesn't hear it ring. I'll wait till he calls me. Are you out for a walk, or are you going somewhere?"

"Me wife said to take the old guy for a walk. I'm not sure if she was talking to me or to Chappie. You know, son, I used to ride as well. Me last bike was a Kawasaki Z900. Did you know it?"

"Yes, I do. I was actually on one in the eighties. It belonged to a friend, and he let me take it for a ride. At that time, it was the fastest I'd ever been on any bike. What happened to yours? It's worth a fortune now."

"I swapped it for an engagement ring in '81. I should have kept it instead of getting hitched. I'm sure it would have given me less shit," he laughed heartily. "I would definitely have ridden it much more. It's strange how the pussy gets less available after you marry it."

Mackie chuckled and checked his rearview mirror but still saw no movement.

"Do you live around here?"

The old guy pointed over the roofs of the houses. "Yes, on the other side of this block. Meself and the battle-axe. Our son wants us to go to the old age, but we cain't sell the house with the friggin' neighbors we have at the back. It seems even the Nigerians don't want to live near Nigerians. They run a... Wait, here he comes now. In the black car. I cain't stand the cunt."

Mackie saw the nose of the black Fortuner emerging from the gate and turning his way. He saw Boer slowly moving from the curb at the bottom of the street, ready to tail the Fortuner. The Fortuner slowly drove past them, and Mackie spotted two large black guys in the front. The one in the passenger seat was glaring at the old man as they went past. Mackie pretended to look at his phone and said to the old guy, "My friend just sent me a location where he is. It's been nice talking to you."

The old man took a step back and looked at Mackie, who noticed something change in his wise blue eyes.

"Yer been waitin' fer him, aven't ye?"

Mackie shifted the bike into gear and nodded at him.

"Go get the fucker, son." He grinned and gave Chappie's leash a tug.

$$****$$

The black Fortuner was heading toward Centurion.

Boer saw the headlight of the Honda two cars behind him and slowed down a bit. He noticed Mackie keeping his distance.

Up ahead, the Fortuner turned into the parking area of a roadhouse. Boer pulled to the side of the road and rolled down his window. Mackie stopped next to him and flipped his visor open. Boer pointed to the entrance of the parking area.

"They went in there. It's the parking area of Burger Box. Piet said this is where they went previously when he tailed them."

Mackie spoke through his open visor, his cheeks squeezed together by the padding of the helmet.

"I will go in and see. Dial my phone so we can talk. I will keep my helmet on for the time being."

His helmet was fitted with a Bluetooth device that allowed him to talk on his phone as well as to fellow bikers in his group when they did tours.

Mackie slowly rode into the parking area and spotted the Fortuner parked ahead. He stopped two bays behind it and answered his phone when it rang.

"They are parked near the entrance to the joint and are busy getting out of the car," he reported to Boer.

He watched them exit the car and walk toward the benches under the roofed area. They took a seat on one of the benches.

"They are seated to the right as you enter. The taller, leaner guy, whom I suspect is Farouk, is dressed in a blue and white tracksuit with white Nikes. The other guy, Nasir, is dressed in black tracksuit bottoms, black trainers, and a red t-shirt. He is shorter and slightly overweight. He was the driver. He looks very much like the guy who did the cutting on the video."

He saw a waitress approach the two killers with menus. She was a very attractive girl with red beads woven into her braids. Farouk immediately turned on the charm, and Mackie could see his gleaming white teeth from where he was sitting on the bike, about twenty meters away.

"The waitress is with them now. I'm going off the phone for a while to take off my helmet and find a seat nearby before I look too suspicious. I will call as soon as I'm seated. Come into the parking area, but stay in the car."

Mackie took off his helmet and put the side stand out. He removed his jacket and locked it in the top box with his helmet. Pulling his white short-sleeved t-shirt down over his jeans, he slowly walked to the restaurant, making sure he did not look in their direction. He walked up to the counter and, from the same waitress who had served Farouk, ordered and paid for a milkshake.

"I will be over there, at that bench," he said, pointing to an empty bench near Farouk and Nasir.

He walked over and sat down. Taking out his phone again, he dialed Boer's number.

"They are going to be here for a while, so make yourselves comfortable. I do not see any security cameras around here. See if you can spot any cameras where you are. Check Google Maps and familiarize yourself with the roads in the area."

Mackie went on Google Maps and did the same.

****

After the previous day's fun at the office, Dan had a spring in his step and couldn't wait to go to work. He couldn't help grinning while eating his cornflakes. His wife saw him grinning and slapped his hand.

"You must not let people at work see you grinning like that. It is unprofessional."

Dan smiled and wiped his mouth.

"Cynthia, I will never forget the sight of that woman being dragged out of the station in cuffs for as long as I live."

Felicity and Dan had hung around his office until Brigadier Flo returned. She stormed past his office to her own, her expensive handbag flapping behind her. They could hear her cursing and shouting at the top of her voice. Felicity had followed her into her office and later told Dan what had happened.

"Who the fuck gave you permission to be in my office?" she shouted at the Major, who was sitting behind her desk with the pile of makeup, lingerie, and sex toys right on top of everything.

She had looked angrily at her belongings and shut up for a few seconds but soon went on the attack again.

"I will have all of you fired. These are my personal belongings, and you have no right to scratch in my drawers. I am phoning the Commissioner right now."

She dug into her latest designer handbag for her cell phone, and as she pulled it out, the investigator standing behind her had taken it from her hands and pulled the handbag from her arm. Before she could protest, another detective had turned her around and clipped the cuffs on her. The Major placed the two warrants on top of her toys and calmly looked at her. He dumped the contents of her handbag next to the pile on her desk and flung the Gucci bag into the corner on the floor.

"This is a warrant to search this office, and the other is a warrant for your arrest. The charges against you will be explained later. You will be offered an attorney as well as a Union representative of your choosing. Right now, I advise you to think before you talk. The charges against you are very serious."

He looked at the two detectives holding her. "Take her away."

They turned her around and almost bumped into Felicity, who was standing behind the Brigadier. She looked at Felicity with hatred and shouted at her.

"You are betraying me. I am your leader!"

Right at that moment, Julie returned from a long shopping lunch and was coming down the passage. Flo had spotted her and lost the last bit of control she had left.

"And where do you think you come from, you fucking white slut? I will have you fired, you useless bitch!" she had shouted as the two investigators dragged her downstairs past all those who had gathered to witness her humiliation.

Some had the courage to clap their hands. Her rudeness and uselessness had been tolerated for too long at Diepsloot. Julie had been motioned into the office, and the Major had interviewed her behind closed doors. Her computer and diary had also been taken for scrutiny. Her cozy job at SAPS was also at an end.

Dan and Felicity had watched from his office window as the Brigadier was loaded into the car below before the whole procession drove out the gate.

Chapter 53

Boer and Piet were parked two spots behind the Fortuner.

He looked over at Farouk and Nasir and saw they had finished their burgers and chips. They were sipping the last of their Cokes.

Mackie phoned Piet, who answered immediately.

"Do it."

He saw Piet get out of the car and go stand next to the Fortuner, pretending to speak on the phone. He had the dead phone to his ear, and Mackie couldn't help but wonder if he wasn't afraid with all that explosive so close to his head. Piet kept an eye on the two killers while pretending to have a conversation.

They were finishing their drinks while the waitress put Farouk's card through the machine to pay for their meal. Mackie heard Farouk trying to get a phone number from the waitress, but she was far too wary of him.

Mackie was astonished to hear him say, "Well, in that case, I cannot tip you."

She took it in her stride and returned to the kitchen. They got up, ready to leave. Mackie had expected one or both to use the restroom before leaving and motioned for Piet to stay where he was. They couldn't afford to let the phone fall into innocent hands.

Once he saw them walking toward their car, he gave Piet the signal. Piet placed the phone on the ground next to the driver's door and moved away from the car. He walked to where Boer was parked and got into the Fiesta. They had a clear view of the driver's side of the Fortuner and watched as the two killers approached their car. Using the remote, Nasir unlocked the doors. Farouk peeled off to the right to get into the passenger seat while Nasir moved to the driver's side.

Just before he opened the door, he looked down. He immediately started scanning the parking area to see if anyone was watching him. He quickly dipped down and picked up the phone. Without hesitation, he opened the door and got inside. He started the car and pulled out of the parking area in a hurry. Boer and Piet could see them laughing about something. Piet was shaking with fury and muttered under his breath.

Boer followed them as they turned onto the road leading back to Eldoraigne. He kept a few cars behind them to stay safe. The road was quiet, with a few cars approaching from far behind and some traffic coming from the front, still a distance away. He glanced at Piet, who was intensely focused on the vehicle in front of them.

"When do you think it...?"

The explosion ripped through the Fortuner. All the windows blew out, and the roof peeled open like a can of beans. The vehicle bounced into the air and veered off to the left, mounting the curb before slamming into a palisade fence, where it finally came to a standstill. Boer slowly moved closer and saw blood and brain matter running down the outside of the doors. Smoke drifted from the blown-out windows, and Boer did not expect any survivors.

"Stop, stop! One of them is still moving!" Piet yelled.

Boer checked his rearview mirror and the road ahead. There were no cars nearby. He stopped the car, and Piet jumped out, machete in hand.

"Go, go! I will go to Mackie on foot. Go now!" he shouted.

Boer realized he couldn't be seen at the scene of the explosion and slowly drove off. In his rearview mirror, he saw Piet walk around to the passenger side of the Fortuner and yank the door open. Boer almost felt sorry for the survivor. For his sake, he hoped he was already dead. He turned down the next road, drove three blocks away, and parked.

His phone rang. He answered it.

"I heard the explosion."

"It was spectacular, but Farouk was still alive. Piet is dealing with him. He told me to go, and he'll make his way to you on foot. I'm parked a few blocks away. Do you want me to wait here?"

"Go back to their house and wait nearby. We still have to get in there as well. I'll wait here until Piet arrives. I have a spare helmet for him."

Mackie called the waitress over and ordered a cheeseburger. She took his empty glass away and cleared the table where Farouk and Nasir had just had their last meal. She looked at him from where she was loading the tray.

"Was that an explosion? Did you hear it?"

Mackie shook his head. "It might be Zama Zamas blasting for gold. They're doing illegal mining all over the place now."

She headed off to get his order, and when she passed him, he asked her to prepare two more burgers for takeout.

He sat back and waited.

****

Maria stood in front of Terror's desk. He was on his feet.

"It is as you expected. Nobody wants to make a move on Manzoni and his friends. Apparently, we need more evidence. Can you fucking believe it?"

Captain Majoba was visibly upset that all their hard work and evidence had been deemed insufficient.

"I have forwarded all the evidence to Colonel Regina. At least Commercial Crimes is still working on it, and they are talking to Leslie Watson from SARS, who is handling it on their side. SARS will not make a move until they are absolutely sure of their evidence, but when they do, it will hold up in court. We have to keep plugging away and be patient."

Maria waited for him to take his seat before she passed him her phone.

"Have you seen these media reports on the raid? It almost feels as if they know more than we do."

He took the phone from her and scrolled through the news items. He looked up at her and, with a sly wink, asked, "Do you know anything about the videos of the party at the apartment doing the rounds?"

Although she had seen it and forwarded it herself many times, she asked Terror, "Do you want copies, Sir? I can send them to you."

He laughed and shooed her out of the office.

"Before you go, Maria, I have to share something with you. Patel has applied to stay with us, even willing to take a demotion. Guess who put a stop to that?"

Maria pretended to think about it for a moment and then answered, "Could it be our esteemed Colonel Diba?"

He raised his hands and shrugged his shoulders. "Who else?"

Maria wasn't worried. Colonel Diba was the one who had decided not to proceed against Manzoni. He would find out soon enough that Colonel Regina Ngoro was also in possession of the evidence.

On top of that, Patel had recorded some of his secret meetings with Diba, and Terror was ready to hand it over to IPID as soon as the time was right.

Chapter 54

The BMW M5 fishtailed out of the corner, speeding up the on-ramp from Mike Pienaar Boulevard.

Kallie had his foot flat on the accelerator, and the technology built into the high-tech car corrected the spin, shooting it up the hill, hitting 180 km per hour before entering the N1 highway. His passengers egged him on as the car accelerated like a rocket ship. All four were high. They had been drinking Jack Daniels all day and sniffing line after line of coke that Kallie had provided at Funani's house in Bellville.

Captain Funani was sitting in front with Kallie, while the two brothers, Rashaad and Shafique, sat in the rear. They were laughing at Funani's antics as he rocked forward and backward, pretending to make the car go faster. He hadn't bothered with a seatbelt. Neither had the two in the back, feeling invincible. Rashaad passed the Jack Daniels to his brother. If their mother could see them now, she would have smacked both of them. As Muslims, they were not allowed to drink alcohol.

The BMW crested Tygerberg Hill, and Kallie looked down at the speedometer. They were doing 295 km per hour. He knew he had to slow down for the turn-off to his house, but he wanted to see 300 on the speedo, so he kept his foot down. Too late, he saw a car in the center lane change lanes and end up 100 meters in front of him, directly in his path.

His reactions, dulled by the alcohol and the drugs, were too slow. Panic set in. He slammed the brakes so hard that the anti-lock brake system lagged for a split second, causing the tail to step out. Kallie overcorrected and hurtled toward the concrete blocks in the center of the highway. The BMW's right front fender struck the angled block and began climbing it. The momentum launched the car up and over. It rolled mid-air before crashing down on its roof in the center of the oncoming lanes, narrowly missing the approaching traffic.

The car skidded along the highway on its flattened roof, scraping across all five traffic lanes. It launched up the ground embankment, hitting a eucalyptus tree and a barbed wire fence. Sparks from the roof ignited the ruptured petrol tank, and the car exploded into a red ball of flames. The occupants were too injured or dazed to do anything about it. Soon, the smell of burnt flesh and petrol smoke hung over the road, drifting over the vehicles that had been forced to swerve and stop.

No one exited from the wreck.

****

Mackie saw Piet walking into the parking area and signaled for him to go to the bike. Piet changed direction and walked toward it, standing nearby as he waited. He seemed calm. Mackie phoned him.

"Yebo," Piet answered pleasantly.

"Are you okay, buddy?"

"I feel great. Oom Mackie, you should have seen that pig bleed. I cut his nose off and then his one ear. Unfortunately, the other one was already missing. He was begging for mercy. The whole time I cut him, I told him it was his payment for the little boys they mutilated. I wish I had more time with him, but too many cars stopped nearby. I slit his throat and walked away. The driver had half his face blown off. He reminded me of a Half Smiley. You should have seen it!"

A Half Smiley was a sheep or goat's head, cut in half and grilled over hot coals—a delicacy in the townships.

"Okay, I'm glad you feel fine. It can sometimes be hard to stomach."

"I'm okay."

"I just want to make sure no one is watching either of us. Stay by the bike, but be ready to move if I tell you."

Mackie took a big bite of his burger and listened to the sirens of police and ambulances screaming past. He licked the burger sauce from his fingers.

"Too fucking late for that party."

He finished his burger and wiped down all the surfaces he had touched with a napkin. Then, he motioned to the waitress to bring the bill. She walked over with the two takeaway burgers and the card machine. She placed the two brown bags on the table in front of him and held out the machine.

"Tap or insert?" she asked.

He took cash from his pocket and handed it to her.

"Here you go. Keep the change."

She smiled broadly and thanked him for the generous tip. Handing him his receipt, she glanced toward Piet, who was still standing by the motorbike.

"Is one of these burgers for that guy?" she asked.

Mackie looked at her and nodded.

She slipped a note into one of the bags and made a cross on it with her pen.

"Will you please make sure he gets this bag?"

She turned and walked away with his empty plate. Mackie glanced toward Piet and whistled softly.

"He's not too bad looking from here, I suppose."

He removed the note from the bag and slipped it into his jeans pocket.

"No time for love. Not yet."

****

In Cape Town, on the slopes of Tygerberg Hill, ambulances and police had arrived at the scene of the burned-out BMW M5.

The fire brigade had been unable to make its way through the log-jammed traffic in time to extinguish the flames. The car was completely burnt out. The fancy perspex vanity number plates had melted and burned into clumps of black soot. The color of the car was no longer visible. The only way to identify it would be to get to the engine and check if the VIN could be recovered. That would take a while, as the damage from the accident would not allow the bonnet to be opened anytime soon.

The arguments between the tow truck drivers began to subside when it dawned on them that not one of them would benefit from the accident. People had died in the wreck, meaning it had to be towed by a police breakdown to their yard for further investigation and to remove the charred bodies of the four occupants.

One of the breakdown drivers spotted a bottle lying near the car. He picked it up and held it aloft. There were still a few tots of Jack Daniels left in the bottom.

He handed it to a policeman standing nearby.

****

Zane woke up and realized he had fallen asleep on the couch with the book on his chest.

He picked up his phone and checked the time. It showed 10:15 p.m. He shook his head to get rid of the drowsiness and listened for sounds upstairs. It was eerily quiet, and the usual sounds of Neil Diamond, which Kallie liked to blast in the evenings at full volume, were absent. Zane was sure the neighbors were very relieved.

He wondered where Kallie was and realized that it was possible he had stayed over for the night wherever they had partied. He would probably be back in the morning with a massive hangover. Zane hoped he would just sleep it off. It was still cold and windy in Cape Town—not a day for work. The wind, born in Pringle Bay, rushed through the natural vortex created by Table Mountain and Tygerberg Hill, blowing ferociously.

He phoned Mr. Delivery and ordered a pizza. Picking up his book, he quickly became engrossed in the adventures of Reacher. It wasn't long before he heard the chime of the gate.

He opened it with the remote and went outside to collect his supper.

Chapter 55

Mackie stopped the bike in front of the Fiesta, and he and Piet got into the car with Boer.

"How did it go, Piet?" Boer asked.

Piet leaned back with his arms thrown over the back of the seat.

"It went chop-chop, Boer," he said with a grin.

Boer looked at Mackie and shook his head.

"As cold as ice."

Mackie smiled and turned in his seat to look at his two friends.

"It's almost over. You two need to get inside and find their cash stash. Try not to be seen, but if you are, pretend to be friends of Farouk. Tell anyone who asks that you have a meeting with him in fifteen minutes and that you'll wait. Get into the house and search Farouk's sleeping area. Look for a safe, take a photo of it, and forward it to me. I'll advise you on what to do.

Boer, you need to get in the back and lie on the floor while Piet drives in. Piet, if the guard at the gate questions you or refuses entry, tell him you're standing in for Petrus today. If he doesn't buy that, tell him you need to show him the files in the boot that Farouk requested. Boer, you slip out the back, subdue him, and tie him up. Get his remote from him. Any questions?"

Piet asked, "Where will you be?"

"I'll be at the property behind theirs. I made a friend who lives there, and I'm sure he won't mind if I launch the drone from there. Wait for my instructions before you move in. My burner phone is on."

Mackie got out of the car, put on his helmet, started up the bike, and rode around to the old Scotsman's house.

****

Felix, the guard at the gate, heard a car honk and looked through the slot in the gate.

He recognized the car and opened the gate. He had been in the middle of searching Gumtree for a car to buy and resumed his search without bothering to look at the driver. He went back into the small Wendy house that served as his office, not noticing the drone hovering about ten meters above him.

Mackie watched as first Piet, then Boer, got out of the car and went up the stairs to enter the house. He slowly guided the drone around the property to make sure there were no surprises.

Boer walked ahead of Piet, going straight from the vast lounge into the kitchen, where he heard someone working. He motioned for Piet to wait and keep watch on the front door and the stairs. When he entered, he saw two elderly Black women standing around a huge butcher's block, preparing vegetables. He greeted them politely.

"Molo, mama. I'm waiting for Mister Farouk in the lounge. He's on his way back from lunch. Can you make me some coffee, please? I take sugar and milk. A sandwich would also be welcome. Thank you."

He needed to keep them in the kitchen for as long as possible while Piet searched for the cash upstairs. He saw that both women accepted his presence without suspicion. The younger of the two walked over to the counter and switched on the coffee maker. He signaled Piet to start searching the house.

Boer walked back to the lounge, keeping an eye on both the front and kitchen entrances while meticulously searching the area. The house was sparsely furnished and contained nothing of personal value, making it easy to search.

Piet had reached the upper floor without encountering anyone. He saw that only two of the four bedrooms were furnished and assumed the larger one belonged to Farouk. He checked under the bed and lifted the mattress. Moving to the desk in the corner, he searched through the drawers and underneath. Then, he entered the walk-in closet and pushed the clothes on their hangers aside, looking for any sign of a safe. He opened the drawers and cupboard doors, then moved to the en-suite bathroom, even lifting the lid of the toilet cistern.

Finding nothing, he returned to the dressing room.

He scanned the space, searching for anything he might have missed. Something caught his eye on the ceiling, and he took a closer look. Faint smudges marked one of the ceiling panels. He pulled the ottoman closer and climbed onto it. Carefully, he pushed against the ceiling tile and slid it aside. He reached into the space and felt around. His fingers brushed against something. Gripping it, he pulled. It was the strap of a sports bag.

He took it down and unzipped it. The bag was filled with used currency, mostly R200 notes.

Zipping it closed, he shifted the tile back into position, making sure to leave no trace of disturbance. He stepped off the ottoman and returned it to its place.

As he entered the bedroom again, he noticed a drone hovering outside the window. With a huge grin, he held the bag aloft and showed it to Mackie. Then, he quickly moved down the stairs, hearing Boer talking to someone.

Peeking over the banister, he saw Boer accepting a tray from a woman in domestic attire. Piet waited until she returned to the kitchen, then descended the stairs.

Boer spotted the bag in his hand. He took a quick sip from his coffee cup, then set it back on the tray before following Piet outside.

"Is that it?" he asked as they made their way down the veranda steps.

"Lots of moola, Bra Boer. Full to the brim."

Piet was clearly delighted. He started heading down the stairs, but Boer grabbed his arm and pulled him behind a pillar.

"Wait. I have a call coming in."

He answered the phone and heard Mackie's voice.

"Are you still undetected?"

"Yes, and we have a bag full of cash."

"Okay, get into the car and wait until you see the security guard step out of his office and open the gate. Drive straight out of there. I'll meet you back at HQ."

"Will do."

He put his phone back into his pocket and relayed Mackie's instructions to Piet.

"I'll drive. We can't risk you getting caught driving without a license at this stage."

The security guard heard someone knocking on the gate. He put his phone down on the table and went to check.

Peering through the slot, he saw a guy on a motorcycle sitting in front of the gate, helmet on.

He scowled. "What do you want? This is private property."

"Farouk sent me. He and Nasir are parked around the corner with a flat tire. He says you must come and help them fit a spare. And you must fucking hurry up!"

The biker revved the engine and disappeared down the street.

Felix hesitated, uncertain. He knew Farouk had a violent temper and wouldn't be happy if ignored. Despite his unease, he grabbed his phone from the desk and opened the gate.

He had walked a few meters down the road when Petrus' car slipped out of the compound, heading in the opposite direction.

Chapter 56

Felicity showed her phone to Dan.

"Look at this. It's all over social media."

He took the phone from her and looked at the videos posted of Manzoni and his associates. Scrolling down, he saw reports and pictures of Rawlimi and the arrest of a policeman in Limpopo in connection with a stolen police docket linked to her and Manzoni. He smiled when he came across the video of the party at the flat, showing Sehloho groping the prostitute. He passed the phone back to Felicity.

He gave her a knowing look.

"I wonder who leaked all of this. Do you know, perhaps?"

Acting indignantly, she placed her hand on her hip and replied, "Captain Dan! Are you accusing me of the leak?"

Avoiding his eyes, she put her phone back into her pocket.

"What do you think will happen now?" she asked.

He leaned back in his chair, placing his hands behind his head.

"Mmm, I think it will have to be investigated. Now that it's out in the media, it will be almost impossible for them to sweep it under the carpet. It might actually be a good thing, you know?"

"I agree. Are we still keeping the vendor's stall going?"

"Yes, we have to until we have everyone in custody. Her fellow stallholders were told that her nephew is watching her stall while she visits her sick aunt. We have to find Farouk soon."

Felicity nodded and set herself a reminder to tell the Contractor to get a move on.

"What will happen now that Rawlimi is gone? Who will take her place?"

"I don't know. They could send someone from another division to take over. But one thing I do know—whoever it is, they can't possibly be worse than her."

Before Felicity could respond, she heard her phone beep. It was a message from the Contractor.

'Car exploded in Eldoraigne. F and N. Go to the double-story house in Shirley Street, Eldoraigne. Gate is open. All Farouk's *hackers are there, plus a very young girl and some illegals. I will forward you some video footage later that will support your case. Tik-tok. Tik-tok.'*

Felicity placed her phone in her handbag and, very calmly, turned to Captain Dan.

"I know where Farouk is. Please come with me immediately and ask Lastborn and John to meet us in Shirley Street, Eldoraigne. They must bring the Constables with them if possible. I will explain on the way."

She stood up, and with Dan in tow—still struggling to get into his jacket—she headed out of the police station.

****

Mamello had his phone to his ear and was pacing the room.

He was shouting like a crazed man, demanding answers while at the same time screaming threats at Manzoni.

"I will kill you! I will kill you! How dare you record me? Do you know who I am? I can take you out anytime I like. I have people who will kill you for nothing. For nothing, I tell you! You come to my country, you make money, and now you tape me? Hey wena, you are a dead man. Dead, dead, dead!"

Spit flew from his mouth, and he had to wipe his phone. When he placed it back to his ear, he realized Manzoni was no longer on the other end. He let out a furious growl and threw the phone across the room, watching as it shattered against the opposite wall.

Immediately, regret set in as he stared at the broken pieces.

His eyes shifted to Sehloho, who sat unperturbed on the couch, watching a video on his phone. He was clearly enjoying the footage of himself with the prostitute—it was the third time he had watched it.

"Sehloho, what the hell are you smiling for? This is serious shit, wena! My wife wants an explanation. She'll be home any minute. What am I supposed to tell her? What am I supposed to tell the voters? How the hell do I explain why we're partying and screwing around with white women? No black woman will ever vote for me again! I tell you!"

Sehloho got up from the couch and slipped his phone into his pocket. He headed for the door, but Mamello grabbed his arm, stopping him in his tracks.

"Where do you think you're going?" he demanded, still gripping Sehloho's arm.

Sehloho jerked his arm free and walked away.

"It's your wife, bra. I'm not married. I'm not sticking around to listen to you two fight. Leave me out of it."

"You are my lieutenant! You are my friend! I demand that you stay here!"

By now, Mamello was nearly foaming at the mouth, his eyes bulging from their sockets with uncontrollable rage. He knew his diminutive size was no match for Sehloho, who was much taller and stronger than him. Helplessly, he watched as his trusted friend abandoned him to face the music alone.

He walked over to where his phone lay in pieces on the floor, gathering up the shattered remains. Realizing it was beyond repair, he hurled the fragments onto the table.

Storming outside, he shouted for his bodyguards. He needed a phone—he had to call Manzoni again. This was all his fault, and he had to fix it.

Just then, he spotted Sehloho's Mercedes AMG exiting through the gate.

He cursed under his breath.

"Sifiso! David! Where are you?" he bellowed for his bodyguards.

He circled the house, but there was no sign of them. Only then did he remember that he had sent them earlier to pick up his cut from the tender he had arranged for the diesel supply to the municipality.

At that moment, he heard the gate open at the front of the house. His heart leaped with hope—it had to be them.

But as he rounded the corner, he stopped dead in his tracks.

His wife's black BMW X3 rolled into the driveway.

His stomach twisted. She was livid.

She looked at him through the side window as she drove past, her expression that of a woman ready to crush a cockroach.

Mamello shook his head, tears of frustration spilling freely down his cheeks.

How had it come to this?

What had he done to deserve this?

Chapter 57

Mackie took beers from the fridge and handed two to Piet and Boer.

They popped the tops and each took a long pull from their bottles. No one had spoken since Piet and Boer had returned to the smallholding. Mackie had checked on Petrus and given him some water when he got home. He was holding up well and seemed content, especially after Mackie told him he would be released soon. He finished his beer and placed the empty bottle on the table. He had been observing both Piet and Boer since their return and was relieved to see that neither seemed troubled by what they had witnessed that day.

"We need to get Petrus out of here. Boer, will you drive his car with him inside while I lead on the bike? Follow me until I stop, then leave him there. Tie his hands in front of him, keep the blindfold on, and put this carpet blade in his hand. By the time he frees himself and gets the blindfold off, we'll be long gone. We'll stop on the way to pick up some meat—I think we need to relax with a braai this evening. We can discuss what we want to do next. Is everyone happy with that?"

"What must I do while you guys are away?" Piet asked.

Mackie turned to him with a smile. "You, my young friend, can count the money, and when you get tired of that, you can get wood ready for the braai. We should be back in about forty-five minutes."

Piet rubbed his hands together and grinned. "I can do that."

Mackie dug into the bag and took out two thick bundles of R200 notes. He handed them to Piet.

"Here, shove this into his pocket. It's about twenty grand. Let him take a piss before you leave. Get the blindfold on properly and get him into the car. Be sure to warn him that he must behave, or he won't be set free. Tell him to stop his internet shit—we will be watching him. Under no circumstances must he ever return to the address in Eldoraigne or talk to anyone about this. I'll wait on the bike. I have a spare helmet for you, Boer."

Piet took the stack of notes to the garage, where Petrus was still tied to the chair. He greeted him cheerfully, waving the stack of cash.

"Payday, Petrus."

****

Maria and Combrink entered Majoba's office.

She closed the door, and they sat down. Rikki Patel was already seated, watching them arrive. Captain Majoba was smiling widely, his excitement evident.

"I just received an alert from OR Tambo airport. Mrs. Manzoni has boarded a plane for Rome with a shitload of luggage. Looks like she's not coming back."

Maria glanced at Combrink and nodded. He tapped on the desk with his finger.

"And I've heard that Colonel Ngoro is on her way here to speak to all of us. She couldn't get through to your phone, Captain, so she reached me. She asked that we all be present when she arrives in an hour."

Terror clapped his hands together. "How can this day get any better? Tell me."

Maria smiled, looking from one person to the other. "How about this? I heard from Sergeant Booysen that when they raided the house Farouk—now known as *the Deconstructed*—used for his shenanigans, they not only netted five hackers and three illegals, but they also found a very young, blue-eyed girl locked up in the basement. She could possibly be the girl who went missing on the West Coast in the Cape a while ago. She's very traumatized but physically okay. She told Felicity her mother sold her to two Nigerian men. She's at the hospital now, where they're checking her out. It's suspected that she may have been raped. And now for the grim part—unfortunately, they also found human remains in a deep freeze in the garage. It appears to be from a small child or children. They won't be able to analyze it until it thaws."

No one spoke. They all sat in silence, lost in their own thoughts.

After a long moment, Terror said, "It's a pity the killers are dead. They should have paid for their sins by sitting in jail for the rest of their lives."

Maria shook her head.

"No, Captain, I don't agree. They got what they deserved. With our justice system, they would have dragged it out for years, gotten bail, and probably left the country at the first chance they got. Besides, from what we can tell, Farouk was tortured while dying. His nose and ear were hacked off before his throat was cut. Clearly the work of a vigilante."

Or the Contractor, she thought to herself with a smile.

* * * *

Mackie signaled to Boer that he was taking over the controls.

They were nearing King Phalo Airport and would be landing soon. There, they would see Piet onto a taxi that would take him to his aunt's village. He sat quietly in the rear of the Beechcraft, his new rucksack stuffed with his fifty percent cut of the loot—*Justice Payment*, as Mackie called it. After about twenty minutes in the air, Piet had overcome his initial fear of flying and was now completely at ease.

"What are you going to do now, Piet?" Boer asked. Mackie had given Piet a spare headset.

Piet gave a shy smile and fingered the piece of paper Mackie had handed him after they returned from releasing Petrus.

"I'm going to visit my mama and make sure she's cared for. My aunt wants her to stay in Transkei. Next week, I turn eighteen and will go for my license. Then, I'll go back to Joburg to finish my matric. I spoke to the couple I rent from, and they're keeping the room for me."

Mackie smiled as he prepared to descend.

"And?"

"Then I'll take my car and see if I can impress a girl who works at a burger place. If she agrees, we'll drive to Cape Town to visit you."

Mackie looked at Boer and asked, "What are your plans?"

"I'm going to get my bike from Oom Jack and go on a long ride. With my half of the money we took from the killers and what I already have, I won't have to work for a very long time."

"Jack is picking us up from the airfield. I'll stay over for the night and fly home tomorrow. I need to figure out how to get back to the smallholding to collect the Isuzu and the bikes. Thanks for helping me load them. Remember, anytime you want to visit, I'll have a bike for you."

Mackie was missing Cara and the life he had created with her on their holiday farm. He was tired of being the executioner for those who thought they could hurt others and get away with it. When he started this journey almost thirty years ago, it had been about the money and some justice. Over time, it had become like a drug that kept him going. But that changed four years ago when he met Cara.

He looked at his two new comrades-in-arms and hoped they would take up the cause.

There were still too many evil bastards who did bad things and got away with it.

There would always be a need for vigilante justice.

Chapter 58

Boer approached his flat in Parow on his bike.

He had a quick beer with Oom Jack and Mackie and had promised to be back later for supper with the two of them and Sweety. He opened the garage door and pushed the bike inside. Taking his helmet and the sports bag with the money they had taken from Farouk's house, he headed inside. It was more than three hundred thousand rand. The rest of the money, he had left in a safety deposit box in Joburg.

He carefully looked around before unlocking his front door. Entering the musty-smelling flat, he dumped the bag and helmet on the kitchen table before opening a few windows to let in some fresh air. He grabbed a beer from the fridge and noticed his cell phone still on the charger. Picking it up, he entered his pin and unlocked it. A message from Devlin, sent a few days ago, caught his eye.

"Solomons is holding me locked up in my..."

His blood ran cold as he listened to Devlin's days-old message. He immediately dialed Devlin's number. It went straight to voicemail. Duncan quickly scanned the internet for news articles reported over the past few days. It wasn't long before he came across an article posted by *The Voice*.

"Slain brother from Elsies found in his flat."

The article stated that Devlin Peters' body had been discovered after an anonymous call to the police. It mentioned that Devlin had grown up in Elsies River and was well known in the area. He had been a friendly person who regularly helped people in need, never turning his back on his neighborhood.

Duncan reread Devlin's message. Then, he sent a voice WhatsApp to Oom Jack.

"I won't be able to make supper, Oom Jack. A friend of mine needs some help. I'll speak to you later. Please tell Mackie I'll be in touch."

He pushed the fridge away from the wall and reached down to the bottom next to the compressor. From there, he pulled out a 9mm pistol and ammo wrapped in a dishcloth. He checked the action and loaded the two magazines. Slipping into a pair of black jeans and a black T-shirt, he put the gun and spare magazine into his leather jacket pocket. Grabbing his helmet and a pair of black calfskin gloves, he headed downstairs to his bike.

He knew Plattekloof well, and less than ten minutes later, he stopped in front of the house Devlin had described. Looking around, he saw no one. It was six p.m., and the thin winter sun was setting over Robben Island. He got off the bike and pushed the intercom button next to the gate.

Zane was sitting on the toilet when he heard the intercom buzz. He wasn't quite done but quickly pulled up his pants and rushed to the control panel in his small kitchen. Kallie hadn't been home for two days, and Zane was worried. He had tried several times to reach his boss on his cell phone but couldn't get through. He had already decided to contact John Roberts if Kallie hadn't shown up by tomorrow morning. Thinking it could be Roberts, he pressed the answer button.

"Who's there?"

There was a brief pause before a voice responded.

"Open up."

Not being entirely familiar with Roberts' voice, he wasn't sure if it was him. Regardless, he opened the gate anyway—he needed to get back to the toilet.

"I'll be out in a minute, Mr. Roberts."

With his pants halfway down, he rushed back to the toilet.

Boer left his bike where he had parked it in the street and entered the yard through the partially opened gate. Seeing no one around, he slowly scanned the house and windows for movement. He made his way toward the front door and climbed the steps to the veranda. Peering through the side windows of the grand double doors, he could barely see through the lace curtains hanging in front of them. He rang the doorbell and took a few steps back, his left hand resting under his T-shirt, ready to pull out the 9mm he had tucked into his waistband.

There was no answer, no sound from inside the house. He had just begun to wonder who had answered the intercom when he heard a door slam around the side of the house. Turning toward the sound, he saw a well-built guy with tattoos coming around the corner, still fastening his belt. Boer saw he was unarmed and removed his hand from the gun.

Zane spotted a large man with a crew cut, dressed in biker gear, standing on the veranda. He stopped a few feet away and looked up at him, recognizing immediately that he had never seen him before.

"Who are you looking for?" he asked warily.

The man took a step down and smiled.

"Mr. Roberts sent me. I have a message for Mr. Jansen."

Zane relaxed and shook his head. "He's not here. I haven't seen him for more than two days. I was going to call Mr. Roberts this evening if he didn't return. Do you work for him?"

Duncan walked down the stairs and held out his hand.

"Yes, I do. I'm Derrick. When will Mr. Jansen be back?"

Zane shook his hand. "Zane. I work for Mr. Jansen—I'm his driver. Come inside, it's freezing out here."

Turning, he led the way back to his flat. As soon as they entered, he closed the door behind them. Before he could turn toward his guest, he felt a powerful arm snake around his neck.

He was no weakling, but every effort he made to shake off his assailant was futile. The blood flow to his brain was cut off. He felt the veins in his head throbbing as his vision darkened. His strength faded, and he slowly lost consciousness.

Duncan lowered Zane onto his bed and flipped him onto his side. Taking three heavy-duty cable ties from his jacket pocket, he secured Zane's hands behind his back with one, his feet with another, and looped the last one around his neck.

He then walked to the kitchen counter and switched on the kettle.

****

Sergeant Fielies and Warrant Officer Nico Brandt sat in the borrowed office of Vredenburg police station.

The Commander had allowed them to use it to interview Jossie April, the mother of the abducted girl who had been rescued from Farouk's house. She sat with her chin on her chest, pretending not to hear them. Her right leg bounced up and down with anxiety. She had her hands folded in her lap, picking at the torn skin of her cuticles. She had been interviewed several times over the past few months and, by keeping quiet as Jimbo and her attorney had advised her, she had always been set free soon afterward.

Warrant Officer Brandt repeated the question.

"Where were you when your daughter was kidnapped? We have warned you that we have new information, and this is your last chance to tell us what you know. Was Jimbo involved in the kidnapping of the child?"

She lightly shook her head. She was struggling to concentrate, and her whole body ached from the withdrawal effects of the methamphetamines. She had been kept in the cell since the previous day and was beginning to suffer badly.

The two police officers from Bellville Hawks were losing their patience, but they still wanted a confession. They looked at her court-appointed attorney, who simply shook his head. They had not yet informed him that they had found the child and had obtained an affidavit from her in the presence of a social worker.

"Mr. Lomas, we are going to terminate this interview with your client, but we will be back in thirty minutes. You can stay here with her, or she can go back to the cell until we resume."

"Why can't you complete your interview now? She has been locked up for more than twenty-four hours. It's inhumane."

"We can hold her for another twenty-four. If you think she's suffering now with withdrawal, you should see her tomorrow. The sooner she talks, the sooner she can go *tik*."

The attorney checked his watch and glanced at his client before answering.

"We will wait here."

The two policemen got up and walked out of the office. Halfway to the door, Sergeant Fielies turned around, switched off the tape recorder, and tucked it under his arm.

They walked to the cells behind the police station to talk to her boyfriend, Jimbo. When they reached his cell, Fielies motioned for the constable to unlock the door, and they stepped inside. He left the recorder switched off and placed it on the bed

324

next to Jimbo. Fielies and Brandt stood with their backs against the cell wall, looking down at him. Warrant Officer Brandt was the first to speak.

"Well, Jimbo, we have good news and bad news. The good news is that Tikkop April has confessed. She says you sold the child to the two Nigerians and that she had nothing to do with it."

Jimbo stretched out his arms and yawned, clearly not falling for it. He looked up at the two policemen and grinned.

"If that was the case, then you wouldn't be bothering to question me, *ne*? I don't know anything about the child's disappearance, and before I say another word, I want a lawyer."

He folded his arms across his chest and leaned back against the wall. Brandt picked up the recorder from the bed and showed it to Jimbo.

"It wasn't switched on. We were just chatting up until now, but unfortunately, you're trying to be clever. So now, you are under arrest for the kidnapping and subsequent rape of Belinda-May April."

Brandt pushed the play button and passed the recorder to Fielies.

"Let's go, Sergeant. Leave this piece of shit to rot."

He waited for the constable to lock the door and, looking back at Jimbo, smiled.

"Pray you get a very good attorney. We found the girl, and she talked. *Hasta la vista*, asshole."

He was pleased to see the look of fear pass over Jimbo's face before turning away. He followed Fielies down the passage and couldn't help himself from singing,

"The final countdown..."

When they reached the charge office, Brandt asked the female constable where the Commander was. She directed him down the passage to an office at the end. They walked to the office and knocked.

"Enter," they heard Captain Deon Le Roux shout.

They stepped inside, and he motioned for them to take a seat. He was a middle-aged career cop with a friendly demeanor. They were relieved. Normally, commanders of these smaller police stations treated officers from the Hawks with suspicion.

"How did it go?" he asked once they were seated.

Fielies glanced at Brandt and decided to answer.

"We were hoping for a confession, Captain, but it looks like Jimbo coached his girlfriend very well. We haven't yet told her or her attorney that we found the girl and that we have a sworn affidavit from her saying that it was them who sold her to the two Nigerians. One of the Nigerians she remembers was called Jamal. She also remembers seeing a BMW logo on the steering wheel of the car that transported her to Gugulethu. The girl says it was a very high car and black. That means we could be looking for a black BMW X5. She clearly remembers it was around 4 p.m. when she was abducted, as she had been watching one of her favorite kiddie shows when her mother called her to the yard. And listen to this—she remembers where they took her, as well as the name of the person she stayed with. It was Cebisile, the *sangoma* who was killed a few days ago. She doesn't remember much after that, except that a skinny man lay on top of her and hurt her between her legs. We suspect she was drugged and raped."

Le Roux shook his head sadly and looked at the two policemen sitting in front of him.

"We've suspected the mother's involvement from the start, but we couldn't find any evidence. What do we do now?"

"We've already given the information to our colleagues in Bellville, and they're scanning footage from traffic cameras on the R27. There are a lot of them if you count the cameras at the entrances of game reserves and those along the route. Once we have footage of the three men and their vehicle, we can correlate it with other footage on the N2 and cameras at Crossroads near Gugulethu. We will find them—you can be assured of that."

"What can I do to help?"

Brandt leaned forward, placing his hand on the desk.

"Captain, you've already helped a lot, but I'd like one more favor. We have the mother and her attorney stewing in the office you loaned us. If you could send in two or three of your biggest men before we go in, it will intimidate her. She's close to breaking point. They don't need to say anything—just stand in the corners and glare at her."

Le Roux smiled and picked up the phone on his desk.

"That's not a problem. Most of my men are large. We have very good takeaway places in Vredenburg."

Brandt and Fielies thanked him and got up from their chairs. They went back to the constable who had unlocked the cell for them. Fielies pulled him aside and, in a low voice, told him what he needed to do. The constable grinned and headed off to Jimbo's cell.

Brandt checked the time on his cell phone and saw that almost an hour had passed since they had left the attorney and Jossie April in the interview room.

"We'll let them wait another twenty minutes. Let's get some coffee."

Chapter 59

Duncan sat with his feet on the edge of the bed, rocking the kitchen chair back and forth.

He sipped his sweet, milky tea while waiting for Zane to wake up. It wasn't long before he saw the first sign—Zane's eyelids twitching. Subconsciously, Zane tried to move his arms in front of him, but the ties kept him from doing so. Suddenly, his eyes popped open, and he began struggling in earnest. It took him a few seconds to realize that someone was sitting at the foot of his bed.

"Untie me immediately! Who the fuck do you think you are? Let me loose!" he shouted at Duncan, who was coolly watching him over the rim of his mug.

Zane fought against his restraints, his face turning red from the effort. When he realized it was futile, he slowed down and lifted his head to look at Duncan.

"What do you want, man?"

Duncan slowly got up from the chair and walked to the kitchen, placing his mug on the counter. Returning to the bed, he leaned over Zane, bringing his mouth within a few centimeters of his ear.

"I want to know where the cunt is who killed Devlin."

Immediately, he saw Zane stiffen, his eyes darting around in panic. Duncan pulled the chair closer and sat down next to the bed. Zane had started to sweat, clearly trying to think of what to say.

The best he could come up with was, "Who is Devlin?"

Duncan reached over and violently yanked the tie around Zane's neck tight. Zane's eyes bulged, and he tried to scream, but all that came out was a faint croak. Duncan leaned back in the chair, folding his arms, his expression cold and detached, as if he were inspecting a dying plant.

Just before Zane was about to pass out for the second time that morning, Duncan sliced the tie with his commando knife. Zane's mouth gaped as he gasped for air, his chest heaving.

Duncan waited for him to recover, pulling another tie from his jacket pocket.

He thought of his mentor, Mackie, and silently thanked him for this method of interrogation. He no longer needed to rely on punches and cuts to get information.

Twirling the tie between his fingers, he made sure Zane saw it.

Zane had recovered somewhat, his breathing gradually returning to normal. Sweat dripped down his face, and fear was written all over it as he watched Duncan toying with the tie. His throat burned like fire, and when he finally spoke, his voice was hoarse.

"You're *The Boer*, aren't you?"

****

Jack and Mikey sat alone around the fire pit.

Jack had stoked the flames after Sweety went to bed and had fetched a bottle of Nuy Red Muscadel from the fridge. They stared into the burning fire, taking small sips of the sweet wine, savoring the rich raisin flavor. In the distance, they heard the air horn of a truck passing a few kilometers away. Mikey was the first to break the silence.

"Where do you think Boer went tonight? He seemed so keen to braai with us. It must be something important for him to change his mind."

Jack nodded and took another sip.

"I'll phone him in the morning to check if he's okay. He seems quite capable of looking after himself. Do you think Boer and Piet will carry on with the work?"

Mikey looked at his friend and smiled. "I'm not sure. I was driven by money and revenge when I was young. They both have money now, and as far as Piet is concerned, the revenge was sweet. We'll have to see what happens in the future. I'll keep in touch with them. Piet told me he wants to finish school, and Boer wants to take a break. Let's see what they decide in a few months. Personally, I think they both don't tolerate injustices against those who can't defend themselves."

Still staring into the fire, Jack asked, "And you, Mikey? What about you?"

Mikey took a few seconds before answering. "I think I'm done with that for good. I have a new life with new challenges, and I'm excited to get on with it. I've told them I'll always be available to give advice if they need it."

Jack scratched his head. He had heard this before, but this time, he felt he could believe him.

"Let's talk about something more interesting. How would Cara feel if Sweety and I came for a visit? I've got the old school bus converted and ready for a road trip."

"Bru, she'd be delighted! It would be great to have you there. I can't wait to show you what Brigitta and Cara have done with the smallholding I bought from old George Travis. I've got two extra bikes as well if you feel like a ride somewhere."

"I like that idea. Are we still on for Bots? I can get some of our crew to leave from here and meet us at the border," Jack said excitedly.

Mikey got up to pour himself another shot of muscadel. He passed the bottle to Jack.

"I think that's a trip for another time. Maybe later in the year when we've planned it a bit better."

"What about a quick trip to Mozambique, then? It's close enough."

Mikey looked at his friend and shook his head.

"No, not Moz. It's not the same anymore, *bru*. It's dangerous, dirty, and there's a cop behind every bush stopping you for no reason other than a bribe. Everything is overpriced and of poor quality. The locals don't see you as a tourist anymore—they see you as someone to rip off. It's changed a lot in the last few years. The youth in that country are unhappy with their government and all the corruption. I can't recommend it to anyone anymore."

****

Warrant Officer Brandt and Sergeant Fielies entered the office where Jossie April was being held.

Her attorney glanced at his watch, his expression clearly showing his displeasure at having been kept waiting. They ignored him completely and took their seats. Fielies switched on the recorder and introduced everyone in the office—except for the three burly policemen standing against the walls. Brandt pulled a page from the docket and showed it to Fielies. It was a meaningless piece of paper, but Fielies nodded enthusiastically. Brandt placed it back in the docket and pretended to search for something else.

Jossie remained seated with her head bowed while her attorney kept looking at his watch. Finally, unable to contain his frustration, he slammed his hand on the table in front of him.

"You've kept me waiting for more than an hour! Can we get on with it? I have another appointment."

Brandt gave him a lopsided grin. "Really? Does it look like I give a fuck?"

The three policemen remained silent, their faces impassive. The one standing behind Lomas suppressed a small smile.

Brandt turned his attention to Jossie April and tapped on the table with his forefinger.

"Miss April, please look up at me when I speak to you. I have something very important to tell you."

Slowly, she lifted her head and looked across at him. He could see she was in bad shape. She clutched her arms tightly to her chest, shivering despite the warmth of the room.

"We have found your daughter. She is alive but severely traumatized. She saw the Nigerians hand Jimbo the bag with the money. She told us you did nothing to help her, which makes you one hundred percent complicit. She identified the car they were driving, as well as their names. She told us the name of the sangoma who bought her from the Nigerians in Gugulethu, along with the address. She gave us a description of the man who raped her. We have apprehended most of the people involved. You are under arrest for the kidnapping of Belinda-May and for human trafficking of an underage child. Is there anything you would like to say?"

Lomas shot up from his seat, pointing an accusing finger at Brandt.

"You deliberately withheld this information to ambush my client into a confession! She will not answer any more questions! I will not—"

"Sit down!" Brandt interrupted. "You're not in court. Advising your client not to answer our questions will only make matters worse for her. If she agrees to testify against Jimbo Van Rooyen, it will help her case significantly. Speak to her. We will give you five minutes."

He motioned to the others to follow him outside, dismissing two of the three policemen. The third was instructed to stay for Jossie April's arrest and booking.

Duncan looked at Zane lying on his side, his hands and feet bound. He showed no emotion and ignored his question.

"This is the only chance I will give you to survive, so think carefully before you answer. One dodgy answer, and we won't have any more business with each other. You will be dead, and I will be gone. Do you understand?"

He twirled the cable tie in front of Zane's face to make his point. Zane licked the sweat from his upper lip and nodded.

"Who gave the instruction to have Devlin killed, and where do I find Boetie Solomons?"

Zane was shocked by how much *The Boer* knew and realized once again how dangerous this man was. He struggled into an upright position, carefully considering his answer.

"My boss, Kallie, told me to contact Solomons and set up a meeting between the two of them. Solomons came back here a few days after the first meeting and picked up a parcel of money Kallie had prepared for him. I handed it to him at the gate. I haven't seen him since, but I know where he hangs out."

He licked his lips, his eyes begging Boer to believe him.

"Where is Kallie?"

Zane shook his head. "I don't know. What I told you earlier is the truth. Three days ago, he gave me the day off and said he was going to a party. That was the last time I saw him. He was driving the BMW M5. I was planning to contact his partner, John Roberts, if he hadn't returned by this evening."

Boer nodded. He believed most of what Zane was saying. His own involvement, however, was probably a bit more than just a facilitator.

"Where do I find Roberts and Funani?"

Zane's surprise showed once again—this man knew too much.

"How...?" He hesitated, then continued. "Roberts is always at the warehouse by the harbor, and Funani stays on Fourteenth Avenue in Bellville. I can take you there."

Boer stood up from his chair and moved to the door. Holding up the remote control, he asked, "Is this for the garage as well?"

"Yes. It opens all the garage doors, as well as the gate. The gate is the blue button."

"Stay here. If I find you've moved or tried to escape, I will kill you."

Boer exited the flat and walked around to the front of the house. It was already dark. Pressing one of the buttons, he heard a garage door open behind him. His eyes widened when he saw the selection of cars inside the triple, double-depth garages—more than four million rand worth of vehicles. He noticed one open bay—most likely the spot for the missing M5.

Pressing the blue button, he watched as the gate opened.

He stepped outside, climbed onto his motorcycle, looked around, and, seeing no one nearby, started it up and rode straight into the empty bay in the garage. He parked it facing outward, put out the side stand, and, leaving the garage, closed both the door and the gate behind him.

Returning to Zane's flat, he found him exactly as he had left him, though he still checked his restraints. He sat down opposite Zane again and silently watched him.

Zane, too afraid to speak, endured the silence for several minutes before finally breaking.

"What now?" he asked quietly.

Boer shrugged.

"We wait. I kill Kallie. Then we go get Boetie. I kill him. Then we get Funani—you can watch me cut him to pieces and let him bleed out. Then we go for Roberts, and so on, and so on, until it's just you left."

Zane began to lose control. Tears ran down his cheeks. He was terrified and humiliated at the same time. He had always considered himself tough, but he had never felt fear like this before. He saw no emotion in his captor's pale grey eyes. He shook his head to rid himself of the tears.

Taking a deep breath, he spoke in a quivering voice. "Whatever you decide to do with me, I ask only one thing—that I get to speak to my mother one last time. I will help you in any way I can. I was just a driver, but Kallie kept pulling me deeper into his business. I had already decided to quit and get away from him. I am not a criminal. I really liked Devlin, and I feel ashamed that I didn't do anything to warn him."

"Why didn't you?" Boer asked. "He could have been alive today."

"I was afraid. I guess I'm a coward. I'm very sorry for my involvement." Zane dropped his head, sniffing.

"Where do I find Solomons?"

"I can tell you where he hangs out or take you there. I will do anything to try and make amends for my part in this."

Boer thought it over. Solomons could wait. He needed to wait for Kallie first.

Checking his phone, he saw no new messages. He pulled the 9mm from the back of his pants and cocked it. Zane's eyes widened, then squeezed shut. He was expecting to die.

Instead, Boer pulled out his commando knife and sliced through the tie binding Zane's feet. Zane's eyes shot open in surprise.

"Get up. We're going upstairs. There's no food here."

Chapter 60

Warrant Officer Brandt and Sergeant Fielies entered the room and took their seats.

Sergeant Fielies switched on the recorder. They folded their arms and looked at Lomas and Jossie April, who was still chewing on a bleeding cuticle. It was Lomas who spoke first.

"Miss April is willing to answer your questions. She is very relieved that her daughter has been found and is still alive."

Brandt gestured for Fielies to proceed. Fielies glanced at his list.

"Where were you when your daughter was handed over to the abductors? Remember, your answers must be truthful if you want any consideration for leniency."

She wiped her eyes with the back of her hands and looked at Fielies. Her voice quivered as she spoke softly.

"I was there in the yard."

Fielies gave Brandt a thumbs-up under the table. *Now they've got her.*

He looked down at his next question.

****

At Diepsloot SAPS, Sergeant Lastborn Tobela took the A4 sheet he had just printed and walked into Captain Dan Mdalose's office.

He placed it on the desk in front of him and stepped back, allowing Dan time to read it.

Dan scanned the report from Cape Town. It detailed the case of the young girl found in Farouk's house. The confession from her mother, along with the arrests of both her and her boyfriend, Jimbo, was confirmed. The three men who had sold her to the *sangoma* had been tracked, and police were actively searching for them. Their names, descriptions, and aliases were all included in the report, with instructions for every police officer in South Africa to be on the lookout. Airports and border crossings had been put on high alert.

Dan knew it was only a matter of time before they were caught. The case had gripped the country, and soon, a member of the public would come forward with their whereabouts. Crimes against children were universally condemned—*even hardened criminals wouldn't stand for it.*

Dan looked up at Lastborn and smiled.

"Get the rest of our team in here. This is very good news."

****

Zane was in the middle of telling Boer about Kallie and Robert's import business when the chime signaled that someone was at the gate.

Boer quickly moved to a window and peered through the shades. Two well-dressed men stood by the gate under the light. He returned to Zane, holding the gun on him as he cut the ties.

"Go onto the veranda and talk to them. Find out what they want. Under no circumstances do you let them in. Go!"

Zane slowly walked to the balustrade and leaned over it. He didn't recognize either of the men.

"Good evening. Can I help you?"

The men looked up at him. The older of the two spoke first.

"Is Mrs. Jansen in?"

Zane shook his head.

"There is no Mrs. Jansen. They divorced years ago. It's just me and Mr. Jansen, my employer, and he isn't here. I haven't seen him in almost three days."

"Can we come in?" the older man asked.

Zane shook his head again.

"No, I'm afraid not. I can't allow anyone onto the premises without Mr. Jansen's permission. I can take your names and number so he can contact you when he gets back. My name is Zane. I'm his driver."

The two men turned away from the gate and had a brief discussion. When they finally turned back, the older man asked, "Does Mr. Jansen own a BMW M5?"

"Yes, he does. He left with it three days ago to visit a friend in Bellville."

The older man turned to his companion, who gave a slight nod. Then he stepped closer to the gate.

"Zane, I'm afraid I have bad news. Mr. Jansen was killed in a car accident two days ago. The car caught fire, and it was only this afternoon that we were able to identify the driver and passengers. I'm sorry to give you this news. The investigating officers will come by early tomorrow morning to see you."

Zane shook his head, processing the information. He hadn't been particularly fond of Kallie, but hearing that he was dead still came as a shock. He looked down at the man delivering the news.

"This is a shock. Who was in the car with him?"

"There were four occupants. Mr. Jansen was driving. The front passenger was Captain Funani, a police officer. It was through him that we were able to confirm Jansen's identity. A police ID was found in the front passenger's shoe—one of the few things that didn't completely burn. Mrs. Funani confirmed that they left her house in Jansen's car. That's how we traced the vehicle. The two men in the back have not yet been identified. She didn't know their names. The investigators will give you more information tomorrow. We were only sent to inform the family."

Zane nodded. "Thank you. I'll be here."

The two men waved goodbye and got into their car. Zane watched as they disappeared around the corner. His mind raced. He was thinking about the fortune in the safe.

Turning back toward Boer, he found him standing with the gun raised, twirling a cable tie in his left hand.

"Assume the position."

Zane walked over and turned around. He felt the tie tighten around his wrists.

* * * *

Mamello peeked through the curtains of his Parktown home.

A mass of people had gathered outside the gate. Most had cameras—some with massive lenses. They were shouting for him to come outside.

Someone spotted him and pointed to the window. Within seconds, every camera was focused on him. Too late, he ducked away.

He walked upstairs to the main bedroom, where his wife sat on the bed.

Glaring at her as he passed, he muttered, "What is wrong with these people? What have I done to them? Why are they chasing me?"

He moved to the window and looked down at the crowd. They were still shouting for him to come out.

At the edge of the park opposite their house, something caught his eye. He squinted and realized what was happening—people were dancing around burning objects.

His face twisted in anger as he recognized what they were burning. His Party's T-shirts. The same shirts his supporters used to wear.

He cursed under his breath.

"I will kill them. Ungrateful fucking moegoes."

He turned to his wife and saw she was crying. He was surprised—earlier, she had berated him, swore at him, and even hit him several times with her handbag. She had called him every insult under the sun, asking herself how she could have ever married such a loser.

He had always known he had married above his social standing. It had taken months of expensive dinners and lavish gifts to win her over.

But now, he feared what her father—*a university professor*—would think of this scandal. He was too scared to even imagine it.

How could that fucking Italian have allowed someone to place a camera in the apartment? How long had it been there?

He shuddered at the thought of more footage surfacing.

There had been several times when he had indulged in the pleasures of those white prostitutes himself. He had accepted multiple bribes from Manzoni in that very apartment.

338

He shuddered and forced the thought away. He turned back to his wife.

"What is the matter? Why are you crying? I made a mistake, and I apologize."

She looked up at him, grabbed a suitcase, and started packing her clothes.

"I'm leaving. My dad is picking me up in ten minutes."

She pulled a folded paper from her purse and threw it onto the bed.

Mamello picked it up, expecting a divorce letter. But as he examined it, confusion set in. It looked like a black-and-white image of clouds.

"What is this?" he asked.

She paused her packing, turned to him, and with venom in her voice, screamed,

"It's a scan. A scan of your three-month-old son. A son you will never see!"

With that, she zipped up the suitcase and headed downstairs.

****

Mikey had fueled the Beechcraft and was completing his pre-flight checks.

He looked up at the sky and was relieved to see the weather had improved slightly. All things considered, he should be home by nightfall. He couldn't wait to hold Cara in his arms. He had already notified her of his ETA. Finishing his checks, he entered the cockpit and started the engines, letting them warm up.

As he waited, his mind drifted back over the events of the past few weeks. He felt satisfied and relieved that it was finally over. He gazed out over the lonely airfield, watching the stillness around him while the engines hummed in the background.

He thought about how it had all started when he was just a young man. The border war, the specialist training he had received—it had changed his outlook on life forever. After his three-year stint in the army, he had tried to fit into normal civilian life, but it hadn't been for him.

Being a vigilante had not been his choice. *The job had chosen him.* And in a way, it had intoxicated him. The thrill, the sense of purpose—it had kept him moving from mission to mission for over thirty years.

But now, it was over.

Thinking about his new life ahead, he smiled, a deep sense of elation washing over him. He turned the Beechcraft into the wind, pushed the revs up, and took a deep breath.

He was ready for takeoff.

Chapter 61

Zane looked at his captor, sitting behind the bar counter. The 9mm lay inches from his right hand. He licked his lips, preparing to speak. He had made a decision.

"I'm sorry, but you can't get revenge for your friend by killing Kallie or Funani. I will show you where you can find Solomons. It's not far from here."

Boer just stared at him, unmoving.

Zane continued. "You need to get out of here before daybreak. The cops are going to be here early. Solomons is not far from here."

Boer picked up the 9mm from the counter and flicked the safety off. Zane's eyes widened at the sharp click. *This is it. I'm going to die. He can't leave me as a witness.*

"Wait. Wait, please. I have to show you something," he pleaded.

Boer pointed the gun at his face. "Show me. I'm in a hurry."

Zane got up from the chair. "Follow me. It's in Kallie's bedroom."

Boer indicated with a tilt of the gun barrel for him to proceed. Zane walked awkwardly, his hands still tied in front of him, toward the master bedroom. He stopped in front of the large nude painting of Kallie's ex-wife and nodded toward it.

"Behind that painting. I know the combination."

Boer lifted the painting off the wall and set it on the floor. Then he turned to Zane, keeping the gun trained on him.

Zane recited the combination from memory. *God knows, I've thought about it often enough these past few days. Every minute of every day, that pile of money has been on my mind. But I'm more than happy to buy my freedom with it.*

"Five. Half a turn back to thirty-seven. Two turns clockwise to fourteen. One turn back to fifteen."

Boer motioned with the gun. "You do it."

Zane struggled with his tied hands but eventually managed to get it done. He turned the lever and pulled the heavy door open, stepping aside so Boer could see inside.

"You can have it all. Just let me go. I can't and won't identify you. I beg you. My mother needs me, man!"

Boer peered into the safe, his eyes scanning the stacks of money, jewelry, and bricks of cocaine. He let out a low whistle and turned his gaze back to Zane.

"Why haven't you taken it all for yourself?"

Zane shook his head. "Kallie would have put The Association on me. I wouldn't have stood a chance. Now it's a different story. With Kallie dead, only you and I know about this stash."

Boer looked into the safe again. Mackie's words echoed in his mind.

"Justice Payment."

He walked to the cupboards and started yanking open the doors. On the top shelf, he found what he was looking for—two large sports bags. He pulled them down and dropped them in front of the safe.

Turning to Zane, he cut the tie around his wrists. Zane immediately started rubbing them, trying to restore blood flow. He looked up at Boer, uncertain.

Boer used the barrel of the gun to gesture toward the safe. He pulled back the hammer.

"Pack it. Money only. Try to put equal amounts in each bag. It will make it easier to carry. Spread the rest of the contents on the empty shelves to make it less obvious that anything was taken. Lock the safe and put the painting back."

****

Enoch sat across the table from his aunt and his mother, while Buhle sat next to him, holding his hand.

She had not let go of him since he had stepped off the taxi an hour ago. She clung to him, too afraid she might lose him again. His aunt, Thombi, had fed him and excitedly shown him where he would be sleeping. She had been just as elated to see him—her nephew, whom she had not seen in more than five years. However, now, as she watched him and Buhle sitting side by side, her expression had changed. A deep sadness had settled over her.

Enoch picked up on her mood, and, releasing his mother's hand, leaned forward on the table.

"What is it? Why are you so sad?"

Thombi glanced at her sister before answering. Buhle nodded, giving her permission to speak.

"A few nights ago, a whole family was gunned down not far from here," she said, her voice heavy. "Three gunmen entered the house at four a.m. and shot everyone inside. Seventeen people are dead. The father, who was the brother of my late husband, his wife, his sister and her husband, and all their children... they were all killed."

Enoch felt his blood rise. Astonished, he looked at his mother, who nodded and wiped her eyes. For a moment, he was at a loss for words. He reached across the table and took his aunt's hands, his fingers tightening around hers as he studied her sorrowful face.

"Does anyone know why they were killed?" he asked quietly.

His aunt shook her head, and for a moment, he misunderstood. But then he saw his mother nod. Releasing his aunt's hands, he turned to his mother.

"Mama, do you know?"

"The police know too," she said. "A neighbor's son saw the men getting into the car that sped away. The car's lights were off, but he recognized it. It belongs to Makoko, the son of the chief of our clan. The passenger was his brother, Molate."

"Did he tell the police?" Enoch asked, astonished.

His aunt shook her head. "No. He told his father, and his father went to the police station in Didiktu. They accused him of lying and locked him up. His son, the one who saw everything, is in hiding. The police are looking for him. They say they will keep his father locked up until Lunga turns himself in."

"Why would the chief's sons be involved in killing innocent people?"

Once again, his aunt hesitated. He looked at his mother, who also shook her head.

"We're not sure," Buhle said at last, "but we think it has something to do with corruption. The family that was killed had all their belongings packed. They were going to load them onto a truck in the morning. They were fleeing Transkei. We suspect they gave evidence against the chief and his family. Everyone knows that the Hawks visited them for a few hours two weeks ago. Somehow, the chief and the local police must have found out. We think they were threatened."

Enoch could barely believe what he was hearing. He had grown up in the hills of Transkei. It was the one place where he had always felt safe. Everyone knew and cared for each other. Children played in the hills and among the huts, never fearing anything. Neighbors visited one another freely, and the old men sat around talking late into the night. People slept with their doors and windows wide open.

It had been his father's job that had taken them to Joburg five years ago, but Enoch and his mother had always planned to return to Transkei one day. Now, for the first time, he feared for his mother's and his aunt's safety.

How can people get away with killing a whole family?

"Do either of you know where I can find Lunga? I have to help him get to safety."

The two women exchanged fearful glances and started shaking their heads. Buhle reached out, her grip tightening around Enoch's hand.

"Enoch, please do not get involved," she pleaded, her voice breaking. "They will kill you. These are dangerous people. Please, I beg you."

Tears streamed down her face as she clung to his hand, desperate to change his mind. Enoch saw how upset she was and forced himself to stay calm.

"Okay, I understand," he said softly. "Let's talk about something else."

****

Much later that evening, Enoch sat on his bed, deep in thought. He opened the soft leather scabbard he had made for his machete. The polished metal gleamed in the moonlight streaming through the open window. Lovingly, he ran his fingers over the blade, unable to resist testing its razor-sharp edge with his thumb.

He got up and moved silently through the house, careful not to wake anyone. Stepping outside, he made his way to the edge of his aunt's property. The night was still, the sky above a blanket of millions of stars, bright and unpolluted.

He took out his cell phone and made a call. It went to voicemail.

In a whisper, he left a message.

"Uncle Mackie, I need advice."

He put the phone back in his pocket and stared up at the stars, his mind racing.

Chapter 62

Dan Mdalose anxiously opened the email he had been waiting for since Monday.

Slowly, he read through it, and a smile formed on his face. He leaned back in his chair and closed his eyes for a few seconds. Having made up his mind, he picked up his phone and called John Robson.

"Good morning, Sergeant. Could you and the rest of the team meet in my office in about five minutes?"

Through the half-open blinds, he saw John look around to make sure everyone was in the office.

"Sure, Cap. They're all here. See you in five."

Dan looked at the three expectant faces on the other side of his desk. He felt immensely proud of them—and even prouder to be their leader. The email he had read earlier was printed and lying on his desk.

"I've received a directive from Brigadier Maputla, our new station commander. He has instructed me to personally congratulate you on the work you did on the child murder case and to thank you for being the best policemen and woman you can be. He says he is especially proud of this small unit. He has also given me instructions to expand our group and promote two constables from the force to detectives. I think we can all agree that the two constables who worked with us on this case should be considered first, but I'll leave that decision up to you."

Dan opened his desk drawer and pulled out two epaulettes, ceremoniously threading them through the bands on his shoulders. He had dressed in his uniform that morning for this very occasion.

"As you can see, I've been promoted to Major. Sergeant Tobela, you have been promoted to Warrant Officer, attached to vehicle theft, but you have the choice to remain in this unit at your current rank until further promotion. Sergeant Booysen, you have been promoted to Warrant Officer. Congratulations to you both."

He could see they were pleased—everyone except for John. Dan knew instinctively that John was about to resign as soon as this meeting was over. The others held their breath, avoiding John's eyes, waiting to see what would happen next.

Dan continued. "Sergeant Robson, you have been selected to complete an Officer's Course with an immediate promotion to Lieutenant. From today, you will be the 2IC of this unit—that is, if you want it."

John looked at the others, unable to believe what he had just heard. He turned back to Dan, who was smiling and holding out his hand. John hesitated for only a moment before standing up and shaking it.

Dan felt relieved and smiled. "Are you going to tell LangFaan, or should I?"

****

Duncan had pushed the seat back as far as it would go.

He stretched his legs out and glanced over at Zane, who was behind the wheel. They were in one of Kallie's cheaper cars—a Mercedes GLC. He had been tempted to take the more luxurious Maybach, but he had decided the SUV would be more practical and attract less attention where they were headed. The pistol rested on his lap as he watched Zane closely.

"Zane, I've decided to throw you a bone. If you help me with this, I'll let you live. When we get there, I want you to go inside and bring him out to the car. Tell him Kallie has another job for him. I'll wait in the car. If you're not out in five minutes, I'll drive myself back to the house and leave you here. I'll hunt you down later. You'll never know when I'll come for you. Do we have a deal?"

Zane didn't need to think about it. He nodded quickly.

"Yes. Thank you. I won't let you down. What will you do with him? People will recognize me with him. They'll link me to it if you kill him."

Boer smiled and patted him on the shoulder.

"Don't worry. If anyone ever asks, you tell them the last time you saw him was when Kallie sent him on a job. Make sure people hear you tell him that Kallie wants to see him outside in the car."

They approached the club in Halt Road, Elsies River. Although it was still early in the evening, the place was already buzzing with activity.

"Drive past and park in that bay."

Zane slid the Merc into the parking spot and switched off the engine with the push button. The remote was in Boer's pocket. Zane sat dead still, waiting for instructions.

"Go inside and find him. You said this is his favorite hangout, so he should be here. If he's not, come back immediately. We'll go to where he lives. Don't fuck this up, Zane. This is a chance that won't come again. You have five minutes. Go."

Boer waited until Zane disappeared inside the club before moving to the back seat of the car. He checked the time on his Rotary Commando.

****

Manzoni was asleep in his bed.

He had started drinking early in the afternoon again, and the alcohol had done its job. He had barely made it to bed before passing out. It had become a daily ritual since his wife, Allegra, had returned to Italy a few days ago.

Any day now, he expected the Hawks to knock on his door and arrest him. The evidence against him was overwhelming, and none of his usual contacts were returning his calls. In just a matter of days, he had become *persona non grata*.

A sharp pain in his ear jolted him awake. His eyes flew open, and he tried to turn his head, but a hand snaked up his throat, gripping his chin tightly. Unable to move, he frantically swiveled his eyes, trying to see who it was.

A large figure sat on the bed beside him, dressed in a black suit, a white fedora tilted on his head.

The man leaned closer and whispered, "*Don Attorio vi manda i suoi saluti.*"

It was the last thing Manzoni ever heard before the sharpened bicycle spoke was driven through the soft canal of his left ear, straight into his brain.

****

Duncan watched as Zane walked out of the club with a man who was clearly unsteady on his feet.

Boetie Solomons was laughing at something Zane had said. When they reached the car, Zane opened the rear door. Boetie leaned in, expecting to see Kallie. Before he realized his mistake, Zane shoved him inside, and Boer jammed the 9mm into his ear, forcing his head against the window.

"Easy. I'm not going to hurt you. I just want to talk. Drive, Zane."

Boetie tried to focus on his assailant, but he had never seen this man before. He had been drinking since early afternoon, and his mind was sluggish. His ear ached where the barrel of the gun pressed against it.

Zane pulled out of the parking spot and slowly drove up the road.

"What do you want to talk about?" Boetie slurred in broken English.

Boer smiled and ground the pistol deeper into his ear. He looked out the window.

"Do you see that guy over there on the pavement?"

Boer relaxed the pressure on the gun just enough for Boetie to move. As Solomons leaned forward to look, Boer swung the pistol and slammed the butt of the gun into his skull.

Boetie crumpled instantly. Boer shoved him forward, pulling cable ties from his pocket. He secured Boetie's wrists behind his back, then looped another tie around his neck.

He pushed the unconscious body onto the floor and sat back, watching him as he stirred.

"Drive toward Yzerfontein," he instructed Zane.

Leaning back against the plush leather seat of the Mercedes, Boer smiled.

It wasn't every day he was chauffeured in a Benz.

349

They had already passed Melkbos Strand before Solomons began showing signs of waking. Soon, he was struggling to get onto the seat. With his hands bound, he had to use his legs to push himself up. A wave of nausea overwhelmed him, and he vaguely remembered someone once saying that it could be a consequence of a hard knock to the head.

Zane became aware of the commotion in the back and stole a quick glance in the rearview mirror. He saw Boer watching as Solomons struggled to sit upright. Eventually, Solomons managed to prop himself up and, wasting no time, started swearing at Zane.

"I will kill you for this, Zane! I will kill you!" he shouted, his voice thick with rage.

Zane met his gaze in the mirror and almost felt sorry for him. Solomons then turned his fury toward Boer.

"And who are you? What do you want with me, hey?" he demanded in his thick Cape Flats accent.

Boer remained calm, his expression unchanging. "Craterface, I am your prosecutor, judge, and executioner. I was also the best friend of Devlin. So today, you must pay with your life."

Boer leaned over and gave the cable tie around Solomons' neck a hard jerk. Sitting back, he watched with a faint smile as Solomons, at first, tried to break free of his wrist restraints. When he realized it was futile, he focused instead on getting air into his lungs. His face darkened to a deep red, his eyes bulged from their sockets, and sweat pooled in the acne scars on his cheeks. The veins in his neck popped like blue roadmaps, and the snake tattoo inked into his skin looked almost alive.

Suddenly, he started to heave. The tie around his throat blocked the sour vomit of brandy and coke from escaping through his mouth. Instead, it was forced into his lungs. Within moments, he had drowned in his own bile. His body gave one final convulsion before slumping against the door.

Boer glanced at Zane in the rearview mirror and saw the horror etched across his face.

"That was fun while it lasted, wasn't it?" he said casually. "Look for a sand road to your left and take it. Drive slowly until you reach a stone structure and stop behind it."

Zane spotted the structure and maneuvered the car off the main road, the SUV struggling in the deep sand. He finally reached a patch of grass and stopped. Boer got out and walked around to the other side.

"Come and help me. We need to drag him into that clump of Port Jackson bushes. Bring the shovel."

With Zane gripping the left leg and Boer the right, they quickly hauled Solomons' lifeless body about two hundred meters into the thick bush. Boer watched as Zane dug a shallow grave in the soft sea sand. At first, he struggled to keep the loose grains from falling back in, but once he hit the damp layers beneath, the digging went much faster. In no time, the grave was about a meter deep.

"That's enough. Let's roll him in. Grab his shoulders."

They watched as Boetie Solomons' body tumbled into the grave. Boer stepped down into the pit and first cut the ties around his wrists, then the one around his neck. He barely managed to step back in time as the sudden release of pressure caused a sickening spray of vomit to shoot nearly to the edge of the grave.

Stepping onto the edge, he looked down at the sagging corpse. "I heard that too much Coke can cause a bit of gas," he mused.

He gestured toward Zane. "Search his pockets. Remove all identification and anything else."

Once that was done, he indicated for Zane to start filling in the grave. He wasn't worried about the tracks they had left behind—the fierce West Coast winds would erase all evidence within hours.

They returned to the car, and Boer climbed into the passenger seat. He looked over at Zane and grinned.

"Have you ever in your life had so much fun?"

Zane slowly shook his head and started the car.

"You won't find this place again, will you, Zane?" Boer asked as they made their way back toward Plattekloof.

351

Zane shook his head again, even slower this time. He was still in shock, and he knew this was something he would never, ever forget for as long as he lived. Deep down, he also knew he would never speak of it—to anyone. *That is, of course, if I'm still alive after today.*

"What happens now?" he asked quietly, not sure if he wanted to hear the answer.

Boer stared out at the passing landscape, taking his time before replying.

"We go back and park this lovely car. Tomorrow morning, you wash it and put it back in its bay. Then you wait for the cops to come and help them with their inquiries. Nothing will go wrong if you stick to your story. Of course, things will go *radically* wrong if you mention me or anything that happened in the past few hours. I will find you, wherever you are. Is there anything you don't understand or need to ask me, Zane? I'm a man of my word, so stop worrying and focus on what you need to do over the next few days."

Zane shook his head and focused on the road ahead. Slowly, he exhaled, and for the first time in hours, he started to relax.

****

It was just past midnight when they returned in complete darkness. They parked the car next to the house, ready for Zane to wash in the morning.

Now, they sat in Zane's flat, both lost in their own thoughts about the night's events.

Boer decided it was time to go. He stood up from the chair and grabbed the bags of money. He tossed one onto the bed next to Zane.

"Go put this in the back of your car. Don't try to bank it. Start a new life. And make sure our paths never cross again."

He turned and walked out.

Opening the garage door with the remote, he straddled his bike. His helmet hung from the mirror, and he took a moment to put it on. He started the engine, letting it idle for a minute before slowly rolling out of the garage and through the open gate.

As he exited, he pressed the button, closing both the garage and the gate behind him. Without looking back, he flung the remote toward where Zane stood, still gripping the heavy sports bag filled with Kallie Jansen's cash.

Boer rode off slowly, keeping the revs low.

After all, this was a very posh neighborhood.

Chapter 63

It had been a week since the report of Manzoni's death.

Combrink and Ruiters were having dinner at the Italian Club in Joburg. They had finished their meals and were nursing the last of a bottle of red wine. Terror Majoba had insisted that the whole team take a week's leave. Rikki Patel had gone to Durban to spend time with his family and to inform them that he was transferring to the Hawks in Parktown. Majoba had taken his wife, Poppie, on holiday to Cape Town—her first visit to the Mother City.

Combrink stared at Maria over the rim of his glass, waiting for her to answer his question. She had kept him in suspense for several minutes already, and seeing the anxious look creeping onto his face, she finally spoke.

"If you are seriously thinking of resigning from the Hawks to work for Interpol, then I think it would be unwise for me to let you live on your own. I have to ask myself how long it would be before some woman in your new office discovered your charms and stole you away from me. So, I have no choice but to shack up with you. Yes, let's give it a go. Cheers."

She clinked her glass against his and watched the smile on his lips turn into a satisfied chuckle. It was at that exact moment that she suddenly realized—*she was madly in love with him*. A small spasm fluttered in her heart, and a tingle ran through her body.

"Wow, that took you long enough. Shall I order some champagne to celebrate?" he asked, one eyebrow cocked knowingly.

"Yes, but only if you can handle the consequences. You know what that stuff does to me."

Combrink shot his hand into the air. "Waiter! Your best champagne over here, please!"

****

Mikey turned the steaks on the fire.

The sun had set, and it was a beautiful evening in the Bushveld. Red lay nearby, his eyes twitching, his tail occasionally wagging. Like most dogs, he loved braais.

Through the smoke, Mikey peered at his wife, Cara, who was deep in conversation with Barry, the new man in Brigitta's life. He suspected the poor guy was being interrogated. A smug-looking Brigitta sat beside him, a sly smile on her lips as she met Mikey's gaze. She was nursing a glass of chilled white wine.

She looked happy.

She wore a flowery summer dress with lace sandals, her hair styled in small braids. The only makeup on her face was a hint of rouge and some lip gloss. She looked beautiful.

Barry was the father of one of the children who had visited the Eco Centre with her classmates. His twelve-year-old daughter, Sophie, had taken a short video of Brigitta while she was giving a presentation. That evening, after dinner, Sophie had told Barry that she had found a wife for him and showed him the video she had recorded. He had laughed, telling her he was quite content being alone, focusing on raising his only daughter.

Sophie's mother had passed away when she was nine—losing the battle against colon cancer just two days after Sophie's ninth birthday.

But Sophie had forwarded the video to her father anyway, along with Brigitta's contact details.

Every morning before school, she had asked him if he had contacted his *new wife* yet. She knew he had been watching the video. One afternoon, Barry finally took the plunge. Leaving his workers in the orchards, he had taken a shower, shaved, and put on a clean set of khakis.

When he arrived at the Eco Centre, all was quiet—no visitors. He hesitated at the entrance, feeling reluctant to go inside. But since he had come all the way, he stepped through the door.

He saw Brigitta standing in front of a row of succulents, her back to him. When she heard him, she turned and greeted him warmly. She looked radiant, her smile as stunning as ever.

He greeted her shyly and asked about the Centre. She grabbed his hand without hesitation and led him outside to a table beneath a tree, gesturing for him to sit.

"Sit here for a while. I'll get us some fruit juice, then we can talk."

At first, he thought her hospitality was a bit strange. But after watching the video so many times, he already felt as if he knew her—and her warmth seemed natural.

As he waited, he looked around, understanding why the Eco Centre had become so popular. It was tranquil, fascinating, and beautifully maintained.

Brigitta returned with a jug of mango juice and ice, placing it on the table. She sat beside him on the bench and poured them each a glass.

Taking a sip, she put her glass down and looked at him.

"What do you want to ask me?" she said, a sly smile playing on her lips.

He was caught off guard, momentarily at a loss for words. He put his glass down and scratched his cheek.

"Well, I was wondering what exactly you do here. My daughter visited with her classmates, and she absolutely loved it. She hasn't stopped talking about it."

As he picked up his glass again, Brigitta shifted closer. He could feel the heat rising to his cheeks. Then she placed her hand on his leg, and he had to fight the urge to jump up. He sat frozen, staring straight ahead.

When she turned her face toward him, he could feel her breath against his cheek.

"You are even more handsome in real life, Barry," she murmured. "Even better looking than in the video. Maybe it's because you showered and shaved for the pretty lady from the Eco Centre, *no*?"

Had she not been gripping his thigh, he would have definitely jumped up.

He turned toward her, and her closeness caused their lips to almost touch.

"What... what video?" he stammered.

She looked into his eyes and whispered in her accented English, "The one Sophie sent me. She say you watch the video of me every day. Sophie say soon you will visit me. And here you are, looking into my eyes. You like, *no?*"

Barry was speechless.

She gave his leg a squeeze.

"Mmmm? You like?"

He nodded slowly. He had never met anyone like Brigitta before. A smile crept onto his face.

She released his leg and picked up her glass.

"You take me to a fancy restaurant and buy me champagne. If I like you *beaucoup*, I will let you kiss me. *Ok?*"

"When would you like to go?" he asked hesitantly.

She gave him a sidelong smile and replied, "When do you want to kiss me?"

Mikey had heard the full story from Cara. He lifted his beer glass toward her, nodding his approval of her choice. He had a strong feeling Barry would soon become part of the family.

Not that the poor guy had any choice in the matter.

Mikey had replied to Enoch's message and was now waiting for more details—information he needed to guide the young man. He had no choice but to help him.

Piet was determined to make the killers of the innocent family pay.

****

Sharon lay on her back, staring up at the unfamiliar ceiling above her.

Well, not completely unfamiliar. She had been looking at it for a good few minutes earlier over the muscular shoulder of her one-night stand. He was now fast asleep and snoring beside her. He had been a surprisingly gentle and experienced lover despite his size, and she had managed to climax multiple times before he finally did himself. He had rolled off her and fallen asleep almost immediately.

She turned onto her side and admired his toned physique, etching it into her memory. Earlier that evening, she had seen him sitting at the bar counter just as she was about to leave the club. She had resigned herself to spending the night alone at home when she spotted him. On impulse, she had taken a seat next to him and openly flirted. He was much younger than her, but in the right lighting, she knew she still looked good. And she had been horny, slightly tipsy, and desperate.

After a few drinks and some flirty conversation, he had invited her to his place in Milnerton—the one-bedroom flat whose ceiling she was now staring at.

She reached for her phone on the bedside table and checked the time. It was almost 4 a.m. *Time to go.*

Carefully, she rolled out of bed and picked up her underwear from the floor. Scooping up her pants, blouse, and shoes, she tiptoed to the bathroom. Once inside, she quietly closed the door and gave herself a quick wash in the basin before dressing.

Opening the door a crack, she peeked out to see if he was still asleep.

She had caught a glimpse of herself in the mirror while washing and was shocked at how old she looked. The carefully applied makeup from the previous evening had all but disappeared, and the heavy drinking and sex had left her looking haggard.

Relieved to see him still asleep, she took a final glance around the bathroom to make sure she had everything.

That was when she spotted something familiar in the cabinet.

Tiptoeing back, she carefully opened the half-closed door and picked up the pill bottle. Reading the label, her legs buckled beneath her, and she sat down hard on the toilet lid.

She opened the bottle and stared at the familiar light purple pills inside. She knew them well. Many times, she had given them to her working girls who had been infected with HIV.

Now she understood why he had insisted on using a condom.

She hadn't been able to wait for him to put it on. She had pushed him onto the bed, climbed on top of him, and taken control.

Standing up, she placed the bottle back inside the cabinet. Closing the door, she looked at herself in the mirror and shook her head in dismay. Tears welled in her eyes.

She scolded herself in a whisper.

"You stupid, stupid old woman."

****

Duncan sat on his bike, parked outside Smugglers Pub.

He hesitated, reluctant to go inside, but he knew he had to face whatever came next. Earlier in the week, he had popped in one evening and spoken to Rory, his dad's friend. Rory had agreed to arrange the meeting for today.

Duncan removed his helmet and unzipped his jacket. Then, taking a deep breath, he stepped into the gloomy interior of the bar. His eyes adjusted quickly, and he spotted them sitting at a table to the left.

He walked over and sat down.

"Hi, Dad. Hi, Rory," he greeted his father and his father's friend.

He was astonished to see how good the old man still looked. It was the first time in decades that he had seen him.

Alistair looked at the bearded young man sitting next to him, his expression one of pure disbelief.

"Dunc... Duncan?" he whispered, barely able to comprehend what he was seeing.

Duncan grinned and held out his hand. "It's me. How have you been?"

Alistair slowly stood up from his barstool. Tears welled in his eyes. He gripped Duncan's hand and pulled him into a hug, his shoulders shaking as he sobbed.

Duncan had no choice but to pat his father on the back, waiting for him to calm down. Over Alistair's shoulder, he caught Rory's wry smile and noticed a tear running down his cheek as well.

Once his father settled, Duncan guided him back to his seat.

"Sit here, Dad. I'll get us a round of drinks."

He walked over to the bar counter. When he thought no one was watching, he wiped away a tear.

How is it that someone you've blamed all your life for your troubles can suddenly seem so important?

He glanced at the mirror behind the bar and saw the two old men at the table, talking excitedly. His father glanced his way every now and then.

Was that pride he saw on the old codger's face?

Duncan picked up the drinks and returned to the table.

He felt good. He was looking forward to his session at the Inn that evening. He knew Oom Jack, Lofty, and Godfrey would be there. Dusty and Tyre would probably pop in too. They would likely discuss next Saturday's ride to Barrydale. It seemed like it would be the last ride for a while, especially since Oom Jack and Sweety were heading off on their campervan tour in a month.

He looked at his smiling father and reached across the table for a fist bump.

They had a lot of catching up to do.

For a moment, his mind flashed to Devlin, and a wave of sadness overwhelmed him.

He shook his head, forcing the thoughts away.

Devlin's death had been avenged. *Justice money had been collected.*

Amen.

Dear Reader

We hope you enjoyed reading our book and found it engaging. Your feedback is very important to us and to future readers.

We would greatly appreciate it if you could take a few moments to write a review on Amazon. Your opinion helps others make informed decisions and helps us better understand what our readers value.

Thank you very much for your support!

Kind regards

The Malherbe Team

www.ingramcontent.com/pod-product-compliance
Lightning Source LLC
Chambersburg PA
CBHW071211250626
47159CB00001B/281